Jennifer Belle's first novel, *Going Down*, was translated into many languages and was named best debut novel by *Entertainment Weekly*. Her essays and short stories have appeared in *The New York Times Magazine*, *Ms.*, the *Independent* magazine, *Harper's Bazaar*, *Mudfish*, and several anthologies. She lives in a lrg rent stab 1BR in GVill w/Emp St Bld vus & WBFP. *High Maintenance* is her second novel. Her web address is:
www.jenniferbelle.com

Also by Jennifer Belle

Going Down

HIGH
MAINTENANCE

Jennifer Belle

VIRAGO

A *Virago* Book

First published by Virago Press 2002

First published in the United States by Riverhead Books
Penguin Putnam Inc. New York

A CIP catalogue record for this book is available from the British
Library

ISBN 1 86049 756 X

Typeset in Palatino by M Rules
Printed and bound in Great Britain by
Clays Ltd, St Ives plc

Virago
An imprint of
Time Warner Books UK
Brettenham House
Lancaster Place
London WC2E 7EN

www.virago.co.uk

For Andrew Krents

ACKNOWLEDGEMENTS

With thanks to Tina Bennett, Julie Grau, Craig Burke, Shari Smiley, Nicholas Weinstock, and Jill Hoffman. Also to Susan Petersen Kennedy, Liz Perl, Louise Burke, Dan Harvey, Lennie Goodings, Antonia Hodgson, Katy Nicholson, Jens Christiansen, Bree Perlman, Svetlana Katz, Elizabeth Tippens, Amanda Weinstock, Debra Rodman, Scott Jones, Robert Steward, Kit McCracken, Dan Ehrenhaft, Doug Dorph, Stephanie Emily Dickinson, David Lawrence, Jayne Jenner, Steve Moskowitz, Ronald Wardall, Charlotte Brady, Paul Wuensche, Patricia Volk, Rick Schneider, David Khinda, Elizabeth Gibbons, Brendan O'Meara, and my family.

And especially to Stefanie Teitelbaum – thank you.

Part I

O! I have bought the mansion of a love,
But not possess'd it, and, though I am sold,
Not yet enjoy'd . . .

WILLIAM SHAKESPEARE,
Romeo and Juliet, III, 2

I

ZEN LOFT — BACK ON MRKT

The morning before I was planning to leave my husband, my friend Violet convinced me to go with her to see a swami in someone's townhouse. I was surprised to see that he was an American guy in an orange dress sitting under a real Picasso.

'When we meditate we keep our eyes open,' the swami said. I was relieved. I didn't want to sit in a strange room with a bunch of freaks with my eyes closed. 'Even when we look deeply inside ourselves, we never stop looking out at the world,' he said.

I sat there for forty-five minutes with my eyes open thinking about my situation and looking around the room. It was a beautiful living room, all very upholstered, with stairs behind me that led to a private garden. The woman who owned it, our hostess, had been proudly running around, fluffing pillows and pouring the swami tea. It wasn't as nice as my apartment.

The question was who would be forced to leave the apartment – me or Jack. Jack owned the apartment, and I didn't. Jack could afford the maintenance, and I couldn't without his help. And Jack had announced that the only way he was leaving the apartment was in a pine box.

I didn't want to leave but I refused to be like my mother, a character from a Jacqueline Susann novel complete with gold ankh necklace, turning a blind eye or cheek or whatever it was to her husband's infidelity.

So I would have to be the one to leave. I had spent five years married to a man named Jack. I had hung all my hopes on a man with the name of Jack. As if my life were a roadtrip in a car with flat tires and the most important thing to have was a jack. I had wanted a jack even though I would have no idea how to use one if my life depended on it.

I sat there crying until someone finally hit a tiny gong with a stick and the swami asked if anyone had any questions. I thought about asking if I would ever have love again, but I didn't.

He looked right at me and said, 'Yes, you will.'

I looked behind me, then back at the swami. 'I will what?' I said.

'Get a boyfriend,' he said sweetly. Everyone laughed. 'As long as you don't get too hysterical about it.'

'I wasn't thinking about getting a boyfriend,' I said. 'I'm a married woman,' I added. At least I was for one more day. I felt stupid for thinking about love when I should actually be more concerned about getting a job and an apartment.

'My advice is to keep your overhead low,' the swami said.

The girl sitting cross-legged on the floor next to me nodded as if deeply moved. A lot of people were nodding and bursting into tears.

'That's especially important for you,' he said to me.

When it was over everyone smiled at me as if I were some kind of meditation celebrity. As if I were the luckiest person to be given the news that I, more than anyone, should keep my overhead low. I felt like I had been given a curse.

Of course Violet never even showed up. I stood there by myself drinking tea and reluctantly hugging people.

'Do you have the time?' I asked a man on the corner when I left the swami.

He extended his arm to raise the sleeve of his suit in a cartoonish gesture and looked at his watch. He told me. I thanked him and began to cross the street, noticing that I actually felt more relaxed and open.

'Get a watch, lady,' he mumbled under his breath.

'What?' I said, turning around.

'Get a fucking watch, lady,' he said, loudly.

'Nice. Nice. Really nice,' I said. It felt exhilarating to have such an intimate fight on the street, even though when I really looked at him I saw he was pimply and didn't look much older than seventeen. People stared. I felt almost wide-awake.

'What do I fucking look like, Big Ben?' he shouted.

I had sat in a strange living room praying for a man to be sent to me. This was something. The swami had already come through. This boy might not be the man I spent the rest of my life with but it was something. A small beginning. I knew from this that I was ready to date again. It was a sort of warm-up.

'You don't look a thing like Big Ben. There's obviously nothing big about you,' I said. 'What time did you say it was?'

'Fuck you.'

'Fuck you,' I said, and walked away.

I bought *The New York Times* and went to a café so I could sit there pathetically circling things like everyone else. I tried to think of what I could do.

I didn't know what I had been thinking ending up in a café at twenty-six with no skills or education. I had gone to NYU for eight days and hated every minute of it. I went the first Monday through Friday, had the weekend off, went back Monday, Tuesday, and dropped out at the end of Wednesday. That's where I met Violet. My father had offered to get me a suite at the Plaza Hotel complete with room service, which was his idea of an apartment, but I had decided to live in a dorm because I wanted to feel like a normal person, and Violet was my roommate. For eight days, I had to overhear her on the phone crying to her parents in Texas that she had fallen off a curb and broken her ankle and that all New Yorkers were the ugliest, thickest-lipped people she had ever seen.

That comment always stayed in my mind. I had always

thought it was good to have voluptuous lips. Her lips were the only things about her that weren't thick. But she was my roommate, my college roommate, and I loved the idea of that. I admired women who stayed friends with their college roommates and had them as bridesmaids at their weddings. I spent eight days bringing her trays of food because she was on crutches and trying to find charm in the fact that she had never seen a Woody Allen movie.

Then I met Jack in an elevator at the Supreme Court at 60 Centre Street. I was looking into changing my name after the *New York Post* ran a blind item about my father on Page Six ('What famous clothing designer was caught with a transvestite prostitute in Riverside Park and punched out a police officer?'), and we got married two years later. After that it always seemed like there was so much to do. The five years just flew by. First of all, we went to his country house every single weekend and that time didn't even count because we weren't in New York. As soon as we hit the Saw Mill it just wasn't my life anymore. There was no sex, no fun, no friends. The most I could hope for was the occasional movie or antique. All I did was listen to the teenage daughter of our closest neighbor talk about all the different places she managed to have sex with her boyfriend without her parents knowing, while I spread jam on saltines in the kitchen, and my husband took naps alternating between the two white couches on the screened-in porch. And then, Mondays through Fridays back in the city, my husband always needed me to do things like buy a chrome orange juicer or interview maids. But at least I hadn't relied on my parents.

Now I couldn't think of anything I could do. I felt a new sense of abandonment, beyond my usual sense of abandonment. It made my old sense of abandonment feel like child's play. I was no longer the house that Jack built. I sat in the café reading the paper. The only thing I seemed to remember how to do was read. I knew how to read although I hadn't learned until I was pretty old, seven. But at least I had learned. I looked to see if there were any jobs for readers.

2

DIAMOND IN ROUGH — NEEDS WORK

When I got off the elevator I found myself facing a large black woman wearing nothing but a huge beige bra and a half-slip. Her dress was hanging behind her desk on a coatrack, soaking wet. She had put pages of the *National Enquirer* on the floor underneath it. 'You're prolly thinking this is a little unusual,' she said. 'But it's raining and I lost my umbrella on the subway. I forgot that he had an appointment.'

It was my first job interview so I really didn't have much to compare it to.

'It doesn't seem unusual at all,' I said.

'Of course I could be sitting here buckass neckid and he wouldn't know a thing.' I liked the idea of a job where the boss didn't know if you were buckass neckid. 'His Honor's ready for you,' she said. She waddled out from behind her desk and punched a code on the door's security system. The door opened. 'Come on, I'll take you there myself.'

Her slip was so stretched out the elastic looked like it was about to break.

'I can find it,' I said.

I walked down a corridor and found my way to the last door.

'Come in,' a man said before I had knocked.

I opened the door and stood for a second. I held my breath. There is nothing more awkward than being in the presence of a blind man. I was more out of place than if I had decided to work construction down some manhole somewhere or if I had gotten a job in a lab with rats. This was a mistake.

'Penny for your thoughts,' he said. 'Don't just stand there. Come in. I'm Judge Garrett.' He was English.

'I'm sorry,' I said. 'I'm Liv Kellerman.' He put out his hand and I went over and shook it. If I had gone to work for my father I would be having a drink right now with Isabella Rossellini, not shaking the limp hand of a blind man. I sat in the wooden chair facing his desk. Behind him was a wall of windows with panoramic views of the East River.

'So what were you thinking about, as you stood in the doorway just now? I have excellent hearing you know, I could hear you thinking.'

I was put off by the question. He made it sound like my brain was a noisy clock.

'Your office has a beautiful view,' I said.

'Yes,' he said, as if he had seen it. We sat there awkwardly for a moment. Then I started desperately describing it, like an insane tour guide. Each of the three bridges and how they differed from each other and the lights – 'like *necklaces*,' I said, and the boats in the river – 'like the *Mayflower*,' I exclaimed, and the Jehovah's Witnesses' clock in Brooklyn, and the cars on the FDR, a helicopter, the sky and smoke from the chimneys and the water towers on the roofs.

'Water towers?' he asked.

'Yes, water towers – like *fat Chinamen* looking down at us from *rice* fields.'

'I see,' he said.

I went on to describe workmen on a plank suspended on the outside of a building.

He sat mesmerized with his chubby hands folded in his lap.

For some reason I described the Woolworth Building even

though it wasn't in our range – 'like the *Emerald City*!' I managed. I felt like Dorothy, trying to be upbeat.

'Well, I'm afraid that makes me the *Wizard*, doesn't it? And you, our Dorothy, and Ms. Howard can play our yellow-bellied lion.'

I had seen Ms. Howard's belly and it was not yellow. He was making fun of me. 'I'm sorry,' I said.

'I'm glad you like the view. Now tell me, are the windows clean?'

They were filthy, streaked with black dirt. I didn't know what to say. I didn't want to offend him.

'They are a little bit smudged,' I said.

'Well, that's very frustrating. I was told they were cleaned last week, but I had a feeling. Do you mind if I take a moment to type a memo to the cleaning staff?'

I shook my head no. Then I said 'no' out loud.

He swiveled his chair to a stack of paper and clumsily put a sheet in a regular typewriter. He touch-typed furiously for several minutes. I was impressed until he asked me to read it back to him and there were hundreds of mistakes.

'If you find an error, please correct it with a blue or black pen. I like my correspondence to be perfect.'

'There aren't any errors,' I said.

He nodded in what he thought was my direction, pleased.

'Now tell me about yourself, Ms. Keller,' he said.

'It's Kellerman,' I said quickly.

As I spoke he took notes on a braillewriter, a clunky antique-looking machine with buttons like a trumpet's. Raised dots appeared on strips of parchment-colored cardstock, like goose bumps on skin. I told him about the apartment I had lived in with my husband and how I had to leave. I told him about the view of the park and the sun on the bedroom floor, the twenty-foot ceilings and the curve of the banisters leading from the mezzanine to the living room.

'It sounds like you're going to miss your apartment more than your husband,' he said.

'Oh, I do, I will.'

It was the truth. We had lived in the apartment the whole five years of our marriage, and I felt like I would never get used to not living there.

'How long did you live there?'

'Seven years,' I said. I deserved seven years' worth of sympathy.

'How old are you?' he asked.

'I'm twenty-six.'

He smiled. 'Twenty-six years old and never been kissed,' he said.

What a jerk, I thought, but then I wondered if it was true. Maybe I had never been kissed. I suddenly couldn't remember kissing anybody. It's impossible, I thought. I had been married, after all.

He pounded away on the prehistoric machine and I watched him. I loved the way I could stare at him openly. You usually don't have an opportunity to stare at somebody like that. I had a new kind of privacy. He had black hair and a full beard and mustache streaked with gray. He was average height with a round, limp body. He wasn't fat exactly, just terribly out of shape as if he had never moved from that spot behind his desk. He was wearing a brown suit and an ugly Italian tie.

'I like your tie,' I said.

'Thank you,' he beamed. 'I always go to the same place and a girl named Shirley chooses all my things. I'll tell her it garnered a compliment.'

'It's really nice.'

'What are you wearing, if you don't mind my asking. I only bring it up because I ask that you dress quite formally for this position. From time to time you will have to accompany me in my dealings with the public. So jeans or anything of that nature would be inappropriate.'

I was glad he mentioned that because now I realized I could wear jeans every day. I looked down at my outfit, a black velvet skirt and a vintage sweater.

'I'm wearing a gray tweed suit and a white silk blouse. It's very appropriate,' I said.

'That's lovely.' He blushed.

He pushed a few more valves and levers on the braillewriter and then leaned back in his chair. I wondered if he would be able to tell if I lay down on the leather couch across the room.

'So,' he said. 'Now you have an idea of what the job entails, haven't you?'

I wasn't sure if I had. 'Yes,' I said.

'Do you have any questions?'

'No,' I said.

'Don't you want to know what the salary is?'

'Yes,' I said.

'I'm afraid it's only eight dollars an hour, which isn't very much, is it?'

I didn't know how to respond to that. If I said it was less than I used to pay the maid it might seem as if I was complaining. 'Could you make it ten an hour?' I asked.

'No, that isn't possible. I realize it's grossly inadequate but the city only pays six an hour and I provide the two-dollar supplement myself.' He said this as if he were the most benevolent man who ever lived.

'That's fine,' I said. 'Eight dollars.'

'Will it be enough for you to live on?'

He asked the question so sincerely and it was such an absurd idea that I laughed out loud. 'I don't think so,' I said.

'Oh, I'm sorry.'

'But that doesn't mean I don't want the job.' There was always the option of getting alimony from my husband or money from my father. Or maybe I could read to other blind people on the side.

'Eight dollars an hour may not seem like a lot of money but, as I explained, some of it comes directly out of my own salary and I require that it fill a financial need for my employees,' he said.

'It fills a need,' I said.

'It doesn't sound like it will fill a need.'

'It does! It fills a need,' I begged. It didn't seem fair that I not only had to take such a low-paying job but I had to prove that I was so pathetic as to have a need that could be filled by eight dollars an hour. A need that could be filled by eight dollars an hour was not a need. A real need, my need, couldn't be filled by a hundred dollars an hour. No amount of money could fill my need.

'Well, all right,' he said. 'As long as the salary will be of help. I'm about to let you in on a little secret. You are not to let anyone know about this.'

'Okay,' I said, relaxing. Maybe his secret was that he really could see and he was just pretending to be blind.

Someone knocked timidly on the door. 'Come in,' he bellowed in a falsely gruff voice.

A bailiff came in and said, 'Time, Your Honor.'

The judge waved him away. 'Shut the door!' It was shut.

'I'm afraid I'll have to cut our interview short, although I've enjoyed it.'

'Thank you,' I said and stood up.

'I hope you've enjoyed it.' He was smiling at the chair next to me.

'Very much, sir.'

'Call me Jerome,' he said sweetly.

Jerome handed me the note he had typed about the windows and asked me to give it to Ms. Howard on my way out. Ms. Howard wasn't at her desk but her dress was still hanging there so I figured she couldn't have gone too far. I waited for a while and corrected all the typos on Jerome's note, and finally just left it for her on her desk.

3

GV PRIME/CHARMING!!!

I left the court building and headed toward MacDougal Street to look at an apartment.

I couldn't wait to sign my own lease without Jack there giving me a million instructions about how I shouldn't mention that he was a lawyer because no one did deals with lawyers, and not to say anything about his country house or who my father was so the owner wouldn't think we had a lot of money, and not to criticize anything in case the owner was sensitive. What Jack didn't realize was that every place we went people liked me more than him, and I had to say, 'Oh, don't mind my husband, he's a lawyer,' to everyone every time he left the room.

I had been excited to start being alone, but by the time I got to MacDougal Street, and Maria, the super's wife, showed up, I was crying.

'This is a good place to be sad at,' she said. She was very fat and wore a gold chain around her neck with the name Maria dangling from it and rubber gloves.

There was an odd makeshift tin fence around the entrance to the building and I wondered if it was some sort of rat guard.

I followed her up the five flights of stairs and into the floor-through railroad tenement flat. The front door was unlocked and opened into the kitchen. I continued crying as she led me through it. It had an old fridge and an enormous stove. 'Oven don't work,' Maria said. 'I have to be honest with you about that.' Between the refrigerator and the stove was a metal shower stall.

I stood facing the stall like a small quaking child looking to a terrible new stepmother for comfort. I couldn't imagine undressing in front of it, let alone standing naked in it. I looked at it and talked to it silently. 'Can I do this? Can I do this?' I wasn't a brave person. The shower had a presence like an angry tree in a Grimm's fairy tale. It looked like an upright metal coffin.

I couldn't take my eyes off it. Its duct-taped hinges. Its tremendous height, beginning a good three feet off the ground and rising to the ceiling.

The opaque plastic shower door had a small duct-tape patch in the middle of it. I peeled it off slowly to reveal a perfectly round nickel-sized hole. It looked like a bullet hole. It had tiny cracks all around it.

I put my finger in the hole.

Maria took her hands off her hips and pressed the gray tape back on the wounded door. 'It's clean,' she said. She opened the shower door and I was hit with the smell of Clorox bleach.

There were no faucets, just little metal spokes jutting out from the shower wall and a pair of pliers lying on the gray-streaked shower floor.

'Good strong water,' Maria said, looking hurt.

I walked into the tiny room next to the kitchen. 'What's that?' I asked, pointing to a small square wooden door in the wall above a full-sized bed.

'That's the window to the air shaft. It must never be opened. Pigeons,' she warned.

'Who do I have to talk to if I want the place?' I asked.

'You tell it to me.'

'I don't have any money right now,' I said. 'Divorce,' I whispered.

'You have a job?' she asked, raising an eyebrow at me.

'Yes,' I said. I hesitated. 'I work for a judge.'

'You a lawyer?'

'Sort of,' I said. 'I'm a reader. But I'm going to be able to pay the rent.'

'Okay,' she said, 'I don't want to walk up no more stairs no more. It's yours.

'How much?' I asked.

'How much you want to pay?'

I felt suddenly grateful. Maria was going to be reasonable. Everything people always said about New York was wrong. It wasn't hard to get an apartment in New York for a good price.

I wanted to look the whole place over before making my offer. I left Maria standing in the kitchen and walked through the little bedroom into the living room, which held a hideous beige couch. There was a trace of sun and a black-and-white dog in the window across the street. I watched a gray leaf fall from a city tree. In New York the closest thing to being in the country is a tree-lined street.

I suddenly had a fantasy that I could fix the place up and every week my husband could come over and I could make a big salad that we could eat sitting cross-legged on the floor and then he could leave.

There were two windows but a large metal sign saying 'Apartment for Rent' was covering half of one of them. It would be nice to have two whole windows instead of one and a half.

I called Maria into the living room. 'Will the sign be coming down?' I asked.

'No,' she said.

'But you won't need it anymore. The apartment won't be available.'

'She stays,' Maria said, meaning the sign.

'I'll give you three hundred a month,' I said.

'Good,' she said. 'Then you add on another nine hundred a month and you can live in here.'

'Twelve hundred is too much. I'll give you nine hundred a month,' I said.

'Twelve hundred,' she said.

'One thousand.'

'Twelve hundred,' she said again.

'Eleven hundred.'

'One thousand and two hundred,' she said, holding up two fingers.

'I'll take it,' I said, and Maria handed me three keys. 'When can I move in?'

'You're in,' she said.

'What about these things?' In addition to the bed and couch, there was a phone, a TV, and a VCR at the foot of the bed on a small chipped chest with an anchor painted on it.

'I'll sell them to you but they belong to the person before you so if he sues you have to give it back to him.'

That didn't seem quite fair. I had seen a case like that on one of those judge shows on television where the landlord had thrown out all the plaintiff's video games and his mother's ashes. 'No,' I said.

She made a sucking sound with her teeth. 'Okay, you can borrow them for fifty dollars.'

'Fine.'

'Fine.' She shook my hand, still wearing the rubber glove, and left me alone there. I cried in the living room for a few minutes and then went to the tiny bathroom to see if there was any toilet paper to blow my nose. I couldn't believe my luck. There, on the tiny wooden floor of the bathroom, was an almost full roll of toilet paper. I started crying again, but this time from a feeling that the universe was generous and filled with abundance. I felt like I was Scarlett O'Hara, not finding one bitter old turnip in the ground, but an entire blooming cotton crop. I was already taking care of myself. I had a job and an apartment.

After the toilet paper excitement wore off I suddenly couldn't stand to be in the apartment for another second. I went for a walk hoping to find some furniture out on the street but furniture is like men – you don't find any when you're looking.

That night I lay in my borrowed/rented bed and stared at the ballerina-shaped crack on the ceiling. I couldn't stop thinking about Jerome. I should have been thinking about who had slept in that bed before me, or about the horrible scene I had with my husband just a few hours before, but every time I closed my eyes Jerome kept walking toward me, waving his white stick. I tried to keep my eyes closed to see what it would be like to be blind, but they kept popping open. I wondered what it would be like to wake up in the pitch-black morning and be able to see only my dreams from the night before. If a blind man got married he would probably never cheat on his wife. Not that I was going to marry Jerome. But I was really going to make an effort to do a good job for him. And I was going to try to be less critical.

4
FNCL DIST — WALK TO WORK

My first week at work I spelled the word 'business' wrong. I sat in the library-style chair in front of Jerome's desk with my legs spread wide apart like a man on the subway. I winked at him seductively and pursed my lips while he continued to complain about my spelling. He kept talking about how it was completely unacceptable to spell a word like 'business' wrong.

'Was it sloppiness or do you really not know how to spell it?' he asked. That was a no-win question.

'I don't know how I could have missed that,' I said. I stared down at the document in question. In the bottom right-hand corner, under my initials, L.K., were the initials J.M.

'Imagine my embarrassment,' he said. 'I felt badly having to check up on you but obviously that was a necessity, wasn't it? I showed it to my former reader, a young lady who has been with me for two and a half years. I am really sorry to see her go. She's getting married next week . . .'

'Well, now I'm here,' I said.

'But I have to be able to trust you not to make foolish mistakes. You represent me. She never made a mistake in two and a half years. She was a perfectionist.' I couldn't believe I was getting jealous of Jerome's other reader. He was pitting us against each other.

'I'm a bit of a perfectionist myself,' I said.

'I haven't seen any evidence of that as of yet. You know, when I showed her the letter you wrote, and she discovered the word "business" spelled incorrectly, she gave me quite a hard time about the woman I had chosen to take her place. I believe the word she used was "trollop." She accused me of only hiring you for your looks.'

'I'm sure you will soon come to see that I am the far better reader. And you can tell that to your mysterious J.M.'

'I'll let Jordan know that you feel that way.'

'Did you tell her your secret?' I asked.

'What secret?'

'You told me you had a little secret that you were going to let me in on.'

'As a matter of fact I didn't. I was getting ready to tell Jordan about it when she announced her resignation. But I have convinced her to stay on for another week or two to help me make the transition. Maybe I'll let the two of you fight it out and the survivor will know my secret. I don't know if I will be able to handle *two* readers. That could almost constitute a harem, couldn't it? If but a small one?'

He looked pathetic slumped in his chair talking about his harem. I considered telling him there was a rainbow out his window even though there wasn't. When someone is blind you will do anything to make their world better. I thought it might give him pleasure to picture a beautiful rainbow. I looked down and noticed that my shirt was buttoned wrong. I unbuttoned the whole thing and started from the bottom. I was wearing a fabulous bra. If Ms. Howard could sit at the front desk in a dingy beige bra then I could sit in the inner chamber in my yellow La Perla. I lifted my breasts out of my bra. I could almost feel my husband's hands on them. I started to cry silently.

'Are you crying?' Jerome asked.

I nodded.

'It's all right. I'm sure you'll be more careful in the future. Would you mind going out and getting us some lunch?'

He sent me to McDonald's and I was happy to be among the seeing, although I still felt the numbness of not being seen. Of being invisible. Businessmen looked at me. I walked with my feet turned out and the belt of my raincoat trailing behind me. I had put my breasts back.

Jerome's ten fingers curled around his Big Mac. He groped for his fries. I had to set it all out on his desk for him. I chewed with my mouth open because he was blind.

I cried silently off and on for most of the day.

'So tell me about this husband of yours,' Jerome said.

'He's older than me,' I said. 'Fourteen years older.'

'And how long did he take to propose? Or, rather, how long before you told him to?'

'He asked me. On the beach,' I said. 'He handed me a seashell with a ring in it.'

Actually what had happened was we had been in bed together and Jack went under the covers and said, obscenely, 'Look what I found in your cunt,' and I felt something sharp against me and then Jack sat up with a diamond ring on the tip of his tongue. 'Well, if it was in my cunt it belongs to me,' I said. 'Hand it over.' He passed the ring from his mouth into mine and that's how he proposed. I always had to make up a story whenever someone asked me how it happened.

'I'm not much of a beach person,' Jerome said.

There was nothing I could say to that.

'How are you getting home?' Jerome, or the Blind Guy, as I was now referring to him in my mind, asked.

'Cab,' I said.

'Oh, because I thought if you were heading toward the subway we could go together,' he said cheerily, as if I would enjoy that.

'I'd be happy to walk you there,' I said.

Cab, cab, cab, I thought.

Suddenly the Blind Guy stood up and gripped the back of his chair. 'I am not a dog!' he yelled. 'You can walk with me if you like, but you cannot walk me.'

'Then I'll just put away my leash,' I said nastily. 'It's an expression I would use with anyone, I'll walk you there. Walk me home. People say it all the time.'

He cocked his head and listened to me, fascinated to know what people did.

He gathered his things and prepared to leave the office. 'Shall we, then?' He clicked his heels slightly.

Gently holding my left elbow, he crept along beside me. He had to tell me how to go. 'The blind leading the . . .' I stopped myself from saying.

'Would you mind if we stopped at a cash machine?' he asked.

'Not at all,' I said. I'm a reader, not a banker, I thought. He led me to an ATM and I watched him punch the numbers, noticing the Braille on the keys for the first time. He withdrew one hundred dollars from checking. 'Did I just request a hundred-dollar withdrawal?' he asked me. He looked nervous.

'No, you asked for two hundred from savings. Some of those bills are fifties.' He became flustered and I regretted my joke. 'I'm just kidding,' I said. 'You asked for one hundred from checking.'

He didn't laugh. He counted the five twenties twice and we continued walking down the street.

We passed a statue of a man I didn't know. It was a regular pigeon-covered statue, but when I saw it I started crying. I had seen it so many times it had become invisible. Which is how I must have become to Jack. But for some strange reason I suddenly felt incredibly jealous of it. It was lucky, except for the pigeons. It got to stand there in an exciting intersection in New York City and not have to feel everything.

I wished I could be a statue. I wanted to be the statue of Joan of Arc without actually having to have been Joan of Arc. I wished I could go straight to statue. I wanted to stand in a triangle in

New York, hard and cold and permanent. Almost lifelike. My whole body, bronzed like a baby shoe. I could stand and watch a girl, I might even say a beautiful girl, walk with a blind judge to the subway. And I thought, I must really hate my life if I can get jealous of a statue.

'Every year one or two blind people die in the subway,' Jerome said. 'When they're waiting on the platform and the train comes to a stop, instead of walking in through the doors, they accidentally walk between two cars and fall into the tracks and get flattened when the train moves again.'

Jerome, flattened. I guessed I'd be walking with him to the subway every day.

'Why don't you get a dog?' I asked.

'Why get a dog, when I have you?' Jerome said affectionately.

5

PIC POSTCARD VUS

I sat in Jerome's chambers looking through his mail. He was late and the tea I brought him from Starbucks every morning out of the goodness of my heart was cold.

The phone rang and I answered it, receptionist-style, saying hello as though I were right at that moment being fucked. There was silence. I said hello again, breathlessly.

'Is this Judge Garrett's new reader?' a woman asked.

'Yes it is,' I said. 'He's not in yet.' I asked if I could take a message.

'He's not there?' The woman sounded very upset. 'He left home forty minutes ago!'

'He'll be here any minute, I'm sure,' I said. I was sure he had wandered off the Brooklyn Bridge.

'Oh my God, have him call me the minute he gets in. I have to try not to worry. I've heard a lot about you,' she said.

'Who is this?' I asked.

'I'm Sarah, Jerome's girlfriend,' she said, proudly.

Girlfriend! I thought.

Just then Jerome came poking and prodding his way in with his too-long sleeves, gripping his stick and his tattered brown briefcase. This was the worst job. His face had a smudge of dirt on it. Was it my job to tell him he had a smudge? No! Definitely not. Sarah could tell him when he got home.

'Sarah, wait, he just walked in.'

Jerome threw down his raincoat and sidled along his desk to his chair. I was glad I had gotten out of it to answer the phone. He said a few words to her and hung up quickly.

'I had a crazy cabdriver,' he said, pronouncing crazy as cwazy and driver as dwiver. This happened more when he was flustered. 'There were no seat belts in the backseat. They are wequired by law to have seat belts. I swear I was almost killed.' I thought about him feeling around for the seat belt, every little bump cause for panic. Nobody put on a seat belt in a cab.

'That's awful,' I said. I couldn't take my eyes off of the L-shaped smudge. 'Why don't you go to the men's room and splash some water on your face and calm down.'

'No, I'm fine,' he said, curtly. He did nothing for a few minutes, which I was beginning to get used to. It meant he was thinking.

'Do you want me to read you your mail?' I asked. My first duty was to pick up his mail. Someone had sent him a postcard, a photo of a happy-looking family on a beach, wearing bathing suits and sunglasses. It was a strange card to send to a blind man. The mother had huge breasts.

'Not now,' he said.

'Your girlfriend sounds nice.'

'Yes . . .' He put his face in his hands. 'Can I ask you a personal question?'

'Sure,' I said. His face was slack and flat from never seeing himself in a mirror. He couldn't practice forming his face into various pleasant, sharp, pursed expressions like other people. I had one I hadn't even debuted in public yet that involved smiling playfully and clenching my teeth like a tiger.

'Liv,' he said, hesitantly, 'I find myself wondering where you live. You've told me so much about your husband's apartment, where you used to live, but I don't know where you are now.'

I felt moved by his wondering that. He probably pictured me

tucked into bed in a straw hayloft like Heidi, or laughing on a futon couch with roommates. For a moment I thought about bringing him home with me and leading him up the five flights of stairs, guiding him around the place, careful not to let him trip on the hole in the kitchen floor. I wondered what his girlfriend would think about him coming over to my apartment with his cane.

I told him it was a floor-through railroad flat in a tenement on MacDougal Street. I lived five flights above a 'restaurant' called King Shawarma. The whole restaurant, the whole block, my whole apartment smelled like rotting flesh. Each morning a new barrel-shaped lamb was placed on the vertical rotating spit with one onion stuck on top like a hat, or with the onion on the bottom and the lamb on top like a seal balancing on a beach ball. The smell invaded everything, settling into the nooks and crannies of my English muffin, coating the feathers of my one down pillow, getting between the stitches of my grandmother's handknit sweaters.

I hadn't smelled it the day I took the apartment. I was crying too hard to breathe.

'I suppose you're sorry you asked,' I said.

'No, on the contrary,' Jerome said. 'I live in a small one-bedroom on the second floor of an elevator building in Brooklyn. And I'm told that I got the apartment for such a good price because it is apparently quite dark.'

I didn't know if he was making a joke. He didn't laugh. 'Liv,' he said. 'I despise myself at this moment.'

'Why?' I said.

'Do you ever have a moment of utter self-loathing?' His voice sounded strangely light. He dropped his chin. 'I'm just not a very good person.'

I didn't know what to say. A recurring image came into my mind – me flying at my ex-husband and violently stabbing him over and over again in the chest. A sort of reflex fantasy.

Another thing that came into my head a lot lately was the time we went to Shakespeare-in-the-Park when we were dating and I packed a picnic dinner with veal Milanese, and cheese, and fruit, and wine, and pasta salad, and pie. So sad to think of myself planning and cooking and wrapping everything in tinfoil.

'Oh, Jerome,' I said. 'I'm sure you're a very good person.'

'Anyway, yes, Sarah is very nice. Do you have a suitor?'

I laughed. I had a lawsuit – I was suing my husband for divorce. I had a Chanel suit, two actually, that I had left in his closet. I had a suitcase. But I didn't have a suit-or. 'I'm not seeing anyone right now,' I said. I shouldn't have said seeing.

'Why do you put up with that? Rumor has it that you are very attractive.'

'When I started that rumor, I believe I used the word "beautiful,"' I said. I had wondered if Jerome had been asking about me. He probably wanted to touch my face like blind people always want to do in the movies. Out of the question, I decided.

'You're probably the sort who likes to be showered with gifts,' Jerome said, obviously amusing himself. 'I'll bet you're quite a handful for a man.'

'Do you shower Sarah with gifts?' I asked.

'Oh, yes,' he said. I doubted it. 'In fact, let's order her some flowers. Would you get the phone book?'

He looked proud. I got the white pages from the windowsill and gave him the number he wanted for a florist in Midtown near her work. On the phone, he demanded salmon-colored roses. Apparently they didn't have salmon. 'No, I don't want pink or peach, I want salmon!' He slammed the phone down on the desk and then fumbled to hang it up. He asked for the number of another florist. Again he asked for salmon-colored roses and bellowed when he was offered champagne roses instead.

'Champagne-colored roses are beautiful,' I told him, although I couldn't quite picture them.

'Her favorite is salmon-colored,' he said.

'Salmon and peach are pretty close.'

'No, they're not.'

It felt ridiculous arguing about colors with a blind man. There was a knock on the door, and Jerome said come in. 'Jury wants to see you, Judge Garrett.' It was the bailiff, bony and bald with a red ponytail. He smiled at me. 'Hi, Liv.'

'Hi, Ray.'

'You look very nice today.'

'Thank you.'

That was the problem with having a job – having to associate with people you wouldn't sit next to on the subway.

'Wait for me outside, Ray, and close the door.'

'You have a little dirt on your face, Your Honor,' Ray said.

'Thank you for telling me.' Ray closed the door loudly. Jerome turned toward me. 'Why didn't you tell me my face was dirty?' he asked.

'I didn't notice it until Ray said it just now,' I said.

'I don't believe you.' He sounded like a miserable teenager.

'It's true, it's barely noticeable.'

'Well, I need you to notice these things, Liv.' He reached around in a drawer and pulled out a black leather dop kit.

'May I watch you in court today?' I asked.

'You certainly may,' he said, blushing. 'We don't seem to be getting much work done anyway. Liv – is that short for Olivia?'

'No,' I said.

'Lavinia?'

'No!' I told him about how I was only three pounds when I was born and nobody thought I would make it and my father stood over the incubator in the hospital and chanted the word 'live' over and over again and a nurse thought that was my name and I did end up living and it stuck. I told him about the picture of me, asleep in my father's left hand.

'You delight me,' Jerome said. 'I look forward to coming to court in the morning.'

'I'm glad,' I said.

I thought of my favorite television commercial. A beautiful woman walks up court steps as a man's voice says, *Jennifer is going back to court today. She's not a lawyer, though she makes as much money as some. She's not a plaintiff or a defendant, but she cares what each one says. She not a judge, although she hands down her share of sentences*. Then we find out that Jennifer is a court stenographer who got her training at the Cittone Institute in New Jersey. Maybe I could be a court stenographer.

'I was wondering if you might –' He stopped abruptly. He looked like he hated himself again. He stood up and walked over to my chair.

'What?' I asked.

'It's just that I wish I knew what you look like.' He reached his hand out. 'May I?'

'May you what?' I asked.

Without explaining, he grabbed my face in his hand. He quickly touched one eye, which remained open, my nose, cheek, ear, jaw, and mouth. He touched my forehead, hairline, and hair. He was beet red.

'You are beautiful, aren't you? Thank you. Sorry.' I giggled awkwardly and he grabbed his shaving kit, briefcase, and judge's robe and left the room.

I sat in my chair touching my face with my hands for a very long time. First it felt cool, then hot. My eyelashes felt short. My eyebrows felt like silk cord. My cheeks felt fat. My bottom lip felt thick. My skin felt like the red velvet wallpaper of a Chinese restaurant. After a while I couldn't feel anything at all. I became invisible. I looked like everybody else.

That night I had dinner at my usual place, across the street from my new apartment at the Olive Tree Café, not to be confused with the Olive Garden restaurant. The Olive Tree was an old Village café with stained glass lamps, slate tables you could write on with chalk, and Charlie Chaplin movies playing round the clock on a white screen on the wall. The Olive *Garden* was a tacky Italian restaurant chain that I wouldn't set foot in for all the all-you-can-eat scampi in the world.

I slid into my usual booth at the Olive Tree, and the waiter came over to take my order. He had silky brown hair and wide eyes. His name tag said, 'Waitress in Training'.

I was staring at a photo of me in a sombrero. My husband had taken it in Mexico.

The waiter picked it up and looked at it. 'Are you a model?' he asked.

In the photo my face is swollen and my nose is bright red because we had spent the whole day in the desert trying to find my sunglasses. My husband had devised a system of marking cacti so we would know what territory we had searched and wouldn't let us stop looking until we found the sunglasses, which we never did. I carried the photo around with me to remind myself that life with him had not always been fun.

'No, I'm not a model,' I said, relishing the word. 'This is just a photo that my ex-husband took of me on the worst day of my life.'

He looked down at it again. 'I thought it was one of your, what do they call it, portfolio shots. I'm serious. I think you look beautiful here.'

'I look awful. I have sunstroke.'

He smiled at me, embarrassed, and I remembered from *The Rules* that men do not like loud sarcastic knee-slapping girls and I suddenly felt old. You should have just thanked him, I thought.

'Thank you,' I whispered.

He got a roll of masking tape from behind the bar, ripped off a piece, and came back to my table. He wrote 'er' on it and put it over the 'ress' of Waitress. 'This was driving me crazy,' he said. 'People are such assholes. I'm new to New York.'

It was never a good idea to date a guy who was new to New York. In fact it was a terrible idea. You never felt more used than when you spent all your time taking some guy who was new to New York to Coney Island, etc., only to find him gone after six months because he missed his mother's gumbo. It was always a waste of time, especially when they also turned out to be gay. I told him I had to go to the ladies' room.

'Good luck,' he said.

He wished me luck because the Olive Tree Café had a comedy club in the basement called the Comedy Cellar. Going to the bathroom there was always a humiliating experience because you had to go downstairs and walk past the stage to get to it. The comedians made fun of anyone taking the long walk to the bathroom.

I could hear laughter as I descended the stairs and felt the dread building in me. I walked quickly down the aisle and saw the pathetic flailing comedian and the clusters of out-of-towners all stop what they were doing and watch me.

'What's your hurry?' the comedian said. My whole body tensed. They never let you just walk by. 'Get out of her way, ladies and gentlemen. This woman pees more than any human being on the face of the earth.' No one laughed. You'd think a man who looked like that, with long red hair past his waist, would just naturally get a lot of laughs without even opening his mouth. 'Don't forget to wash your hands this time,' he said.

'I didn't come down here to use the bathroom,' I said. 'I came down here to give you a message. Your mother just called and said you're forty years old and it's time you got your own apartment.' The whole audience exploded in laughter. I walked triumphantly to the ladies' room. When I was done I had to walk past him again but he didn't stray from his act.

Then he came upstairs and said, 'Hey, you're a pretty funny girl.' When a comedian tells you you're funny it means he really hates you.

'I just want to be able to pee.'

'Yeah, well, I just want to be able to survive,' he said. He looked so miserable that I decided I would never use the bathroom there again, I would start using the bathroom at Caffe Reggio, just down the street.

I turned my attention to the screen and watched Charlie Chaplin. He was unicycling on a highwire with three monkeys jumping on his head. One monkey's tail curled into his mouth. I laughed out loud. The comedian gave me a nasty look.

When I got home I shoved my wedding video into the VCR and watched myself say my vows. Love had made me strong and sure and honest. 'For as long as we both shall live,' I watched myself say. I rewound and watched his vows. 'Forsaking all others . . .' I rewound. 'Forsaking all others . . .' I rewound. 'Forsaking all others . . .' I paused the tape and saw his face frozen on the filthy television screen. I marveled at his Academy Award-quality performance. 'Forsaking all others.' 'For as long as we both shall live.' I watched it over and over again.

Violet called and asked what I was doing.

'Nothing. Watching TV,' I said. My husband was frozen on the screen with his lips pursed about to say the 'for' of 'forsaking.'

'What are you watching?' she asked.

'Nothing. Flipping around.'

'I hope you're not watching the wedding again,' she said. Violet didn't like the video because she thought she looked fat. For a moment I hated her for accusing me of doing something that sad and pathetic.

'I don't do that anymore,' I said. The pause time on the VCR ended and the tape started to play. 'Forsaking all others' boomed through my bedroom.

I quickly hit the mute button. 'You've gotta stop watching that thing. You're not married to him anymore!' Violet announced as if I wasn't aware of that fact. I thought about saying it wasn't my wedding video, it was just a soap opera or something, but it was midnight and she would know it was a lie. 'I can't help it,' I said. 'It's my favorite movie. If I had a video of my divorce it would make a great double feature.'

'Promise me!' she said.

'I promise,' I mumbled. I had no idea what I was promising.

'I had a Hitler sighting,' she said. She was referring to her ex-boyfriend, David, who had recently grown a little square of hair over his lip and moved to her neighborhood. Everyone who lives in Hell's Kitchen sees each other at least twice a day because there are only two diners, the Westway and the Galaxy. 'I walked into Westway and there he was wearing bike shorts and carrying a briefcase. What an outfit. I ran out but I think he saw me.'

'You'll wind up face-to-face with him sooner or later.'

'Not if I'm careful.'

I watched the strange muted groom on the television screen step on the wineglass wrapped in its red linen napkin. I watched the silent rabbi mouth his gobbledygook. I watched the spellbound groom raise the nine-hundred-dollar veil of the beautiful, laughing-like-an-idiot bride, and then, the way I am surprised by the end every time I watch *Gone with the Wind*, I am shocked to find that that bride that that groom is about to kiss is me.

I got off the phone, turned up the volume, and fell asleep to the sounds of the reception, and Violet running like a linebacker to catch the bouquet.

The next morning I had been looking forward to sleeping late because Jerome didn't need me until twelve-thirty, but I was awakened by the phone ringing. It was my ex-husband calling from an airplane. I had made the mistake of leaving my number with his secretary. 'Did I wake you?' he asked.

'Not at *all*,' I declared, like a sophisticated divorcée.

'It's only nine-fifteen your time,' he said, self-importantly, as if my time were somehow inferior to the time of the rest of the world.

'Well, I've already had breakfast and made love,' I said. I stretched my arms and smiled when I said this like Scarlett O'Hara when she wakes up after a tumultuous night with Rhett. Then I said, 'Why are you calling me?' very curtly. Talking to him was like eating already chewed food.

'Come on, be nice,' he said, 'I'm calling you from a plane.'

My call waiting went off and I made him hold on while I got it. It was Sprint trying to win me back from AT&T. I decided to stick with AT&T after considering my options for a while and then clicked back to my ex-husband.

'Well, I should go, this is costing me seven dollars a minute. I just was thinking about you and I had a feeling that I should call.'

I hated when people had a feeling like that for no reason. Especially someone on a plane. It creeped me out.

'Well, I'm fine.'

'Shows you I'm still a good guy.'

I didn't say anything to that.

'Liv, have you put any thought into what you're going to do for a career?'

'I'm going to think about it right now, hold on,' I said. I put the phone down next to me on the bed. I tried to force myself to think about a career.

'Liv . . . Liv . . .' I heard him say into the phone.

The night I finally left him I stood waiting for the elevator with my pathetic luggage and the tourist's straw hat we had bought together in Mexico. I was a tourist in that building, in that life. I should have taken a picture. Then I would have seen that I was not the worldly sophisticated woman I thought I was, a woman with a past, a newborn divorcée. I would have seen myself holding my hat in one hand and a garbage bag of shoes in the other, with a certain wronged expression on my face, feeling at once very old and very young, as he stood screaming in the hallway, 'I'm a good guy, Liv! I'm a good guy! Goddamnit, Liv! I'm a good guy!' He had followed me out to the elevator in his blue bathrobe and his hairy legs and his leather slippers. I could hear him screaming as I went all the way down in the elevator, 'I'm a good guy, Liv.'

'I'm back,' I said into the phone.

'That wasn't funny,' he said. 'Comedienne should not be one of your career choices.'

'What do you suggest then?' I asked. 'How about divorce attorney? Maybe I'll go to law school.' Suddenly this conversation was making me feel worse than our whole marriage.

'Well, you do love to argue and you're pushy enough,' he said laughing. 'You're a pushy New Yorker.'

'I take that as a compliment.'

'You're so pushy you could be a real estate broker,' he said, laughing hysterically like a seal. 'A bro-kuh.'

Now he was being just plain insulting. We had made so much fun of the man who had sold us our apartment, a sad little man named Sandy.

I got off the phone. I knew that he had only called because he was bored on his flight and wanted to try using the airplane phone. He probably wanted to impress the person sitting next to him.

I went to my window and looked at the beating rain. Then I put on a T-shirt and panties and opened the front door. I wanted to see if anyone had *The New York Times* lying in front of his door so I could look at the help wanted ads again. I didn't know why I was bothering because this wasn't exactly the kind of building whose tenants read the *Times*. I dashed up one flight and saw a pair of child's rain boots, neatly lined up on someone's doormat. They were green rubber and looked like they might belong to a six-year-old boy. I didn't think there were any children in the building.

The boots looked so incredibly sweet that I thought I might cry. I wanted to hold them. I wanted to remember the feeling of a small green rubber boot. I picked one up and then the other. Then I brought them down to my apartment and locked the door behind me. My heart was beating loudly.

I sat on the floor of my living room with my back against the wall and held the little boy's boots in my arms. I put my hands in them and made them take little steps. It was time to get on with my life. I couldn't sit here forever with my hands in a pair of stolen boots.

I got dressed, brushed my teeth, and returned the boots to their mat. Then I grabbed an umbrella and went down for the paper.

6

BLCNY OVRLOOKS RIV

'Judge Moody is retiring and there's going to be a little party for him this afternoon here in the building,' Jerome said. 'I would like you to escort me there. It will be our first official outing together. It will be like our first date, won't it?' He looked straight in my direction with a bold blind look on his face.

Ray the bailiff had warned me about the party already and I had come in appropriately dressed for once. I wasn't wearing a suit but I was wearing a really nice black-and-white velvet vintage dress.

'I'm afraid it's going to be boring, isn't it?' Jerome did this very English thing of saying something and then tagging a little question onto the end of it, therefore putting the burden of the conversation back on you. With other English people you could just nod or shake your head but with Jerome you had to answer.

I didn't say anything.

'Isn't it?' he asked again.

'I don't know. I've never been to a judge's retirement party,' I said. 'Have I?' I added.

'No, I don't suppose you have, have you?'

'No.'

This was typical of our conversations.

At five o'clock, Jerome flipped back the glass on his watch and felt the time. 'Shall we?' he asked.

I stood up and started to the door. He met me there and grabbed for my elbow. I felt like a nurse taking a patient for tests in another part of the hospital. I did not want to be a nurse. 'Velvet!' he said. 'Lovely.'

We walked into the party and just stood a little to the right of the entryway. No one noticed our arrival and I really didn't know what we were supposed to do. How did a blind man mingle? I wondered. I decided to describe the whole room. 'We're in a sort of a hall,' I said, 'with very high ceilings and a mosaic floor with a geometrical star pattern and portraits of judges on the walls.'

My husband was right, I really could be a real estate agent. I sounded just like one. A Seeing Eye dog and a real estate agent weren't that different. You led people places and barked. 'As you can see the hall has the grand dimensions of a United States courthouse, yet it's somehow warm and cozy as a country cottage,' I said, practicing my new career. 'Isn't it just drop-dead to die for?' I added in a Long Island accent.

'Would you please stop that,' Jerome said. 'That's terribly annoying.'

'The space has marvelous *bones*,' I said. An old woman with osteoporosis who had shown Jack and me an apartment had said that to us and I had always remembered it.

'What on earth does that mean?' Jerome asked.

'I'm not sure,' I said. 'My ex-husband thinks I should be a real estate agent. What do you think?'

'I think it's a vile idea, isn't it? I can't think of anything less relaxing than being in the company of a budding real estate agent.' I wasn't aware that it was my job to relax him. 'On the other hand, you'd probably be very charming at it, and I understand you don't have to be a good speller, do you?'

It was true you didn't need any skills or an education. If you grew up in New York and got divorced, it seemed inevitable. You had to do it. But you usually did something else first. All the brokers who had shown us apartments had first failed at something else. One had been an investment banker, one a CPA, one had owned a consignment shop called Crème de la Crap. I wondered if it was possible to skip the doing-something-else part and just go into early partial-retirement as a real estate agent at twenty-six. Certainly failing at marriage was enough to qualify. It didn't seem like a bad idea if I was just going to end up doing it anyway.

'Actually I really am going to go to real estate school,' I said. 'I've been keeping an eye out for something to, you know, do, and that seems like the best thing.' I shouldn't have said eye out.

'Really,' he said, flustered. 'You neglected to mention that, didn't you?' His hand dropped from my elbow. He didn't know if I was kidding or not and I didn't really know either. Standing in that hall with all those judges made it feel almost official, like a ceremony. I felt as if I had made a vow. 'You promised me a year, Liv, and you've only given me a month,' Jerome said.

My husband had promised me a lifetime. 'Well, I start in two weeks,' I said. I had no idea when I started but I wondered if it was somehow true.

'Good for you,' Jerome said, bitterly.

We stood in silence until an old man wearing his robe open to reveal a Hawaiian shirt finally walked over to us.

'Jerome, Bob Moody here.'

'Congratulations, Bob,' Jerome said. 'We've been trying to get rid of you for a long time, haven't we?'

'I'm the last person in this room who should be retiring. I look fifteen years younger than all of you.'

I laughed. For some reason I really liked judge humor.

'Is that true, Liv?' Jerome asked me.

'You all look pretty old to me,' I said.

Jerome put out his hand very close to his side like a robot and Judge Moody shook it. 'Well, Bob, this is a happy day for all of us, isn't it?' Jerome said cheerfully. Jerome introduced me and said, 'Liv is my new reader and she is also, I just found out, an aspiring real estate agent. Isn't that right?'

'That's right,' I said.

'What exactly do you have these young readers do?' Judge Moody asked. 'Liv, what is it you do?'

'I'm not really sure,' I said.

'My bidding,' Jerome spit out.

I rolled my eyes. 'Congratulations on your retirement,' I said.

'Well, I'm not quite retired yet. I still have one very happy last task to perform. I will be conducting a very special wedding ceremony,' Judge Moody said. 'Jerome, are you bringing Liv to the wedding?'

'That would be lovely,' Jerome said. 'But I don't know if a wedding would be Liv's cup of tea right now, would it?'

'Thank you,' I said, 'but I can't.' I was afraid it might involve somehow dancing with him.

'Well, anyway, Liv, I should introduce you to Andrew Lugar,' Judge Moody said. 'He's standing right over there.'

'Why?' I asked. When you feel like a nursemaid, you don't expect to be introduced to people.

'Well, you're in real estate,' Judge Moody said, 'and Andrew's an architect. Today's a very big day for Andrew.'

I had just told Violet that I thought Asian babies were the cutest kind of baby and she told me that she thought I would marry a Japanese architect. She was always making totally wrong predictions which annoyed me because I actually thought about them afterward.

Andrew Lugar walked over to us. He wasn't Japanese but he was short and wore a dark suit. He stood tensely with his weight on one leg. He introduced himself to Jerome and me.

'What were you talking about with those clerks?' Judge Moody asked.

'They were discussing whether they had sex on the first date,' Andrew said. He turned to me. 'What about you, do you have sex on the first date?'

Judge Moody wagged his finger. 'Andrew, what kind of question –'

'Overruled,' Jerome said. 'Liv, you may answer the question.'

'I only have sex on the first date if I really don't like the guy and I know I don't want to see him again,' I said.

'Good for you!' Jerome said.

Andrew burst out laughing. I asked Jerome if he wanted any cake. He patted his stomach and said, 'No thank you, I really shouldn't.' His stomach wasn't really his problem. He should have patted his hips and thighs.

'I'd like some, would you?' Andrew said.

'Okay,' I said, trying to sound like I didn't care about cake one way or the other. My father always insisted his models eat cake on their birthdays and not throw it up after because he said if you don't have cake on your birthday you'll be hungry all year. I extended that to, if you don't have cake anytime it's offered you'll be hungry all year.

Jerome squeezed my elbow and released me. 'Go ahead,' he said.

I followed the architect to the cake. It was covered in shredded green icing and little plastic golf flags and a little plastic golfer.

'So, how do you know Judge Moody?' I asked.

He cut me a rectangle of green cake and flipped it onto a paper plate.

'Maybe I should bring a piece to Judge Garrett,' I said.

'He said he didn't want any,' Andrew said. 'Have you been out on the balcony? You should see the view.'

We stepped out on the small curved balcony and leaned on the wrought-iron rail.

'How did you say you know Judge Moody?' I asked.

'He's my father-in-law.'

My eyes went automatically to Andrew's left hand. There was no ring. He watched me do this.

'Looking to see if I'm wearing a ring?' he asked.

'What? No,' I said.

I was glad he wasn't wearing one and that I hadn't forgotten to look. Violet was an expert left-hand looker, but I always forgot. I once wasted a whole plane ride talking to a man wearing three wedding bands.

'I was wondering if I could call you to discuss real estate.'

'What sort of real estate questions did you have?' I said.

'I'm looking for a loft I can live and work in.'

'A live/work loft,' I said.

'Right. I found one I liked but they wouldn't allow dogs. I have dogs. Do you have any pets?'

'No,' I said.

'Well, do you think you could help me find a loft?'

There was no reason to try to impress a married guy.

'I'm not really a real estate agent,' I told him.

'Well, I'm not really married,' he said.

'Oh, you're not?' I said. I could feel my face get hot.

'No, I just live with someone,' he said.

He was totally rude and unattractive with awful brown glasses that made him look like a lesbian. He pulled his wallet out of his back pocket and handed me a business card. 'Call me if you hear of anything.' He grabbed my hand and I pulled away from him. 'What would you do if I picked you up and threw you off this balcony?' he said.

'I don't answer hypothetical questions,' I told him.

'We could have a drink.'

'Is that some sort of a threat?' I said. I felt confused, like I was one beat behind in the conversation.

In one quick movement he grabbed my arm, turned me around, wrapped his arms around me, and lifted me up. I screamed and he laughed. He had me up in the air facing the party. I could see Jerome through the French doors talking to some men who were taller than him.

'Put me down,' I screamed. No one could hear me.

Andrew turned around so I faced the river. He pressed the fronts of my legs against the railing. He held my upper body over the edge of the balcony and laughed. For a moment I thought he really was going to send me over but we just stood like that with my hair blowing in my face. I kept my eyes closed. He shimmied his arms lower on my body and dangled more and more of me over the edge. I got dizzy thinking about my bracelet falling off.

'Well, if you're not going to do it, I really should be getting back to Judge Garrett,' I said, calmly.

The jerk put me down and I went back inside.

And people say it's hard to meet a man in New York.

M y legs shook as I walked up the stairs to my apartment. I couldn't get him out of my mind. How could a man just lift a person up like that? How could I just get lifted?

It had felt almost natural being with Jerome at Judge Moody's retirement party. He had stayed to attend the wedding Judge Moody was performing and it felt strange leaving alone, being out on the street, walking without his hand on my elbow. I had gotten used to Jerome grabbing my elbow like Henry the Eighth grabbing for a turkey wing. I get attached faster than anybody.

As soon as I opened the door, the phone rang and I started to regret answering. It was Violet, and I didn't want to talk to her because we always spent hours on the phone and lately neither one of us had anything even mildly interesting to say. I was through talking about my ex-husband. I didn't want to tell her about Andrew Lugar, the lifter.

I didn't even get a chance to speak. She was rattling on about how she had taken Valium the night before and had sex with a stranger at a roof party. 'He was so sexy and European. Such a mensch,' she kept saying.

Violet liked to use words like mensch all the time even though she was a Wasp from Texas and had absolutely no idea what mensch meant.

'Do you think he'll call?' she asked.

I couldn't believe she thought there was even a remote chance that he would call. He would never call. 'He'll call,' I said. 'He'll definitely call.' Finally I said, 'Well, you're not going to believe what happened to me. I consider it a new low point.'

'What?' she asked, completely interested in any story that started with that.

'I was lifted,' I said. I told her the whole story and we sat on the phone in silence, shocked that a person could just lift another person like that. This was so much better than our usual conversations.

7
LIVE/WORK OK

The next day I squeezed in with a million Japanese people and took the elevator up to the top of the Empire State Building. It was raining and visibility was low, but that hadn't stopped the tourists. I wished visibility were even lower. I loved it when there was zero visibility and you stood up there in a cloud. You knew New York was there but you couldn't see it.

I walked past the concession stand with its rows of stuffed King Kongs and stood outside in the misty rain. I put fifty cents in a telescope machine. I aimed it toward my old apartment, where I used to live high up with my husband. I swung the machine fast over the broccoli patch of Central Park and over to the East Side. I could travel from the Hudson to the East River with a flick of my wrist.

Then the lenses went blank and I put another fifty cents in. This time I saw nothing but color. I pulled my face away. It was an enormous rainbow. The crowds around me gasped and clapped like it was the Fourth of July. I gasped and clapped, too. I had never seen one before, but looking at it now made me feel like I should never have bothered to look at anything else. I should have always been looking at rainbows. It was the most beautiful thing I had ever seen. God had thrown down a scarf.

I couldn't imagine New York without it. It would have to stay. 'Why does that happen?' I heard a little boy ask.

I waited for the answer but there wasn't any.

In minutes it started to fade, getting muddy in the center at the height of its arc. Clouds were interfering with it. I started to get angry.

I put quarter after quarter in and followed the rainbow through the lenses. When it faded completely I found myself staring at a familiar shape. It was the shape the curtains made in the glass doors leading to the balcony in the bedroom of my husband's apartment. The broker had called it a Juliet balcony. There were the curtains, the doors, and my giant flowerpots. I could see right into my husband's bedroom.

We had sex on that balcony once. I had been drunk and my knees had wobbled and the city spun. I didn't know we were being watched by Japanese tourists.

I had stood on that balcony in a white hotel bathrobe when he was at work and waved, pretending to be Marilyn. Now I wondered who had waved back.

Again the lenses went dark. I went to the concession stand to get more change so I could keep watching the balcony. I half-expected to see my husband standing out there. I half-expected to see myself.

The next morning I rushed to the newsstand expecting to see pictures of the rainbow on all the front pages. I bought the *Times*, the *News*, and the *Post* but all I found was a war, and a sports guy who had picked up a prostitute. I turned reluctantly to the weather pages, thinking at least it would be there. But it wasn't. Yesterday's rainbow wasn't news in this world.

I read my horoscope and dumped the papers in the garbage can. Then I tried to remember the horoscope that I had just read but I couldn't. It had completely evaporated from my mind.

I couldn't bring myself to go to Jerome's. The thought of sitting there staring at him all day with him not even able to stare back depressed me. I looked in the mirror. I had to be seen today. By somebody. That wasn't too much to ask.

I spent the morning walking around looking up at the tops of buildings. New York had a high blue ceiling. I looked up into windows. With all those windows there had to be somewhere I could work. There had to be someplace where I could be of use. In this whole city there had to be a job where the people had vision.

At noon I went to Il Cantinori, an Italian restaurant on Tenth Street that I used to go to with my husband.

The maître d' recognized me and gave me a great table near the front. The floor-to-ceiling windows were swung completely open and my table was practically on the sidewalk. I was half in and half out. Half here and half everywhere else. The noise of the city outside – men working construction on top of scaffolding, car alarms, honking – mixing with the soft music inside and the ringing of cell phones mad me feel like nothing was going on or ever had, or would, that I didn't somehow know about.

Suddenly I was distracted by a woman at the next table making strange sex noises over her soup. 'Ummmm, ummmm, ohhhhh,' she moaned.

She was sitting alone. Only now I wasn't sure that it was a woman. Short fingernails. A plain gold wedding band. Men's brown oxfords.

'Hi, I'm Dale,' the person said to me. 'How aaaaare you?'

'Hi,' I said, going back to the menu.

'This soup is so good.' Dale was wearing big blue jeans with a blue work shirt tucked in like a postman. Dale was fat and even rounder and softer than Jerome, with tight short curly black hair. 'This soup brings me right back to Italy,' Dale said.

Fat people always love to talk about Italy.

'Italy is perfect. The food and the wine! Everyone is so elegant. The women wrap themselves in long wool capes. It's so beautiful.' Dale stopped and raised a finger. 'Shhh, you hear that?'

I listened. I could hear everything and nothing. I shook my head Dale pointed to two businessmen. One was talking about a meeting he was having with a co-op board about an apartment he was trying to buy. 'They're tough,' he said, 'and without board approval, there's no way we can move in there.' The other laughed. 'Wear a good suit.' 'No,' the first man said, 'the problem is Jenny plays the cello.'

'You see that. All anybody talks about in this town is real estate!' Dale whispered, dipping bread into a plate of oil.

I hated when people called New York a town.

Without my asking, the maître d' brought over a plate of the pasta I used to get with my husband. It embarrassed me. I felt like an impersonator, pretending to be my old self. I felt like a trespasser, as if I had broken into my husband's apartment and pulled my chair up to my old place at the dining room table. I didn't want my husband's old pasta. I was Miss Havisham afraid of splattering tomato sauce on my gown.

Dale stood up, walked over to the two men, and handed them a business card. 'Pardon me, gentlemen, how aaaaare you? I couldn't help overhearing. I'm sure you won't have any problem getting board approval but if it doesn't work out please give me a call.' They looked up in disbelief.

Then Dale put a card down near the edge of my table. 'It was very nice to meet you,' Dale said, putting out a chubby hand. I shook it.

Through a gap between the buttons of the blue work shirt I caught a glimpse of a stark white bra. Woman! I thought. Dale looked me straight in the eye. 'I'm sure I'll see you again.' She leaned in closer. 'I love having that soup when it's that time of the month.'

'*Grazie*,' she said across the restaurant to the waiter, and left.

'What a freak,' the man buying the co-op said.

The card said 'Dale Kilpatrick Licensed Real Estate.'

My check was almost fifty dollars. The maître d' had taken the liberty of charging me for everything he had brought over. I needed a real job.

'Hi, how aaaaare you?' Dale said, when I walked into her office. She was sitting behind a desk with a complete set of Tony Robbins motivational tapes on a shelf behind her.

'Great,' I said.

'Grrrreeeaaattt!' she said.

She looked me up and down. I hadn't worn anything special to meet with her, just jeans and a Chanel No 5 T-shirt I had bought on Canal Street and a long pin-striped jacket. I suddenly wished I was wrapped in a long wool cape. I didn't know why she was making me feel self-conscious. She was wearing the same blue uniform as the day before. I decided it was just that I wasn't used to a sighted interview.

'Let me axe you a question,' Dale said. 'Why do you want to be a real estate agent?'

'I'm divorced,' I said. 'I had to move out of my apartment. It was a really beautiful apartment.'

'I think so many women in New York get into real estate for that reason,' Dale said. 'We don't want to end up homeless bag ladies collecting aluminum soder cans.'

The homeopathic doctor I had gone to right before I left my husband told me that my body was filled with aluminum. I was more metallic than anybody she had ever met. 'I bet you beep when you go through metal detectors at the airport,' she had said. 'Yes I do,' I told her, even though I didn't. I liked the idea of it.

'Anyway I know how you feel. When I was a kid,' Dale said, 'we lived in a walk-up in Queens.'

'Oh, that's awful,' I said.

'No, that's not the bad part. My father beat me and then he made me wait out in the hall. The hall was dark and smelled like cat piss and garbage. They wouldn't let me into the house. I had to wait in the hall for whole days sometimes and into the night. I wasn't even allowed to have my own house key. That's why I got into real estate. Look,' she said. She pointed to a Peg-Board on the wall with dozens of keys hanging from tiny hooks.

'When I was a kid,' I said, 'we traveled a lot, from hotel to hotel, and I had to stay in my room and sometimes it wasn't even on the same floor as my parents' room.' I wished I hadn't told my own hard-luck story. Dale didn't look too sorry for me.

But I somehow knew how she felt about being in the hall. When I was a child my shrink told me that I was a nomad, which she explained meant turtle without a shell.

'Anyway, that's why I like to sit here in my beautiful office and surround myself with beautiful things,' Dale said.

I looked around the shabby office. It was one square room with a bathroom. Water dripped in the sink. One wall stuck out to create a partition for no reason and was painted orange with a yellow stripe. There were five wooden school desks in a row and a bridge table in the middle of the room with a computer on it.

Another woman sat at one of the desks with her back to us. She shuffled through papers. She had long ruined bleached blond hair and a baseball cap. She wasn't wearing a wedding ring. She didn't acknowledge me in any way.

'Oh,' I said, pointing to a wall lined with shelves that were crammed with strange knickknacks: vases, lamps, figurines, glass bottles, two old rotary phones, three sets of salt and pepper shakers – a squirrel and a nut, two red chili peppers, and two feet. It looked like a junkyard.

'Those are for sale,' Dale said. 'This isn't just a real estate office. We're a real estate *gallery*. I'm currently interviewing to hire, you know, a gallery guy.'

'You mean a curator?' I asked.

'A what?'

'A curator. Someone who chooses the art in a gallery.'

'That's what they call it? I like that word!' Dale said. 'I never heard of that.' She grabbed a paperback dictionary and looked it up. '"The director of an institution such as a museum,"' she read. 'This isn't exactly a museum. Yet.'

I laughed, and she gave me an angry look.

'They still call it a curator,' I said.

Dale rambled on about her successful SoHo art gallery. 'We could use a smart kid like you,' Dale said. She gave me a brochure for a real estate course at the Pennsylvania Hotel on Seventh Avenue. 'You have to be sponsored by a broker in order to get your license. When they axe you who's sponsoring you, give them my card.'

'Thank you,' I said, suddenly feeling grateful to be sponsored like a starving African child with flies crawling on my distended stomach.

'And what's my salary going to be?' I asked.

The blond woman snorted.

'There's no salary!' Dale said, enthusiastically. 'The great news is you're an independent contractor. You get paid a commission! Most firms only give you twenty percent of every deal but I'm willing to start you off at fifty percent.'

'That sounds great,' I said.

'Grrreeeaaattt! Well, I really think you lucked out. You found your way into a great firm,' Dale said. 'I think you're going to fit in very well.'

'Thank you,' I said, suddenly planning never to come back.

'We're going to make millions,' Dale said.

The blond woman snorted again. 'Shut up, Lorna,' Dale said.

'Oh, one more thing, there's a dress code,' Dale said. I tugged at my Chanel No 5 shirt. It had risen up a little over my stomach. 'You should dress as though you're working in a high-end law firm, or a Madison Avenue art gallery.'

Or a run-down real estate office and garage sale, I thought.

'Look at you,' Lorna said to Dale. 'Look what you're wearing. You look like a bus driver. You look like Ralph Kramden.'

She looked more like a postal worker, I thought.

'You look like a postman,' Lorna said.

'Lorna, that's enough. Things are going to be changing around here now,' Dale said.

'What do you care what we wear?' Lorna said. She pointed to the wall of junk. 'This place is like working at Sanford and Son. I love working at the town dump. Oh, and for your information, all firms start you at fifty-percent commission.'

'It's okay,' I said.

'Shut up,' Dale said, to Lorna. 'When I get dressed up to go out I can look more feminine than all of youse. In a short dress

and heels . . . Ummmm, I look good. Every man I pass looks at
me. I could get more men than both of you put together.'

'Yeah, right,' Lorna said.

'You're really axing for it,' Dale said.

'What are you going to do, fat man, fire me? I think you have
to actually pay a person in order to fire them.' She stood up. 'It
stinks in here. I'm leaving,' she said.

'Pay no attention to her,' Dale said. 'She's just jealous.'

From the window behind Dale's desk I could see Lorna
already walking up Greene Street. I had never seen anyone walk
so fast in my life. She led with her head and shoulders like she
was straining on an invisible leash. People moved aside to keep
from getting hit.

'I have to apologize for my associate,' Dale said. 'She's a very
unpleasant person. I'm just letting her work here because she
owes me money. Have you ever used a computer?' Dale asked.

'No,' I admitted.

'I'll teach you.' She led me to the computer and I sat too low in
a wooden chair. 'This is the Mac.' The keyboard was covered in a
thin clear plastic cover like an old lady's couch. She punched the
keys through the plastic layer until the screensaver of the New
York City skyline under sparkling stars disappeared and an animated frog in a pond came up. She showed me how to use the
mouse and I sat for twenty minutes double-clicking and drag-
ging the frog from one lily pad to another. If I missed he fell in the
water and splashed. If I made it, he ribbited happily.

'You're a natural,' Dale said.

I know how to use a computer now, I thought to myself. I
didn't have to sit in the dark reading the calories and fat grams
on a potato chip bag to Jerome. I had to admit it felt sort of good.
I felt like I could make millions.

Dale walked over and stood behind me, wearing a sickening
aftershave.

A fat woman with a ponytail drooping down her back walked
in. She had dark skin like a gypsy and sad eyes like a child at
bedtime.

'Harri, meet the kid,' Dale said.

'I'm Liv,' I said.

'Pleased to meet you,' Harri said. She took a bag of Doritos out of a shopping bag and poured them out on one of the desks, making a big pile of them.

'Harri's my partner,' Dale said. Harri was wearing the same gold band as Dale. 'Liv's our new young lion.'

'Oh yeah?' Harri said.

8

NO DOGS, NO BKRS

In order to get my license I had to take a forty-five-hour course and two tests – the test for the school and the test for the state. I signed up to take the course in five days straight for nine hours a day.

Why not? I thought. I was so depressed it wasn't like anything could make me feel worse. What difference did it make where I sat and brooded for five days? Might as well get licensed for it. The first day was on what would have been my husband's birthday if we were still together.

When I walked into the lobby of the Pennsylvania Hotel I gasped. There were dogs everywhere, dogs of every shape and size. It took me a minute to realize that the Westminster Dog Show was happening across the street at Madison Square Garden.

The place had turned into a dog run. It felt strange and exciting like when a pigeon flies into an expensive restaurant.

But the more I looked at the dogs, the more grotesque they seemed – fluffed and powdered and drinking water from Evian bottles. They were more like trained seals than dogs. More like stewardesses working at the St. Louis hub than unneutered animals. They all looked like JonBenet Ramsey.

I made my way to the elevators, past a Shih Tzu having his portrait painted, and got on with four Bedlington terriers. On the ninth floor I followed an arrow on a handwritten sign that said 'Empire Real Estate School.'

An obese woman with a slight beard sat on a stool outside the door with a clipboard. I told her my name. 'You're six minutes late,' she said. She wrote a – 6 next to my name. 'You're only allowed to be out of the room for a total of twenty minutes while class is in progress or you're disqualified,' she said, looking down at me like I was worst-in-show.

I took a seat in the front row, which was the only seat left. The room was filled with women, a few fags, and some middle-aged men. A couple of people were all dressed up. I wished I was back in the lobby.

The woman sitting next to me smiled and stared at me until I turned my head and smiled back at her. She was tall and wore a hat with an actual feather and no wedding ring. I was miserable sitting in the front and I twisted around to see if there was any way I could move back.

'If you're looking for where the action is, it's up here,' the teacher said, pointing to himself. 'Trust me.' He was very small and Jewish with a New York accent. Wedding band.

'We're talking about chattel marriages,' he said.

'Chattel marriages,' I repeated like a parrot.

He hooted. 'Not marriages. *Mortgages*.'

'Sorry,' I said.

'Will you mortgage me?' he asked, bending down on one knee in front of me. I couldn't believe it.

'No,' I said.

'Actually I'm very happily mortgaged already.' He flicked an invisible cigar and stood up.

I wrote the words 'Chattel Mortgage' on the legal pad I had stolen from Jerome's office. One day while he was sitting there, I just piled a bunch of pads, boxes of pens, and a stapler into a shopping bag. Chattel Mortgage. The words looked soft and valuable like champagne.

'Chattel,' he instructed, 'from the French for cattle.'

'Hi,' the woman sitting next to me wrote on her pad. She tilted it toward me for emphasis.

'Hi,' I wrote on my pad and tilted.

'I'm not listening,' she wrote. 'Already bored.'

'Me too,' I wrote.

She wrote back a two-page dissertation. Her name was Valashenko and she had been a model on the cover of *French Vogue* when she was twenty-one. A gentleman friend, a sort of a benefactor, who was also a psychiatrist, had encouraged her to get into this line of work, but she had certain misgivings. Then, a leak, pouring down from the ceiling of her closet, had been the final straw. She needed money and a new apartment. She realized she had nothing and she couldn't get any more miserable so she signed up for real estate school. She wrote that she was only wearing one contact lens and couldn't see a thing. 'I'm divorced,' she squeezed in on the bottom of the second page.

I underlined the 'me too' I had already written. Divorce was my only résumé item. It was my whole story.

When we went out on our lunch break I could see that she was at least fifty. She kept her hat on the whole time. She couldn't decide what to order. She counted the dollar bills in her wallet.

She wasn't happy with her pasta special.

'I have eaten in all the finest restaurants in the world,' she said.

'Send it back,' I said.

'I never do that,' she said. 'I don't think I could do that.' She tried to take a bite.

'Don't eat it if it's bad.'

'It's not good,' she said, distressed.

'Just tell the waitress it's not good and get something else,' I said, amused.

'I can't!'

'Do you want me to do it?' I asked.

Finally when I was almost done with my egg salad she called

the waitress over. 'I'm really sorry to bother you but' – she looked down at the pasta – 'I'm . . . I'm . . . I can't do it,'-she said to me.

'You can do it,' I told her.

'I'm just not happy at all,' she blurted out to the waitress. She looked like she was going to cry. It was amazing how badly she had handled it.

The waitress whisked away her plate and brought her a menu. She squinted at it with her good eye.

At that moment I knew that I had what it took to be a real estate agent. I wouldn't think twice about sending back food. Valashenko wasn't going to make it, and neither were most of the people in that class. The man in the bow tie, the woman who ate bags of McDonald's, squirting dabs of ketchup on individual fries while the rest of us took notes, the Indian man with the English accent who kept asking how much money he could expect to make, the girl in the last row who reeked of cigarette smoke and brushed her hair, the failed lawyer interested in doing land development deals Upstate. One girl, a young lion type like myself, told a story about how she worked as an agent's assistant, showing apartments at Zeckendorf Towers, and a man told her he would only take the apartment if she went for a swim with him in the rooftop pool, and she did but he didn't sign the lease. I knew from that she wouldn't make a dime.

But I would. I could do it with *no* contact lenses. My husband was right – I was pushy enough – and Dale was right – I was a natural.

We got back from lunch twelve minutes late. Now I had a negative 18 next to my name.

'We're talking about multiple listings,' the teacher said.

'Multiple listings,' I repeated carefully.

'Very good, for a minute I was worried you were going to say multiple orgasms,' he said. He laughed at his own joke. It was why I had always hated school – the teacher always focused on me.

He went on to talk about the fact that you had to be a licensed agent to sell cemetery plots. 'Real estate is real estate no matter what you want to use it for,' he said. 'It doesn't matter if you are selling six feet or six thousand square feet. Maybe that would be good for you,' he said to me. 'Working in a cemetery. You seem glum enough.' He was smiling at me. 'You look like you're at a funeral.'

His comment surprised me since I had faced real estate school so bravely. I thought I had been sitting there with a pleasant, upbeat expression on my face.

I thought of myself taking the train to Long Island every day and working at a Jewish cemetery. Trudging through dirt in a long black skirt with lace-up shoes.

'I think I'd rather sell million-dollar lofts in Tribeca,' I said.

'And I think you will,' he said. 'I think you will.'

For the next five days I learned about liens and fees and bonds and fiduciary responsibility. The words were so beautiful and sounded so promising, my heart sank a little each time one was explained. But there was always another to take its place. They looked like Fitzgerald titles written on the blackboard. Tender of a contract, binders and good faith, consideration, promissory notes, lot and block numbers, easements, options, time is of the essence, meeting of the minds, renunciation, abandonment and breach, earnest money, usury, blanket mortgages, wraparound mortgages, covenants. Estoppel, enough already.

I couldn't help but think if I had known any of this when I was married we might have stayed together. We would have had puffing and steering to talk about. I already felt like a different person.

For forty-four hours and forty-one and a half minutes, I sat next to Valashenko and ate Dunkin' Donuts and Pepperidge Farm, passing them around to everyone behind me.

I also went to the dog show, standing in the back because I couldn't sit anymore. I had spent some time getting to know the contestants, and I felt like I had to support my friends.

'When are you taking the test?' I wrote to Valashenko. I had counted down the last ninety minutes on my pad in thirty-second increments. My whole body hurt from sitting so long.

'Next Tuesday,' she wrote.

'Me too.'

I got all one hundred questions right on the class test, even the math, and on Tuesday I went for the state test. I sat in a big room with a hundred people. Valashenko wasn't there.

A few weeks later a slip of pink onionskin paper came in the mail saying I had passed the state exam. I received a license and a 'pocket card.' I was so excited I wanted to call my husband but I called Dale instead and told her I was ready to work.

'Grreeeaaattt!' she said. 'I have a listing for you.'

On my first day as a licensed real estate agent I ate peas for breakfast right out of the can, standing in my kitchen, and got to Dale's by ten.

I sat at my desk, terrified, calling Violet whenever Dale left the office.

'So you don't know what you're supposed to do?' Violet asked.

'I have no idea,' I said. 'They didn't cover that in real estate school.'

'You should canvass,' Dale said when she came back in and hovered around my desk.

'Great,' I said, as if I were looking forward to it. I wasn't sure canvassing was something to do with real estate or with her art gallery.

'Grrreeeaaattt!' Dale said. She placed two huge books on my desk and put her hand on them as if they were Bibles. 'This is a co-op book,' she said about one, 'and this is an upside-down phone book She looked proud, as if she were presenting me with a homemade upside-down cake. 'Pick a building you would like to conquer and call all the people who live in it and axe them if they want to sell or rent. That's how you get listings. You can usually get two commissions that way, selling their apartment and then selling another apartment to them.'

I looked up my old address and found my husband's name.

Then I picked a building on West Broadway and left messages on twenty-five answering machines. If an actual person answered I hung up. My next task was to write my name on the bottom of a stack of 'temporary' business cards.

When I got home I got undressed and a single pea fell out of my bra. I had gone to work with a pea in my bra and not even known it. Some princess, I thought.

The next morning I woke up late and did some X (Excedrin). I had learned in real estate school that as an independent contractor I was allowed to make my own hours. I felt independent. I was even ready to return the video I had brought with me from my husband's house, *The Long, Long, Trailer* starring Lucille Ball and Desi Arnaz.

When I rented it the girl with the glasses five sizes too big in the video store said she and I were the only two people in the history of the place to ever take it out. My husband and I didn't get a chance to watch it in the heat of our battle, so I packed it in with the rest of the things I was taking with me. Every night in my new place, I intended to watch it but I couldn't. I hadn't watched a video alone, except for my wedding video, in five years. I couldn't watch *The Long, Long Trailer* without my husband's arms around me. I had had it out now for sixty-seven days. I was ready to return it.

I took a cab to the Upper East Side and walked into the video store. I looked around nervously for a minute, thinking I might see my husband there, but of course he probably wouldn't be renting videos at noon on a weekday.

The girl with the big glasses was there behind the counter next to the shaved-bald man with the tiny glasses. 'Hi, Liv,' the girl said.

'Hi,' I said. I took the video out of my bag. The girl punched my name into the computer.

'Hmmmm,' she said, frowning at the screen.

I felt like I was getting bad news about an ultrasound. Jack should be here with me holding my hand.

'You don't have an account with us anymore,' she said.

'I'm on my husband's account,' I said.

'Hmmmm,' she said, punching keys. 'No, he took you of account.'

I couldn't believe it. I stared at the Polaroids of dogs taped counter under a basket of tiny Milk-Bones.

I hadn't even been planning to sue him for one drop of alimony.

'I'm sorry,' she said, tortured as if she were our child caught up in the divorce and we were going to have to start shuttling her back and forth between our apartments. 'Did you want to open your own account?'

I shook my head no. 'I don't think this video store is big enough for the both of us.' I put the video back in my bag.

The girl stretched out her hand. 'Were you going to return *The Long, Long Trailer?*' she asked.

'No, I think I'll keep it out another day or two,' I said and left the store.

When I got to the office Dale informed me that I was late. 'I expect you here by ten,' she said. 'It's your job to open up and get the messages off the machine.'

'I thought I was allowed to make my own hours,' I said.

She glared. 'This is a small firm, Liv. You have to think of yourself as an entrepreneur or a mogul.' Then she gave me the other secret to getting listings. 'Call everyone you know and tell them that you're a real estate broker now. And always start every phone call with the words "good news." "I have good news, I'm a broker now."'

'I'm only an agent,' I said. I had just learned in real estate school that you had to be an agent for a minimum of two years and complete a certain number of deals, and then take a ninety-hour course and pass another set of exams to be a broker.

'It doesn't matter. Tell them you're a broker, it sounds better. And you work for a top firm. Call all your friends and relatives.

Are you any relation to the designer Peter Kellerman?' she asked.

She was talking about my father.

'No,' I said.

I sat at my desk and considered calling my father. I really missed him and I had read on Page Six that he was in New York. I hadn't been able to face calling him since I had left my husband. He had spent a quarter of a million dollars on the wedding. It reminded me of when I went around our building when I was a kid selling raffle tickets for my school and lost the envelope of three hundred and eight one-dollar bills. I walked around for weeks hardly able to breathe. But when I told him he just hugged me and wrote a check for three hundred and eight dollars.

I decided to call him and tell him about the divorce. Maybe he would kill Jack. I would tell him I only had one rented video to show for the whole marriage. As soon as Dale left the office I called him.

'Hi, Dad,' I said, resisting the urge to call him Daddy.

'Hi, Liv!' he said. 'I called you but Jack said you were away on a vacation.'

I couldn't believe what a coward Jack was.

'Is everything okay, Liv?'

'There's something I have to tell you,' I said. My wedding gown, which he designed specially for me, with its Peter Kellerman label, hung practically still-warm in my husband's closet. I took a deep breath. He waited patiently.

For a moment neither one of us said anything. Lorna stampeded into the office. 'It stinks in here,' she said.

'Who's that?' my father asked.

'No one,' I said.

'Something really stinks,' Lorna said.

'Where are you?' he asked.

I tried to think of the kind of place where you would find someone like Lorna. A diner, the subway. 'Jury duty,' I told him.

'So what is it?' my father asked. 'What did you want to tell me?'

I couldn't bring myself to tell him about leaving Jack. And I certainly couldn't tell him that I was living in a tenement and working in one, too. I couldn't imagine one of my father's friends coming to Dale's office and perusing the junk shelf. I would have to get listings some other way.

'I'm sorry I haven't spoken to you in so long,' I said.

'No, I'm sorry,' my father said. 'I go to Paris tonight but I'll see you the next time I'm here.' My heart felt tied-off like a sausage. 'So I trust everything's fine?'

I took a deep breath. 'It's okay,' I said. 'But the other day I got jealous of a statue.' I thought from this he would know there was something wrong.

'What statue?' he asked.

'You know, just a statue on the street,' I said.

'Well, you've always been like that, Liv. Jealous of inanimate objects. You were jealous of my mannequins when you were a child. Remember the time you were jealous of the turkey?'

On Thanksgiving all the children felt sorry for the turkey but I felt excited for it. Everyone always said how beautiful it looked. It was carved and served and eaten and everyone always said how good it tasted. It had a wishbone. It could make a whole family happy just b dying. It had a purpose.

'That's true,' I said.

'So, I'll call you when I get back.'

'Great!' I said, as if I were talking to Dale and not to my father. 'How's Mom?'

'She's fine.'

'Is she still in Nice with Aunt Emma?'

'No, she's in London now but she's leaving for L.A. tonight.'

'Great!' I said.

'I love you,' my father said.

'Thanks,' I said. 'Me too.'

When I hung up I thought how unlike me it was not to run to him crying about everything. Everybody did. His models came to him with their deflating implants and eating disorders and money mishaps and heroin hassles. They clustered around him like giraffes at a leafy tree.

Dale walked back in, and Lorna stood up and said, 'I thought we weren't allowed to make personal calls.'

'Did you call your parents?' Dale asked.

'Not yet,' I said.

'Call your father right now. It's the best way to get clients.' She looked like her mouth was watering over all these clients.

'My father's very busy,' I said.

'Jesus, Liv, I didn't think I'd have to do so much hand-holding. Just call him. What does your father do anyway?'

'Uh, he's a judge,' I said.

'Grrreeeaaattt!' She stormed over to my desk and picked up my phone receiver and shoved it at me.

I dialed.

'Judge Garrett's office, may I help you?' a sexy voice asked. It was his new reader. I wondered what she looked like and if he had touched her face yet, and if she let him walk to the subway alone. I actually missed Jerome. I found myself thinking about him, hearing his weak voice in my head. I wondered if he hated me for leaving him.

'May I speak to him, please?'

'May I ask who's calling?' she said territorially.

'Liv Kellerman,' I said.

There was a pause. 'Oh,' she said. 'I've heard a lot about you. Hold on, please. *Jerome*, it's Liv,' she whispered.

Then I heard Jerome's English accent. 'Yes, Hello? Liv, is that you?' Jerome had a way of making every phone call seem like it was transatlantic.

'Hello . . .' Suddenly I didn't know what to call him. 'Dad' seemed all wrong. I couldn't say Jerome or Judge Garrett. 'Your Honor,' I said. Dale, who had pretended not to be listening, looked up at me from her desk.

'Your Honor is it, then?' Jerome said. 'Well.'

'How have you been?' I asked.

'We've been managing. You know you left me in a bit of a lurch with your sudden departure but my new reader is lovely.'

'So you don't miss me then?' I said. Dale raised an eyebrow at me as if she could tell she was losing money.

'Does that mean you miss me?' he said. I could see Jerome there, sitting limply as if he were in a wheelchair.

'Ummm, maybe a little,' I said.

'Yes, I see,' he said. 'So to what do I owe the pleasure?'

'Well, I passed the real estate test,' I said.

'Congratulations, I'm sure that's quite a feat, isn't it? Have you grown a fin on your back yet? I bet you have, haven't you?'

'Yes, a fin, and I have another row of teeth coming in,' I said. Dale didn't look pleased with the turn the conversation had taken. 'Anyway, I wanted to give you my work number in case you know anyone you could refer to me,' I told him.

'You're at a top firm,' Dale whispered. I nodded at her.

'All right, shoot, then,' Jerome said. I heard the Braille machine clicking as I gave him the number. 'There was someone who came by and said he was looking for a loft. Who was it? I'm sure it will come to me,' he said.

I was sure it wouldn't.

9

WALK-UP — BUT WORTH IT!

The next morning Dale told me to show an apartment for her. She walked over to my desk and handed me keys. 'They'll meet you out front.'

I was excited to have something to do outside the office but I felt wary.

'Why can't *you* show it to them?' I asked.

'Look at this, the kid's already turning down business. What do you care why I don't want to show it to them? I'm doing you a favor by letting you do it. If you rent it you get the commission.'

Now I knew there was something wrong with the situation. 'I'm happy to do it, it's just that I had a lot of canvassing planned for today,' I said.

'You have to do it,' Dale said. 'The landlord won't allow me on the premises. We had a falling-out. He's a real scumbag. He's a crook. I can't deal with him. You have to do it. I just want to get someone in that loft.'

She came up behind me and put her hands on my shoulders and squeezed them. She was wearing her men's cologne, which made me instantly sick.

I stood up and grabbed my coat.

'And tell them there's absolutely nothing else. They have to take this one. If they don't take it tell them I axed you to axe them if they really want to move or if they're just wasting our valuable time. They said they didn't want anything cookie-cutter. Tell them it's this or nothing.'

I walked over to Watts Street thinking now I really was a real estate agent. It's what I did, if anyone was to ask. Or axe.

I found the young couple standing right in front of the building. Just standing there nervously and expectantly, reining in two enormous white poodles. It was almost pathetic, like the people you see at cafés in the Village who are clearly waiting for blind dates.

I introduced myself.

'I'm Dale's . . .' I couldn't think of the right word. I didn't want to be associated with her in any way. They just stared at me. The woman was wearing a big black fur Buckingham Palace guard's hat. She shook my hand.

'Thank you for coming out,' she said. 'I'm Cheryl and this is my husband, James, and these are . . .' I didn't catch the dogs' names. Her husband looked like an overgrown prep school kid. I could tell right away that Cheryl was going to be making the decision. James had less say than the dogs.

'It's very close to the dog run,' I said. If you considered about a mile close.

Cheryl beamed. She took off her hat. She had short spiked blond hair underneath.

'Get ready for a hike,' I said.

'Oh?' her husband said.

'Didn't Dale tell you it's a walk-up?'

He shook his head. 'How many floors?'

'Six,' I said brightly.

I opened the door and we headed up, dogs first.

'We just got married,' Cheryl said. 'Yesterday.'

When we finally got to the top we stood sadly in the rectangular loft. 'It's very bowling alley,' Dale had said.

Even the dogs didn't like it. They waited by the front door.

For half an hour the couple named all the bad things about the loft and then convinced themselves of why those bad things weren't that important.

'How much did you say it was?'

'Five thousand a month.'

'Five thousand a month for an apartment?' James mumbled.

'It's a loft,' I said.

'We have to make a decision quickly,' Cheryl said. 'Everything we own is still on the moving truck. After the movers loaded our things onto the truck, our other deal fell through. We just can't bring ourselves to put our things in storage.'

They said they would take it.

As soon as I got back to the office they called to say they had changed their minds. I hung up and told Dale. 'Assholes!' she said. 'They don't know what they want.' She glared at me and clicked her pen for five minutes. Then she said, 'Call them back.'

'They don't want it, Dale.'

'Call them back and convince them to take that loft. If you don't do it, I will,' she threatened.

I felt sorry for the spike-haired girl. I hated the thought of Dale calling her. But I also felt sorry for the loft. It was too good for them. It was better off standing there clean and empty, hopeful that someone interesting would live there, instead of this sad, unappreciative little-rich-kid couple with their entitlement complex and their unexercised dogs. A new apartment was a great thing, a symbol of hope, like a time capsule, a daffodil, a perfect egg. As bad as the loft was, it deserved better. Dale grabbed a ring of keys and stormed out of the office in her Hush Puppies.

I didn't care if they lived there or not.

I called the couple. 'Cheryl, I was thinking maybe you should consider.'

'We just don't know what to do,' she said.

'I understand. It's very hard,' I said.

'It's all happening so fast. It's too much change too fast.'

'I know exactly how you feel,' I said. 'I'm divorced,' I added

'I'm sorry,' she said.

'I thought we were happy but then my husband started taking Prozac and stopped having sex with me,' I said.

'That's awful.'

'Yes. You're lucky you don't have to do this all alone.' My voice quavered.

'You're right,' she said. She said they would take the loft.

We signed the leases that night in the office. 'I'll need a check for the first month's rent, and two months' security.'

'That's fifteen thousand before we even move in,' James said.

'And a check for my commission,' I added.

'Which is?'

I tried to act like I was just figuring out the commission right then and there and that I hadn't done the math a million times on a pad at my desk.

'Uh, let's see, that's nine thousand,' I said. I would get to keep half of that and Dale would get the other half.

'Nine thousand *dollars*,' James said, horrified.

'No, nine thousand *beans*,' his wife responded, so I didn't have to.

'Yes, fifteen percent of the first year's rent.'

James handed me my commission check and said a very reluctant thank-you. They were moving in the next day. They rushed off to make the final arrangements.

I headed to Dean & DeLuca to buy a gift basket for their house-warming present. I lined a basket with burlap and filled it with apples, lemons, a pomegranate, grapes, cheese, tea, a honey bear, chocolates in a moon-shaped box, and house-shaped cookies. I tied a bow around its handle.

The next night Dale took me out to dinner to celebrate. We went to Lucky Strike. Lorna was supposed to join us but she never showed up. I put the gift basket on the chair between us. I was going to deliver it right after. I ordered a salad.

'Have a steak,' Dale said, but I stuck with my salad, thinking that I could have another dinner after this one somewhere else and wash the memory of Dale out of my mind.

Dale picked a broken brick-red crayon out of the glass of

crayons on the table and wrote the word 'winner' on the white paper tablecloth. Then she drew arrows pointing to me. 'You've earned the most money out of the three of us this month,' she said.

She wrote 'Liv,' 'Lorna,' and 'Dale' on the tablecloth and wrote how much each of us had made that month. Lorna had $0 under her name. Dale had $0. I had $4,000. Dale drew stars all around it. 'Four thousand is not bad for your first month,' Dale said.

'Actually, it's four thousand *five hundred*,' I said.

'There's a five-hundred-dollar listing fee which goes to the house.'

'You never told me about a listing fee.'

'I didn't? Why would I forget to do that? I must be in love or something.' I ignored that comment and crossed out the $4,000 and wrote $4,500 next to it with a gold crayon. I drew my own stars. 'Why do you think I would do something like that?' Dale continued. 'Someone must be bewitching me.'

'I guess so,' I said.

'Have you ever answered a personal ad?' Dale asked.

'No,' I said.

'I have a little confession to make. I've been, well, *corresponding* with a bi-curious girl from Brooklyn.'

'What about Harri?' I asked. I knew Dale was making it up. It was a terrible mistake to come here. The place was filled with models. People were staring trying to figure out if Dale was a man or a woman.

'Harri doesn't have to know anything about it. When you've been married to a person for twelve years you need a change, you need to break your lease and take a sublet once in a while. I like young girls. Nineteen, twenty-one, nothing over twenty-two. Don't look at me like that, I haven't done anything wrong. *Yet*,' Dale said. 'What I was thinking about doing was getting a room at the Paramount Hotel and just meeting her. Do you think it's a good idea? She's a lot younger than I am.'

I thought of this bi-curious girl showing up at the Paramount seeing Dale there and being bi-disappointed.

'I don't know, Dale. Why don't you take Harri to the Paramount?'

'She's even younger than you are,' Dale said. She looked at me trying to gauge my reaction. 'You're not the only young girl in world.'

'I'm not that young,' I said.

'You know I had a dream about you last night if you can believe that,' Dale said. 'The kid's in my dreams now. I was running to catch up with you but my legs were chopped off at the knees. You were encouraging me, though. You axed me if I was okay. What do you make of that?'

I took it as a very bad omen that Dale was dreaming about me. I cringed. 'Dreams don't really mean anything,' I said.

'There's something I have to tell you. My friend Paula told me not to do this but I really want to get it off my chest.' Her chest heaved.

The waitress put down my salad and Dale's steak and I started eating as fast as I could.

'Do you want to hear what I have to say? I don't know, maybe it's just that I'm getting my period. Maybe I shouldn't say anything,' she said.

I stood up. 'I should really take this over to James and Cheryl. It's getting late and I want them to have it.'

'That's my champ,' Dale said. 'The winner!'

'Thanks, Dale,' I said, and I was grateful. I had done my first deal, a rental deal, but a deal nonetheless. I had made forty-five hundred dollars.

I grabbed my heavy basket and walked with it awkwardly, holding it out from my side, to the building on Watts Street. The streets of SoHo were empty, gloomy. I felt like Little Red Riding Hood.

But when I got to the building it was burning. The firemen were using the extended ladder to break the windows. I stood across the street with Cheryl and her husband and dozens of spectators. They had arrived home from the supermarket and found the fire trucks. It was a four-alarm fire. They lost everything, pictures, jewelry, computers, work, all their unpacked boxes.

A fireman said they suspected arson. 'Probably set by the landlord for the insurance money. We see it all the time,' he said.

The couple stood holding each other.

I put the basket at their feet.

'Where are the dogs?' I asked, frightened.

The husband shook his head and pointed toward their top-floor windows.

Cheryl was crying.

'I'm sorry,' I said.

'You knew this was going to happen,' James said.

'No, I didn't,' I said, horrified. Dale had forced me to bring the deposit checks to the owner. She said she couldn't face him. I wondered if she knew the building was going to burn. Dale had already deposited the commission check.

'We want our commission back,' James said.

'You have to talk to Dale,' I said.

'Fuck you,' he said. He bent down and grabbed the honey bear the basket and threw it at me. It just missed my head. I tried to talk to them but he kept cursing at me. Then he hurled the basket at my feet.

'Stop it,' Cheryl cried. 'Stop it.'

'Come into the office tomorrow,' I said and turned to leave.

I wondered what it would have been like if I had lost everything in a fire, my husband, my apartment, my things, instead of just walking away from it all the way I did. Same difference.

As I walked home to MacDougal Street I looked at all the buildings I passed. They each seemed human and alive, each with a distinct personality. Some were gracious and pale, like geishas. Some hid behind masks of gargoyles. Some were hard workers with sleeves rolled up, showing graffiti tattoos. Some had windows sealed up with brick like Jerome. Some were sad, with small streams of urine at their feet like pools of tears.

I talked to them as I passed. I loved my new friends, the buildings. I felt like one of them. I was made out of brick and concrete,

my spine was a cast-iron column, my rib cage was a cage elevator from am old hotel, my heart was a radiator, my head was a
penthouse, my breasts were bay windows, my two lungs air
shafts, a boiler room was between my legs. I imagined myself on
fire. I felt sorry for the poor building burning on Watts Street, not
the two newlyweds holding each other on the corner.

My shrink had been right. I *was* a nomad. But I wasn't a turtle
without a shell. I was a shell walking around without my turtle.

It really burned?' Dale said, the next day in the office. She
looked like a kid who was about to get in trouble.

'They want their money back,' I told her.

'The commission is nonrefundable,' she said.

'But Dale, the landlord burned their apartment down the day
after they paid it,' I said. 'Their dogs are dead.'

'I know, that's pretty bad,' Dale said, as if it were a slight
inconvenience like forgetting to get them a copy of their mailbox
key. 'But this is New York and the commission is nonrefundable.'

'It isn't right, Dale.'

'Let me axe you this – is the owner of a gun store responsible
if a man buys a gun and commits murder with it? And is a travel
agent responsible if she sells a plane ticket to someone and the
plane goes down? And let me axe you another question – how do
we know they didn't cause the fire themselves? Maybe they left
the coffeemaker on when they left the loft or maybe their dogs
found a way to turn on the stove.'

'I don't think the dogs turned on the stove or made coffee,
Dale.'

'All I'm saying is we really don't know what happened and
it's not our problem. Here's a hot tip, Liv. *Everyone* wants their
commission back. *Nobody* likes their apartment after they've
moved in. If you returned the money every time someone had a
complaint, you'd be broke. You can't be in the business of returning commissions.'

I hated Dale so much at that moment I decided I wanted to give back the commission.

'I think we should give it back.'

'We?'

'Yes, we. We should give back the whole nine thousand.'

'The whole thing?' Dale asked, as if she were talking to a crazy person. She shook her head and sat at her desk, thinking. She put her finger in the air. 'Were they smokers?'

'No, Dale.'

'Well, it's against company policy to refund a commission, so there's nothing I can do, but what you do with your half is up to you. If you want to let a couple of rich kids run you around, be my guest.'

'At least I did a deal.'

'You haven't done the deal till you've spent the dough,' she said. 'But I'm still proud of you. Disappointed but proud.'

While this discussion was taking place, Lorna sat at her desk the whole time, smirking and snickering to herself.

'Well, as soon as you give me my half I'm giving it right back them. What would you do, Lorna?' I asked her.

'What would I do?' she mimicked. 'This conversation is making me sick. What would I do? I wouldn't have handled a fucking cursed bad-luck death-trap doomed apartment to begin with,' she said.

'Give the kid a break, she's had a rough night,' Dale said. She smiled at me. Then the phone rang and Dale answered. 'Yes, James, how can we help you?' she said. 'First let me express my sympathies for *your* fire in *your* apartment. Well, I'm sorry you feel that way. Let me axe you a question. What can we do to help you and Shirley turn this situation around and get something positive out of it? What? That's what I said, you and Cheryl.'

Dale smiled at me, pointed to herself and gave the thumbs-up sign to show she had things under control.

'Yes, and our most sincere condolences on the loss of your beloved pets,' she continued. 'We'd like to do whatever we can to help you through this trying time. Will you be needing to look at other apartments? You might want to consider buying instead of renting in this market.' She listened for a moment. 'I see. Well, I'm looking at the document you signed right here on my desk.' She looked down at her chocolate muffin. 'I'm sure that you're aware that we could sue you for that, but perhaps we could work something out. I see. Well, if that's the way you feel about it. It just goes to show that bad things happen to bad people for a reason. Goodbye,' she said, and hung up.

'He canceled all the checks,' she said. 'Cheap bastards. Their house burns, their dogs die, and they have time to worry about canceling checks. And here we are feeling sorry for them and getting ready to refund their monies. People don't give you a chance to be good person in this business. Next time get certifieds,' Dale said.

10
NONSTRUCTURAL WALLS

Three days later I had my own listing. Dale had given it to me. I stood on Laight Street looking at my watch, waiting for my five o'clock appointment. I was feeling slightly nervous that the man wouldn't show up because he hadn't sounded too sure where Laight Street was, or what a loft was, or what he needed it for. He said he had gotten my number from Judge Garrett. Dale had been glaring at me during the whole phone call. She didn't think I was 'qualifying' the customers carefully enough. 'Axe how much money he has,' she whispered. I ignored her. She snapped her fingers at me which is always how she tried to get my attention when I was on the phone.

'Axe!' she screamed.

'Do you and your wife have the funds for such an expensive loft?' I asked. 'You would have to put down twenty-five percent as a down payment.' Didn't Dale know that people just lie?

'Hold on a second,' the man said, 'I have a call.' He put me on hold.

'Oh, that's plenty,' I said. 'You're *more* than qualified.' I looked at his name, which I had written neatly on top of the client sheet. Fred Freund.

Fred Freund came back on the line. 'Now, you were going to describe the loft to me,' he said.

I looked down at the listing sheet in a panic. I hadn't been allowed access to the loft. I hadn't even seen it yet. 'It's very large, a large, vast space,' I said. Dale had scribbled 3000 and a square with a line going through it. 'It's three thousand square feet,' I said. Under description there was just one word, 'Strange.' 'It's a little bit hard to describe,' I said. 'It's one of a kind, Mr. Freund.'

The man let out a theatrical laugh like a kid pretending to be a vampire. It made me smile. I got off the phone as quickly as possible.

I had taken a cab to Laight Street, even though it wasn't far from the office, so I would be there on time. I had to get out in Holland Tunnel traffic and cross Canal Street using the pedestrian walk-over. Hundreds of cars honked. A sculpture, a giant orange metal knot, loomed pointlessly in the middle of the traffic circle. This man was not going to take this loft, even if he did show up. My new beeper went off. Since Dale had given it to me I had to tend to it constantly like a Tomagochi toy, pressing its buttons and changing its batteries. She always punched in her number followed by 911 to let me know it was an emergency.

A man came up behind me and said, 'Hello.' 'Hello,' I said. He didn't say sorry I'm late.

'Don't you recognize me?' he said.

It wasn't my client, Fred Freund. It was Andrew, the lifter, the architect from Judge Moody's retirement party. He wasn't wearing a suit as he had been when we met. He was wearing blue jeans and a blue denim shirt with a tie. A very bad look. 'No, I'm afraid I don't,' I said. The good thing about living in New York is that even though you constantly run into people as if you were living in the smallest of towns you can blatantly pretend that you've never seen them before in your life.

'You don't remember me from the party?' he said.

'What party?' I could still feel his hands on me.

'Moody's party at the courthouse. Are you sure you don't

remember me, Liv? I thought it was a very up-*lift*ing experience.'
I hoped he would go away before Fred Freund showed up. I
hoped he wouldn't make a scene.

'Ooooooh, yes, now I remember,' I said. We both just stood
there. 'I'm waiting for a client,' I said.

'It's me,' he said, 'I'm your new client, Fred Freund.' He did
the vampire laugh and I smiled again in spite of myself. I
clutched the keys. Maybe it wasn't safe to go upstairs with him.
He was certainly less imposing standing on ground level than up
on a balcony. Here on the sidewalk he wasn't even much taller
than me. He looked at me with an expression I recognized from
somewhere but couldn't quite put my finger on. Something I
had once seen a long time ago, maybe in a movie. Oh yes, I
remembered, it was adoration.

As we got into the elevator I accidentally called him Andrew.

'So you do remember me,' he said. 'Should I carry you over
the threshold?'

'If you lift me I'll call the police,' I said.

When we entered the loft I was horrified to see some sort of
bamboo tiki hut built right in the center of it. There was a little
door to get into it. In fact there were doors everywhere. Dozens
of little doors lined the entire loft on both sides.

Andrew and I stood looking at it in disbelief. 'This place is
awful,' Andrew said.

'I think it's fantastic,' I told him. 'I love this . . . structure.' I
pointed to the tiki hut. He marched around opening every door
like a child. Behind each door were massage tables and shiatsu
mats and sinks built right into the floor.

'What do you think these are for?' Andrew asked, looking at
the sinks, as if it were some kind of sex thing. 'Bidets for very
short people?'

'Pedicures,' I said.

He laughed as if that were hilarious.

'What would you be using the loft for?' I asked.

'Luckily, I was thinking of opening a Korean whorehouse, so
this place is perfect,' he said.

'Well, the maintenance is very low and it's seventy-two percent tax deductible.'

'Look at this,' Andrew said. I couldn't see him. 'I'm in here,' he said. A door opened a crack. I opened it and walked into a tiny wooden sauna.

Andrew's tie was on the floor and his shirt was rapidly coming off. He ladled water onto coals that sizzled.

'What are you doing?' I asked him.

'This feels so good,' he said. He sat down on the redwood bench and closed his eyes, with his chin up in the air as if there were sun. I stood holding the door open. 'Are you in or out,' he said with his eyes closed.

'I'm in,' I said. I sat next to him on the bench and felt the heat of the room. I took off my boots. I took off my coat. Another strange job, I thought. I pulled my sweater up so that my stomach was bare. He stretched his arms up over his head and then out so that our fingertips almost touched. I wondered what would happen if we had sex on the bench.

'I'm very interested,' he said. 'You're a great salesperson.'

'Maybe you'd like to come back and bring your girlfriend or wife or whatever,' I said.

'We're not married. I told you all this at the party. I live with someone. But it's ending.'

'So, I've been put on a waiting list of some sort?'

'Oh, come on, Liv, this is so great. Don't ruin it,' he said. 'Let me rub your feet.'

I yanked my feet up off the floor and folded them under me. 'No.'

'Come on, I just want to rub your feet, what's wrong with that?'

'Absolutely not. Do you have any other questions about the loft?'

'I have thought about you every day since I met you,' he said.

'But you live with someone,' I said, in a naive sexpot voice, like Marilyn explaining why she keeps her panties in the fridge.

'Well, Liv, sometimes life is complicated,' he said, solemnly.

Then we both were solemn, sitting in the sauna, sweating. Andrew ladled water on the coals.

His chest was covered with black hair and his skin was dark.

'Can I take off my pants?' he asked.

'No,' I said.

He smiled at me and I started warming up. I began to thaw. I closed my eyes and relaxed into the heat, the way you do in Los Angeles when you finally admit that the weather *is* really great, in spite of yourself. Andrew was like Los Angeles, a studio lot, a break-away façade of a building. A fake dorsal fin emerging from a man-made lake, without the shark attached.

Once, when I was a child, my shrink said, 'Your mind is playing tricks on you.' I pictured my mind as a mean little boy, taunting me in a horrific Halloween costume.

'I have a client waiting downstairs,' I said.

'You're kidding,' he said, as if that were the rudest thing he had ever heard.

'No, I'm not,' I said, nastily. 'This isn't a date.' I stood up and pulled down my sweater.

'A date?' he said, exaggerating the word. 'I think it is a date.' I wished I hadn't said the word 'date.' 'Look, Liv, I know you're just recently separated and I'm still living with . . . someone.'

'Someone?'

'But sometimes things happen, Liv, and there's not that much we can do to fight it. I have been completely and totally in love with you since I met you.'

I sat back down. I had to admit I was flattered by Andrew. But I was flattered by the bums who hung around the chess tables in Washington Square Park. It didn't take much. And then I wondered if Andrew was somehow right about all this. Maybe he knew something I didn't. Maybe love had a black, hooded, grim reaper quality that you couldn't avoid. It seemed so important to him.

'Well, what do you want us to do about it?' I asked.

'What?' He looked scared for a second.

'Do you want to kiss me?' I looked deep into his eyes.

'No!' he said.

'What! No?' I grabbed my coat and my shoes and his gay tie by accident.

'No, Liv, I don't want to kiss you until I figure out what we're going to do.'

'Do about what?'

'About Jordan,' he said. His eyes darted guiltily over to his gym bag on the floor for some reason, as if she were inside it, cut up into pieces.

'Isn't that a man's name?'

'I like it, it's sexy,' he said, smiling.

'You have to go,' I said.

'I'm not going.'

'I have another client coming.'

'I'll wait for you here,' he said.

Out on the street I realized I hadn't thought about my husband once in over an hour. Even that brought sadness. Soon our marriage would hold the importance of a one-night stand.

I leaned against the building and waited for my client, a woman named Jean Small. She had sounded scared on the phone, asking questions as if she were being coached. When I asked her what she did for a living she said that she wanted to open an art gallery. Maybe she could go into business with Dale, I thought. She had just inherited a million dollars. She said it with dread in her voice, as if she had just inherited a crippling disease.

'That's great!' I had said on the phone.

'Well, it's actually a really big responsibility,' she whimpered

I was glad Jean Small was late. I needed time to think about Andrew. A guy wearing jeans and a T-shirt stood a few feet away looking at me. He had a bike messenger's bag across his chest, a blue cardigan, and dirty enormous sneakers. He was the kind of man I avoided at all costs, squirrelly. Every time he looked at me I looked away with a disgusted expression on my face. Bike messengers are the worst thing in New York. They're more violent than cops. They're more hated than real estate agents. The only thing possibly lower is someone who sells memberships at a gym. I wondered why he was just standing there.

'Are you waiting for someone?' the man said awkwardly.

'Yes,' I said toughly.

'I think we might be waiting for each other,' he said.

'I don't think so,' I said, as nastily as possible. 'I'm waiting for a woman.'

'I'm Jean Small.' He looked in a pocket notebook. 'You're Liv?'

'Yes,' I said, confused. Then I realized he was a woman after all. She just looked like a man.

'Oh, I'm sorry, right this way.'

'I hope this loft is big enough,' Jean said. 'I'm looking for a place for the gallery and I need to be able to live there, too. It has to have enough rooms in case I want to have a baby.'

A *baby*? I thought in disbelief. Some people have so much confidence, they think they can have a baby anytime they want no matter what they look like. 'Oh, this place has plenty of rooms,' I said. 'Are you married?'

'No.'

'Do you have a . . . boyfriend?'

'No. But I might want to have a baby.' She said this with the confidence of Miss America.

'Of course,' I said. Jean made Dale look like Marilyn Monroe.

'Now, where are we?' Jean took out the pocket notebook again and turned to a list of addresses. 'Since my windfall I've been under a lot of stress.'

We entered the loft and faced the tiki hut. 'What's that?' she asked.

I decided to call a spade a spade. 'It's a tiki hut,' I said. 'Isn't it great?'

'I don't know.'

'It is,' I said.

'It's a lot of dough to plunk down.'

'Yes,' I said. 'It's a great loft.'

She opened the door to the pedicure room. 'What are those for?' she asked, pointing to the sinks.

'Pedicures,' I said, as if every loft had them.

The next door was the door to the sauna.

'Well, you've probably seen enough,' I said.

'What's that room?'

'That's a small sauna. Probably best not to go in there.' I paused. 'The heat escapes.'

'Okay,' she said. We turned to leave. 'Hi,' I heard Andrew say behind me.

Jean and I both jumped. We turned around again and found him standing there. He had gone ahead and taken his pants off after all. He had a white towel around his waist with a yin-yang circle printed on it. I wondered where he had found the towels.

'Welcome to my loft. I'm the owner, Fred Freund.' He put out his hand and Jean shook it.

'Can you show me the kitchen?' she asked.

'Sure, follow me.' He wandered around looking for the kitchen. 'Here it is,' he said, pointing to a mini-fridge and a microwave on a shelf. 'Can I fix you something?'

'No thanks,' Jean said. 'Do you mind if I have another look around?' She walked around opening doors.

'You better leave,' I said to Andrew, when she was out of sight.

'You're the most beautiful woman in this loft,' Andrew said.

'Shut up.'

'I'm just kidding. You're the most beautiful woman I've ever shared a sauna with.'

'Get dressed,' I said.

'I want to give you a pedicure.'

'But you don't want to kiss me.'

'I do want to kiss you. It just isn't a good idea right now.'

'Please get dressed and leave. This is unprofessional,' I said.

'It wouldn't be right for me to kiss you,' he said. Then he kissed me. It was shy and careful, eyes open. Very unlike him, I thought. It was not what I expected. His towel tented up in front.

Jean came back toward us and Andrew took a bag of Orville Redenbacher popcorn from a basket on the shelf and put it in the microwave.

'Well, thank you,' Jean said. 'It's very interesting but I don't see how it could possibly work. And it's a lot of dough.'

'You're probably right,' I said.

'Maybe I could bring an architect by. And my lawyer.'

'Sure,' I said, guiding her to the door. I couldn't stand to look at her another second.

'Maybe you could show me some other places. My accountant says I have to buy something soon for the tax deduction. I guess it's time to leave my studio apartment,' she said sadly, like Jackie O leaving the White House.

'Sure, great, I'll call you,' I said, and shut the door.

I heard the buzzer from the microwave go off.

'Andrew!' I called. It sounded like I had been saying his name for years.

'Yes, honey,' he said sweetly.

'I really think you should go now.'

'When will I see you?' he asked.

'I don't think it's a good idea.'

'But I want to see this loft again.'

'That other client just bought it.'

'I'll only leave if you agree to go out with me.'

'No, not while you're living with . . . someone,' I said.

'Fine, I'll go. But we are going to see each other again and you're just going to have to trust me. I'm going to call you.'

He got dressed cooperatively and got into the elevator eating popcorn from the bag.

When I left the building I was almost surprised to find him gone.

I went back to the office and let myself in with my own key. The phone was ringing and Dale and Lorna were nowhere in sight. I answered. 'Liv Kellerman.'

'Hello,' a man said. 'I'm calling about an ad for a three-thousand-square-foot loft on Laight Street. I'd like to see it.'

The man's voice was beautiful. Deep and resonant like an actor's.

'What's your name?' I asked.

'Ving Rhames,' he said.

'Oh really?' I said, haughtily. It was clearly Andrew. Only he would make up such a ridiculous name. 'You sure this isn't Fred Freund?'

'Uh, yes,' the man said.

'Isn't Ving a sort of strange name?' I said.

'Uh, I guess so,' the man said. 'Could I take a look at that loft?'

'Ving, Ving, Ving,' I said. 'Vingy.'

'Excuse me?' he said.

'And what is it you do, Mr. Ving?'

'It's Ving Rhames. I'm an actor,' he said, humbly. 'My girl-friend and I want to move out from Los Angeles. I'm starting a film in New York next month.'

'Yes, Ving, I'm sure you are. Did anyone ever tell you you're a pretty good kisser?'

'Have we met?'

'Yes, I believe we have.'

'Miss, is there some sort of problem?'

'Yes, Ving, there is a problem. You live with someone.'

'I live with my girlfriend.'

'Well, until you leave her, we won't meet again,' I said, and hung up.

But I couldn't help feeling a little bit in love. I left the office and hailed a cab. When I got in the driver punched the meter and the celebrity recording came on. 'Hi, this is designer Peter Kellerman.' It was my father's voice right there in the cab. 'Do you know what accessory is an absolute must with any outfit? That's right! A seat belt! So buckle up for safety and I'll see you at the Tonys.'

I couldn't believe it. The cabdriver would hear from my father more often than I would. Maybe I could get my father to make a special recording just for me. 'Hi, Liv, this is your father, designer Peter Kellerman. Don't forget to brush your teeth before you go to sleep, lock your front door, never go out with a man who lives with his girlfriend, good night, sleep tight, and I'll see you at the Tonys.'

'See you at the Tonys, Daddy,' I whispered.

The next morning I turned to Page Six of the *Post*. Emmy award-winning actor Ving Rhames was in town apartment hunting. 'New York has some insane realtors,' Mr. Rhames said.

II

2½ BATHS

On the day I left my husband he said, 'I still think you're beautiful. This morning, when I woke up, I looked at you under the covers, and I prayed you wouldn't wake up and start speaking.' I thought about this as I got ready for my date with Andrew Lugar. I put on makeup and regretted it.

When I was a little girl my father used to put makeup on me. He would prop me up on the butcher-block counter in the kitchen and direct me to open and close my eyes and mouth as he tickled me with soft brushes and lined my eyes and lips with pencils that he kept in a green plastic tackle box. He worked quickly, sometimes letting me choose the length of my lashes or the color my lips would be. 'Let me see, let me see,' I would say, looking sideways to try to see my reflection in the chrome tea-kettle. Finally he would hold up a mirror and I would stare at myself. He would hold the mirror patiently, letting me look for as long as I wanted to. With my lips painted like a gypsy's, I felt alive. With my cheeks pink as an ice skater's, I felt fresh and vibrant. I could see myself more clearly, see each feature distinctly – my nose smelled more, my tongue tasted more, my eyes actually looked back. I was not just the pale blurry mass I usually saw, until my mother came home and scrubbed at my face with a washcloth.

One day my mother said I was too old for him to be putting makeup on me. 'That doesn't even make sense,' I said in pre-teen scorn, 'I'm too old for makeup, that doesn't even make sense.'

Maybe I wouldn't even go out with Andrew. I changed my sheets and made my bed. Then I got into bed and looked at my body under the new comforter I had bought because it was called the Vienna. I lay on my side and imagined what it would feel like to have a man's body pressed up behind me. I imagined it would feel good.

I got dressed and ran downstairs when the buzzer rang. But it wasn't Andrew. It was a Chinese-food delivery boy who had pushed every buzzer in the building and was trying to carry his bicycle and the bags of food with him up the stairs. I sat on my stoop.

It was early. I sat there trying several different positions, leaning back on my elbows, hands on my knees, etc. A few people walked by and looked at me, which made me wonder if I looked wildly inappropriate like the statue in SoHo of the giant woman with eight sets of breasts, so I went across the street to Caffe Reggio and asked Mick, the waiter, if he thought I was wearing too much makeup.

It was too dark in the café so Mick took me outside to get a better look at my face in natural light. 'You look fine,' he declared seriously. He smelled like beer. I decided to check myself one more time in the bathroom.

The bathroom at Caffe Reggio was tiny and black so you couldn't see if it was clean or not but you could smell that it wasn't. It was smaller than an airplane bathroom.

I thought about how I had sat next to my husband on the airplane while he read an Elmore Leonard novel. He was completely absorbed in it, even laughing out loud from time to time. He read for hours not looking up or speaking. I had never seen him like that.

He wouldn't look up. 'Does he want any tea or coffee?' the stewardess said to me.

Finally he finished it and said, 'The heroine of this book is so fucking great. I love her.'

'Well, why didn't you marry her?' I said.

'Jesus, Liv, don't tell me you're jealous of a fictional character. She's a character in a book. She doesn't even exist!' he said, completely exasperated.

I would have loved to be a tall blond action spy character in a book.

'That's ridiculous, I'm not jealous,' I said. I wanted to rip the blond bimbo on the cover into tiny pieces. I hated her. 'You're crazy,' I told him.

'I'm not even allowed to read,' he kept muttering under his breath. 'She won't even let me read a book.' He turned to the man reading a newspaper in the seat across the aisle from us and said, 'You're lucky you're allowed to read.' It was bad enough I was jealous. He didn't have to humiliate me in first class. He left the book in the seat pouch on the plane.

It was too dark to see myself in the Caffe Reggio bathroom mirror. Without thinking, I leaned on the sink with both hands. I had my hands on the filthiest sink in New York. I removed them from the sink as quickly as possible and knocked something off it with my right hand. I bent down and felt around on the black floor until I found the object. I couldn't tell what it was. I thought it might be part of the sink itself, a piece of plumbing. I stood up and found myself holding a gun in both hands.

Somebody banged on the door and screamed, 'Get out of there, fucking junkies.'

'Just a minute,' I called. I put the gun in my pocketbook and went back to wait for Andrew in front of my building.

It was exhilarating to walk with the gun. I kept my hand on it as much as possible. I moved carefully. I felt like a mother kangaroo with a full pouch. I didn't know if it was loaded or cocked or stolen or freshly used or even real for that matter. It was small and black and professional-looking and it felt very very real.

Andrew was standing on the top step examining the names on the buzzers.

'Hi,' I said.

'Hi,' he said. 'Let me look at you.' He walked down the stairs and sort of held me at arm's length like a grandmother. 'You look great. Do you want to get a coffee?'

Cheap, I thought.

'How about that place?' He pointed across the street to Caffe Reggio. We went to the café and sat in the front near the door.

'Hello! What can I get for you?' Mick said, winking and looking Andrew up and down.

Andrew ordered American coffee and I got a hot chocolate, which I hoped Mick would put whipped cream on even though I didn't ask for it.

'Well,' Andrew said.

'Well,' I said.

'There's something I have to tell you,' he said.

'There's something I have to tell *you*,' I said back.

'Oh?' he asked. 'What is it?'

'I'm exactly the wrong kind of person to have an affair with,' I said firmly. I felt proud of myself for saying it.

'That's too bad,' he said. 'Because I am so crazy about you I can't think about anything else. I don't know what to do.' His voice was low and sincere-sounding. 'I know this isn't your problem,' he added.

There was a noise like cracking in the back of the restaurant. People were looking around for what had caused it. Then the old tin ceiling started to buckle a little and the people sitting at the tables under it suddenly stood and moved to the front. They were two couples and a group of three girls grabbing their coats and coffees and menus and taking tables near me and Andrew. A stream of water started to pour down. It was like being on the *Titanic*, everyone moving to one side of the ship.

'Whoa,' Mick said.

The brown-painted tin ceiling got a little lower and lower and then a giant white object came crashing down like a dirigible falling from the sky. It was an old-fashioned bathtub with a wet, naked girl sitting in it covering her head with her hands. It landed between tables, its four clawed feet breaking off under it. The noise, like a thundering brass band, was still reverberating.

The girl in the tub was thin with long brown hair up in a barrette. She looked like she was about my age. I had seen her in the café before. The side of her head was cut and bleeding but she didn't look too hurt.

For a moment no one did anything. It didn't even seem that strange. In New York, the eye learns to adjust quickly.

Mick called 911. 'Yes,' he said, sounding official, 'we have a bit of a situation here. A falling bathtub sort of a thing.'

'Does anyone have a . . . towel?' the girl said.

'That's a nice tub,' a man said. I noticed that the claws on the clawed feet had been painted with red nail polish.

The man gave the girl in the tub a sheepskin coat to cover herself with and Mick gave her a Caffe Reggio T-shirt, which she tried to squirm into.

'Don't move,' the man told her.

'I knew that would happen,' she complained. 'They took out my shower and put in this tub.'

'She's in shock,' a woman said, stirring sugar into her tea. She went on talking to her friend.

'Yeah, pretty tough break. Not the type of thing you expect to happen when you pour in the old Mr. Bubble,' Mick was saying to her. Then they both started to laugh.

'Nice place,' Andrew said. I noticed that he had gotten a good look at the girl's breasts. Of course everyone had.

'Could we have the check?' the woman who had diagnosed the shock said.

'Yes, I'll be right with you,' Mick said.

'I don't think we should have to pay,' the woman's friend said.

'Yup, yup, you do have a point there,' Mick said. He put their check on their table anyway. He looked at me and Andrew.

'Having a good time, folks? It's like fucking Niagara Falls in here. Very romantique.'

The two women got up and left without paying. An NYU student writing in a composition notebook asked for a refill.

'Can I have a cookie?' the girl in the tub asked Mick.

'I don't know about that. They might be a little waterlogged,' he said. 'We can give it a try.' Water was pouring down on the chrome pastry case. He opened the glass door and placed an assortment of Italian cookies on a small plate using a pair of tongs. He brought them to her. 'I'll get you a hot chocolate. That'll warm you up,' he said.

'Maybe you should ask if there's a doctor,' I told Mick.

'You don't need a doctor, you need an architect,' Andrew said. He walked over to where the girl was sitting in the tub, careful not to let any debris get on his tasseled loafers, and looked up the hole. There was wood and tin and dirt everywhere. The girl looked up the hole, too.

'They should have reinforced your floor with scuttle beams,' he explained to her. Then he said something I couldn't hear that made her laugh.

'You don't need an architect, you need a lawyer,' Mick said.

Andrew came back to our table and we sat there for a long time and watched the girl get carried to the ambulance. The man who had given her the coat asked for it back.

We said goodbye to Mick. 'Sorry about that, folks,' he said.

Andrew walked me to my building. 'Did you have fun?' he asked. 'I had a lot of fun,' he added.

'I think that was probably an omen,' I said.

'Yes,' he said. 'It was an omen that we should get naked and take a bath together as soon as possible.'

'So what are we doing?' I said.

'Dating, I guess,' he said, smiling. 'Are you saying this wasn't your idea of a great first date?'

If I was going to be a mistress I'd be needing dinner & a movie.

'Can I call you?' he asked.

'I don't think so, Andrew,' I said, dramatically.

'I'll take that as a yes,' he said. 'We'll figure everything out.'

He kissed me. Then he took off his glasses and kissed me again. I put my bag on the street at our feet, remembering my gun. He kissed me hard and passionately. He was only a few inches taller than me. It made me feel strong and equal and I kissed him back.

'I have to walk the dogs. I'll call you when I get home,' he said. He kissed me again, taking my bottom lip between his teeth and biting a little. I watched him walk down the street toward the subway.

A little boy in a stroller passed by me. He was being pushed by his mother. He was wearing a sweater with a mouse and hearts on it. He looked like Cupid in his chariot. The little boy pretended to shoot me with a toy gun. 'Kill, kill,' he said, pointing the gun in my direction. His mother wasn't paying any attention. 'Kill, kill,' he said to me. I pulled my gun just slightly out of my bag and pointed it at him. 'Kill, kill,' I said back. The little boy looked surprised and laughed. I put the barrel of my gun in my wide-open mouth for a second like a lollipop. Then the little boy put the barrel of his gun in his mouth like a lollipop. His mother looked down at him, embarrassed. I put my gun away quickly. Then his mother noticed me and smiled.

When I got home I sat on my bed for a while, squinting one eye and aiming at various things. I really wanted to shoot something but I was afraid of the noise it would make. I needed a silencer. I walked around the apartment holding the gun and then I put it down on the windowsill and tried to watch TV. I couldn't just leave the gun there.

I opened my jewelry box filled with the things my ex-husband had gotten me and nestled the gun in the center. But it was too beautiful and valuable and real for that box. It dwarfed the antique garnets and pearls and the replacement diamond engagement ring. Before we were married I had thrown the original one Jack had gotten me out of a speeding car window during a huge fight and he had to get me an even nicer one. The gun made it look like a Cracker Jack prize.

Violet called to ask how my date with Andrew went.

'Is he there right now?' she asked.

'No,' I said.

'Did he lift you this time?'

'No.' I told her about the girl in the tub falling through the ceiling.

'Was she really fat?'

I thought that was a strange question.

'I want to hear everything. Let's have dinner,' Violet said.

'I don't think I can go, I've got this gun here.'

I told her the whole story and I felt her reach a new peak of jealousy.

'That's so fantastic,' she kept saying.

'It's the most incredible feeling,' I said.

'Meet me at Life Café in twenty minutes,' she said, 'and bring the gun.'

As I sat in the café waiting for Violet I thought that maybe I was meant to kill myself. That day at lunch my fortune had said, 'An important letter or message is on its way to you.' And then I found the gun. I felt like crying. Not me exactly, but my face. My face felt like crying, as if my face had a mind of its own. My cheeks felt smooth and cool like the calm before a storm.

I started making a pro-and-con list in my mind. Killing myself pros: no risk of getting married and divorced again; no more New Year's Eves; no more craving phantom sex; no more underwires poking through expensive bras; no more waking up early; no more Dale; no more Violet . . .

Violet rushed in with new highlights, tiger stripes of strawberry and brown in her blond hair. She looked completely different. 'Nice highlights,' I said.

'What do you mean?'

'I like what they did to your hair.'

'I didn't get it highlighted,' she said, defensively. 'It always looks like this.'

I couldn't take my eyes off her new hair.

'So, where is it?' she asked, in a hushed voice.

'I can't just whip it out,' I said.

'You have to let me borrow it,' she said. I didn't think that was a good idea. Violet got very violent at work. She was the most hostile waitress imaginable, accidentally spilling boiling soup on people all the time and dropping steak knives on them.

'What do you want it for?' I asked.

'I just want it in my apron when I work. When I reach into my apron for a straw or a Sweet'n Low, I want to feel it in there.'

She'd probably get drunk and let some guy hold it. 'It's pretty dangerous,' I said.

'I have to see it. Follow me into the ladies' room.' Without looking at me she stood and walked toward the ladies' room. I stayed seated. I suddenly didn't feel like showing Violet my new gun, the way I didn't like to discuss the size and shape of my ex-husband's penis with her. I wished I hadn't brought it. I started thinking about fingerprints. Mine were already on it along with the prints of the guy before me. I knew I was being childish. I put my bag over my shoulder and headed for the bathroom.

I took it out of the bag. 'Here it is,' I said.

'Is it loaded?'

'I have no idea,' I said.

She looked down at it but she didn't take it from me. She seemed cowed by it. 'You should really take that back,' she said.

'Take it back where?'

'Turn it in or something,' she said.

'Yeah, you're right,' I said, slipping it back into my bag. 'I'll do that.'

Later when I was walking past Caffe Reggio, Mick came out. 'Did you hear what happened?' he asked. 'Some dumb cop left a gun in the john and someone found it and walked off with it. He took it out of his holster when he took a crap.' Mick started laughing. 'Makes you feel safe, doesn't it?'

'Who found it?' I said.

'I wish I had. That cop was so embarrassed, he would have paid any amount to get it back. But I wouldn't have given it to him, because it was so fun watching him squirm.' He put on a dumb-guy voice. 'Duh, did anyone happen to find a gun?'

'Was he cute?' I asked. I could be like Prince Charming sliding the gun into every holster until I found the perfect fit.

'Why? Would you date a copper?'

Mick had a point. 'Of course not. What kind of sick person would want to walk around with a gun?' I said.

12
CENTRL HEAT

The next day at Dale's I was alone in the office so I took out my gun. It was square and made mostly of black plastic. It had the word 'Glock' printed on the handle. I couldn't believe how light it was. I weighed it on the mail scale. One and a half pounds. I could send out announcements to my friends and family, bouncing baby Glock, one pound eight ounces.

The trigger had a tiny piece of plastic sticking out of it, like a fin. I wondered what it was for. I put it in the zippered compartment of my bag and left for an appointment with a new client.

On my way, I ran into a coffee place to get an iced tea but I had trouble communicating what I wanted because I absolutely refused to say the word 'grandissimo.' If everyone else in New York wanted to go around saying words like 'venti' and 'grandissimo' like a bunch of idiots, they could, but I wasn't going to.

'An extra-large iced tea,' I said.

'We don't have extra large,' the boy behind the counter said. He was working in Rollerblades.

'The largest size you have,' I said.

'Would you like grande, gigante, or grandissimo?'

'The biggest,' I said.

'Grandissimo?' he asked, really slowly.

I nodded, reluctantly.

He brought me the iced tea. 'One grandissimo iced tea,' he announced. I searched through my bag for money.

A pudgy black man, obviously a bum, came in and walked up and down studying the jars of biscotti behind the counter. He ordered a small coffee and grabbed a pile of napkins. Then, when the boy rolled away, he took the contents of the Daffy Duck tip mug, a five-dollar bill, masking it with the napkins. He was slow and fumbled but managed to get the money into his pocket.

The boy behind the counter had sweat stains under his arms.

He gave the bum his coffee and the bum said, 'I ordered a grande.'

'Oh, sorry,' the boy said and went to change it.

I noticed a pen on the counter and I grabbed a napkin and wrote, 'That bum stole $5 from the tip mug,' and drew an arrow pointing to the thief.

The thief gave the boy the five-dollar bill and the boy gave him change. The thief dropped a nickel in the empty tip mug and it made a loud sound bouncing off the bottom. When the boy rolled back I said, 'Excuse me,' and held the napkin up so he could read it. Instead of taking the napkin from me he just stood there slowly reading it, silently mouthing the words.

'Oh,' he said. He looked at the empty tip mug.

The thief was still standing there taking more napkins.

He rolled over to the thief and I put two dollars on the counter and started to leave.

'There was five dollars in the tip jar, man,' the boy said to the thief.

'Maybe she took it,' the thief said, pointing at me.

'Oh yeah? I don't think so,' the boy said sarcastically, showing the thief my note.

'Bitch,' the thief yelled at me. 'You bitch.'

'Oh, like I really care what your opinion of me is,' I said.

'You should mind your own business, bitch.'

I unzipped my bag and pulled Glock out for a split second.

'Oh shit,' he said. He ran away. Holding the gun like that made me terrified. It felt the opposite of safe. It gave me vertigo.

Once, when I was young, I wanted to impress my father, so I told him I could go on the roller coaster alone. He said I was too small, but I insisted. He called me a tough cookie. As soon as the ride started I became terrified and started to cry. I felt my face go slack with concentration. Just when I thought I was going to die the ride slowed to a stop. My father had paid the man to stop the ride seconds after it had started. My father climbed up and got me, while the other riders screamed complaints. I wrapped my arms around his neck like a little monkey.

I walked away from the coffee place quickly and when I finally started to slow down I saw something beautiful leaning against a building. It was a child's legless wooden piano painted cobalt blue with Chinese pink, yellow, and lavender roses on it. I picked it up and touched the keys, which really played. It was heavy. I played something I remembered from all my piano lessons, 'Yankee Doodle.' I put it under my arm like an attaché case. I headed to White Street for my appointment with my new gun and piano.

Noah Bausch, my client, was waiting when I got there. He was looking up at the building with his hands on his hips. He had on shorts and a goatee. The richer they were, the sleazier they looked. We waited there for his wife and daughter. Recently I had been spending a lot of time with married men waiting for their wives and babies to stroller up.

I stood there sexlessly holding my child's piano. I was trying to practice sounding interested without flirting. I didn't want to alienate the wives. I hadn't mastered the technique and usually ended up somehow flirting with the wives and alienating the husbands until we were all pitted against each other.

I tried to assume the same neutral expression I had when I used to baby-sit. Baby-sitter and real estate agent were the only two jobs I could think of where you really weren't allowed to be sexy.

'So you're a writer,' I said, not caring.

'Yes! And you play piano.'

'Not professionally,' I said.

'Well, I *am* a writer. Short stories mostly. I love the form.'

Is it true what they say, I wanted to ask, the shorter the story the shorter the . . .

'That's great. I love short stories,' I lied. I didn't ask if they were published.

'And your wife?' I asked.

'Audrey's a *top* literary agent,' he said.

'Is she your agent?'

'No, as a matter of fact she's not my agent, she doesn't think it would be ethical,' he said. I could tell by the way he said it that he had no agent. 'Of course, ethics probably isn't a big issue in your line of work.'

'No, it isn't.'

He looked at his watch. 'She's always late.'

'I am not late,' she said, coming up behind him. She was taller than he was and anorexic with dark circles under her eyes.

'Where's Flannery?' he asked, accusingly, as if she had misplaced their child.

'I convinced LaLa to stay late,' she retorted.

She put out her hand. 'Hi, I'm Audrey Bausch,' she said, grandly. I switched the piano to the other arm and shook her hand. 'What a cute piano,' she said. 'Is that for Flannery? She'll just love that.'

'Uh, no,' I said. 'It's for my . . .' I couldn't think of a child it could be for. 'Self.'

'Oh,' she said, with fake embarrassment.

'Flannery, what an interesting name,' I said.

'She's named for Flannery O'Connor,' Noah Bausch said, proudly.

He obviously thought that naming his child Flannery would help his short stories. Flannery will get you nowhere, I thought.

'Aud, not everyone wants to spoil Flannery with presents everywhere we go,' Noah snapped.

'Well, the last agent gave her that tea set and I just assumed . . .'

'Let's not turn this into a big argument,' he said.

The crazy thing was, it was this more than anything that made me miss my husband. A couple fighting made me more jealous than their hand-holding in the master bedroom, or their loving, knowing glances across the marble bath, or their quick kiss and tummy rub in the elevator. I missed the arguments. I wanted to join in like a swinger.

'Where were you?' Noah asked his wife.

'Dentist,' she said.

'You know, I've actually been thinking about finding a new dentist,' I said. 'Is your dentist good?' Since the separation I wanted all new doctors, but I shouldn't have been asking their advice. It made me look ungrounded not to have a dentist.

'*Ours* is wonderful,' Audrey Bausch said.

'I don't think he's a very good dentist,' Noah Bausch said.

I just stood there like a baby-sitter. 'Well, should we go up?'

The only thing the Bausches agreed on was their dislike of the loft. It seemed I had forgotten to mention that the loft had a tin ceiling and they had been instructed by their kinesthesiologist that living under a tin ceiling caused cancer, because tin couldn't breathe so all the bad vibrations stayed inside and ricocheted around like stray bullets. They stood united in their hatred of tin. 'I'm terribly, terribly sorry,' I said.

That night I had a dream that Dick Van Dyke and I were sitting on a bench holding hands, in love, and Mary Tyler Moore wanted me to leave. Even though she wasn't really his wife, they were just actors, she still wanted me gone. She didn't want me in their sitcom.

In the morning I made an appointment with the Bausches' dentist, Dr. Blum. I told him I had let my husband have the dentist in the divorce. I explained that I didn't want the same picks and drills, however sterilized, that were in my husband's mouth, in mine. He said that was very understandable and to come right over.

I sat in his tiny ground-floor office on Washington Square West, tilted back, mouth wide open. I tried not to look up into his giant nostrils. I looked past him, hovering over me, and realized I was facing the street. The window had no shade, any passerby could stop and watch me.

'It's lucky you're not a gynecologist,' I said, with my mouth full of his hands. Leave it to the Bausches to have a cheapo dentist. My husband's dentist had an attractive female hygienist who made entertaining jokes about her boyfriend.

A man walked by, glancing at me through the window. Then another man. Why didn't he just move his chair right out to the middle of Washington Square Park? I wondered. Give me my cleaning under the arch. Everyone who walked by looked in and smiled, glad not to be me. I had never been more vulnerable. This was worse than people who went to gyms and did the StairMaster in the window. I was sure the next man to walk by would be my husband.

But the next man wasn't my husband. It was Dale. She sauntered by in a khaki safari outfit and stopped short as soon as she saw me. I pretended I didn't see her there, even though she was waving wildly.

'Is he a friend of yours?' Dr. Blum said. I shook my head no. 'I always get the crazies. My wife left me and took the window treatments and now the crazies always come and stand right there where that crazy's standing. At home I get the pigeons and here I get the crazies.'

'I get pigeons and crazies, too,' I mumbled.

'It seems we have had a lot of the same life experiences,' he said.

I didn't think I had the same life experiences as an old balding dentist.

Dale broadly mouthed the words 'I'll wait for you here' and pointed to herself and to me and downward to indicate that spot on the sidewalk.

'She had the nerve to try and sell me my own window treatments that I had already paid for. She said they were hers because she designed them. She'd only leave them behind if I gave her four thousand dollars for them. So I would essentially be paying for my own window treatments twice. I'm telling you, my wife is the penultimate hard-ass.'

I wondered who the ultimate hard-ass was. I knew it wasn't me. I wished I had taken down the custom-made curtains I had agonized over in my husband's living room and hung them in my new apartment. My new ceiling was half the height of my old one. If I hung those curtains my new windows would look like two small boys wearing their father's pajamas.

Suddenly I missed those curtains more than anything. I wanted to wear them myself with the curtain rod still attached like Carol Burnett playing Scarlett O'Hara.

My husband never even appreciated them. He would wake up in a rage if one beam of sunlight entered the room without his express permission.

Mrs. Dr. Blum, the penultimate hard-ass, had the right idea.

'I wish I could see you again before your next cleaning in six months,' Dr. Blum said. The hair on his knuckles made bumps under his latex gloves. I hesitated. 'Spit,' he said.

'I have a boyfriend,' I said quickly. The way I said it I almost felt like I did have a boyfriend. An image of a man was coming to my mind but I wasn't sure who it was.

'I thought you said you were just recently separated.'

'I am,' I said, flashing a smile, suddenly feeling strangely successful. I was sure I had a boyfriend, I just couldn't quite place him at that exact moment. Then I realized the man I was thinking of was Andrew and I stopped smiling.

'Well, you know where I am.'

'Yes, I'll wave to you when I pass by,' I said.

Dale stayed right outside the window like a lawn gnome for the rest of my appointment and I was forced to walk with her when I left.

'This is great!' she said. 'How are you? What are you doing now?'

I couldn't think fast enough.

'This is so lucky that I found you. It's kismet. You know how you've been complaining about your apartment?'

I didn't recall complaining.

'The smell and the hole in the kitchen floor and the way the floor is so slanted every time you put a glass on the table it rolls off?'

I guess I had mentioned one or two details.

'Well, an apartment just opened up in my building. Right next door to Harri and me! We can be neighbors.'

'How much?'

'Only eighteen hundred.'

'That's more than I'm paying now.'

'You can afford it. You're going to make a lot of money working for me. And you need that kind of motivation in this business. You have to need to make money.'

'Why don't you rent it to someone else and get a commission?' I asked.

'First rule in real estate,' Dale answered. 'Don't shit where you eat. Come on. We might as well jump on the subway. I'm in Chelsea.'

First we had to stop and get Dale a slice of pizza and then we managed to get on the subway going downtown instead of uptown. Two native New Yorkers, real estate agents, experts on the transit system, constant givers of directions, people who would feel almost confident walking through Central Park at night, familiar with every single block, mews, and alley, heading the wrong way, straight to Brooklyn.

We got off at Chambers and walked upstairs and then down to the uptown platform. We sat on a bench with just a tiny strip of wood separating us.

'This is fun,' Dale said. 'I feel like I'm seeing things in a whole new light.'

'That's great.'

'You're great,' she said.

Our train came, and Dale and I got on through separate doors.

I sat and Dale stood over me. 'If you take the apartment we can ride back and forth together on the subway all the time,' Dale said.

The whole time I tried to think of somewhere I had to be. Any excuse to get out of going to Dale's building. There had to be a job somewhere that didn't involve going on the subway with your boss.

We entered an old, run-down building with a shabby lobby.

'Is it a walk-up?' I asked.

'Would I live in a walk-up?' Dale said, indignantly.

We got in a tiny groaning elevator that had a round window in the door like a ship's porthole. First we went down instead of up, the porthole going black like we were underwater. Then we slowly churned to the fifth floor.

'I'll show you the available apartment first,' Dale said.

Dale opened the door with a key. I thought about what it would be like to live next door to Dale with her own key to my apartment. Maybe it would be okay with my gun. We walked into a small square room with another small square room connected to it. One room was painted white and the other black. It would be like living in a domino. 'That's the kitchen,' Dale said, pointing to the black side.

The white side had a pole going from floor to ceiling right in the center of the room.

'Oh, this is great,' I said. 'I love poles.'

'I know the pipe is a little awkward but you can work around it.'

'No, actually it's really great because I'm a stripper in my spare time and I need a pole at home to practice on.'

'No place is perfect, Liv,' Dale said, as if I were a client.

The pole divided the room in such a way that it would be impossible to put a bed in it. You could have a couch and two chairs with the pole in the middle, but no bed.

'I'm serious, this is perfect,' I said, 'because I have a bed that happens to be in the shape of a donut so I can saw it in half and put the pole in the center of the hole.'

I put my hand out to lean on it.

'Careful!' Dale said. 'That's the heating pipe. It's burning hot. It isn't insulated.'

'That's too bad because I've always wanted to hang the American flag in the exact center of my room and if the pole's hot the flag might burn.'

'Okay, fine. I just wanted to offer you the opportunity but I see you're just wasting my time. I thought it would be nice if we were neighbors, that's all.'

'How high is the ceiling?'

'Ten feet,' Dale said, as if I were actually interested.

'Ten feet? That's funny because I wouldn't touch this apartment with a ten-foot pole and that's exactly what we've got here.'

'Fine,' Dale said.

'Does your apartment have a pole?'

'Come on, I'll show it to you.'

'Harri, we're home!' Dale announced. I followed her down a dark, narrow corridor that opened into a tiny living room.

Harri was lying on the couch watching a large television set. She wore a huge white T-shirt that said 'Get out of my way I'm shopping' on it in big black letters. She clutched an old piece of flannel material that looked like a child's security blanket. The children's movie *Freaky Friday* was on. 'Harri, look, I've brought our star.'

'Hi, Liv,' Harri said, not taking her eyes off the TV.

'I told you to cover the couch with a sheet if you're going to lay on it all day,' Dale said.

'This isn't the office,' Harri said. 'Here, you aren't the boss. I'll do what I want. If I want to take a shit on the couch I will.'

'What do you pay for this place?' I asked.

It is totally acceptable in New York to ask someone their rent. In New York it's rude *not* to ask a person's rent. Asking what someone pays for their apartment is a very New York thing. It's an L.A. thing, too, but it was started by the New Yorkers who moved there.

'Only four hundred,' Dale said, excitedly. 'It's been in Harri's family for years. We decided to stay here and use the money we save to spend a month in Italy every year. In fact I was thinking of axing you if you'd like to come with us.'

I pretended she was joking and laughed.

'No, I'm serious. You should come. I want us to be more than just boss and employee. I want us to be a team.'

'Can I use the bathroom?' I said. I didn't think I should use the couch.

'Of course,' Dale said. 'Harri, show the kid where the powder room is.'

'It's right in there,' Harri said, pointing behind her.

'Thanks, I'll find it,' I said.

The toilet seat squished under me, making a sound. Owl figurines, a shelfful of them, eyeballed me. A white wire rack hung from the back of the door displaying winged maxi pads for heavy flow.

Dale's apartment was worse than mine. She sat on this toilet every morning and then showed marble bathrooms to people all day, standing by like a bathroom attendant. Bathrooms with Jacuzzis, and mounted televisions, soft recessed lighting, twin pedestal sinks, fish swimming in bowls, cabinets filled with Kiehl's and Chanel, fat scented candles, sea salts, ginger scrub, savon de Provence.

'Why did you bring her here?' I heard Harri whisper.

'I was showing her the apartment next door.'

'Were you hoping I wouldn't be here?'

'You're going to make me hope that,' Dale answered.

'I just wish you would show some discretion.'

'You're crazy. She's my employee.'

Independent contractor, I thought. Suddenly I thought of an excuse for why I had to leave immediately. It was airtight.

'I have to go,' I said, leaving the bathroom.

'Why?' Dale asked, suspiciously.

Then I gave my excuse. ' 'Cause I want to,' I said.

Harri laughed. She got up off the couch and showed me to the door.

Out on the street I looked up at Dale's building. It had an ornate façade, but when you turned the corner you could see that it was really just an old tenement. The front was just slapped on. My building was a tenement but it was an honest one. I had a fire escape outside my window, like an ugly jagged scar down my chest, but at least it was real. People always take after the buildings they live in the way they look like their dogs.

I stood next to two boys waiting to cross the street. They were about seventeen, wearing jeans as long and wide as skirts. They were looking at two girls walking away from them.

'That shit looks good,' one said.

'I didn't get to see her face,' his friend said.

'You don't have to see her face,' he said. 'That shit's going to be bent over anyway. You just have to like the back of her head.'

They laughed, and for a minute I remembered what I liked about men.

13

HRDWD FLRS

I was relieved to open the door to my own apartment and smell the smell and feel the slant. At home I was lopsided like the people in the commercials who should have had a V8. I kicked off my shoes. My apartment was so messy, pieces of paper and cellophane stuck to the bottom of my feet. At least my next-door neighbor was a crack whore and not Dale.

I lay on my bed and thought about my husband's curtains. I knew I was better off without them. I wondered if the women he brought home noticed them.

The phone rang and I answered. 'Hello?'

'How's my future wife?'

It was Andrew. I had wondered when he would call. 'Who is this?' I asked.

'It's me,' he said.

Water was running. 'Are you calling me from the shower? Your girlfriend must be home.'

'Nooooo. I'm washing dishes,' he said. 'I just ate a baked potato. How was your day?'

'I went to the dentist,' I said, as if I were Mrs. Bausch talking to Mr. Bausch.

'You sound down,' he said.

'I'm not,' I said. How did he know that? I didn't even know when I was down and when I was up.

'What's wrong, honey?' he said.

'I miss my apartment. I miss my windows. I miss my views. I miss my carpeting.'

'Ohhhh, poor baby,' he said. 'Do you miss your husband?'

'No. I miss my curtains.'

'That certainly says a lot about your marriage,' Andrew said.

Andrew listened for an hour while I talked about my old apartment. I told him everything, and he listened patiently, asking questions about the moldings and the lighting and the beams. 'I knew the building, it was a great one,' Andrew said solemnly, as if he were trying to find something to say about a person who had just died. It was comforting talking about it. There should be funerals for apartments. There should be apartment obituaries in *The New York Times*. There should be apartment mourners support groups.

The water ran steadily. 'That's a lot of dishes for one potato,' I said.

The next night as soon as I got home my buzzer rang. It was Andrew. I shoved all my mess into my closet. Papers poked out from under the cheap louver doors like bear claws. As a child I would lie in my bed and stare at the crack under my bedroom door expecting to see the claws of a bear trying to get in.

Andrew was sweating from lugging four enormous garbage bags up the stairs. He was wearing black pants and a black turtleneck and a hilarious black beret with the little stem sticking straight up in the center like a tiny erection. The beret emphasized the arbitrary place on his forehead where his hair began.

'What?' he said.

'Nothing,' I said. '*Tres chic.*'

He took off the beret and went straight into the kitchen to look at himself in the only full-length mirror, to make sure nothing had happened to him en route. He washed his face in the sink, wetting his hair, and dried off with a dish towel. He picked up my hairbrush and brushed his hair in short, organized strokes like he was doing the box step. I just stood there watching in disbelief. He examined his teeth close up in the mirror, unabashedly.

'What are you doing?' I said, finally.

'I want to make sure I look good for you.' He went back to the living room and I followed. 'Well, aren't you going to open them?'

I looked in one of the garbage bags. Yards and yards of gold silk.

'It's just like my . . .' I said in disbelief.

He pulled my husband's curtains out of the bags. The curtains from every single room.

'Did you want the rods, too?' he asked, concerned. 'I could go back.'

'How did you . . .'

'Never mind. I have my ways. I'm an *architect*.' 'Architect' was pronounced like 'President of the United States.' 'I couldn't bring you the windows or the views but I did bring you your curtains. And I also have another little souvenir here for you.' He pulled a few square feet of my husband's pale wool carpeting out of his duffel bag. 'I lifted up the couch in the living room and took it from there. I put the couch back so he'll never know it's missing. It will be hilarious if he ever moves the couch and sees the hole. I wish we could be there when that happens.'

I held the carpet in my arms. When I was eleven I couldn't decide what color carpet to have in my room. I liked pink and red and blue and yellow. My father didn't feel I should have to choose a color. He had squares of every color put down like a patchwork quilt.

'Now you can put the carpet on the floor by your bed and feel happy when you put your feet down in the morning. Let's go try it out.'

He walked over to the bedroom and laid the carpet. It fit almost perfectly between the wall and my bed.

'Now what are you going to do with the curtains? Hang them or hold them for ransom?' He picked up the phone pretending to hold a gun to the curtains' head. 'Hey, buddy, listen and listen good. We got your curtains and if you ever wanna see 'em again you better do what we say. You want proof we got 'em, listen to this. Say something!' he screamed at the curtains. He put the phone to the curtains and rustled them. Then he talked into the phone again. 'Did you hear that? Huh, wise guy? Did you hear that? We got 'em all right.'

He did an imitation of my husband coming home and looking at the naked windows. 'Heeeyyy,' he said, sounding confused. He stood with his legs spread apart and his hands on his hips and scratched his head. 'Something's different.'

Then I started laughing. I laughed so hard it was almost painful. Andrew was relentless. Tears poured down my face and I gasped for air. A person only laughs that hard a few times in his whole life. Andrew continued his curtain monologue until I finally begged him to stop.

I was nervous having sex with Andrew. I hadn't been with anyone other than my husband since our first date. The closest thing I had come to human contact with another man was when Dale rubbed my shoulders.

The room spun as if I were drunk. I held on to him and he only stopped kissing my face long enough to bite my earlobes.

'I don't have any condoms,' I said.

'Oh well, we don't need any,' he said.

'We can't have sex without a condom.'

'Well, that's okay, I've got some.'

'Oh, so you brought your own?' I said.

'You think I'm going to break and enter a man's house, steal his idiotic curtains, bring them home to you, and not stop along the way for condoms?'

When we finished I held my breath and expected to cry. The first night I had sex with my husband I cried and locked myself in the bathroom for an hour. He wrote funny notes and stuck them under the bathroom door but it just made me cry harder. After sex with Andrew I didn't feel like crying at all.

'My earring's gone,' I said, when I tried to soothe my ear with my fingers.

'Yes, I know. I swallowed it,' he said. 'I'm really sorry.' I loved that he had swallowed it. I wanted to feed him the other one.

'That diamond could feed a village of starving children for a year,' I said.

'That's funny, it didn't fill me up at all.'

'Well, you'll have to search your stool every day until you find it.'

'Maybe you should search my stool every day.'

'I don't think your girlfriend would want me coming over every morning and rooting around in your shit.' I sort of liked the idea of the diamond stud my husband had given me lodged in Andrew's shit. When he gave them to me at the Rainbow Room I didn't think they'd end up in another man's digestive tract.

'No, I'll have to move in here until we find it.'

I struggled out of his arms and got out of bed to look at my ear in the mirror. It was red and swollen but still intact. And the carpet felt like a sandbar under my feet. So soft and warm, safe and forgiving.

He pulled me back into bed with him and we kissed for a long time, urgent, intense kisses, as if his girlfriend were waiting just outside the door and our days were numbered. But it felt like my husband was out there with her. Andrew was living with someone, but I was getting a divorce. For some reason it felt like the same thing.

'Won't your girlfriend wonder why you didn't come home last night?'

'She thinks I'm dog-sitting, but I don't start until tonight. I'm dog-sitting for a week on University Place. You can stay there with me for a whole week.'

'A whole week,' I said.

A whole week, in dog years, was seven whole weeks.

'I love your smell,' he said. 'I love our sex.'

'*Our* sex,' I repeated, thinking of Mrs. Bausch saying '*our* dentist.' 'I love it, too,' I said. 'Except for the biting.'

'I know, but I can't help myself.' He climbed on top of me and pulled the covers over us.

Every man I have ever dated has been a black belt in some form of martial art or another. It is a strange coincidence, to find myself being flipped over onto beds and futons by various men. I don't seek it out, it just happens. It's like my friend Violet dating six men in a row named David.

Unfortunately, Andrew also liked to bite me. His teeth repeatedly clamped down on my ear, on the lobe or sometimes higher up on the skinny part. He clamped, released slightly and clamped again. When I resisted he ground his teeth into me harder and made noises that echoed in my head. Noises like you make for a child when you are pretending to be a monster eating something. *Nyum nyum nyum.*

My answering machine went off. It was Dale in a grumpy morning voice saying that she and Harri were going to Venice without me and I was in charge of the office for an entire month. I had only done one rental deal and I was in charge of the office. 'Our flight leaves tonight at seven from JFK.' She gave all the flight information. 'If you change your mind about coming with us, call me. Or come to the airport. I have a ticket for you.' I wondered if Dale had a scene in her head of me running through the airport screaming, 'I love you, Dale, don't leave without me.'

'Are you going to go?' Andrew asked.

'I have to dog-sit,' I reminded him. 'I have to supervise and make sure you don't bite the animals.'

Andrew rolled on top of me and we had *our* sex. He put his teeth on my ear but he didn't bite down. I relaxed. I'm having sex, I thought. I couldn't remember what I had been worried about.

In a daze we left my apartment to get something to eat. I suggested crepes at Les Deux Gamins but Andrew wanted pizza. We stood at a high round table eating slices. The crust was so delicious I could barely bring myself to swallow. I had never tasted anything like it. And the oregano on my tongue, and the colors, and the music the chiming bells made from the church on the other side of the street! I had never even really noticed a church there before.

My ear was so red and swollen I felt like I had an American Beauty rose tucked behind it. It was beating faster than my heart. I was proud of it. I felt like everyone could see our sex.

Andrew held my hand.

'What if someone who knows Jordan sees us?' I had never called her by her name before.

'I don't care,' he said.

Then I saw his jeans. They were mine. He was wearing my jeans. I stopped walking and stared at them.

'What?' he said.

'Are those my jeans?'

'No.'

'Yes, those are my jeans. Are you wearing my jeans?'

'Yes, honey, so what?' he said, tauntingly.

How could he wear my jeans? He was so much fatter than I was. And he was taller than me, if only slightly. I was mortified. I refused to take another step with a man wearing my jeans. My jeans should have been much, much too small for his barrel shape. It was the most insensitive thing any man had ever done. 'Those are my . . . big jeans,' I said, lamely. 'How did you squeeze into them?'

'I didn't have to squeeze. They slid right on.'

'That's impossible.' I wanted him to take them off and go home to his girlfriend in his underpants.

'I couldn't believe they fit," he said. He laughed. I didn't see how he could ever be attracted to me again knowing he could wear my jeans. But then he kissed me and rubbed my jeans up against me.

It was strange to see my jeans with an erection in them. 'I'm going to wear them all week,' he said.

14
ALL ABOUT WNDWS

I turned and started walking toward the office. I had to get to work. With Dale gone, I was in charge of an entire real estate firm. I had so much to do. I sat at Dale's desk and looked out the window at sparrows flying in and out of the open metal tube of a traffic light – probably the best bird real estate in New York.

Lorna walked in. 'Something stinks,' she said.

'Actually, Lorna, nothing stinks.'

'Yes it does. And now that I'm in charge we're going to have the windows open.' She took a joint out of her knapsack and lit it.

'Actually, Lorna, Dale put me in charge, and I don't think you should smoke pot in the office.'

'Why would she put you in charge? You've never even done one deal.'

'Yes I have.'

'The towering inferno doesn't count.'

'That's beside the point,' I said. 'She put me in charge and I would really appreciate it if you didn't smoke during business hours.' Lorna continued to smoke her joint.

'I know why she put you in charge,' Lorna said. 'Because you're sleeping with her.' She started to laugh hysterically. I was more taken aback by the sight of Lorna laughing for the first

time than by her comment. Dale's line rang and we both jumped
to answer it. I won and Lorna screamed, 'Fuck you' at the top of
her lungs and stormed out.

The call was from a woman with an English accent named
Juliet Flagg who had seen the sign hanging in the window
behind Dale's desk. Dale had forced me to make the sign
myself – 'Dale Kilpatrick Real Estate Gallery,' written crookedly
on neon-pink oaktag. She wanted me to come over and appraise
the sale price of her loft on Liberty Street.

I took a cab there. Juliet Flagg opened the door wearing a
wedding gown that I recognized from the window of Morgane
Le Fay, which was right around the corner from the office. She
had long red hair parted in the middle. Her hair was jagged on
the bottom like the teeth of a jack-o'-lantern.

I stood in the doorway.

'Please come in, I don't have much time,' she said.

She turned in her dress and I followed her. Sheer white fabric
exposed the delicate structure of the bones of the bodice and the
texture of the crinoline. It had the perfect balance of soft to hard,
like ice cream on a cone.

'So what do you think?' she asked.

'It's the most beautiful gown I've ever seen.' I felt disloyal to
my father.

'I'm glad you like it, but I was talking about the loft. I just
bought it this morning – the gown, not the loft. That's when I saw
your sign hanging in the window. I had called another estate
agent to come give me an appraisal but she sounded a bit strange
so I thought I should get two opinions. I'm afraid it's all been a
bit rushed.'

Suddenly I became competitive. I took out my leather organizer and started to make notes in the section I had labeled
'exclusives.' I couldn't stand the thought of another real estate
agent in this loft. 'Has the other agent been here yet?'

'No, but she'll be here any minute,' Juliet said.

'You should get out of that,' I said.

'But she's already left her office. I can't get out of it now.'

'No, the gown. I don't want you to ruin it,' I said, in the caring tone of a full-service broker. I was determined to get this listing.

'Get out of it? I just got into it. They had to lace me all up in the store. The wedding starts at two. And that's in less than an hour. In fact we should really get started.'

Her loft was in a converted office building. The floors were the original gorgeous mosaic marble and an old-fashioned brass mail chute was built into the wall just as you entered her foyer. You could mail letters right from inside your own apartment. The bathroom was done all in wood like a treehouse and the shower was built into the corner of the room against two glass walls. The walls were clear glass, floor to ceiling. You would shower naked on the twelfth floor looking right down onto traffic.

'I know it's a bit odd,' Juliet said, 'but that's an office building across the road so if you make sure to shower before nine or after five, they're the only ones who can see you.' She pointed to a row of gargoyles on the building across the street. 'So, how much do you think I could get for it?'

I had no idea. It was an apartment even my father would like. It was fantastic. What I did know was that she was making a terrible mistake to sell this loft. She would miss it when she got divorced and was out mailing letters on the street like any commoner. She would long for it desperately when she had to shower alone in four dull tiled walls. Which was I first, a woman or a real estate agent? If I was a woman first I would stop her from making the worst mistake of her life.

But I had to give her an answer. 'Six hundred thousand?' I asked.

'Don't you need to know the maintenance?'

I had forgotten that. 'Sure,' I said, casually, as if I was so good at my job I didn't need to know trivial little details like maintenance. 'What is it?'

'It's high. Twenty-two hundred a month.'

'Oh, that is high,' I said.

'But you haven't even seen the roof deck yet.'

A roof deck was an incredible thing. You rarely saw a roof

deck without a rainbow flag hanging off it indicating gay pride. Gay men had conquered all the best outdoor space. They had the best taste and the most money.

'I really do love this place,' Juliet said. She had the passion in her voice that people only got for their apartments. 'I hope I'm doing the right thing.'

I didn't know if she meant marrying or selling. She looked at me so pitifully, I felt like Dr. Kevorkian selling her apartment. It was like a murder/suicide, giving up a loft like this just to marry a man.

I could go to their wedding and object. I could make it my mission, as an almost-divorced woman, to object at all weddings. Each morning I could go to City Hall and start objecting. I could object all day. If anyone tried to catch me, I'd throw rice in their faces and run. My disguise would be a tasteful Peter Kellerman hat with a small veil. I'd stop hundreds of weddings every week. Finally the Lone Objector would be apprehended and my husband would have to come bail me out and he'd say something like, 'Liv, I always told you if you like objecting so much you should be a lawyer.' I'd be tried before Judge Garrett and he'd say, 'First you spell business wrong, then you become a real estate agent, and now this!'

Juliet looked upset. 'I know this is going to sound strange,' she said, 'but I just can't . . .'

'I don't think you *should* sell,' I blurted.

'What? No, I was going to ask you to cut my hair in back. I went crazy and cut it myself this morning and I know it looks terrible. And I trust you.' She handed me a pair of scissors.

Once I dated an Italian man whose grandmother forced me to cut her hair in her kitchen. It was gray and stiff as a board. Her scissors were dull and wouldn't cut through. I tried to protest but she insisted I continue hacking until it looked like pointed icicles hanging off a roof. When she saw what I had done she said, 'I curse you,' and made a jabbing motion with the scissors near my heart.

'I'm not good at that,' I said.

'Please, I don't want to get married with my hair a disaster.'

'I can't,' I pleaded. 'You could go to Tom at Tortolla Salon, just a few blocks away on Franklin Street. He'll see you right now if I tell him it's an emergency.' I remembered Tom telling me that he didn't like to see women who cut their own hair because they were usually terribly disturbed control freaks.

'Please try,' she said. 'I have to wait here for the other agent.'

I figured if I didn't cut her hair the other agent would. 'Who's the other agent?' I asked.

'A woman named Vashinko, or something like that.'

'Oh, Valashenko? I know her,' I said. I felt happy for Valashenko that she had passed the test. But I didn't feel too threatened. There was no way she would be able to cut Juliet's hair either. 'She's not very good,' I said. I couldn't believe I could say anything bad about poor Valashenko. I was getting to be as bad as Dale.

'She's not?'

'No, she's awful,' I said. 'I wish you would go to Tom. You should leave right now and go to Tom. I'll call him for you.'

She felt nervously at the back of her hair. 'Maybe I should,' she said.

I pulled one of Dale's exclusive agreements out of my bag. It was typed in all caps and it stated that Dale Kilpatrick Real Estate Gallery had the exclusive right to sell her apartment for a year.

'A year?' the woman said. 'I was hoping it would be sold by the time I get back from my honeymoon.'

'Oh, I'm sure it will be. I'll go back to the office and run some comps on the computer so I can price it correctly and I'll begin advertising right away. I'll just need the keys and a number where I can reach you with offers.'

She said she was leaving that night after the wedding and she'd be gone for three weeks. 'I'll call you when I get to my hotel,' she said.

She signed and we rode down in the elevator together. She got into a limo. 'I'm nervous,' she said through the rolled-down window. I had the incredible urge to lend her my gun. Something borrowed.

'You'll be fine,' I told her.

'I know. He's the loft of my life.'

I laughed. 'You mean the love of your life.'

'Yes, that's what I said, isn't it? The love of my life.'

I gave the driver the address of Tortolla and waved. The limo started to pull out. Suddenly I remembered that it was Monday and Tortolla was closed. I started to panic. 'Wait,' I screamed. The limo drove off. 'Wait, wait,' I screamed and ran after it. It stopped at a red light and I caught up to it.

Juliet rolled down her window. 'Maybe I can cut it myself,' I said, panting. 'I was just thinking you really don't have time to go all the way to Tom. I can just do it now.'

'I don't know,' she said.

'Please, let me.' The driver pulled over.

Juliet took an alligator manicure set out of her carry-on bag. I helped her out of the limo and stood behind her, clasping the tiny gold scissors in my shaking hand. I took an inch of her beautiful red hair between my fingers the way Tom did. I snipped tentatively and the hair fell. I made delicate little cuts all around. The tiny red hairs sprinkled down on the back of her dress. I brushed at it furiously. 'There,' I said.

She got back in the limo and they drove off.

When I was a child, my shrink told me something I never forgot. At the end of our session, right out of the blue, she said, 'Liv, if you had been caught by the Nazis and put in a concentration camp, you would have survived.' 'How?' I asked her. 'By finding a way to make yourself useful.' She had told me that fifteen years ago but it had bothered me ever since.

Just then Valashenko walked past me in her purple felt hat. She saw me and stopped.

'Hi, Liv,' she said.

'Valashenko,' I said. She looked older and tired, like a camel. Her eyes were bigger and she looked like she had grown another layer of skin. Her hair looked like I had cut it. I felt so terrible I could barely look at her. 'You look wonderful.'

'Well, things have been hard but I finally got my license and I'm going to pitch my first exclusive. If I don't make money soon I don't know what I'll do.' I could tell she was still wearing only one contact lens.

'Maybe your family could help you.'

'Hah, my family would never help me. Liv, I grew up with the Hasidim. They sat shivah for me when I became a model. To them I've been dead for thirty-five years.'

'Maybe I could take you out to lunch sometime next week,' I offered.

'Oh, I'd love that. You're the only nice person in this business.' She leaned down to kiss me on the cheek and walked toward Juliet's building. I was still holding the signed exclusive in my hand. I watched her ring the buzzer and adjust her hat in the door's reflection. She rang the buzzer again and stood there patiently. She rang the buzzer a third time and I turned and walked quickly away.

I knew I was doing the right thing. I would do a much better job selling this loft than Valashenko, and my allegiance had to be to its owner. If she was going to make the worst mistake of her life and sell her loft, then the least I could do was get her the most money I possibly could. I walked faster, fueled by fiduciary responsibility.

Now that I had my own exclusive, I couldn't seem to walk fast enough. I couldn't wait to get back to the office. People were in my way. Everyone's shoulders were rounded. The pace of New York was getting so slow it was practically at a standstill. I wanted to be in a city where people moved quickly. I would have to move to Hong Kong, where men didn't laze around all day commenting on women and holding basketballs.

When I got back to the office Lorna was sitting at her desk smoking a joint. I couldn't believe how unprofessional it was to sit there doing that in the office. 'Something stinks,' I said.

'I know, what is that?' Lorna said.

'Your pot,' I said.

'The pot is what's making it smell better in here.'

'Lorna, how much do you think a two-bedroom loft on Liberty with an unfinished roof deck would go for?'

'How big?'

'About sixteen hundred square feet.'

'Okay, so we'll say it's two thousand square feet. What's the maintenance?'

'It's quite high,' I said, as if I had already thought of everything. 'It's twenty-two hundred a month.'

'And why do you want to know this?'

'I'm just curious.'

'Well, I'm not here to baby-sit you so figure it out for yourself.'

'I'll look it up on the computer.'

Lorna laughed. 'That's a good one. Listings on the computer! That's funny. Where do you think you are, Corcoran?' Most companies, like Corcoran, Halstead, Feathered Nest, Smoothe Transitions, or Douglas Elliman, had thousands of listings on their computers. It turned out all Dale had on the computer was that program to help you learn how to use the mouse.

The phone rang and this time Lorna was the first to answer it. It was Dale calling from Venice. 'Yeah-yeah-yeah, ciao,' Lorna said. 'Could you tell your darling new employee that I'm not here to do her work for her?'

'Ask her who's in charge,' I said.

'Who did you put in charge, Dale, me or your new lover? Fine. Well, I can't stay on the phone all day, I have to try to get some of my own work done around here so I can afford to take trips to Italy and waste time,' she said and hung up. She took one last drag on her joint, strapped on her knapsack, and headed toward the door.

'Well?' I asked.

'We're both in charge,' she said, slamming the door behind her.

For some reason, I was starting to like Lorna. In a way, I liked her more than Violet. At least Lorna was totally honest. There was something comforting about all that nastiness, like brown water gushing out of my sink. You knew it was bad, you didn't have to wonder.

I had even been tempted to show her my gun.

As soon as she left Dale called back. 'How aaaaare you?' she asked.

'I thought I was in charge, Dale.'

'You are, of course you're in charge. I just couldn't tell Lorna that. She has a lot of seniority. Can't you try to be understanding?'

'I don't care,' I said.

'Do you miss me?' she asked. I didn't say anything. 'I'm just kidding,' she said. 'Harri and I are having a wonderful time. How's business?'

'I've got good news for you!' I said. I told her about my exclusive. 'I could really use your help with it.'

'That's great! You're the emperor with the golden touch.' She lowered her voice. 'Liv, I wish you were here.'

'Me too,' I said. 'By the way, it's King Midas and the golden touch and the emperor's new clothes. Anyway, it's a sixteen-hundred-square-foot –'

'I'm serious, come to Venice. Harri's going home early, it will just be the two of us.'

'You need me to stay here and manage the office,' I said. 'I have to ask you how to price the loft.'

'I'll pay for everything. Venice is so beautiful. Bella. Bay-la.' I could see she wasn't going to help me. 'Listen, kid, I think I have little bit of a crush on you.' Oh no, I thought. 'There, I said it.'

'But, Dale, I'm not gay,' I said.

'I know, I know,' she said.

'I'm straight,' I said. I drew a straight line on the listing sheet on my desk.

'I know.'

'I mean I'm very flattered. Extremely flattered,' I said. 'And I respect you as a businessmanperson.'

'I know you could have anyone,' she said angrily. 'You should have a real sugar daddy, an older Italian man.'

'Are you going to fire me now?' I asked jokingly.

'Of course not, I love you,' she said, and hung up.

I sat at my desk cringing. I knew I was going to get fired. No exclusive in the world was worth even having to talk to Dale on the phone. I tried to put Dale out of my mind and concentrate on my first night dog-sitting with Andrew.

Just then he called. 'Are you coming over?' he asked.

'Yes,' I said. I suddenly felt confused. I thought it had been definite. 'Do you still want me to?'

'Yes, of course. I just thought maybe you had changed your mind because I left three messages for you and you didn't call back.'

I laughed. 'Lorna doesn't take messages,' I said. I would have to talk to Dale about voice mail. I noticed the three while-you-were-out slips Lorna had put on my desk. The first said, 'I'm not your fucking secretary.' The second said, 'Your boyfriend sounds like a loser.' And the third said, 'Get a life.'

'Hurry home,' he said. 'The girls and I are waiting for you.'

'What's the address?' I asked.

He gave me the address of a building called the Cedarton on Tenth and University and told me to hurry. 'I can't wait for it to be morning so we can wake up together,' he said.

The whole way to University Place I thought about sex. Just that morning I had had sex. I still felt it, felt him, between my legs. I felt like a woman who is proud of her walk-in closet, feels richer, more feminine, opulent, even though few people have ever stepped inside it. I knew I looked different because every bum on the street and man in a black jeep with music blaring out of it commented on my appearance. I thought I was looking pretty average but the men of New York apparently thought otherwise.

15

WEA/80'S 3BR — THIS WON'T LAST

Andrew greeted me at the door with two dogs. He showed me around the apartment we were going to be staying in for the week. He moved the white Fisher-Price baby gate aside so I could get into the living room.

'Does she have a baby?' I asked.

'That's for the dogs,' he said. I sat on the couch and the dogs jumped up next to me. They were gleeful to be let in.

'Whose apartment is this?' I asked. Maybe Andrew had girl-friends all over New York.

'My friend Lauren's.'

'And why are you dog-sitting for her?' I asked with a polite question mark.

'That little one was a stray I found,' he said. 'But my dog Ajax didn't get along with her so Lauren said she would take her if I agreed to dog-sit occasionally.' He still didn't tell me who she was.

The room was filled with whimsical Salvador Dalí-style fur-niture. Exaggerated shapes, high backs, a wavy clock. A velvet couch that looked like it came right out of the SoHo Starbucks. 'She really knows how to decorate,' he said. No, she doesn't, I thought. I wondered if he was going to spend the whole night complimenting this woman. 'Isn't this a great apartment?' he asked. No, I thought. He was an architect, how could he think this was a great apartment?

'It's all right,' I said.

The bedroom had a Lifecycle at the foot of the bed. I pictured the friend as tall and thin, biking during commercial breaks.

Andrew flipped me onto the bed and climbed on top of me.

'I thought we were going to go out to dinner to celebrate my new exclusive,' I said.

'We're celebrating right now. Congratulations,' he whispered in my ear. 'I'm proud of you.' I hated when men said they were proud of me. He didn't even know me. Being proud involved an investment on his part. He hadn't exactly carried me in his womb for nine months or put me through college. Next he would want a cut of my commissions. 'I missed you so much today,' he said.

'Did you buy condoms?' I asked.

'I'm sure there are some around here somewhere.' He reached over my head and opened a tiny drawer in the built-in head-board. He pulled out a condom.

'Have you looked through her underwear drawer, too?'

'Of course,' he said. 'I'm a man, Liv. I'm not going to stay alone in a woman's apartment and not look in her hamper.'

'Did you say her hamper?' I asked. He laughed. 'And?'

'They're really nice,' he said.

'Silk?'

'No, cotton, but really nice.' Cotton isn't really nice, I thought. I was wearing silk.

One of the dogs, the big one, crawled under the bed.

Suddenly I realized why I wasn't enjoying dog-sitting with Andrew as much as I thought I would. We weren't in his apart-ment. We weren't in his bed. These weren't his dogs. You learned about a person by looking around his apartment. You saw his magazines and dishes in the sink. You saw if he made his bed or not and if he had a Brita water filter. You saw if he used Dial soap or Dove, his CDs, books, cereal, screensaver, if the picture of his mother was framed or not.

My job was to look at apartments all day long. I was more familiar with the apartments and dogs of strangers than I was with Andrew's. By the time I retired from real estate I would have seen every single apartment in New York, except Andrew's. You just couldn't know a person until you knew where he lived.

The only thing I knew about Andrew's apartment was that there was a grandfather clock. I had heard it chime when we were on the phone. But where? In the living room, dining room, a corridor, or foyer? I knew it had to be somewhere near the kitchen. I wondered if the clock belonged to him or to his girlfriend. I could picture it, big, brown, and Roman-numeralled. I didn't even like grandfather clocks. I couldn't think of anything more depressing to have in your apartment. Why not just put a sign up saying, 'Time is flying by, with each ticking second you are closer to the grave, and this clock is going to last a hell of a lot longer than you are.'

He pulled off my clothes as I lay there limply. He put on his friend Lauren's condom and slid inside me.

'Andrew, where's your grandfather clock?'

'It's in your cunt,' he said. 'And it's going to chime on the stroke of twelve.'

'I'm serious, where is it?'

'I don't know, it's in the hall outside the kitchen.' He rammed into me. 'Don't think about grandfathers,' he said.

I thought of the real estate term grandfathering, grandfathered in. A person was grandfathered in if he was already living in a place when the rules got changed. You could be grandfathered in to an Artist-in-Residence building without an A.I.R. certificate. You could be grandfathered in to a rent-controlled lease. If a person had a preexisting greenhouse on his roof and a new law was passed saying that greenhouses were illegal, his greenhouse could be grandfathered in. People were constantly finding ways to get grandfathered in all over the place. Andrew already had a preexisting girlfriend. If Andrew and I ever married, his girlfriend could somehow be grandfathered in to our bed.

Andrew came on top of me and the dog crawled out from under the bed and went into the other room.

'You make an interesting sound when you come,' he said.

'But I didn't come,' I said.

'Yes you did.'

'No I didn't. I didn't even consider coming.'

'You came and when you came you said, "*Oy vey*."'

'First of all I did not come and second of all I did not say the words *oy vey*. I've never said *oy vey* in my life.'

'You definitely said *oy*. You might not have said *vey* but you said *oy* a couple of times.' He imitated an old Jewish woman coming. '*Oy . . . Oy . . . Oy vey!*'

'I did not say *oy*.'

'Don't be embarrassed. I love all your sounds. I loved when you said *oy*. You are a beautiful Jewess.'

'Don't ever call me that again,' I said.

'Why?' he asked.

No one had ever called me a Jewess before. I didn't look particularly Jewish. Cabdrivers always thought I was Indian or Italian. It occurred to me that Andrew was the first Jewish man I had been with. I liked that he was Jewish. I felt intensely intimate with him, like a Hasidic couple after they have said their marriage vows and are allowed to be alone in a room together for the first time. It felt like the first time. I felt skewered to him like a shish kebab.

He propped himself up on his elbow and traced my eyebrows with his finger.

Lying there with our faces so close together I fell in love with his looks. He didn't seem as hideous as I had once thought. His cheeks no longer looked so munchkinlike, as if his grandmother's invisible hand were permanently squeezing them. They looked delicious, like fruit I wanted to bite. His eyes looked scared and tired and hurt and happy. His forehead looked smart. His hair looked grown-up and responsible. His lips looked so cute and Jewish saying the word oy over and over again.

'Are you a mensch?' I asked. When I was a child, my shrink

told me to marry a mensch when I grew up. I thought it was a nationality like Mennonite or Swede or Californian. When I got home I got out my atlas and asked my father where Mensches lived. 'Upper West Side,' my father said.

'No, I am not a mensch,' Andrew said, smiling.

'Maybe you are.'

'I tell you what. I won't call you a Jewess if you don't call me a mensch.'

'Mensch is a good thing,' I said. 'What do you think it means?'

'It means nebbish. Wimp. Limp dick.'

'It means family man.'

He got another condom out of the drawer and climbed on top of me again. We fucked for a long time, with his mouth on my ear. This time I didn't think about real estate. I thought about the mensch I had inside me.

And I remembered the time I stood on line at the post office buying Love stamps for my wedding invitations. The only thing I was sure of in all my wedding plans was the need for Love stamps. That made it somehow more official to me than the vows or the license or the rings. While I was on line a handsome man had smiled at me and I had smiled back. The line snaked around and he was several people ahead of me but we kept smiling. I was in love with my fiancé and I was there to buy Love stamps but I thought at that moment that I could have joined this man where he was on line and left with him, saving the Love stamps for a later date.

Then an old woman went up to the postal clerk and said, 'How much is it to mail a letter?'

'Same price as last month,' the man told her. 'Do you want to buy more than one stamp this time?'

'No,' the woman said. 'I don't know how much longer I'll live.' It made life seem so short all of a sudden that I stopped smiling at the handsome man and I thought, I love Jack and I might as well only take that one since I don't know how much longer I will live.

But my marriage had died an early death and I had outlived it and now I was with Andrew and he was a mensch. He was making me come. I listened to the sounds I was making. I had never felt so close to anyone. I pulled my head away, forcing him to let go of my ear and buried my face in his chest. I started to cry.

'Why are you crying?' he asked, pleased.

I didn't know. Maybe it was the release of letting him fuck me. Or the tension of it. When I was a child my shrink had told me that no two people ever cry for the same reason, like snowflakes.

'*Oy Gevalt*,' I said.

'I can't remember the last time I fucked like that. Twice in a row like that.'

'You're a mensch,' I said. Tears were pouring down my face. 'Maybe I should go home.'

'Please stay here with me tonight, Liv. Please stay with me all week.'

We took the dogs for a walk and sat holding hands on a bench in the pebble dog run of Washington Square Park, sharing a big bottle of water.

16
SUB-O

In the morning I got to the office first and got the messages off the answering machine. One was for Lorna. I copied down the information and erased the message.

'So who's that freak who kept calling you yesterday?' she said when she got in. 'Your boyfriend?' Her voice was filled with disgust.

I couldn't believe she wanted to attempt girl talk.

'Maybe,' I said.

'I need a joint,' she said. 'I went to visit my friend Mario in the hospital. He only has three T cells left. He's hitting on all the female nurses, trying to pinch them and shit. All of a sudden he likes girls. The AIDS has made him straight. They finally figured out a cure for homosexuality – dementia. He can't remember he's gay. It cured him.' She laughed. 'How ironic, if you think about it. His boyfriend's furious.'

'That's funny,' I said. Lorna was always telling you how many T cells everyone had left.

'So what's he do?' Lorna asked.

'Who?'

'The freak you're seeing.' Women, no matter how much they

hate each other, always are friendly enough to talk about each other's boyfriends.

'He lives with a woman,' I said.

'So?' She pulled a joint out of a cigarette pack and lit it. I tried not to be judgmental about the joint.

'So, he's not really my boyfriend. I have to stop seeing him.'

'He's not married,' she said. 'Who cares if he's living with some idiot. She doesn't have the exclusive. All men are gay anyway.'

'So you think I should keep seeing him?' I asked.

'How do I know? It's been a long time since I left junior high. Why's your ear all swollen?'

'Sex,' I said.

'He fucks your ear? Maybe you should tell him he's not doing it right. His dick's probably so small your ear's the only part of your body that's tight enough.'

'Hey, Lorna,' I said. 'You got a message.' I held it up like a dog biscuit.

'So?'

'So I was thinking what do you say we make a deal? I'll give you your messages if you give me mine.'

'You know, Liv, this is the real estate business, not some mom-and-pop Hallmark store. This isn't a fucking florist, it's a brokerage for Christ's sake. This isn't a fucking not-for-profit charity shit. Where do you think you are? We don't sell fucking Beanie Babies here, we sell property in Manhattan.'

'So what do you think?'

'Okay,' she said. I put her message neatly on her desk, smoothing it a little.

Then I called every real estate firm in the downtown area and told them about my exclusive. I had learned in real estate school about multiple listings. There was something called the Downtown Brokers Association. You were required to share your listings. I could take another broker and her customer to my listing and if her customer bought it we would split the six-percent commission. And I could take my customers, once I got any, to

their listings. It was called co-broking. No one had ever heard of
Dale Kilpatrick Real Estate Gallery but I described the loft to a
dozen secretaries, giving my phone and fax numbers.

Within the hour seventeen brokers called me to make appointments to bring their customers to the loft. The pages of my
organizer filled. And faxes started coming, descriptions and floor
plans of their listings. I was in business.

I sat at my desk trying to come up with a headline for my
first *New York Times* ad. FINCL DIST EXCL PH/LOFT OF MY LIFE/2000SF +RF
DECK, OWN MAILCHUTE, I-OF-KIND SHOWR, I wrote on my pad. Lorna
came over and looked at it. She crossed out Fincl Dist and wrote
in Tribeca.

'Own mail chute? That looks ridiculous,' she said.

I crossed it out. 'Thanks,' I said.

'That and a token . . . You should ice that ear. Great, now I'm a
nurse,' she said, walking out the door.

I took the clip out of my hair so it fell down over my ears. I
called Noah Bausch. 'Good news,' I said. I told him they could be
the lucky first to see the loft.

'Where is it?' he asked, excited.

'Liberty Street.'

'Liberty Street?' he said, as if I had just named an exit in
New Jersey instead of a chic downtown address. 'Where's that?'
he asked. I could tell he was working his mind to its full capac-
ity.

'Southern Tribeca,' I said. 'Tribeca is where Nobu is.'

'Yeah, but Liberty's way south of that.'

'It's a few blocks south of Nobu.'

'Can you even get cabs down there?'

'Of course. The market is moving farther south,' I said. I made
the 'market' sound like a band of gypsies.

We spent forty-five minutes arguing about whether Liberty
Street was officially in Tribeca.

'It's Tribeca slash the Wall Street area,' I acquiesced.

'If you could move the loft north about fifteen blocks it would
sound perfect.'

'Well, I can't physically move the loft,' I said as if I were speaking to a small retarded child. 'It's in a great building.'

'But it's not in Tribeca.'

'Well, where do you think it is then?' I asked.

'Chinatown slash South Street Seaport,' he said.

I hated Noah Bausch so much at that moment I swore I would never let him set one foot in the loft. It made me physically sick to think of him writing his inane Faulknerian short stories in the third bedroom, looking quizzically at the gargoyles between each presumptuous omniscient third-person sentence, and then looking back down at his old-fashioned yellow legal pad because he's far too literary to use a computer and none of his twenty-six antique Underwoods works, and leaning back so smugly in his leather desk chair that it tips over backward and he cracks his head open on the marble mosaic floor.

'Well, it's fine if you don't want to see it,' I said. 'I just wanted to offer you the opportunity.'

Of the seventeen brokers who made appointments, fourteen showed up, and two people made offers. With every showing, I adjusted the price based on 'feedback' from the other brokers, until I arrived at a final price of seven hundred and fifty thousand dollars. I couldn't believe how easy it was; I just stood at the door jingling the keys and looking at my watch to let them know I had a lot of other buyers coming.

When my ad came out in the *Times*, fifty-two people called about the Loft of My Life, including Noah Bausch.

'Why didn't you tell me about this loft?' he asked.

'I did. That's the one I told you about. You said it was in Chinatown.'

'Well, we'd be interested to see it.'

'I'm sorry,' I said, 'but I already have *several* offers. You could have been the first,' I added. 'What a shame,' I added further. And 'What a shame,' I added again to that. 'How's the writing going?' I asked with a voice full of sympathy.

'Fine,' he said, sounding small and tortured.

That weekend I showed the loft to the people who had

answered the ad in the *Times*, my customers, and one man and his fiancée made an offer. 'How old are you?' I asked the man. He looked like he was about sixteen. 'Twenty-six,' he said. He gave me his business card. Senior Vice President, Solomon Brothers. Amazing. His mother and father, the Zeislofts, came to the showing, both architects, and his fiancée's mother and father, the Meads, also both architects, came, too.

'My boyfriend's an architect,' I announced.

'This is where I can put the collection,' his fiancée said. She was totally unattractive.

'Oh? What do you collect?' I asked with a look of pure concentrated interest on my face I used to use at business dinners with my husband. African masks? Tibetan kilims? Grecian urns?

'Snow domes,' she said proudly. 'I have over a thousand.'

'That's fantastic,' I said, actually clapping my hands. A thousand snow domes junking up my loft. I was sorry I asked.

'We're going to get a see-through refrigerator,' she said. 'With shelves that rotate like those cake display cases you see in diners.'

Juliet's refrigerator was fine. Who would want to wake up in the morning and have to try to catch up with the milk? My refrigerator didn't even work. It was dark inside like Howe Caverns. It was huge with rounded edges like a Love bus from the seventies. I had finally given up on it completely and put my shoes in it. Shoes on the top shelves, sweaters on the bottom, socks in the butter and condiment side trays, bras and panties in the meat and vegetable compartments. The freezer still worked though, so it made a nice combination freezer/armoire.

I was beginning to notice that people in this business cared more about refrigerators than anything. A Sub-zero refrigerator was more important than the maintenance, or ceiling heights, or school district.

The family of architects invited me to dinner at Montrachet and talked excitedly about the loft. I did math in the ladies' room on toilet paper. I would get the whole six-percent commission if I sold it to these people instead of to a customer brought by

another broker. I would split six percent with Dale instead of
three percent. Thirty-nine thousand dollars split with Dale was
nineteen thousand, five hundred each. I couldn't wait for Juliet to
call so she could accept their offer and I could start the paper-
work to present to the lawyers and the board.

When I got back to the table the waiter suggested the pigeon.
I almost considered it. My father always said if you were afraid
of rats you should eat one. I thought of the pigeons screaming
from deep in their throats in the air shaft out my window. Maybe
if I ate one I would feel different toward them as they woke me
up each morning. Maybe now that I was a real estate agent I
could handle eating pigeon. Any broker worth her salt should be
able to eat her city's Official Bird.

'Well?' the waiter asked. I choked on a sip of red wine and spit
it out on the white tablecloth. 'Oh, excuse me,' I said.

They looked at me pityingly.

Nineteen thousand five hundred, I thought.

I chickened out and ordered steak. I wondered if Andrew had
walked the dogs yet.

'To Liv,' Mr. Mead, the girl's father, said, raising his wineglass.
'For finding our kids the perfect place.' We all raised our glasses.

'Thank you,' I said. I hoped nothing horrible would happen,
like it burning to the ground.

'And now you have to sell our place,' he said. He and his wife
looked at each other.

'What!' the daughter said.

'We want to sell the apartment and get a building,' he said.
'And we want to give Liv the exclusive.'

I smiled and tried to act calm and professional. This would
mean three deals right in a row. This is what they called a
rollover, or a tripleheader, or something like that. Whatever it
was called, in the end I would get three commissions out of it.
The three deals spun in my head like pictures on a slot machine.
I imagined the gift baskets I would have to make. Gift baskets
replete with snow domes and Dom Pérignon. Perhaps a picture
of me in a Cartier frame. I felt like making myself a gift basket. I

let the waiter refill my wineglass. Lorna would die. I couldn't wait to see her face when she heard about this.

'Does your firm handle townhouse transactions?' he asked.

'Of course,' I said. 'I'm very familiar with townhouses. I can show you some wonderful townhouses.'

I *was* familiar with townhouses. When I was a child my shrink's office was in a townhouse. I had a Barbie townhouse. I had been given a chocolate townhouse one Easter by a relative who didn't believe Jewish children should get chocolate rabbits. In the eighth grade I made out with Darren Sullivan in his father's townhouse, on his father's bed, watching one of his father's porn videos called *Sex World*, a sort of X-rated version of the TV show *Fantasy Island*. My whole life was one townhouse after another. I was sure I knew more than enough about them.

I ate orange sorbet and cookies and hugged everyone goodbye on the street outside Montrachet. I felt as close as family. I felt that blissful awkward confusion you feel with your in-laws when you are first married, wondering if you should call them Mom and Dad.

When I got to the Cedarton, Andrew was waiting for me, sitting at the kitchen table eating a bowl of cornflakes and soy milk.

It was our last night dog-sitting together. I felt suddenly panicked, as if I would never see him again after tonight. I didn't know what would happen. Would Andrew call me from the kitchen while he washed dishes and see me from time to time for an hour or two right after work? I wondered if he missed his girlfriend. If they would have home-from-dog-sitting sex. If she would cook something special. I had never cooked for Andrew. I had eaten steak at Montrachet while he ate cereal and fake gray milk.

'Where were you?' he asked suspiciously. He had a lot of nerve being annoyed with me when he was the one who lived with his girlfriend.

'I sold the loft and my clients took me to Montrachet.'

'What'd you eat?' he asked sulkily.

'Steak.'

'Steak,' he said, as if I had put another man's dick in my mouth. 'I bet you'll pass a big load tomorrow.'

'That's disgusting,' I said. Men who talked about passing loads really weren't my type. 'Did you walk them?'

'Yes. They also passed a couple of big loads.'

'Andrew, I have an idea. Why should we stay here when I have the keys to somewhere better?' I said. 'The loft is so beautiful, I want you to see it.'

'I want to stay here,' he said.

'Come on,' I said, pulling on his arm. I told him the address on Liberty. 'We can take a cab and be there in ten minutes. I want you to see the roof deck.'

'I said no.' He stood and walked into the bedroom.

I followed him. Suddenly the apartment with its gated-off living room and sterile exercise equipment became unbearable.

'Well, I'm going there,' I said.

'No, as a matter of fact you're not,' he said. He threw me down on the bed and clamped my left ear between his teeth. I kneed him as hard as I could from that position. It didn't really hurt him but it made him jolt upright, and I managed to get out from under him. I grabbed my bag. 'Bye,' I said, and ran down eight flights of stairs instead of waiting for the elevator.

It turned out to be an unnecessary measure because he hadn't bothered to come running after me. Out on the street I felt like a complete idiot. I had been famous for scenes like this in my old dating days. When I stormed out I expected a man to catch up with me, take me in his arms despite my struggling, and kiss me, apologizing as hard as he could for whatever it was that he had done wrong. Usually, however, I just sat on a bench crying and finally went back to whomever I had run from, finding him sleeping soundly in bed or finishing his meal in the restaurant or watching the end of the movie, his arm resting contentedly over the back of my empty chair in the movie theater.

I stood in the doorway of the Cedarton not knowing if I should reconsider and go back up. I missed Andrew and the dogs. Why did I have to act like this? I wondered. Now he would never leave his girlfriend. I stood under the building's awning nervously hoping he would come looking for me. Inside the lobby, the elevator doors opened but no one came out. I remembered the ultimate failure when I was a child – leaving a sleepover in the middle of the night, parents called, sleeping bag rolled up and tied.

But maybe it was for the best that I had driven him back into the arms of his girlfriend. I deserved better. I deserved a man who didn't talk about passing big loads, who followed after me, and lived alone in his own apartment with his own condoms. A man who was single and didn't bite. And I deserved a fridge with food in it instead of clothes, and a loft like Juliet's.

I walked for over an hour until I got to Liberty Street. Practically Brooklyn. I opened Juliet's loft with my key, marked with the initials LOML for Loft of My Life on a small piece of masking tape. I had learned in real estate school never to put the address on the key.

I turned on all the lights, touching the mail chute as if for good luck. I called my answering machine to see if Andrew had called but he hadn't. I opened the door to the walk-in closet and slid open the built-in drawers. Everything was perfect. I had never seen anything like it. Juliet had used a label maker to indicate her many different styles of leggings – Ankle lengths, Bikers, Capris. Her panties were divided into Thongs, Bikinis, and something called Hipsters, and her T-shirts were listed as V's, Scoops, and Tanks. The hamper was also built-in. Andrew would have had a field day in here.

I got undressed and went into the bathroom. I looked at the shower with its glass walls. The gargoyles were illuminated with soft white light coming from between carved marble pillars, and the empty office building across the street was lit with fluorescents, flickering randomly. I loved this bathroom. I would never get bored in here.

I turned on the shower and stepped into it, bravely. It was like jumping out the window without falling. I pressed my whole body against the glass wall facing the street, the way a child smushes his face against a school bus window. My wet nose and breasts and stomach and pubic hair flattened. I felt like Spiderman. I forced myself to look down. It was desolate. Then a cab pulled up and a dog jumped out, then a man, and another dog. It was Andrew, carrying his duffel bag, his white sneakers glowing in the dark.

He looked up at the building and I stepped away from the glass wall and right out of the shower. I was sure he hadn't had time to see me. I wondered if he would remember that I was in the penthouse and figure out what buzzer to ring. I took a towel from the shelf marked 'Bathsheets' and wrapped myself in it. Twice.

Andrew rang the downstairs buzzer. The top of his cute blurry head appeared on the video security screen.

'Yes?' I answered. 'Who is it?'

'Bellevue, here to pick up an insane lunatic,' he said.

'There's no one insane here,' I said. I heard other people answering their buzzers. He must have rung all of them.

'It's Fred Freund,' he said.

'I don't know a Fred Freund.'

He picked up one of the dogs and put her face close to the camera. 'Big bad wolf,' he said. I laughed. He was the big bad wolf. I buzzed him in and waited in my towel for the elevator to open.

'Let me give you a tour,' I said.

'Just show me the bedroom,' he said.

'My tour starts here,' I said, opening the door to Juliet's walk-in closet. 'Allow me to present the hamper.' I walked all over the loft with Andrew following me.

'Guess what's going to go here,' I said, pointing to the shelves in the dining room.

'What?'

'A thousand snow domes,' I said.

'What the hell is a snow dome?' he said. 'You mean snow cone?'

'You know, a snow globe.' I made a shaking motion with my hands. 'A souveniry thing.'

'Like from the airport? Oh my God,' he said. '*One* would be too many.

The dogs lay on the couch. They loved it. They stayed there while Andrew and I climbed the spiral staircase up to the roof deck. The view was incredible. If Andrew had been blind it would have taken me all night to describe it. Andrew yanked my towel off and spread it on the wooden planks for us to lie on. I was naked. 'I'm cold,' I said. He took off his turtleneck and I put it on and curled up next to him on the towel. On our backs we looked at satellites and helicopters and the gold angel on the Municipal Building. This was the closest I ever needed to get to camping.

Then we went back downstairs and got into Juliet's bed, one dog at the foot and one dog under.

'You know I don't think I've ever felt more at home,' I said.

'That's because we're together.'

Actually I was pretty sure it was the loft. It was the first night I hadn't missed my husband's apartment.

'I can't believe I'm not going to be sleeping with you tomorrow night,' Andrew said.

'Yeah, what a shame,' I said, nonchalantly. 'My earlobes will get some rest.'

'Soon we'll be together all the time. I promise,' he said.

'Yeah, yeah,' I said.

I fell asleep, looking forward to seeing Andrew's face in the morning when he got into the shower.

Three weeks later Juliet Flagg came back from her honeymoon and we closed on her loft. The mortgage was in place, the letters of recommendation were in order – both buyers, although young, had gone to Harvard and had their parents as guarantors, and I had provided twelve perfect board packets to the co-op. I put them in shiny green folders I bought myself, because Dale didn't have any in the office.

She had ashtrays and knickknacks, a dozen vintage juice

glasses, 1950s blenders, Bakelite radios, Tony Robbins motivational tapes, and a roomful of flea-market art, but no envelopes or folders.

I also had an accepted offer of eight hundred thousand dollars on the architects' apartment with its Vulcan stove, smooth pocket doors, leather chairs in the shape of giant baseball gloves, and faux forest of trees on wheels hiding the service entrance. They liked a townhouse I had shown them on Harrison, across the street from Independence Plaza, and if that didn't work, I had a list of fourteen other houses to show them.

17
E-I-K

That night Andrew called and said he and Jordan had had a terrible fight and he was going to sleep at my place. When he got there he said, 'You know it would be really nice if you had some food in this house.'

'Why?' I asked. I was getting to like not having food in the house. I had the biggest kitchen in the world – New York. I flung open my window and leaned out over MacDougal Street. 'There's all the food you could want, right out there.'

'I'm just saying it would be nice if you could make me something.'

'Like what?'

'Like a cheese sandwich, for Christ's sake. We'd also save a lot of money.'

'Andrew, do you consider yourself cheap?' I asked.

'No, I consider myself fiscally responsible.'

I went across the street to the deli and bought a tiny jar of Hellmann's, a half-loaf package of Pepperidge Farm white bread, American cheese individually wrapped singles, and one plum tomato. It came to fourteen dollars and ninety-nine cents. I brought the bag back upstairs and spread the ingredients out on the kitchen table. I tore off a piece of paper towel to use as a plate and I made Andrew his cheese sandwich. I cut the sandwich in half and presented it to him. 'Thank you,' he said.

'So tell me about your fight,' I said. I wondered if he had told Jordan that he was leaving her. If he had told her about me. This would be the start of an all-night talk. We would plan everything now, when he would leave, what he would say to her, what he would take with him and what she would keep. He would bring one dog and leave one dog. He would leave the grandfather clock. And we'd decide where he would put his clothes. I'd clear out some shelves. We'd have to make room for his desk and his drafting table.

'What fight?' he asked.

'Your fight with Jordan,' I said.

'Oh, it was a big one. A new couple just moved in downstairs from us and when I left they were standing in the hall, shaking.'

'They could hear the fight?'

Andrew laughed. 'The whole building could hear the fight. We *screamed* at each other.'

'Really?' I asked.

He looked at me as if I were crazy. 'Haven't you ever had a fight with anyone?' For some reason that remark wounded me. Did he think I wasn't capable of a fight? I was sure I had had many fights with neighbors shaking.

'I think you should move out right away, Andrew. Move in here.'

'You don't move out over one fight, Liv.'

'I'm sorry,' I said. 'I wasn't aware that this was your first fight. I was under the impression that you were in a troubled unhappy miserable relationship. An adversarial relationship.'

When I was a child, my shrink said my parents had an adversarial relationship. 'What's that?' I asked her. 'Well, Liv,' she said, 'If your mom died how do you think your dad would feel?' 'Happy?' I asked 'That's right. And if your daddy died how do you think your mom would feel?' she asked. 'Happy?' 'That's right,' she said.

'It's not a relationship, Liv,' Andrew said. 'It's a relation*shit*.

I'm just saying you don't move out because of one fight. I'm afraid it's not that easy. You need to give me more time. You have to be patient with me, Liv. I need more time than most people. There's a way to do this and leaving after one fight isn't it.'

Andrew finished his sandwich. 'Do you want another one?' I asked. He shook his head no. 'It was great,' he said.

Since I didn't have a working fridge, I had to throw out the rest of the cheese, bread and mayo. I had used the whole tomato.

I got into bed with him. 'I wish things were different,' I said.

'What things?'

'I wish I was tall. I wish I didn't have to think about you sleeping in bed with your girlfriend.'

'I usually don't sleep in bed with her. I have a futon on the floor of my study.' Andrew hardly ever told me anything about Jordan. The only thing I knew about her was that she was a vegetarian and wouldn't even wear leather. When I tried to imagine her all I could picture was a giant frown.

'Do you think I'm short?' I asked.

'I like short women.'

'So you think of me as a short woman?'

'No, I don't think of you as a short woman. I think of you more as a tall midget.'

'Well, you're the one who can wear my jeans.'

'Touché,' he said.

'Touché?' Touché is not a romantic word. Touché is a word you don't expect to hear in bed. 'It's a good thing you don't break up with a person over one word,' I said.

18
PRE-WAR GEM — BING & BING

The next morning I sat in the office and read the *New York Times* real estate section. One of the city's biggest firms, The Corcoran Group, had taken out a full-page ad. The ad featured a photo of Barbara Corcoran herself, very pregnant and wearing a suit with a short skirt. She was smiling radiantly. To me, it was more radical than Demi Moore, naked and pregnant on the cover of *Vanity Fair.* The single most successful woman in New York real estate, attractive, rich, pregnant, proud, and well dressed. Nothing was going to stop her from being that way. Nothing was going to stop her in her short blond Cathy Rigby Peter Pan hair. She was a cross between an Olympic gymnast and a boy who wouldn't grow up, flying over the city's rooftops every night. A woman like that *had* to have hair like that. She made it seem like a woman couldn't sell real estate until she knew what it was like to *be* real estate for a perfect upcoming Gerber baby. A bird building a nest and buying and selling nests, too. It made me want to get pregnant and be a better real estate agent. She was pure energy, drive, and confidence, Florence Henderson, Helen Reddy, and Doris Day. I wondered if Barbara Corcoran had ever dated a man who lived with another woman. I wondered if Barbara Corcoran ever had to ice her earlobes after sex to reduce their swelling. She probably thought she deserved better than that.

Just then Dale walked in. It was her first day back from Italy. Once when my father came home from a trip to Italy, I had spelled out 'Welcome Home' with uncooked macaroni glued onto construction paper and hung it on the front door. I wondered if I should have made a sign for Dale.

Dale had gained weight and was wearing a leather jacket and black leather gloves even though it was warm out. I had never noticed how much her face looked like the face of a dog or a wolf. It made me feel compassion for her. She entered a room the way Lorna did, her head first and then her body.

I quickly put down the newspaper.

'*Buon giorno*,' she said. 'Did you get my postcards? What's that?' She grabbed the paper and studied the Corcoran ad. 'What kind of a sick fuck would put herself in the paper like that?' she said. 'Can you believe this woman? She looks ridiculous. Does she even realize how ridiculous she looks?'

'I think she looks good,' I said.

'Are you crazy? No one wants to see Barbara Corcoran pregnant. Who cares? She pronounced 'Corcoran' a little like 'cockring.' 'You wake up Sunday morning, you want to buy an apartment, you don't want to look at that. Right now all of New York is axing themselves, Who cares?'

Right now, I thought, all of New York was axing themselves how to convince the Corcoran Group to list their apartments. 'I admire her,' I said.

'Great. Yesterday I was riding in a gondola on the Grand Canal in total ecstasy and today I have to come here and see that first thing. It's an assault to my senses. Get this filth out of here.' She threw it back down on my desk. 'Get that pornography out of here.'

My phone rang and I picked it up. 'Suck my cock,' a man whispered into the phone.

'Hi, Andrew,' I said.

'Hi,' he whispered.

I laughed. 'Can I call you later?'

'Sure,' he whispered, and hung up.

Dale walked back over to my desk and got the newspaper. Then she sat at her desk looking at the picture of Barbara Corcoran. 'Who was that?'

'No one, just a friend,' I said.

'Well, it looks like I got back just in time, before my whole business went to hell. That's some welcome back you gave me. If you're such a Barbara Corcoran fan maybe you should just march right over there and take Lorna with you.'

I imagined Lorna walking into the Corcoran Group offices an saying, 'Something stinks.'

'Or why don't you stay here and *I'll* go to the Corcoran Group Dale screamed. 'Maybe I'd actually make some money if I worked with professionals.'

Dale sat at her desk, pouting. She opened all her drawers and shut them. Then she started furiously writing something in a notebook. She tore out the page, ripped it up, and threw the pieces in her wastepaper basket.

She picked up the phone and called Harri. 'Harri, it's me, pick up the phone,' she said. 'Hi, honey,' she said brightly. 'No. No, I'm not. The office is filthy. I guess when the maid goes away for a few weeks, the princesses let the whole office fall apart. Yes, I guess certain people think they're very high and mighty with their exclusives and their mysterious phone calls. Yes, someone has gotten a big head.'

'Someone has gotten an even bigger stomach,' I mumbled.

'What did you say? Hold on, Harri. What did you say?'

I looked up. 'What? Nothing.'

'Harri, I'll call you back,' she said and hung up. 'This was hardly the welcome I had in mind.' She stormed out, her leather gloves in her teeth as she struggled into her too-tight jacket.

Dale was right about the office, it was a mess. Lorna and I hadn't cleaned it at all. There were empty soda cans and coffee cups everywhere and ashtrays filled with the tiny remains of Lorna's burnt white joints, smaller than Barbie-doll shoes. We had thrown while-you-were-out slips on Dale's desk, not even making them into a welcoming pile.

I got a garbage bag from the storage closet and walked over to Dale's desk. I bent down and picked up her wastepaper basket. Then I picked out all the torn pieces of paper and sat at her desk arranging them. I matched her long, slanted lettering until I had everything lined up. I taped it together.

New Rules
1. There is going to be a mandatory weekly meeting for all sales associates Mondays at 9:00 A.M. All those late and/or absent will be finde $100. No exeptions ifs ands or butts.
2. A new dress code is in affect. NO JEANS!!!
3. I, Dale Kilpatrick, am going off sugar and I would appreciate no sugar products to be brought into this office as a matter of curtesy.
4. Dale and Liv. Liv and Dale. Dale loves Liv. Liv loves Dale. D.K. and L.K. Liv Liv Liv Liv Liv.

I wondered if Jerome had written things like that about me on his Braille writing machine. I emptied her basket into a garbage bag and a balled-up while-you-were-out slip rolled onto. the floor. I uncrumpled it. It was a message Dale had taken for me before she left for Italy but never given to me. It was from Jerome.

I't was good of you to come,' Jerome said.
  'Yes,' I said.

'I hope it wasn't too much of an inconvenience to come here to the office. I would have been happy to take you out to lunch.'

Jerome was always hinting that he wanted to take me to some restaurant in the Village I had never heard of called Ye Waverly Inn. It sounded ridiculous. He probably had a discount coupon.

'Actually it wasn't inconvenient at all. I just sold a new exclusive of mine not far from here on Liberty Street.'

'Liberty Street. That sounds like an ideal place to reside. Do you have any apartments available on Easy Street?'

He was no longer paying me to laugh at his jokes so I just sat there. 'I brought you something,' I said.

I handed him a souvenir replica of the Empire State Building. Jerome had never seen it. I put it in his hands. 'It's the Empire State Building. It looks like this, only bigger,' I said.

The man could only see what was placed in his hands.

'You make me jealous when you say it like that,' he said, feeling the miniature building. He put its point to his temple. 'Sharp.'

'What are you talking about?' I asked. I got the nervous feeling I got every time Jerome tried to get inappropriate.

'You act like you like this building more than you like any person,' he said.

'I do.'

'You're so arrogant.'

I liked when Jerome told me about myself. I liked when anyone did, but I especially liked hearing these things from a blind man. It seemed more meaningful. I felt proud to be arrogant. I decided to emphasize this feature from now on. What else am I, besides arrogant? I wanted to ask.

'I am not arrogant,' I said.

'Yes, you most certainly are. You're arrogant but you're also kind.' He held the building over his head like a trophy, victoriously. 'I'd like to go to the top with you someday,' Jerome said.

'I can see into my ex-husband's bedroom if I put fifty cents in the telescope machine.'

'You mean the bedroom you and he used to share?' Jerome asked.

'Yes.'

'I bet loads of tourists used to watch you, didn't they?' he asked.

'Only when I stood in the window naked,' I said.

'Does it turn you on to think of someone watching you?'

'What do you think?' I said, as arrogantly as possible.

'I think it does,' he said. I was arrogant and kind and I got turned on being watched.

'If I like being watched and you're blind I guess we wouldn't make a very good couple.'

'Oh, I don't know about that. You might find it vewy fweeing.' He was making his r's into w's because he was flustered. 'Sometimes people who like being watched also like not being seen.'

I wanted to be seen. I had experienced invisibility. Jerome was wrong. 'You're right,' I said out of kindness. If anyone could make blindness sexy it wasn't Jerome.

'Anyway, I guess you're wondering why I asked you here,' he said.

'Okay.'

'Remember when I told you I was working on something but it was a secret? Well, here it is.'

He patted a cardboard box on his desk in front of him. It had the Sir Speedy Copy Shop logo printed on it.

'I have completed a novel,' he said, sighing. 'I don't have my hopes up about it, of course.'

I remembered being told not to get my hopes up as a child. I would bear down inside myself, pushing like a woman in labor, trying to keep my hopes down in the pit of my stomach, where I thought they were.

'I was wondering if you would consider reading it. I know it's a big favor to ask, isn't it?'

I wondered if he had written anything about me.

'I'd be happy to read it,' I said.

'Remember to be totally honest.'

I pulled the box toward me and put it on my lap. I opened the lid.

The Weight of Truth by Jerome Garrett. I turned to the first page. It just said *To*.

'What does this mean?' I asked.

'What?' Jerome said, leaning forward.

'The word *To*.'

'Oh, I haven't decided to whom I shall dedicate it yet.'

'It's always pathetic when the person dedicates it to his mother and father,' I said, thinking he should dedicate it to me for reading it. 'What about your girlfriend?'

'She hasn't been the most supportive person when it comes to my writing.' I'm sure, I thought. 'And we're not married, you know.'

I had overheard a woman in a restaurant once say that the worst thing about not being married was having no one to go to your parents' funerals with. But having no one to dedicate a book to was up there.

'Maybe you should just pick some random initials. To L.R. To D.P.W. To C.S.H.'

'To M.S. – My Self,' Jerome said.

'To M.E. – Me,' I added.

'To M.M. and I. – Me, Myself, and I.'

'To Y.T. – Yours Truly.'

'To N.O. – Number One.'

I flipped to the last page. 'Four hundred and seventy-six pages!' I said.

'It's very kind of you,' Jerome said. 'And thank you for the gift.' The crude little Empire State building was prone on his desk.

'I'll let you know when I've finished it,' I said, tucking the manuscript back into the box.

Later, in Abingdon Square, I saw an old man walking a black cat on a leash. He walked out of the lobby of one of the two big Bing and Bing buildings that stood catty-corner to each other on the edge of the small park. He walked the cat over to the baby swings, removed its pink leash, and placed the cat in the center swing. I watched as he pushed the cat in the swing for ten minutes, standing beside parents pushing children. Child child cat child child. I thought of Jerome never getting to see a sight like that. What was the point of living in New York, sightless?

There was so much fog, the Empire State Building loomed, eerily half-invisible, like the Headless Horseman.

When I got home I took out my disposable daily contact lenses and added them to the pile I kept on the corner of the sink like seashells. They were dried and curled in on themselves. I didn't know why I was performing this experiment. It felt important, like keeping baby teeth. I just couldn't bring myself to throw them out, the way I kept old negatives in a drawer somewhere. I felt like I could develop the contact lenses later and see everything again. Feel things I hadn't been ready to feel the first time I saw them.

My phone rang and I answered it before I realized it could be Dale.

'Hey, it's me, Dale. How aaaaare you?'

'Fine,' I said.

'Listen, I'm sorry about the way I acted today. I have my period and I'm all crazed. You know how it is, we're both women here.'

'Of course,' I said.

'I know I shouldn't say this, Liv, but I have certain feelings for you. Certain feelings of love and lust. Now I've said it and we can forget it even happened.' She sounded all hyped up like a salesman whose vacuum cleaner had exploded during the presentation. 'All right, kiddo, I'll see you at the office tomorrow.' She hung up before I had a chance to say anything.

Then the phone rang again.

'Hello?'

'Hi, how aaaaare you, it's me again, Dale. I'm calling to axe you not to tell anyone about this if you don't mind.'

'Of course I won't!' I said, a little too quickly. It wasn't like this was something to brag about. I wasn't exactly going to hire a pilot to write 'Dale Loves Liv' across the sky.

'Sorry to inconvenience you.' She hung up.

In the morning I got to work early but Dale was already there. She had a cold sore on her lip. She was interviewing someone who was going to be our new receptionist. A grotesque drag queen sat submissively in the wooden school chair with the attached desk. She had long brown nails with rings on every finger but her ring finger.

'This is Janet,' Dale said, brightly. 'Janet, this is the kid.'

'The kid?' Janet asked.

'I'm twenty-six,' I said.

Janet laughed. 'Well, she's a kid to us,' Dale said.

'Not to me. I'm twenty-one,' Janet said, clenching his legs together. 'I really want to reenter the workforce as a woman.'

'Well, that's certainly understandable,' Dale said. 'Thank you for coming in, I'll let you know by next week.'

Janet struggled to get his long legs out of the desk chair. He looked miserable. You could see his Adam's apple right through his turtleneck.

I heard him say the words 'Oh God' as he clumped down the stairs in his high heels.

'I cannot believe myself,' Dale said. 'I saw an ad in the *Voice* – Pre-op Transsexual Gal Friday – and I called. Harri would kill me if I hired her. I'm gonna do it. I'm gonna do it.'

'What is her job going to be?' I asked.

'She'll answer the phone and if anyone comes in she'll axe them if they want coffee. We're going to have coffee here now. In fact a lot of things are going to be different around here from now on. What, you don't think it's a good idea?'

'No, I think it's a good idea,' I said.

'What are you, crazy? I'm not hiring a drag queen. Do you think I'm completely out of my mind?'

I made myself look busy at my desk.

'Where's Lorna?' Dale said. 'Why isn't Lorna here yet?'

My phone rang and I picked it up quickly. It was Violet. 'Let's have breakfast, I'm depressed,' she said.

'Who's that?' Dale said.

''Which apartment were you calling about? I asked her.

'Huh?' she said. 'It's me, Violet.'

'Yes, I can show that to you today,' I said. 'I can meet you there now, if you like.'

'Where, at the Waverly?'

'Yes, it has a working fireplace. What line of work are you in?'

'Are you being kidnapped?' Violet asked.

'Oh, so you're more than qualified.' I felt Dale staring at the back of my head. 'Twenty minutes?'

'I'll meet you there,' Violet said.

'Okay,' I said and hung up. 'I'll be back in an hour,' I told Dale. 'I'll go with you,' she said and followed me out the door.

When we got out on the street I said, 'I better go back upstairs and make sure I have the right keys.' I figured I could quickly call Violet and tell her I couldn't meet her and then tell Dale the client had just called and canceled.

'Okay,' Dale said.

Dale started to follow me back inside.

'You can wait here, I'll get them,' I said.

'I don't mind going up.'

'You don't have to,' I said. But she came upstairs with me and I rummaged around in my key drawer. I grabbed keys to a loft on Elizabeth Street. I hoped the owner wasn't there.

We left the office again. 'Dale, it's silly for you to come with me,' I said.

'I want to see the kid in action.'

'I just think it makes me look bad if you come with me on my showings. I think it looks bad to my clients.'

'They're *my* clients,' Dale corrected. 'They're not your clients.

We walked silently to Elizabeth between Houston and Bleecker. We stood in front of the building facing a lot where construction was going on. The owner had wanted me to tell the clients, Dale's clients, that a very tall building wasn't going up. I was supposed to say that a community garden was going there, but when they dug the foundation and started pouring cement that became impossible.

'What time are they supposed to be here?' Dale asked.

'Eleven,' I said. We both looked at our watches. It was eleven. Dale pointed down at the sidewalk.

'You know what those are?' she asked. There were little glass bullet-shaped objects everywhere. 'They're crack vials. You should get rid of those before the client gets here.'

'This woman will never know what they are,' I said.

Dale rocked back and forth on her heels clutching her leather legal pad holder and clicking her pen.

'I don't want my clients to see a place with crack vials on the street. A true professional would do whatever it takes to make the deal. I think you should sweep them up.' She ran her tongue over the cold sore.

'I don't exactly have a broom,' I said.

'Why don't you run upstairs and get one?'

'I don't think I should use the owner's personal broom on the street,' I said.

'Do you expect someone to pay four thousand dollars a month to live in a crack den?' Dale bellowed.

I bent down and picked up the crack vials one by one and shoved them in my pocketbook.

Dale looked at her watch. 'These people are such time-wasters. They never think our time is valuable. They don't mind keeping us waiting all day.'

'She usually isn't late.' As soon as I said it I knew I had made a mistake. I had asked the 'client' on the phone what line of work she was in. Now I had made it sound like I had shown her apartments before. 'Well, at least her husband isn't ever late. I've worked with her husband but never with her.'

I wondered how long Violet would wait for me at the Waverly. She was probably mad.

'Well, I guess we can give her another five minutes,' Dale said. 'About last night.'

'Dale, don't worry about it.'

'It was wrong of me. I shouldn't have told you that I wanted to sleep with you. It was unprofessional.'

I noticed a vial I had missed a few feet away. I went to get it.

'You know what my fantasy is?' Dale said.

To have sex with me, I thought.

'You see those buildings?' She pointed to a row of three dilapidated four-story tenement buildings, each with its own 'For sale' sign. 'I'd love to buy one of those and make it into an artists' residence. Where artists could create.'

'You want to build an artists' colony?' I asked.

'That's right. Harri and I could live on the top two floors and have the office on the first floor.'

That only left one floor for the artists.

We stood there until eleven thirty. She looked at her big man's watch one more time.

I didn't know why I was going through with this. I didn't care if I got fired. It was like a contest of wills standing there side by side with Dale on a terrible block waiting for an imaginary client. Like a poor man's feminist production of 'Waiting for Godot.' Like my marriage. I wasn't going to give in first.

'We've been here a half hour. You sure you're meeting her here?'

'Of course,' I said.

'And what's her story again?'

'Her husband's a Wall Street guy and he wants a place downtown,' I said. 'They're relocating.'

'And what does she do?'

'Ballerina,' I said.

'I don't think she's showing up,' Dale said.

'Maybe I should wait a few more minutes.'

'Come with me,' Dale said. 'I want to show you something.'

'Where?' I said. She had taken me to a Norma Kamali sample sale before she went to Italy and watched me try on bathing suits in the open dressing area. I wasn't going to do that again.

'Just right around the corner,' she said. We walked around the corner. Dozens of claw-foot tubs and antique sinks were for sale on the sidewalk. 'Isn't that beautiful?' Dale asked. 'All those old remnants.'

It was beautiful. Oh no, I thought, Dale and I are thinking alike.

'It's like a porcelain garden,' she said.

We stood there looking at it.

'Why do you think your client didn't show up?'

'I don't know,' I said. 'I'm really annoyed. I'm sorry you had to waste your time.'

'Maybe there was no client,' Dale said.

'What do you mean?'

'Maybe you were talking to one of your boyfriends and you were making plans to meet him for a little afternoon delight.'

'What? Dale, you're crazy. Of course there was a client.'

'What was her last name again?'

'Nemchineva.' It was the name of my ballet teacher who taught classes in the Ansonia when I was five.

'I don't know why I just don't trust you anymore.'

'Dale, this is because of the way you feel about me.'

'How dare you accuse me of that,' Dale screamed. 'Give me your keys to the office. You're fired. The kid is fired,' Dale announced.

'Dale, I think you're going to regret this.'

'Gimme,' she said.

I reached into my bag, past the gun, and searched through the crack vials for the keys to the office and gave them to her. She walked off jangling them, taking long strides like Art Carney in Jackie Gleason's body.

When I got home I stood in my vestibule on MacDougal Street and read Dale's postcard from Venice. The picture was of those two famous angels by Raphael, a blonde and a brunette, one with crossed arms and one with her chin in her hand. Dale had written 'Lorna' over the blond angel's head and 'Liv' over the brunette's head.

I didn't read the postcard. I didn't read any of Dale's postcards that came, one a day, for the next three weeks. And I didn't return her phone calls. She left messages saying how sorry she was for firing me, that she had meant to fire Lorna, not me, that she had her period, jet lag, low blood sugar, severe depression. The last message said it all. 'Hi, Liv, it's me, Dale. How aaaaare you?' There was a brief silence and then she just hung up.

Part II

Clown. Sayest thou that house is dark?

Malvolio. As hell, Sir Topas.

Clown. Why, it hath bay windows
    transparent as barricadoes,
        and the clerestories toward the south
    north are as lustrous
        as ebony; and yet complainest thou of
    obstruction?

Malvolio. I am not mad, Sir Topas. I say to
    you this house is dark.

WILLIAM SHAKESPEARE,
Twelfth Night, IV, 2

19
BREATHTAKNG VUS OF PRK

On my way to my first day at the Smoothe Transitions real
estate company I saw a black man on the street selling
incense and a few books. On the table was a picture of an Indian
man in a cardboard frame. He looked like a real swami. The
swami was naked from the waist up and sat cross-legged with an
orange cloth wrapped around his bottom half.

'How much?' I asked.

'You like that?' the man asked, smiling.

'Yeah,' I said. 'How much is it?'

'You can have that one,' he said. He handed it to me.

When I got to my new office on Fifth Avenue and Eighteenth
Street, I waited at the front desk while the receptionist, who
wasn't a drag queen, answered and redirected calls. There were
framed black-and-white photographs of old New York on the
walls. One was of the downtown skyline before the World Trade
Center was built. It was like looking in the mirror as a child and
finding two teeth missing.

Finally my new boss, a woman who was shorter than me and
looked like she was about twelve, came out from behind a closed
door and walked me across the office. It was a huge rectangular
loft with desks and people everywhere. Along one wall was a

row of windows facing a gray air shaft. The place was painted a disturbing shade of aqua. It looked dingier than I remembered it looking at my interview. My boss showed me to my desk.

'Here it is,' she said proudly. It was a shelf with a file cabinet under it that I was supposed to share with another woman. There was no clear dividing line on the shelf indicating where her portion stopped and mine started. It was like sitting on the subway next to a stranger, with her shopping bags and rolls of fat spilling onto your tiny seat. On the subway I could choose to stand. It would be hard to stand up every day at work.

There was one computer in the middle for us to share and the cord from the computer stretched across my half. We were back to back with another shelf. The woman who was going to be my shelfmate picked up her phone and started talking into it the minute she saw our boss even though it didn't ring and she hadn't dialed any numbers.

'You'll probably want to spend the morning getting settled in,' my boss said. I suddenly couldn't remember her name. My chair was the only one in the whole office without arms. 'You don't look that happy,' she said. That was the problem with having a boss who could see.

I had thought about trying to get a job with Corcoran but I admired Barbara Corcoran so much I knew it would ruin it if I worked for her. Smoothe Transitions wasn't as big a firm as Corcoran but it was still really good, and of course it was a million times better than Dale's. Samantha Smoothe, the president, kept to herself in the uptown office. The closest I might ever come to meeting her was passing by the life-size cardboard cutout of her that leaned against the wall a few feet from my desk.

I had only had one other interview. It was with a handsome gray-haired man named Steve Levin at a small but elegant firm in SoHo. 'You remind me of my daughter,' he said, just as I was about to leave his office. I had felt flattered. I liked reminding rich, successful real estate moguls of their daughters. 'That's Jennifer,' he said, pointing to a picture in a silver frame of a girl wearing a sweater.

'She's pretty,' I said. She really looked familiar. Jennifer. Jennifer Levin.

As soon as I closed his office door behind me I realized where I knew her from. Jennifer Levin. The Preppy Murder victim. The girl Robert Chambers strangled in Central Park with her own bra. Jennifer Levin had been around my age. It could have been me that night. Although I would never have sex in the park at night because I was too afraid of rats. But when you have sex with a guy, even if he's a jerk, you don't expect to end up dead on the cover of the *Daily News* the next day.

I stood frozen in front of the receptionist, thinking of something Andrew had said to me just the week before. 'For Halloween I can be Robert Chambers and you'll be Jennifer Levin.' 'That's not funny,' I said. That morning I had had rough sex with Andrew and a moment ago I had been sitting face-to-face with Jennifer Levin's father. From now on, in her memory, I would be more careful.

'Are you okay?' the receptionist asked me.

'That's Jennifer Levin's father,' I said dumbly.

She showed me a petition to keep Robert Chambers from getting early parole, and while I signed it I wondered, if I were dead, if my father's receptionist would ask people to sign a petition for me. I didn't think she would. My cousin died right after he was born and my father always secretly criticized my aunt Emma for not moving on with her life. My eyes filled with tears.

I wanted to go back in and tell him not to worry. I wouldn't let what happened to Jennifer happen to me. I would break up with Andrew. I wanted to show Mr. Levin my gun, to let him know I could take care of myself, but I didn't have the guts to go back. That's why I had chosen to work at Smoothe Transitions.

'So, what can we do to make you happy?' my new boss said. She had an actual crest of some sort on her navy blazer. Who dressed like that?

I remembered in real estate school the teacher said all we needed was a phone and a pair of comfortable shoes.

'All I need is a phone and a pair of comfortable shoes,' I said.

She looked down at my black high-heeled boots. They were Via Spigas that my father had sent me. It took weeks before I could get used to walking one block in them.

'Well, make a lot of money for us and you can have any desk you want,' she said. 'Except mine, of course.' She laughed and I laughed, too, trying to regain my wits. 'If you need anything just holler. I have an open-door policy.'

She left, and the woman I shared the shelf with hung up her phone without saying goodbye to the person she was pretending to talk to. Her things were taking up most of my half, including her big coat. I really hated her.

I put my picture of the swami on my part of the desk next to the woman's coat, and she looked at it. It didn't go with the rest of the office. The swami stared out with piercing eyes.

'Who's that?' she asked.

'A great swami,' I said. She looked over her shoulder as if she wanted to see if anyone had heard me say that. She looked almost scared.

'Are you going to keep that there?' she asked.

I noticed a picture of a gray-and-white Shih Tzu wearing a barrette pinned to the bulletin board in her corner.

'Yes I am. I consider him one of the secrets to my success.'

I introduced myself confidently. She had a Post-it on her telephone with the words 'My Number' written on it and her seven-digit phone number. I figured if she couldn't even remember her own phone number she wouldn't pose much of a threat.

'I'm Carla Lerner,' she said. 'I've been here for almost six months. I think you'll like it, it's a great company. Kim's great.' She had a long face and plain brown hair. She looked jowly.

'Who's Kim?' I asked.

'Who's Kim?' she mimicked. 'Kim's our boss. The woman who just brought you over to your desk.' She looked at me as if I would be no threat to her if I couldn't remember the name of my boss.

'Oh *Kim*, I thought you said Tim,' I said. 'Oh, yeah, Kim's great.'

Around us people screamed into phones. I recognized Marti Landesman, one of the most infamous brokers in New York. I suddenly realized I had no idea what I was doing. I didn't really know how to use the computer. I didn't know anything. Working here was going to be completely different from Dale's perverted little office. At least here no one was chain-smoking marijuana and I could use my phone as much as I wanted.

I called Violet and gave her my new work number. She was just lounging around at home deciding what to order from the Westway diner for lunch. We had a whole conversation in which she asked me long complicated questions about how I was feeling and I gave one-word responses like 'bad,' 'hell,' and 'miserable,' so Carla Lerner wouldn't know what I was saying. Then Violet had to get off the phone.

'Are you sure you're okay?' she asked again.

'No.'

'Do you have money for lunch?'

I sighed. I would never start a new job without money for lunch. I would never leave my house without money for lunch.

'I'm taking you into the bathroom with me,' she said. I could hear her peeing. 'Liv, this is frustrating. It's hard to have a conversation like this. You're not telling me anything. What's it like there?'

'Suffocating,' I said.

'Call me later.'

I hung up reluctantly, letting go of my last link to the outside world.

'I guess you're not too happy here,' Carla said, as if I were the only homesick girl at camp.

I sat in my armless chair staring at the swami. I took off my boots and crossed my legs under me, sitting like the swami on my desk chair. I smoothed my skirt over my knees and touched my thumb to my forefinger on each hand. I had to relax. It was really freaking Carla out.

I looked into the swami's eyes. I had never considered myself a spiritual person but maybe I was one. I called on the great real estate forces to help me. Steve Levin, Donald Trump, Barbara Corcoran, St. Francis (the real estate saint). Carla Lerner's phone rang and she answered it. 'I'll call you back,' she whispered and hung up. I could feel her staring at me. I closed my eyes and the noise of the office softened. My fingers started to tingle. The muscles in my neck relaxed. Then my head snapped back sort of involuntarily. I wondered what was happening to me. I had never been in a trance before. I sat that way for quite a while and then suddenly I was filled with the feeling of knowing what I was supposed to do.

'Carla,' I said, softly.

'What,' she said.

'Do you think you could find another place to put your coat?'

Her face managed to go from long to longer. 'Why? Is it bothering you or something?' she said.

'Yes it is,' I said. 'It's taking up half of my desk.'

She moved it over in her direction a quarter of an inch. 'How's that?' she asked.

'Not quite good enough. I want you to get it off my desk.'

She grabbed her coat and stormed over to the coatrack. When she came back I pointed to her tape dispenser, her mini-fan, and her Snackwell's cookies. 'Your stuff is still on my desk.'

She moved her things over, walked back to the coatrack, put on her coat, and left. I picked up the wastepaper basket from next to her chair and put it on my side of the file cabinet, next to me. I figured that was enough work for one day.

'Five hundred thousand dollars! Five hundred thousand dollars! That's an insult,' a man was yelling into a phone on the other side of the office. 'Tell your client he's insulting the owner. Is he aware that he is going to insult the owner?' He had one of the more deluxe freestanding desks reserved for the successful 'power brokers.' His voice sounded furious but his face looked happy. He looked happy to be there, yelling at someone on the phone. I was jealous. I couldn't wait until I could start screaming at people like that.

I opened my organizer and turned to my 'clients' section.

These were the clients I had stolen from Dale's. I dialed Noah Bausch's number and left a message that I was no longer with the Dale Kilpatrick Real Estate Gallery because Dale Kilpatrick was insane, and now I was with Smoothe Transitions from where, I was sure, I could better serve them. Two pigeons landed on the ledge outside the air shaft window near my desk. Worse than Carla Lerner, worse than almost anything, now there were pigeons.

20
XXX MINT PIED-À-TERRE

There are a few things I always do with a man to endear myself to him, things I've done with all my boyfriends, such as jumping up and down a little at the thought of going to the zoo. Before I left my apartment with Andrew, I spent a long time fumbling with the zipper of the red rain jacket my husband had given me. It had been his, but I got him to give it to me by telling him that it looked like a woman's jacket and that he looked like a woman in it. I stood there fumbling with the zipper like a little girl even though I could easily have zipped it quickly.

Andrew turned around a few times to look at me trying to zip the thing. 'Are you having a problem there?' he asked. He had a big smile on his face. I wouldn't think that my zipper trick would work on someone like Andrew, but of course it did. He came toward me as if he intended to help me with my jacket.

'I can do it myself,' I said. 'See!' I zipped it all the way to the top.

He came over to me and kissed me. 'I just love you,' he said. It was the first time he had said it to me. But he didn't say, 'I love you.' He said, 'I just love you.' Just-love wasn't the same as love. It sounded so offhanded and fleeting.

'I know you love me, too,' he said.

'What are you going to do about your girlfriend?' I asked him.

'I'm going to leave her.'

'When?'

'Liv, I need time. Why do you have to push like that? You just got me to tell you that I love you and that I would leave her. We just said I love you to each other. Why can't we just enjoy that?' He unzipped me. 'Come on, let me see you try to zip this thing again. It was kind of turning me on.'

'I thought we were getting pizza,' I said. 'We so rarely dine out.'

He followed me down the stairs and out onto the street. We walked down the street in silence. 'When we're married, you're going to be so proud walking down the street with me,' he said. 'When we're married, you'll be proud every time you walk down the street just knowing you've got my ring on your finger and my money in your pocket.'

I laughed. 'When we're married, every time you walk down the street, it will be like a small parade with all the private detectives I'll have following you.'

'I want to take you to a restaurant.' He criticized every restaurant we passed for blocks. Finally we ended up in SoHo at Fanelli's.

'Is this dark enough for you?' I asked.

We sat in the back at a table covered with a plastic red-and-white-checked tablecloth. He reached over and took my hand.

The waitress came over with water, silverware, and napkins. 'Andrew?' she said.

'Hi,' he said. 'How are you?'

'Fine, except for working here. How are you? I just saw Jordan on the street the other day and she said you guys were good.'

He was still holding my hand on top of the table.

'Uh,' Andrew said.

'Oh, I'm sorry,' the waitress said, noticing our hands.

'Who is Jordan?' I asked in a loud, shocked voice. I stood up. Andrew laughed nervously. 'Oh, my God, you have a girlfriend?' I said. 'You bastard. How could you do this to me!'

'I'm really sorry,' the waitress said. 'Oh, my God.'

I stormed over to the bathroom. 'She's just kidding around,' I heard Andrew say behind me. In the ladies' room, I laughed out loud.

When I returned to the table, Andrew ordered a veggie burger without onions. The waitress looked miserable taking our orders, especially when he said, 'No onions.' I ordered soup. The waitress brought us wine on the house. 'Are you still acting?' he asked her. She got very animated practically reciting her whole résumé for the past few years the way all actors do. When she finally left us alone, Andrew said, 'Liv, tell me what our kids will be like?'

'We won't be having any kids,' I said.

'Yes, we will. You've probably already planned what they'll be like.'

I had worried that they might be hideously ugly with munchkin cheeks.

'Well, they'd be short,' I said.

'And what else?'

'They'd probably be crying all the time and saying things like, 'Mommy, why does Daddy live with that mean woman uptown instead of at home with us?' and, 'Mommy, why do we have to hang up when we call Daddy and that mean woman answers the phone?' and things like that.'

'Liv, I'm trying to have a serious conversation with you.'

'They'd say, 'Mommy, why does Daddy only take us to the most dimly lit McDonald's and why do we have to wear these strange disguises and why do you hire all those men to follow Daddy and take those pictures of him?''

'I just adore you,' Andrew said.

As soon as we finished our meal, Andrew wanted to leave. The waitress put our check down between us on the table. He didn't make a move for it. 'I'll get this,' he said, finally.

'That's a good idea,' I said.

'Oh, so you just expect me to pick up the check?'

'Andrew, I'm the *mistress*,' I said, in a really loud voice, so the waitress could hear. 'I'm the mistress for Christ's sake, the *other* woman. The other woman doesn't pay for anything. You don't even buy me presents. Where are my presents? Where are my chocolates? Where are my flowers? You never even buy condoms.'

'Okay, okay,' he said, smiling. He stood up. 'Walk me to the train.'

We kissed by the Spring Street stop and said goodbye and then I walked around SoHo by myself for a little while. I realized my heart had been pounding the whole time I was with him. When I got home my face was still flushed. My phone rang. It was Andrew.

'Liv,' he said. 'Did my breath taste funny when we kissed?'

'What!' I asked. It had tasted awful and garlicky from the veggie burger.

'When I got home Jordan said my breath was funny and all I could think was, Oh no, I kissed Liv and I tasted terrible.'

'You tasted fine,' I said. He sounded tortured, miserable.

'I've just been sitting here, running the whole thing over and over in my mind.'

I told him his stupid breath was fine, and we got off the phone. Then I realized he must have gotten pretty close to his girlfriend, if she could tell him he had bad breath.

The first thing I thought of when I woke up the next morning was that I was in love with Andrew and I believed him. He was going to leave Jordan, which would be better for both of them. He wasn't doing her any favors by staying with her if he was in love with me. I decided it would be for the best if he left Jordan by Friday.

I called his number, but Jordan answered so I hung up. She had a nice voice. It sounded young and sweet. I had expected her voice to be so frigid it would freeze the phone line. Icicles would form on the receiver. But she just sounded normal. A few minutes later he called back. 'Did you just call here?' he asked.

'Yes,' I said bravely.

'Tell me you love me,' he said.

'I love you,' I said.

'Oh, my God, that's great,' he said. 'That's so great. I love you, too.' We had moved past just-love.

'How's your girlfriend?'

'You tell me – how *are* you?' he said.

'I'm talking about Jordan. Where is she?' I asked.

'She's walking the dogs.'

'I've been thinking about something, Andrew. I think you should leave and move in here by Friday. Just get out of there quickly, and then we'll figure out what to do from there.'

'By Friday,' he said.

'Yes, Friday,' I said.

'That sounds like a good idea,' he said. 'I'll think about that.' It all seemed so simple now.

'You know what I wish, Liv?'

'What?'

'I wish I could carry your cunt around in my pocket like a change purse, and always have it with me. A beautiful, soft velvet change purse.'

'You sound like Jeffery Dahmer,' I said.

He laughed. 'I've got to go, I'll call you from the office.'

I got to work just in time to hear Carla Lerner describing a loft. She was holding a photograph of the living room and gushing about the location. 'And it's got those, you know, poles,' she said. 'It's got twelve white poles . . .'

'Columns,' I whispered. 'Not poles. Cast-iron columns.' The apartment Dale had shown me in her building had a pole; this loft had columns.

'Twelve cast-iron *columns*,' she said, exaggerating the word as if it were something exotic, as if she had just learned Greek.

'Thanks,' she mumbled, when she got off the phone. We didn't say a word to each other for the rest of the morning. I spent about an hour recording my voice-mail greeting. 'This is Liv Kellerman at Smoothe Transitions,' I said over and over. I liked the sound of it.

I couldn't wait for my first message from Andrew on my new voice mail. Jordan was visiting her parents in Connecticut and he was coming to my place for the whole night.

21
BACHELOR PAD — CONV MDTWN LOC

Right before we had sex, Andrew got up and pulled something out of his bag. I wondered if he was going to try to tie me up. He brought it over to the bed. It was one of those things doctors use to test your blood pressure.

'What do you have that for?' I asked.

'I want to see if my blood pressure gets too high when we fuck,' he said.

'I'm flattered,' I said.

'I tried to do it this morning when I was jerking off but I couldn't do it by myself.'

'Why didn't you ask Jordan to help you?' I asked.

'She wasn't home. We have very different schedules.'

'Why don't you jerk off at your doctor's office and have him test it?' I asked.

'I already thought of that but jerking off isn't as strenuous as fucking you. I thought about trying to fuck my doctor right there in the office so she could test me properly but I want to try this method first.'

He went back to his bag and pulled out a silver stethoscope. 'I just love this thing.' He put it around his neck.

'How much did this stuff cost you?' I asked.

'A lot,' he said, but you can't put a price on health.' I couldn't imagine Andrew buying anything, let alone something expensive.

He put the wide black pad around my upper arm and fastened it with the Velcro strips. It was too tight, but I didn't say anything. Then he unfastened it and made it tighter around my arm.

'It's much too tight, Andrew,' I said. He pumped the thing up in his hand, ignoring me. He held my wrist and looked at his watch.

'Not bad,' he said.

'What happens if your blood pressure gets too high when we're having sex? Are you going to stop having sex with me?' I asked, smiling.

'No, honey, we'll just have to modify.'

He put the black rubber tips of the stethoscope in his ears and put the cold metal mouth on my chest. He tucked it under my left breast. He smiled. 'I can hear your heart,' he said, like a little boy. The blood pressure meter was still wrapped too tight. 'I can hear that you're in love with me.'

'I need a second opinion,' I said.

He moved the metal disk around my chest. 'Breathe in,' he said, 'breathe out.'

'You're giving me a headache,' I said. I moved it to my nipple.

'This isn't a toy,' he said. He ripped the pad off my arm and placed it around his own. Then he fucked me, stopping every few minutes to check the meter. He made me hold the pump and give it a few blasts from time to time.

He wore the stethoscope in his ears the whole time and as soon as he came he listened to his own heartbeat.

In the morning, Andrew climbed tentatively into the shower. He was getting the hang of how to manage the faucets with the large pliers. After he got the water running I went into the living room determined not to look in the bag he always carried around, the royal blue gym bag. I looked at the way it sat on the floor by the door, wrinkled in certain spots, smooth in others, some compartments zipped all the way, some only part of the way. I studied the bag as if I were preparing to describe it to a police sketch artist.

I got very close to it and squatted. The metal tab at the end of the zipper of the main compartment was sticking straight up. I gingerly unzipped Andrew's bag and pulled out the plain brown notebook, noting exactly how it was positioned.

I opened the book and looked down at Andrew's neat architect's block writing. *Got up, made myself a baked potato, gym, had sex with Liv K for the 3rd time,* it said. I wondered how many Livs he knew that he had to use my last initial. I was on the same list as a potato.

I heard Andrew sigh in the shower. I turned to the next page. I *was brilliant in the S.B. meeting. I am a fucking great . . .* The water stopped and Andrew pushed open the metal shower door. I closed the book, put it in the bag, panicked momentarily trying to remember which direction it had been facing, then turned it around, adjusted a ball of sweat socks, zipped the zipper, and turned the metal tab on the end of it so it was sticking straight up. I stood and moved away from the bag.

Andrew came into the living room wrapped in a yellow towel. His eye went to the bag. I was still nervous about the placement of the notebook.

'I killed something in your shower,' he said.

'Thank you.'

'What did you do while I was in there?' he asked.

I hadn't thought about that. I should have had the TV on. 'Looked out the window,' I said. The window was closed. Ominous heavy ropes swayed and banged against the fire escape.

'How is it out?'

'Nice.'

'I could go out and get us some bagels.'

If he went out I could lock the door and read more of his journal. 'That's a great idea,' I said.

Again his eye went to his bag. 'Or we could go together,' he said.

He went back into the kitchen and put on my deodorant and pulled on his underwear, jeans, and turtleneck.

'I'd rather stay here,' I said. I turned on the TV and sat on my bed.

Andrew finished getting dressed and opened the front door. 'Be right back,' he said. I went to the door to lock it. His bag was gone.

I was desperate to keep reading that notebook. I had to know more about the sex life of Liv K. I couldn't wait to get my hands on it again.

Andrew's journal was the first book I had enjoyed since my divorce. The most terrifying thing about living alone, I had decided, was reading. Lying alone in bed and reading a book, noisily turning the pages, glancing guiltily at the clock. With every half hour that ticked by, while I lay alone and read some book about a fat girl or a girl in England, I had the feeling that I was ruining my chance to have a life. I should be out Rollerblading or smoking a cigar in a lounge somewhere, trying to meet men. At the very least I should be reading at a bookstore and making eye contact between sips of latte. Reading in bed with my husband had been different. Alone, I might as well have been reading by a penlight in a coffin six feet underground. Reading is what it must feel like being dead.

Nothing had changed since I was a little girl reading all day in the hammock my father had installed in my bedroom. When I was a child I won a contest at my library for reading the most books. As a prize I got to choose any book so I chose the most exotic title: *The Wind in the Willows*. I was so excited. What a disappointment. Some prize. It was a childish book about animals, and I hated all books about animals. All I got for reading all those books was another book. A book no one in his right mind would like.

But now I had the next segment of Andrew's diary to look forward to.

We ate our bagels sitting next to each other on the side of my bed. 'It's my mother's birthday and I want you to meet her,'

Andrew said. 'Do you want to come with me to Virginia?'

'Won't she tell Jordan that you brought another woman to meet her?' I asked.

'No,' he said without elaborating.

After a while I said, 'Does your mother like Jordan?'

'She's never met her. I haven't brought Jordan down there. I think it's better that way. Although I think she suspects I'm a fag, living with a man named Jordan.'

Andrew was the only man I had dated, including my husband, I was sure wasn't a fag.

I called Violet as soon as he left to tell her that Andrew wanted to introduce me to his mother. 'He's taking me to Virginia in his girlfriend's car.'

Violet was silent on the other end of the phone.

'Isn't that great?' I said.

'Ohhh,' she said.

'Oh what?' I said after a pause.

'Don't go,' she said.

'Why not?' I said.

'I just have a feeling you shouldn't,' Violet said. I hated when Violet had a feeling. She waited a moment for me to react to her feeling as if her feeling would mean something or be in any way accurate this time when it never had been in the past. I didn't react. 'I think it might get really' – Violet paused as if summoning her intuitive powers – '*intense*.' She sighed, collapsing from exhaustion, as if the spirit she had channeled had just left her body. I pictured her in flowing scarves and a turban on her head looking deeply into a bowl of Häagen-Dazs.

'Just don't get married,' she said grimly, almost nastily, as if I married every man I met and she had to buy me an expensive gift each time. As if Andrew weren't living with someone and it would be perfectly easy for us to get married over the weekend.

'I said he was taking me to meet his mother, not the justice of the peace,' I said.

'I know,' she snapped. We didn't say anything for a while. I got off the phone as fast as I could and lay on my bed staring at the ceiling. I wondered if we would just go down for the day or if we would sleep over. I wondered if she had a guest room or if we would stay at an inn. If there was a guest room I would probably stay in it, and Andrew would sneak in to see me in the middle of the night. I figured out when I was expecting my period. I wondered what I should wear and if his mother would like me. All mothers liked me. I planned some things to say to her.

The next day I went to Tiffany's and bought a ceramic honey pot, in the shape of a beehive with bees painted on it, for Mrs. Lugar's birthday. I brought it to the office, swinging it in its baby-blue bag. I plugged a typewriter in at my desk and typed up a rental lease on a Blumberg form. At the bottom I put in a rider stating that the tenant had to pay four hundred extra dollars a month to have the owner's plant caretaker come to the apartment to water the plants once a week. 'The plants cannot be moved!' the owner had screamed. My phone rang.

'Liv Kellerman,' I said.

'Do you miss the feel of my cock in your cunt?'

'Andrew, why can't you just say hi like other people?'

'Hi,' he said. 'Do you miss me?'

'I can't talk now, I'm closing a deal,' I said. I had wheeled my chair over to Maria Lorta's desk all morning to help her look at pictures of wedding gowns. 'Where are you?' I asked.

'Virginia,' he said.

I didn't say anything.

'But I'm going to make it up to you. I'll be back tomorrow and I can stay at your apartment for the next few days.'

I was still fuming at eight that night when I brought a man who had his own seat on the stock exchange – whatever that meant – into a stunning loft on Canal Street. He wore pale cowboy boots and carried a matching ostrich-skin briefcase. On the way up in the elevator, he pinched my shirt between his thumb and forefinger to see what it was made of, if it was silk. It wasn't. 'Sorry,' he said, 'I just had to know.' It was one of the rudest things that had ever happened to me in an elevator.

'So what do you think?' I asked, after he had looked around for fifteen minutes. It was truly one of the most magnificent places I had ever seen. It belonged to a famous artist I had never heard of and it had enormous windows looking out on the Hudson. The sunsets would be incredible. You could watch the Circle Line go by.

'It's dark,' he said. I looked at him in disbelief.

'It's nighttime,' I said. 'The loft is flooded with sun in the day.' I tried to smile. I had to remember apartment hunting was stressful. People got nervous. They weren't themselves.

'But I *work* during the day,' the man said, sounding frustrated, as if I were the stupidest girl he had ever met. 'I'm only home at night. If it's sunny during the day that doesn't do me much good.'

'I don't have any lofts that are sunny at night,' I said.

'But that's the only time I'm home and I want light. I put that on my list.' I had given him the Smoothe Transitions Wishlist to fill out. The buyer was supposed to list the qualities he was looking for in a loft in order of importance. I opened the shiny Transitions folder and looked at his list. Sun was number one.

'That's why I brought you here,' I said. 'You have direct south and west exposures. It doesn't get any brighter than this.'

'But look how dark it is in here,' he said. 'Your ad in the paper said, "Bring your sunglasses." I clearly don't need to put on my sunglasses .'

It was like showing Jerome an apartment. I felt like I was in a production of *The Taming of the Shrew* set in a Canal Street loft. I was supposed to admit the sun should shine at night, after the market closed. Just for him.

'You're absolutely right to be upset, sir. I don't know why it isn't sunnier tonight. I just can't understand it.' I looked out across the dark Hudson River to the lights in Jersey. 'Maybe the sun is hiding behind a cloud.'

'I'll just have to find another broker,' he said.

'That's probably a good idea, sir. I hear the sun sets later on the Upper East Side, maybe you should try up there. And I believe Corcoran handles night sun, why don't you give them a call?'

'I think I will,' he said walking out, leaving me to pull down the special heavy-duty shades the owner had installed to protect his art from all the sun.

22
ARCH DESIGNED

Andrew came to me when he got back from Virginia and apologized. I didn't ask if he had gone with Jordan.

When we woke up he said, 'I'm having an early day and I want to come here after work. Give me your key.'

'I'm not giving you my key,' I said. At the last minute I agreed to keep my door open all day so he could let himself in. I figured it wasn't any more dangerous than having the door locked, because it was so easy to break in. I made my bed before I went to work, something I never did.

When I got home I looked for signs of him. His gym bag was on the bedroom floor but he was gone. It was too risky to open the bag and look for his diary without knowing when he was coming back. He could walk through the door at any time, unless I locked it, which would seem suspicious.

I undressed and got into the shower. I wouldn't read it, I decided. I would do whatever it was I did when I was home alone.

I got out of the shower, wrapped myself in a towel, and went into the bedroom. The bag was there. I decided to ignore it. I took my new flesh-colored bra out of the tissue paper it was gently wrapped in and tried it on. It fit perfectly. In the mirror I saw the bag again on the floor. I couldn't stand it anymore. I locked the front door and went back to the bag. I squatted beside it and unzipped it carefully. I reached into the bag and pulled out the diary.

I know Liv loves me, I read. *We came simultaneously last night. I told Liv that the one time Jordan let me go down on her she did the Sunday Times crossword during it the whole time . . .*

'What are you doing?' Andrew said.

I jolted to my feet. Andrew was lying on the bed, on his side facing away from me. I had walked past the bed twice in my bra and not seen him lying there. I was still holding the diary. If he turned over he would see me with it. I bent down fast and shoved the thing back in his bag. He rolled over to face me. He was wearing a green silk paisley ascot of some sort. I stepped away from the bag as if it had a car alarm going off inside it.

'I watched your wedding video,' he said sleepily. 'That jackass you married has the personality of a piece of cardboard.'

'What!' I said. I was horrified. 'You shouldn't snoop through my things.' I was vulnerable as a bride. I didn't want people tuning in anytime they wanted to. It was like Dorothy's future boyfriend watching her trip to Oz on video one day and making snide comments about the scarecrow. It was *my* dream from *my* tornado concussion. My father was in it, and my mother, and my aunt Em, and of course Jack.

'I was hoping it was a porno,' he said.

It was, I thought.

'When we get married it's going to be different,' Andrew said.

'Are you going to be wearing that scarf?' I asked.

'Come here,' he said.

'That's a girl's scarf. You look like a cross-dresser in that thing.'

'This is a man's scarf. I thought maybe I could tie you up with it,' he said.

In bed Andrew overwhelmed me. That was the thing that made him better than other lovers. He would leave me confused. I felt like I was in the wrong decade. Having 1940s sex in the present time. I always felt like dusting off my bottom afterward as if we had been doing it on a metal desk in a small office belonging to a private eye in old New York. I had the impulse to hand Andrew his hat when it was over, even though he didn't wear one, and adjust my own invisible garter belt. When I was with him I felt like a blonde.

After we had sex I said, 'Don't throw the condom on the floor. Give it to me and I'll throw it in the garbage.'

'I think we can stop using them,' he said. 'I want to shoot a baby into you.' He rolled on top of me and kissed me and bit my neck a little. His words ran through my mind. No man had ever said that to me before. It was the most romantic thing I had ever heard.

'If anyone were to give me the AIDS virus, it would be you,' I said, taking the condom from him. It was limp and empty. Andrew had come. I had witnessed the veins of his thick neck pop out and his chin point up in the air like a bull terrier's. I knew he had come, but the inside of the condom was completely dry. I wondered if he had managed to slip the condom off. Having sex with Andrew was like having sex with the magician David Copperfield.

'Did you come?' I asked him.

'Mmm, yes,' he said, smiling.

'Inside me?' I asked.

'Honey, no,' he said.

'Where's the come?' I asked, pinching the condom's reservoir tip.

'I can come without ejaculating,' he said.

'What!'

'It's a technique I learned from my Qi Gong master.'

'Did you come or not?' I said. I was getting angry.

'It's not good for men to ejaculate every time they come. You release your power that way. You lose strength. It's the worst thing a man can do. It took a lot of practice but now I can have as intense an orgasm without sacrificing anything. And I can keep fucking all night if I want to.'

I was so angry I could barely speak.

'You wouldn't want me to feel all . . . *spent* now, would you?' he asked.

'Yes I would, Andrew,' I said. 'I would like you to feel spent.'

'Most women would be happy,' he said. 'I still have all of my energy.'

'You're so cheap you can't even give me your come,' I said. I just sat on the edge of my bed holding the rubber. It was the same color and texture as my new expensive bra, which I was still wearing. Its cups had stretched out during the sex and formed little reservoir tips of their own. 'You withhold even that.'

'What am I depriving you of, a mess on your belly? Don't worry, I came great.'

'How do I know you weren't faking?'

'How do *I* know *you* weren't faking?'

'That's a woman's prerogative,' I said. 'I want you to ejaculate, Andrew. If we have sex again, I want a mess on my belly.'

'I want my baby in your belly,' he said. He rolled on top of me and fucked me hard for less than a dozen strokes before he came and collapsed on top of me. 'Satisfied?' he whispered. 'If I hold you upside down for half an hour there's more chance of getting a boy.'

'No one's holding me upside down,' I said. I felt his come wet my thighs and the bed under me. 'It would probably be better if we had a boy baby. There's less chance you'll molest it.'

'Now I'll probably be too tired to work tonight.'

'Good,' I said. 'Andrew, you shouldn't have come inside me without a condom.'

'I thought you wanted me to ejaculate. You don't even know what you want. I'm glad I did it. We're going to have a beautiful baby boy together.'

He got up and started getting dressed. I hated being left behind in my apartment. It was somehow easier to part on the street in the midst of New York. It made it a more equal parting. I got up and pulled a velvet shirt on over my head. 'I'm leaving with you, I'm going out,' I said.

It was raining when we got out on the street. The tops of

buildings were fogged up. There was red mist glowing in the distance from the giant neon umbrella of the Travelers Insurance offices. I looked for the Empire State Building, for the World Trade towers, for the moon, but they weren't there. Like David Copperfield, Andrew had made them disappear.

I had seen a magician shoot an arrow with a scarf tied to the end of it through the stomach of his assistant and into the bull's-eye behind her. I wondered if Andrew had shot a baby into me.

23
CORNER APT, EXPSD BRK

Andrew and I stood in Minetta Lane, kissing. It was mid-night. My back was against a wall and Andrew stood in front of me with his legs spread apart.

I didn't want him to come up to my apartment. I was trying to convince him that he needed to have a place I could come to.

'Where are we going to make out tomorrow night?' I asked. 'We've kissed on every corner in the Village. Maybe we should try something new.'

'Tomorrow we're going to kiss on the corner of Fifty-ninth and Lex and the next night we'll try Thirty-third and Third. I also have a couple of nice spots picked out for us near Lincoln Center.'

I remembered a cabdriver telling me that Thirty-third and Park was the most dangerous street in New York. More accidents occurred there. For some reason I remembered his name, Ishmael.

'How about Thirty-third and Park?' I said.

'Any place you like.'

'Okay, your bed.'

'It might be a little crowded.'

'I showed Maya Lin that house,' I said. I pointed to a four-story house on the corner with a wrought-iron gate. Maya Lin was the young architect who designed the Viet Nam Veterans Memorial in Washington, D.C. I looked at Andrew's face to see if he was jealous that Maya Lin was looking to buy a whole house. He didn't look jealous at all. 'She wants to turn the whole building into her offices.'

Andrew nodded and smiled at me.

'She's really nice,' I said. I hadn't actually shown her the house. Another woman in my office had. 'Are we still getting together tomorrow night?' I asked as casually as possible. Two dates in a row was rare.

'Yeh-hes,' he said in a high falsetto. He kissed me hard and forced my mouth open wider than normal. He pressed his tongue into my mouth.

A big peach overstuffed chair was across the street. It was missing its cushion but it still looked comfortable. In New York you never see a couch or a chair on the street with its cushions intact. You see bums carrying peach cushions off to their carts like ants carrying crumbs. Even though I would normally never touch anything on the street that was upholstered, this chair looked very inviting. I wanted to sit on Andrew's lap in the chair and pretend we were in his apartment. I wanted to straddle him in that chair.

'When was the last time you went to the dentist?' Andrew asked.

For a second I was taken aback. That is the last question in the world anyone wants a date asking them. It's almost worse than 'Have you ever been tested?' I had been to the Bausches' dentist not too long ago. When my husband and I started talking about getting a divorce, I wanted to be in perfect physical condition for our fights. I went to every kind of doctor. I went to massage therapists. I also got constant manicures and pedicures and wore exquisite bras and panties all the time. Once a salesgirl in a lingerie store asked me why I was buying all those things. 'Are you going someplace special?' she asked. 'I'm going to war,' I replied.

'When was the last time?' Andrew said again.

'Just a few months ago,' I said. 'Why?'

'I think you have a cavity.'

I was horrified. 'What?'

'You have a cavity, you should go have it taken care of.' He kissed me again.

'I don't have a cavity,' I said. 'I've never had a cavity.'

He probed my mouth with his tongue. 'You have one now. I can taste it, honey.'

'Well, stop kissing me then.'

'I don't want to stop kissing you, I just want you to make a dentist appointment this week. I love your taste. And I love your smell.'

He buried his face in my neck. A man walked past us and looked at us. I wished Jordan would walk by. I wished Jordan would walk by in her plastic shoes carrying her ugly canvas tote bag and we could have a big scene and put an end to this whole thing. Andrew could stay at my house that night and go get his dogs and his things in the morning. I would buy a toaster so I could make toast with his eggs. We had been kissing in that small alley for over an hour and only one man had passed us the whole time. The chances of Jordan walking down Minetta Lane at midnight were pretty slim.

'Come on, let's go upstairs and I'll give you the rest of your checkup,' Andrew said.

'I don't think my insurance will cover it,' I said.

The next day I was desperate to go to the dentist. I called the Bausches' dentist at eight and got the answering service and then called again at nine. 'Dr. Blum has no appointments available today,' the receptionist said.

'Please,' I said. 'I really have to see him today.'

She told me all the other days he was available.

'I have to come in today,' I said again. 'It's an emergency.'

'Are you in pain?'

'It's an emergency situation,' I said. 'Why don't I just come in and wait in case someone cancels?'

'I'm sorry, there's already a waiting list,' she said.

I went anyway and waited in the dentist's office for most of the day, talking on the patient courtesy phone and reading articles in *Glamour* about kissing.

Finally I was escorted to the chair. 'Dr. Blum?' I asked, before I was even seated. 'Is it possible to detect a cavity in someone else's mouth by, you know, kissing?' I felt like a teenager.

The dentist laughed. 'I don't usually perform a dental exam by kissing,' he said. 'But I can if you want me to.'

He seemed to think I was coming on to him. 'I was just curious,' I said. 'So, can you?'

'No,' he said. 'Of course not.'

As he worked I closed my eyes and imagined he was Andrew.

'I don't know what the big emergency is,' he told me. 'You have a cavity but it isn't deep.'

He smiled at me as if he were on to my little plan to come up with any flimsy excuse to see him again. He still didn't have any curtains.

He filled the cavity with an invisible white filling, and I sat patiently in the chair waiting for him to finish. 'Now go home and kiss whoever you want,' the dentist said.

That night Andrew lay on top of me kissing me. 'How did you get an appointment so quickly?'

'What appointment?' I asked. I had brushed my teeth as soon as I got home to get the dentist taste out of my mouth. I didn't want him to know I'd been to the dentist.

'You had your cavity filled. I'm proud of you. Open your mouth and let me see,' he said.

'No,' I said, and clamped my mouth shut.

'Come on, open up,' he said.

I shook my head no like a little girl. I could feel him hard against my leg.

'Open your mouth, like a good little girl,' he coaxed. Then he pinched my nose closed with his thumb and finger. I couldn't breathe. I made noises of protest through my closed lips. Finally I was forced to open my mouth.

He put his finger in my mouth and felt the tooth I had just had filled. 'That's what I do with my dogs when I want them to let go of a ball,' he said. He kissed me gently. 'I love playing dentist chair with you.'

'Dentist *chair*?' I said.

'I meant Dentist,' he said. 'Liv, we're going to have so much fun when we're married.'

Suddenly the not being able to breathe episode of a few moments before began to leave my mind. 'When are you going to leave Jordan?' I asked.

He lay next to me, silent. 'I really want to,' he said.

'Then do.'

'I can't right now.'

'Why not?' I asked, genuinely interested in what reason he was going to give tonight.

'Jordan has found a lump in her breast.' He said it with reverence as if he were saying, 'Jordan has won a Pulitzer Prize.'

'Did she have a biopsy?' I asked, coolly.

'Her doctors are taking care of it. She's in good hands.'

Yeah, yours, I thought.

I didn't say anything for a while. I had never considered Jordan's breasts in all of this. I had never thought about what they looked like. I wondered if Andrew had discovered the lump the way he had discovered my cavity. Suddenly my cavity seemed like very small potatoes.

'You're not doing her any favors by staying with her,' I said.

He sighed sadly. 'Maybe you're right. But I can't leave her now with all of this happening. I can't do that to her.'

'Why not?' I asked.

'It just wouldn't be the right thing to do,' he said.

'But I think it would be the right thing to do, Andrew. Sometimes a crisis like this can make a person strong. You should tell her the truth about us.'

'If you think I should hurt her like that now when she's going through this then you have shit for blood,' he said.

Who talked like that? Who said things like 'shit for blood' in normal conversation? 'I hope you're joking,' I said. I couldn't believe what he had just said. It sounded like something a mafioso would say before hacking off a thumb. 'If you're not joking, I think you should leave.'

He got up, slid on his loafers, and walked out the door.

Later that night he called me.

'I'm sorry,' he said. 'You and I are supposed to get married and have children. I know that. I can feel it. I feel like we're meant to do that. And I know that by not leaving Jordan I'm interfering with the history of the world. We're supposed to be together.'

'So what are you going to do?'

'Well, right now I'm going to go to sleep and tomorrow I have a big meeting.'

'Do you want me or not?' I asked.

'Yes, I want you. I love you.'

'Then do something about it,' I said.

'Honey, tell me what it will be like when we live together,' he said sleepily, demanding his bedtime story.

'Well, you'll come home every night after work and I'll check through your pockets for phone numbers and lipstick-stained hankies and . . .'

'We'll need a big apartment.'

'Yes, we'll need room for the twenty-four-hour armed security guard I'll have to hire to make sure you don't bite me.'

'Maybe we'll even take over your husband's apartment. Force him out and live there together.'

'Yes.' I missed my apartment so much I hadn't even let myself fantasize about living there again. And to live there with Andrew!

'Why don't you move in here in the meantime,' I said.

'Liv, we'll never make it in your tiny place. We have to wait until we have time to get a big apartment.'

'I can't wait that long,' I said, and hung up.

24
MNTH-2-MNTH

Every morning I scalded my hand from the steam of the teakettle and told myself that the next time I would use an oven mitt. I scalded my right hand first, and then I scalded my left. The steam was soft and pretty and harmless-looking. I turned off the only burner on my stove that worked. The kettle was shaped to look like a rooster. The oven mitt, with its price tags still attached, looked like a rabbit. I stood naked in my kitchen running cold water on my hands feeling like I was in the middle of an Aesop's fable unable to find the moral. The slowest, stupidest, vainest animal. Certainly the one most easily fooled.

I got to the Monday meeting twenty minutes early so I could get a bagel and a seat. There were only eight chairs around the conference table and twenty or thirty agents always attended and had to stand crowded into the corners of the room and spill out into the hall. If you sat you looked punctual and eager. If you stood you looked busy, too busy even to sit, as if at any moment you were expecting a call that would produce the offer that would close the deal that would get you into the 'Millionaires

Circle.' I usually missed the meeting altogether and came in at the very end with my hair wet.

On the last Monday meeting of every month Kim handed out the ribbons, including a First Deal ribbon to new agents who had completed their first deals for the company. I was expecting my First Deal ribbon for a condo I sold to a fat woman after showing her twenty apartments in one weekend. She made us stop between every apartment for soup and hot chocolates. I had actually expected my ribbon the month before for the high-end rental I had done in Tribeca but Kim said they only gave out ribbons for sales, even though my commission for the rental had been as high as most sales. I didn't push the issue. There had been a big holdup on getting the commission for the rental because I had accidentally left the certified check for $10,000 in the back of a cab. I had closed and received commissions for selling the architects' loft and then selling them the house on Harrison Street, but that hadn't counted because I had technically stolen them from Dale.

Then I wasted three weeks showing apartments to a couple who owned three small dogs. All they talked about was their dogs. They brought the dogs to all the showings to make sure they responded well to the space. They ended up buying a $1.4 million loft from another broker in a building that didn't allow dogs. 'How could you do that?' I asked. The woman burst into tears. 'We sent them to live with my parents. I'm so unhappy. The broker convinced us to put ourselves first,' she wailed.

I had zero respect for people who sent their dogs to live with their parents. Violet had done that. Her dog had swallowed a used condom from her bedroom floor and she had to take him to the vet and spend a lot of money. Then she sent him to live with her parents in Texas but she still referred to him as 'my dog.'

In addition to wasting time with the dog couple, I was also spending night and day with Audrey and Noah Bausch. I was really beginning to despise them. They were my Moby Dick. I wanted Noah Bausch stuffed and mounted over my nonworking fireplace. Everyone was buying and selling except the Bausches.

New York real estate was like a giant game of musical chairs. When the music stopped everyone grabbed an apartment but Noah Bausch.

But now I had done a sale and I would get my ribbon. Some of the agents, like Carla Lerner, hadn't gotten their First Deal ribbon yet, but most of them had. With all the ribbons pinned to the bulletin boards over everyone's desks, the office looked like livestock stalls in a county fair. I thought it was the most ridiculous thing in the world but everyone else seemed so happy to get theirs. I wore a suit.

In the second grade I got dressed up for a bake sale that was taking place in my school's gymnasium at lunchtime. I wore a velvet skirt, a red-and-white-checked blouse, and Mary Janes. I felt excited about the bake sale. When I got to school a mean girl named Harriet said, 'Look, Liv got dressed up for the bake sale,' and everyone laughed. I hoped nobody would think I got dressed up for my ribbon.

I sat alone at the table and spread vegetable cream cheese on a bagel and bit into it. The cream cheese was crawling with onions that would give me bad breath all day. I put the plastic knife back in the cream cheese and continued to eat alone at the conference table as professionally as possible.

'All agents to the conference room for a sales meeting,' Yvonne said over the PA. I sat up straighter in my seat. The agents piled in.

'Well, you're here early,' Kim said to me. She wore a sort of junior suit. She didn't even really look like a grown-up. 'All right, all right, let's begin,' she said. 'I'd like to start by asking Tony Amoroso to tell us what he does every morning.'

Tony had been the Downtown salesman of the year for five years in a row.

'Go on, Tony. I really think everyone can learn something from what you told me you do every morning to start your day.'

Tony's wife stood behind him holding a pad and pen. The more successful agents hired their own assistants and paid them a salary out of their own pockets. Tony had hired his wife. I felt sorry for her, one for being married to him, and two for being a real estate agent's assistant. He was the only agent at Transitions Downtown with his own office. He was also one of only two male agents in any of the Transitions offices who was straight.

'Well,' Tony said. 'Every morning I walk on the treadmill in my bedroom for thirty-five minutes.'

This was already more than anybody wanted to know about him. I pictured him in his undershirt and boxer shorts or worse, some sort of robe, walking in place while his wife was busy getting his work clothes together.

'And I listen to motivational tapes while I exercise. You know, how-to-sell-ice-to-the-Eskimos sort of things.'

A couple of agents close to the door left as if they had just been beeped.

'I've asked Tony to bring in some of the tapes and we're going to post a sign-out sheet at the front desk so you can borrow them,' Kim said.

A black woman holding a beautiful downy baby walked into the conference room.

'I know many of you have been anxious to meet my daughter,' Kim said, taking the baby from the woman. 'Everyone, this is Dakota,' she said, raising her voice several octaves. I wondered if she was named for the building or the state. A few agents ooohed and aaahed and three more left the room. She handed the baby to the agent on her left, who held her on her lap for about a second and then passed her on to the next agent.

'Now, we have some ribbons to hand out. Melanie gets a yellow ribbon for biggest deal of the month.' Everyone clapped as Kim tossed the yellow ribbon across the table at Melanie. It was big and ruffled with a pin on the back and the words 'Bigge$t Deal' in the center. 'Adrienne gets a red ribbon for most deals closed.' Again, everyone clapped. Adrienne handed me Dakota so she could accept her ribbon properly.

'The blue ribbon for most overall money earned this month goes to Tony. Big surprise,' Kim said. Two more agents left and the rest of us, including Dakota, clapped.

'And finally a green First Deal ribbon goes to Liv Kellerman for successfully completing a condo sale.' Everyone clapped and a few people looked around to see who I was, even though I had already been there two months. 'Liv,' Kim said, 'We ran out of green ribbons, I'm really sorry, but you'll get it as soon as they come in. I told Yvonne to order more ribbons.'

'That's okay,' I said.

'Congratulations anyway,' Kim said. I sat there holding her baby. I remembered being on a plane with my husband going to Mexico City. He was asleep with a blanket over his head and the woman across the aisle from us, a fat Mexican woman with many children, stood up to take some of them to the bathroom. She hovered over me for a moment and then thrust her large fat baby at me. I held the baby for twenty minutes, rubbing its back, until she finally returned. My husband never woke up. I wanted him to wake up so I could say, 'Honey, look, we have a baby.' I felt like an impostor, like Lucille Ball carrying a whole cheese in a baby bunting to get it through customs. I thought about keeping the baby and telling my husband it was just a cheese. For days after, I felt the baby's weight in my arms.

I noticed Carla Lerner had left the room when my name was announced. She was in a bad mood because she had stupidly locked herself out on the roof of a building and no one had found her for seven hours.

Kim stood and came around the table to collect Dakota from me. I wondered if Kim had gotten a ribbon that said First Baby on it. She announced that a prize of a one-hundred-dollar bill would go to the first agent who canvassed the Sunday *Times* each week and got at least one listing from it.

There were only about nine of us left in the room now so Kim brought the meeting to an end and I went back to my desk, ribbonless and childless.

There is one thing I remember about my marriage that makes my body curl up on itself like peeling wallpaper when I think about it. I think about this one night when my husband bought theater tickets and I was getting dressed to go. I had terrible period cramps which I usually don't have and I had a bad headache but I was so happy because he had planned this night for us. He sat on the bed and watched me brush my hair and put on a necklace. He watched me apply lipstick. 'You look beautiful,' he said. I felt beautiful going down in the elevator with him, sliding into a cab, sitting next to him in our orchestra seats. I felt beautiful all night. What a fool I was.

I left the office and got on the downtown six train. The train was completely empty. I stood at the end of the last car like a little kid looking out the back windows at the blackness and occasional red light bulb. The word 'Will' was etched jaggedly into the dark windowpane. I had heard some idiot on the news say that this was a new form of graffiti known as 'scratchitti.' 'How will New York solve its scratchitti problem?' the newscaster had said. It sounded like a skin disease. I wished this boy Will, whoever he was, was here right now. 'Hi, Will, I'm Liv,' I said ludicrously out loud as if I were really introducing myself to someone.

I took my keys out of my bag. The key ring had a retractable blade on it I used to neatly cut apartment listings out of the Sunday real estate section. I scratched my name on the subway window under the word Will. Will Liv.

When I got home I did something I hadn't done in a long time. I lay on my bed crying and sort of wailing the words 'What have I done' over and over like a lunatic. I didn't know why I was saying that. I hadn't done anything. 'Oh no, oh no,' I cried. 'What have I done?'

Then my mind stopped crying before my body did. My body continued bucking and shaking with sobs even though my mind had lost interest in the whole thing and was, almost, still. 'You haven't done anything,' I told myself. 'You just missed a few clues.'

On my twenty-first birthday, when I was first dating my husband, he gave me a present. He handed me a rectangular wrapped box. I opened it slowly.

'Oh, it's Clue,' I said.

'I thought we could play it together,' he said. 'It's silly I know, but I thought it would be fun.'

'Oh no, it's great,' I said, telepathically telling him never to do this to me again. The next day my friends said it was as good as over. 'If a man gives you a board game for your birthday . . .' they said.

I still had the game. I pulled myself up off my bed and took it down from my kitchen cabinet. We had opened it together but never played it. We couldn't because you needed at least three players, a sort of ménage à Clue.

I lifted the lid off the box and picked up the sealed plastic bag containing the little game pieces. The revolver, the lead pipe, the candlestick holder, the knife, the wrench, and the rope. They were all metal except for the rope, which was white plastic.

I ripped open the bag and held the six loose pieces in my fist. I went to the windowsill to get a can of ginger ale since my refrigerator still didn't work. It was warm but I opened it. Then I did a strange thing. One by one I popped the game pieces into my mouth and swallowed them down with the ginger ale. With the pieces inside me, I was sure the mystery could somehow be solved.

25
W/D IN BSMNT

The next morning I woke up exhausted. I felt strange from the dream I had just had. I dreamed that the swami from the photo on my desk came to me and asked me to open my mouth wide. Then he reached into my mouth and started pulling yards and yards of white silk cord from my throat. He kept yanking and yanking and the cord continued coming up. The swami pulled like a longshoreman. Finally I woke up.

I wondered if the swami had gotten the last of it out of me. I had a terrible taste in my mouth. I went into the bathroom and threw up into the toilet. My bathroom was so small I had to kneel at an awkward angle with my legs out the bathroom door into the kitchen. After, the white plastic rope game piece floated in the toilet water.

I got myself together in time to go to see a loft for rent. The building was on York Street, which was nothing more than a small alley tucked behind Beach Street. The American Thread Building loomed over it. The loft I was looking at was on the fifth floor and was essentially a walk-up even though there was a manual elevator. 'You can use the elevator,' the landlord said, 'but you have to bring it right down and then walk back up.'

'Of course,' I said, not understanding that at all.

'I'm glad you understand,' he said. 'You'd be surprised how many people can't understand such a simple concept. If you take the elevator up to your floor then no one else in the building can call it down. My wife and I live on the top three floors and we bring the elevator up there at night for security purposes but it's here for the tenants the rest of the time. It's a great convenience.'

It took me a few minutes to figure out that would only be useful for bringing things up so you wouldn't have to carry them or for freighting old people.

'So it's basically a walk-up,' I said to the landlord, making a note on my pad.

'Well, there *is* an elevator,' he said angrily. He was about seventy and wore a baseball cap that said 'Empire Trophies' on it and had a picture of a trophy in the shape of the Empire State Building. White hair poked out from the back of the cap. He wore a shirt with a tiny golf flag over his right nipple and new-looking jeans and sneakers. He was pretty thin.

My father had dressed like that one Halloween when I was a kid saying he was going as 'a regular Dad.' He took me to a party and I felt proud but halfway through he got bored and put on a long Indian feather headdress and spent the rest of the night doing Cher imitations.

The landlord took us up slowly and stopped at the number 5. He slid the metal elevator gate open and unlocked the door facing us. We stepped off the elevator right into the loft. I started to look around.

'This is a beautiful loft,' I said. It had barrel ceilings, one bathroom, and an island kitchen right in the center. But it was dark. As dark as the planetarium.

'I bought the building in 1969,' he said.

'A pioneer,' I said like an idiot. I was off today for some reason. Maybe it was the metal Clue pieces banging around in my stomach.

'We've been living here ever since. Put in a roof deck, small swimming pool, small antique cage elevator that's just for the top three floors.'

'So you have your own private elevator.'

'Put that in recently, about twelve years ago. Never had one regret about buying this place. You hear about Letterman buying a loft on North Moore? What's his name, David?'

'Yes, David Letterman,' I said slowly and authoritatively as if I were speaking to someone with Alzheimer's. I was beginning to sound more and more like a broker. 'He paid two million for it.' I didn't know exactly how much he had paid but I knew it was something like that.

'As a matter of fact it was closer to three. In 'seventy-two I could have bought that loft for five thousand dollars. Didn't think it was worth it at the time.' He smiled at me. 'This building used to be a Greek foods warehouse.' He pointed to the old wooden floor, which had giant black rings on it. 'Can you guess what those circles are from?'

'No,' I said, flirtatiously, as if only he in all his wisdom could tell me.

'This floor was used to store heavy barrels of olives,' he said.

I took one last look around the loft. I considered doing that thing I had seen other brokers do where they walk the length of it trying to space their feet so that each step represents a yard. I decided against it and just drew a little picture of the loft on my pad. 'Would you let someone build a darkroom?' I asked. I had a client, a man with long hair, who wanted to put in a darkroom.

'I don't think so,' the landlord said.

'Well, I think I can rent it right away,' I said.

He didn't look bowled over by this news. 'If you don't someone else will,' he said. 'Come on, I'll take you down.'

I followed him into the elevator and as we descended I looked up through the grillwork to the top of the elevator shaft.

'A lady baker lives on the third floor,' he said. 'Bakes pies and things. A lady writer was living on the fifth floor in the loft I just showed you, but she fell in love with the painter on the second floor so she just moved in with him. That's why we have the vacancy.'

He released the lever and we came to a bumpy stop. He

handed me keys and I took them gratefully. I was relieved. Now I could show it at my own convenience without involving him in any way. I got out of the elevator and he closed the doors between us.

'If you want to take a look at the basement, go right ahead,' he said. 'We have, what we consider to be, quite an unusual feature.' He grabbed the lever, pushed it all the way forward, and rode all the way

I hesitantly took the stairs down to the basement wondering what this unusual feature could be.

At the foot of the stairs I saw it. A shiny white washing machine and a shiny white dryer with a stack of plastic laundry baskets standing next to them. There were no slots for coins. They were free! If you lived in this little building, underneath the old rich landlord and his wife, you got to do your laundry absolutely free. That was probably where the man from the second floor met the woman from the fifth floor. They probably made jokes about the episode of 'The Odd Couple' where Felix rendezvouses with the Pigeon sisters in the laundry room.

Clothes were thudding gently in the dryer. Sex took place in this building. New sex and old sex. A new couple and an old married one. I pictured a beautiful young couple having sex in the second-floor loft, and then washing their sheets for free. I pictured the landlord and his wife embracing in their small swimming pool.

I put both my hands on top of the dryer and felt the warm massaging motion. I was suddenly filled with hope. I stood that way for a long time, almost praying. A smell of baking cookies wafted toward me.

I was startled when the dryer suddenly stopped. I hadn't realized how noisy it had been. I wondered whose clothes were in there. Women's panties? Men's blue pajama bottoms? Baker's whites?

I opened the dryer door as quietly as possible and bent down to peer in. I reached in and pulled out a big peach towel. I spread my arms wide to fold it and put it on top of the dryer. Then I reached in and pulled out another peach towel and carefully folded it and put it on top of the first one. The dryer was filled with four more peach towels. I folded them all quickly and left.

I walked all the way to the office composing the ad in my head. It was Wednesday and if I got it into the computer by four o'clock it could still make it into the Sunday paper. I would have to find a way to convey that this was the only building in New York with a free washer/dryer in the basement. 'W/D incl' didn't seem to convey enough. Sweet-Smelling Loft. Downy Soft Loft. 1700 sf of Heaven. Loft of Love. Nothing seemed quite right.

When I got to my office, there was a sign on the door saying that the elevator was broken, so I walked up nine flights. When I reached the top the receptionist signaled me over. I was so out of breath I had to brace myself on her desk. 'There's someone here to see you,' she said.

'Who is it?' I asked. I was a little upset because we weren't supposed to have drop-in clients. We were too upscale for that, unlike firms like Dale's that welcomed any homeless person or college student to come in and get free real estate advice.

'I don't know who he is,' she said. She looked worried. 'He seemed sort of . . .' She stopped talking.

'Sort of what?' I asked.

'Aggressive,' she said.

'Is he in the conference room?' I asked hopefully. I hoped whoever he was he wasn't sitting in my tiny cubicle next to Carla Lerner looking at my picture of the swami.

'He insisted on sitting at your desk.' She handed me a tall stack of toilet paper rolls. 'Would you mind putting these in the bathroom? I can't leave the phones now.'

I slowly walked up the aisle between the cubicles. There was hardly anybody in the office probably because no one wanted to climb up nine flights just to get to work. I walked up to my desk holding the rolls of toilet paper in my arms like a janitor. There was Andrew sitting in my chair reading a Faulkner novel.

'What are you doing here?' I asked.

'Hi,' he said.

'Why are you here?'

'God, this guy is good. Listen to this.' He read a sentence but I didn't listen to it. I wondered if he had gone through my Rolodex.

'Andrew, I don't have time to listen to Faulkner.' And I didn't have time to listen to Andrew if he wasn't going to leave Jordan. Andrew was a time-waster, as Dale would say.

'I wanted to take you to lunch.' He swiveled around in my chair and faced the dirty air shaft window with two pigeons pecking each other on the sill which was white from bird shit.

'I'm only at this desk temporarily while they finish the construction,' I said. Andrew stood and looked around. There was no construction being done anywhere. 'Anyway I'm really busy right now.'

'I can wait,' he said. 'There's something I want to talk to you about.'

Carla Lerner walked in and said hello, expecting an introduction. She was out of breath from the stairs. She stared at us. 'Hello,' she said again.

'These have to go to the bathroom,' I said, shoving the toilet paper at Carla. 'We're going to lunch.' I led Andrew out of the office and practically ran down the stairs to the street. 'I suppose you were hoping to eat lunch in my bed,' I said.

'Not at all,' he said. 'I want to take you to my favorite Italian restaurant. *The New York Times* only gave it two stars but I think it's much better than that.'

I followed him a few blocks east to some business-looking place and watched while he fussed over the menu. The waiter took our order. Then Andrew s beeper went off in his blue duffel bag. He hoisted the bag onto the chair we weren't using and got the beeper out. 'I'm sorry,' he said, standing, 'I'm going to have to get this.'

He went to the other end of the restaurant and down a flight of stairs. His bag was still on the chair, unzipped. I reached into it and got his journal. I opened it and flipped through to find the last entry.

The waiter came with my artichoke and Andrew's soup and I closed the book, keeping my place with my finger.

For a moment I considered just putting it back without reading it. Reading it was a lose/lose proposition. I couldn't question him about the things he wrote or the cold clinical tone he used. I didn't want to know his thoughts. I just wanted to sit there and try to feel beautiful. I hated him for writing in that thing. '

Once when I was a little girl I got to my shrink's office early and had to sit alone in the waiting room. I could hear everything that was being said behind the closed door. Every week after that I got there early so I could hear more. I would stop breathing and lean forward in my chair, trying to quiet my heartbeat. By the time the sad crying woman would come out of the room I was exhausted. I always gave her a consoling look. One time I heard her say, 'I hate that morose little girl who waits outside every week. I know it's wrong to hate a child but I do.' I ruined it by asking the shrink what 'morose' meant. The next week the walls were lined with cork.

I couldn't stop myself. I opened Andrew's book.

Today I called Liv from the study instead of the bedroom. I lit candles.

That sounded strange, like a game. Like Clue. 'Colonel Mustard in the study with the candles.'

I pulled down my pants before I called her this time. I got hard as soon as she said hello. She rambled on about some story that happened to her friend's dog and I squirted vaseline lotion onto my cock and stroked myself to one of the best orgasms I have ever had. It was so good I couldn't keep myself from ejaculating. I couldn't hold back. It was like a hailstorm. My cock was unbelievably hard. She was actually saying the words 'The vet said Bad Doggie' at the moment I shot. She told me some sexy little story without having any idea at all what she was doing. What I was doing. I shot all over my computer screen. I have to buy screen cleaner. As soon as I finished I told her I had to take a call and got off the phone.

As I read I reached out and peeled off an artichoke leaf and dipped it in the creamy vinaigrette. I brought it to my lips and a drop of the white dressing fell on the page. I wiped it off with my napkin but it still showed, like a come stain. Then I looked up and saw the top of Andrew's head coming up the stairs. I calmly closed the book and slid it into his bag even though what I wanted was to open the book and say, 'Would you mind explaining this part to me? I didn't know my phone number had been changed to 970-LIVV.' I should have charged $1.99 a minute.

My stomach felt sour and I was sure I was going to throw up.

'Sorry I took so long.' He sat back down across from me and picked up his spoon like a weapon. 'Why are you blushing?' he asked.

'I'm not blushing,' I said.

'Yes you are. You look like you were doing something naughty under the table.'

'That sounds like something you would do,' I said.

'I'm not the one blushing,' he said. 'Can't we just try to have a nice conversation for once? What's your favorite television show?'

I didn't say anything. It was definitely *I Love Lucy* but I wouldn't even sully Lucille Ball's name by saying it in front of Andrew. 'I'm not going to tell you.'

'All right, then what's your favorite color?'

'What?'

'Tell me your favorite color.'

'That's stupid,' I said.

'I want to know.' He smiled at me.

'Yellow,' I whispered. I could hardly speak. My hands were stiff in my lap as if they were still holding the diary. My mind was still reading it.

'Yellow? Why yellow?' he asked.

I shrugged.

'Yellow's nice,' he said. 'What shade?'

'All shades,' I mumbled. 'Mustard. Taxicab. Warning sign. Lemon.' I couldn't believe we were sitting here having such a ridiculous conversation after what I had just read. I was so confused. 'What's yours?' I asked.

He thought for a moment, seriously. 'Probably yellow,' he said.

'It's hard to believe we both like yellow so much,' I said. Then everything struck me as funny and I started to laugh.

'What's so funny?' he asked.

'Is this what you wanted to talk to me about?' This was the end, I thought. This had to be the end, like a wadded-up tissue on a bedside table.

I chewed on a few more artichoke leaves. Then I knew I was going to throw up. I quickly excused myself and ran down the stairs to the ladies' room. I hung my head over the toilet and heaved over and over again. I wiped my mouth and looked into the bowl anxiously. There was the lead pipe floating in a slow circle.

When I got back to the table Andrew asked me what took me so long.

'There was a line,' I said.

He looked around the empty restaurant. The only other people eating there were two nice-looking businessmen. One was saying, 'Jenny's grandmother is in the hospital so we're going to Montauk for four or five days to be with her.' He sounded so sincere and solemn as if he really cared about this Jenny and her grandmother. I wanted a man like him.

'Liv,' Andrew said.

I shifted my gaze from the married man back to Andrew. 'Yes?'

'I'm ready to leave her,' he said.

'Jordan?' I asked.

'Of course Jordan, who else would I be leaving?'

The waiter cleared away our appetizers. My bristly artichoke heart lay on the plate uneaten. I tried to turn the page of his diary in my mind.

'You're kidding,' I said. It was an unromantic thing to say. I had rehearsed this moment so often, heard those words in my ears, 'I'm leaving Jordan. I'm ready to leave her.'

'I'm not kidding. I love you. I want to be with you.'

'How do I know you're telling the truth?'

'Liv,' he said, exasperated, 'I'm not lying.'

'Have you told her?'

'I will tonight.'

'I know a loft you could rent,' I challenged. 'Available immediately,'

'Where is it?' he asked.

'York Street.'

'You mean York Avenue? I don't want to live on the Upper East Side.'

'Not York Avenue,' I said. 'York Street.'

'Where the hell's that?' he asked.

I suddenly wondered if the York Street loft was too good for Andrew. I had often thought this about my clients, that they weren't good enough or interesting enough or attractive enough to live in the places I showed them. I wanted someone like the businessman and his wife Jenny to live in the York Street loft.

If Andrew wasn't good enough for the York Street loft, I reasoned, with its free washer/dryer and fresh-baked cookie smell and its olive barrel circles on the floor like a wedding ring quilt, then maybe he wasn't good enough for me.

'I'd like to see it,' he said. 'I'd like to see it right away. Do you have the keys?' he asked.

'I can't show it to you right now because I have another appointment,' I said. Until this moment I had forgotten that I had an appointment with a girl named Storm, the daughter of one of my parents' Beverly Hills acquaintances. When she called I thought she was acting as a spy for my father and he had found out that I was selling real estate, but it turned out she had found me completely by accident. Her father was living in Texas and wasn't in touch with my parents so I didn't feel in danger of being outed. I still hadn't been able to bring myself to tell them.

'I can come along with you and then we can look at the York Street place,' Andrew said.

I finally agreed to meet him later that afternoon. It would give me some time to think.

26

FLRTHRU ARTIST LOFT — 7 SKYLTS

Storm got out of a black limousine all by herself even before the chauffeur could hold open the door. She was dressed as a bag lady as usual in an old black wool coat and strange little flat elf boots. She had told me on the phone that she had just been left at the altar in front of four hundred people at the Beverly Hills Hotel after giving up her 'absolutely adorable bungalow in Beachwood Canyon.' She looked awful.

'Hi, you look great,' she said.

'You do, too,' I said.

'Oh, you're sweet,' she said. 'So, is this it?' she asked, looking up at the building. 'It's not what I imagined.'

We were standing on West Street and Gansevoort in the heart of the meat-packing district.

'What did you imagine?' I asked.

'I really like Park Avenue a lot. Is there anything there?'

'You said you wanted a loft.'

'Oh, I do!' she said.

'There aren't any lofts on Park Avenue,' I said. 'This building has a doorman.' I pointed to a man in a uniform slouched over a Formica desk in the lobby.

'This is so exciting, let's see it,' she said.

I took her up to the second floor and we were greeted by the owner, a middle-aged woman. She showed us the kitchen first. It had a half-fridge and one narrow counter.

'Where's the kitchen?' Storm asked.

'This is it,' the woman said. Storm laughed as if the woman was kidding.

She took us into room after room. It was a huge square loft, easily three thousand square feet. The price was low for all that space.

She took us into a bedroom and put her finger to her lips. A gray-haired man was sleeping on the low austere platform bed.

'We're night people,' the woman said as we headed toward the door. 'The person who buys this place has to be able to sleep through anything.'

'Why's that?' Storm asked.

'Well, of course you get the noise from the West Side Highway but you can put in double-paned windows,' I told Storm quickly.

'We've already got them,' the woman said. 'No double-paned windows in the universe are going to help this place.'

'What do you mean?' Storm asked.

The woman looked at me helplessly.

'New York's a noisy place,' I said. 'If you want quiet you have to stay in Beverly Hills.'

'Look,' the woman said, 'I have to be honest with you. Every night at four A.M. the place downstairs gets their delivery.'

'Delivery of what?' Storm asked.

'It makes quite a racket.'

'What gets delivered?' I asked. Now I was curious.

'Carcasses.'

'What!' Storm said. She looked like she was going to pass out.

'Oh, not people, dear, cows. Cow carcasses. They come in at four off trucks on conveyor belts. It makes a lot of noise, sort of a thud, thud, thud sound. If you're interested in buying the place we suggest spending the night here one time to see if it's for you.'

I pictured Storm rising from her four-poster canopied bed,

leaning out the window and getting splashed in the face with cow blood. She'd have to sleep with a butcher's apron on over her silk negligee.

'Okay, thank you very much,' I said.

As we left the building Storm gathered her coat up around her, afraid it might trail on the sidewalk.

We took her limo to the next loft on our tour. We sat in silence. The limo was sort of cheapo, nothing special.

Finally I said, 'Storm is an interesting name.' Interesting if you're the son of a weatherman who grows up to be a weatherman.

'It was one of the names Margaret Mitchell considered for Scarlett O'Hara,' she said.

'How interesting,' I said. Scarlett O'Hara, Storm Shapiro. I think Margaret Mitchell made the right choice.

The next loft was on Greenwich Street near Christopher. There were wall-to-wall windows on two sides and sun poured in on the floor, making it look like someone had spilled light. After the noise from the West Side Highway, it seemed silent. All you could hear was the soft sound of a basketball bouncing somewhere outside.

Storm relaxed. She moved around easily. She walked over to a long elegant table surrounded by chairs upholstered in velvet. Every chair was a different color.

'I love these chairs,' she said. 'It would be so fun to entertain with them.'

'You're not furniture shopping,' I said. 'Look at the loft itself.'

She walked past a half-bathroom. 'Oh, look at this powder room, it's so cute,' she said. She pointed to a tile that said 'W.C.' hanging on the door.

The bedroom had white built-in bookshelves arranged like library stacks along an angled wall.

'These will look so great with books on them,' she said. 'I love this loft, I really, really love it. It's a lot nicer than the dead cow loft.'

'Well, I have one more place to show you today,' I said. I

wanted to get her out of there before something bad happened.

'I'm going to put those chairs over there so you see them when you first come in.'

'I don't think these chairs are for sale, Storm.'

'We'll see.'

I followed her to the kitchen and she opened the refrigerator. 'Oh, Parmesan cheese,' she said. She took out a small plastic container. I was going to make a stop at the store for some Parmesan later. Do you think I could take this?'

'I don't think so,' I said.

'I'm sure the owner won't mind,' Storm said. I hoped the owner wouldn't walk in and find us looking in her refrigerator.

'I think you better just go to the store.'

Storm started opening cabinets and found a box of baggies. She filled a baggie with some of the Parmesan cheese, knotted it, and put it in her purse.

'How much is this loft?' Storm asked.

'Eight hundred thousand. I already sent the financials to your father.' It was hard to believe the daughter of a millionaire had to steal cheese.

'I don't think I have to see anything else,' she said.

I had planned to take her to the loft of the actor Judd Hirsch from the television show *Taxi*. It was an overpriced loft that had been on the market for years but it was a great loft to show because for one thing it made all other lofts look like a good deal and for another thing there were a million photographs on the walls of Judd Hirsch posing with Danny DeVito so it made me look like broker to the stars.

'I'll talk to my father and I'll call you tomorrow,' Storm said. I watched her get into the limousine and drive off. Then I jumped in a cab and went to meet Andrew.

27

DEAL FELL THRU — OWNER ANXIOUS

Just as Andrew and I were about to walk into the York Street building a model walked across our path like a black cat. Her lips were pink and shiny as if she had just eaten watermelon. She was six feet tall and dressed in Andrew's and my favorite color with her stomach exposed and bones jutting out all over the place. She was beautiful but freakish like something that could be hanging in the window of Mayhem, the Halloween shop on my block. I tried to picture myself that tall and skinny but I couldn't. I tried to picture myself as a skeleton but I imagined my bones thick and soft like Styrofoam.

'You're prettier than she is,' Andrew said.

'No I'm not.'

'Oh, you are. Your body is so, I don't know, chewy.'

Andrew walked around the loft.

'So this is where you want me to live.'

'I don't care where you live.'

'Where would I walk the dogs?'

'By the river, I guess. Hudson River Park.'

He lay down on the bed in the far corner of the loft. It had a flowery green comforter on it. He looked like a dog lying in a field.

'Let's see how well we make love here. If the sex is good I'll
know it's the right loft for me.'

'That's what all my customers say.'

'Come here.'

I went over to him on the bed and sat on the edge of it. I
couldn't believe how much I wanted to fuck him. He took my
arm and started kissing the underside of it. The keys to the loft
were clenched in my fist. The first rule in real estate is never put
the keys down for any reason. He grabbed some flesh in his teeth
and bit down gently.

There is a photograph of me as a child. I'm about six and I'm
holding a tiger cub in my arms. The cub is almost as big as I am.
My hand is in its mouth, and I am laughing. On the back of the
photo my father wrote, 'Liv in love with a tiger, India.' I could-
n't recall ever having held a tiger. I couldn't remember being in
India but my father assures me I was and that it is really me
there in the photo, sitting on that bench, holding the baby tiger.
'You were brave,' my father told me. 'Braver than all the other
children.'

Andrew pulled me down and kissed my neck. He bit my ear.
'Stop it,' I said.

He bit down harder and harder. It was much harder than he
usually bit. It took me a moment to realize how seriously he was
biting me. I started to see white. I screamed but he covered my
mouth with his hand. I struggled and felt my ear tear. He bit
and sucked until I stopped moving and lay limp underneath
him. I imagined I was in India with buildings that looked like ice
cream sundaes and monkeys grabbing cans of Coca-Cola right
out of the hands of children in the streets. I imagined I was being
bitten by a tiger and that I was brave.

'You're bleeding,' Andrew said.

I stood and went into the bathroom. Blood was pouring down
my neck and my earlobe was dangling. My small diamond stud
was still in place in the dangling portion. I couldn't feel anything.

'I have to see a doctor,' I told Andrew. I grabbed a roll of paper
towels from the island counter in the kitchen and went around

turning off the lights and wiping blood off the floor. 'If you did one thing to hurt this loft, I'll kill you,' I said. There was blood on the comforter. I would have to come back later and try to get it cleaned before the owner saw it.

I opened the front door.

Andrew sat on the bed.

'Let's go,' I screamed.

Andrew jumped up, grabbed his bag, and followed me out. I locked the door with the keys I was holding and started to cross the street with Andrew following me.

'Where are we going?' he asked.

'You know what?' I said. 'You're an animal.' I finished crossing the street holding my ear onto my head. I couldn't feel anything there.

'I didn't mean to bite you that hard.'

'Get away from me,' I screamed behind me. 'Stop following me. Get away from me, you fucking . . .' I paused to think of the right word. He was still behind me. 'Nutjob!' I screamed.

I ran one block north on West Broadway and into the SoHo Animal Clinic.

The waiting room was tiny. I maneuvered myself past a small Asian woman holding the leash of an enormous Great Dane and a shepherd who seemed to be there by himself.

A young black man wearing round gold glasses sat behind the reception desk. There was a bulletin board behind him with Polaroids of dogs and cats and their names written in Magic Marker. Shakespeare. Hudson. Ladybug. Teddy. Puja.

'I've just been bit,' I said. My voice did not sound brave.

'Oh God, okay, just take a seat for one second, I'll get a doctor,' he said. He ran out from behind the desk and up a flight of stairs. I sat next to Andrew.

'Don't you think you should go to a doctor for humans?' Andrew said.

A woman in a white coat came down the stairs and looked at my ear. 'What have we got here,' she said. She was young with a brown ponytail.

'Come with me.' She led me into an examination room on the same floor as the waiting room. Andrew followed us in. 'Why don't you sit in the waiting room,' she told him.

The doctor helped me up onto the metal examining table and told me to lie on my side. She pulled on latex gloves, covering a diamond ring. She wiped blood gently off the side of my face. She put a blue ice pack on my ear. 'Do you know the dog who bit you?' she asked.

'Yes,' I said.

'Has it had all its shots?'

'Yes he has.'

'Did he bite you for a reason? Did you antagonize him?'

I nodded.

'Does he have a history of vicious behavior?'

'Yes.' I smiled.

'You must really love dogs if you can still smile after this. Is there any chance he has rabies?'

'I don't think so.'

'You don't think so or you're sure?'

'I'm sure,' I said.

'You're sure,' she said. 'What's the dog's name?'

'Andrew.'

'Andrew? That's too cute a name. Maybe they should rename him Tyson.'

'Maybe they should rename him Marv Albert,' I said.

The vet laughed. 'Do you know Andrew's owner?'

'Yes, I do.'

'And what's the owner's name?'

'Her name is Jordan,' I said.

'Okay, it sounds like you know her. I just have to check to make sure you know the owner well enough to know if her dog might have rabies. If Andrew does this again she might have to put him down. Have you had a tetanus shot recently?'

'I don't know,' I said. I was pretty sure I hadn't.

'I'm going to give you one.'

I felt like I was going to pass out.

'Roll over,' she said. I lay on my back.

'I'm going to stitch you up here,' she said. 'It won't be hard to reattach the lobe but the OR won't be ready for another ten minutes. This is going to hurt just a little.' She gave me the shot. I yelped a little bit.

'All done,' she said. 'I'm going to bring you upstairs now. Hold that on your ear.'

We walked out of the room and I saw Andrew and the Asian girl and the Great Dane. The shepherd was gone. I didn't say a word to Andrew.

He stood and started to follow.

'Stay,' the vet said.

Andrew stayed.

We walked up the stairs. I felt like I was floating.

'I'm afraid you're going to have to wait in here for just a few minutes. I should probably send you to Saint Vincent's but the ear should really be reattached as soon as possible.'

She walked me into a room lined with cages. Most were empty but there was a Dalmatian puppy yapping and pushing his face into the metal, one very groggy mutt, and three cats. She brought a folding chair into the room and told me to sit in it.

I stood up and stuck my fingers in the Dalmatian's cage. He chewed on them and barked.

'It's okay,' I told him. 'We're going to be fine. They're going to let us go home soon.'

The vet stitched my ear back on with black thread as if I were a rag doll. She gave me a small cup of orange juice and sent me downstairs with an enormous white bandage taped onto the side of my head and my diamond earring in a plastic baggie like another Clue piece. I wondered what my ear looked like under the bandage. Pointed like a Doberman's? Droopy like a basset hound's? Wrinkled like a shar-pei's? Long like a rabbit's?

'Stay away from that bad dog,' she said. I made the man at front desk give the bill to Andrew, who was still waiting. He wrote out a check.

The street was empty. I hadn't realized how late it had gotten. There wasn't any traffic on Canal Street. I stood trying to get a cab, ignoring Andrew.

'Come on, Liv, I'm sorry. I didn't mean to do that, you know that,' he said.

'You should be put to sleep,' I said. 'The vet said if it happened again you would have to be put down.'

'Let's go back to your place, and you can put me to sleep.'

'Andrew, I mean it, it's over. Get away from me.'

'I'm not leaving.'

'Leave me alone, Marv Albert.' There weren't any cabs. I felt dizzy and walked over to a building so I could lean against it for a minute.

'The vet told me to make sure you got something to eat. She's worried about your blood sugar level.'

I started to walk again and he walked right along beside me with his hand on the back of my neck. He did seem sorry. We walked along MacDougal Street, crossed Houston, and continued until we came to the Olive Tree Café. They were making a movie and the street was flooded with strange white light. Minetta Lane was crawling with crew members. Huge trailers vibrated.

'Let me buy you a hamburger. All of a sudden I have an immense craving for red meat. The least I can do is buy you dinner.'

I looked at Andrew standing there in his blue architect's shirt.

'Please, Liv.'

He looked nervous. I felt weak. Maybe a hamburger would give me the strength I needed to finally end it once and for all. I could explain to him that after this it would be impossible for me ever to see him again.

'We can go to the Olive Tree,' I said. 'It's right here.'

'So this is the restaurant you always go to, the Olive Tree? What is it, Middle Eastern?'

I looked up at the stained-glass Jewish star in the window. 'I think it's Israeli.'

'You're such a good Jewess.'

Maybe Andrew wasn't a mensch. 'What kind of restaurant did you think it was?' I said

'I thought you went to that Italian chain. The place with all-you-can-eat fettuccine Alfredo.'

'That's the Olive Garden,' I said. I felt insulted that Andrew pictured me eating bottomless bowls of cream sauce every day.

Andrew ordered us hamburgers. 'Liv, I'm sorry,' he said. 'I intended for us to have nice gentle sex, I didn't think it would end up with you getting stitches. If it makes you feel better, I'll take the loft. You'll get a commission. We can start over.'

'I'm not talking to you,' I said. 'And this isn't about a commission.'

'If you were a judge and you saw how cute your ears are, you would let me off scot-free.'

When I was a child my father and I used to play a game called 'Tell it to the Judge.' I sat on his desk wearing his bathrobe and my mother's white bathing cap, holding a yellow Fisher-Price mallet. 'Today I ate too much ice cream, Your Honor,' my father would say.

'Tell it to the judge,' I'd answer.

'But, Your Honor, you are the judge.'

'Oh, yeah,' I'd say, as if I had forgotten. 'Guilty!' I'd scream laughing.

'Your Incredible Beautiful Honor, I admit I love my daughter too much.'

'Tell it to the judge.'

'But you are the judge, remember?'

'Yes I am, and you are guilty, guilty, guilty as charged! I'm afraid you will be going to jail now, Daddy.'

'Your Honor, I'm having a terrible problem. I have to go to Paris for six weeks but I can't bear to leave my wonderful daughter. Who can I complain to about that?'

'Tell it to the judge. Hey, wait a minute, I am the judge. Guilty, guilty, guilty as charged!' I'd roar, banging my mallet and laughing.

'Admit it, Liv, you can hardly blame me,' Andrew said.

Two comedians sat in the booth behind us talking about how much they wanted to get out of comedy. They were like a couple of gangsters desperate to get out of the mob.

'Because of comedy I lost my marriage. Went into bankruptcy. Every night my kids beg me to promise that tonight I'll tell my last joke,' the older one of the two said.

'So what are you going to do if a deal comes along? I mean if they want you to be on *Make Me Laugh* you've gotta take it. You can't just tell them fuck you,' the younger one said.

'Why can't you ever just one time let me eat in peace without harassing me about my life,' the older one said. 'I was happy just sitting here for five minutes and now I have to go commit suicide down there you fuck.'

Once a waitress at the Comedy Cellar got to work early and hanged herself from a pipe on the ceiling.

I looked at the Charlie Chaplin movie playing on the screen across from our booth. Charlie Chaplin was trying to cut a giant leather shoe with a knife and fork on a plate in front of him.

28

CHELSEA/SEMINARY BLK —
PARLOR FL W/PVT GRDN

I met Storm Shapiro at Tea & Sympathy, a tiny English restaurant on Greenwich Avenue. I had a splitting headache and the idea of tea and a little sympathy sounded good.

The restaurant was the size of a garden shed. I got there before Storm and asked the grungy English waitress for the table by the window.

'You alone?' she asked.

'I'm meeting someone.'

'Outside with you then,' she said. 'Come back when you're both here.'

I stood outside and waited. I tried not to get my hopes up but I was certain that Storm was going to buy the Bank Street loft. I had sent her father all the financials and he faxed me a note saying that if Storm wanted it, it was 'okay by him.' And she did seem to want it. I had already called the owner and she had agreed to throw in the multicolored velvet chairs in the asking price. My cut of the commission would be sixteen thousand dollars. I really needed it. I needed the money enough to endure another lunch with Storm.

A little black girl, about nine or ten, wearing dark glasses, was being taught how to walk down the street with a white cane. She tapped it with a lot of style in her denim mini skirt and her hair tied into a pompom on top of her head. A young woman walked closely behind her, guiding her a little, showing her how to feel for the curb. The little girl walked confidently, jauntily. Tap tap tapping.

Storm arrived on foot. 'Oh, this place is soooo sweet,' she said. She was wearing her same awful striped shirt.

We went in and I asked for the table by the window.

'Oh all right,' the waitress said. 'Hey, what happened to you?' I hadn't done a very good job replacing the bandage that morning. It looked all lumpy and mangled.

'My boyfriend bit my ear off.'

'Oh, that's awful,' Storm said. 'You're kidding, right?'

'No, it's true,' I said.

'He bit your bloody ear off?' the English waitress said.

I nodded.

'You're missing an ear under there then?' She talked louder, as if I were deaf.

'No, I got it reattached.'

'What a prick,' she said. 'Ear-biting wanker.'

'It's just awful,' Storm said, as if it were the worst thing she had ever heard.

Storm and I sat at the tiny table.

'Listen, this is a table for four so if four people come in I'm going to have to move you,' the waitress said.

'Storm,' I said, 'I have great news.'

'What?' she said, hopefully.

'The owner has agreed to throw in the beautiful velvet chairs.'

'Oh, that's wonderful.' She had forgotten all about my ear. 'I'm so hungry,' she said, looking at the menu.

The waitress brought us pots of tea. Mine had a scene from *Romeo and Juliet* on it and hers was shaped like a monkey.

'These are so sweet,' Storm said.

'They are sweet,' I said.

'So sweet.'

'Sweet,' I said.

'Yours is sweeter.'

'Do you want to switch?' I asked, kidding.

'Okay,' she said. I gave her my *Romeo and Juliet* pot and took her monkey.

Two women walked into the restaurant with a small child. It was obviously a grandmother, mother, and daughter.

'I'm afraid you're going to have to move,' the waitress said nastily. 'I told you so.'

I picked up both of our pots and we moved to a table crowded in the middle. My head felt like it was going to split open. My ear was itching under the bandages.

'Do you have any aspirin?' I asked the waitress.

'You're not in hospital, dear, this is a restaurant, isn't it?' she said.

'So,' I said to Storm. 'What do you think? Do you think you want to live in this loft?' I said it with a certain serious wonderment like a salesgirl at Chanel.

'You know, Liv, you have the best job. I think I'd like to do what you do.'

I couldn't imagine Storm even saying the word 'job' let alone having one.

'Real estate agent,' she said, as if trying it on for size. 'I like that.'

The waitress brought me a shepherd's pie and Storm a bowl of dairy-free vegetarian soup. She hardly ever ate anything, which is why she always had horrible breath.

'So do you want your father to make an offer on the loft?'

'Yes,' she said, 'I'll call him and tell him to make an offer. I really want it.'

'That's great,' I said. 'I think you're making a smart decision.' I sat back in my chair, relieved.

'Can I see one of those little drawings of the loft so I can figure out where I'm going to put everything?'

'You mean a floor plan? Sure.' I took a xeroxed floor plan out of a folder in my bag and handed it to her. She looked at it. I wanted to go back to the office and call her father and start the ball rolling.

'It's kind of a funny shape, isn't it?' she said. I was really starting to despise her.

'It looks like a normal shape to me,' I said. It just looked like a long rectangle with an angled edge on one side, like the Citicorp building lying on its side.

'What's this pointy part?' she asked.

'That's the bedroom, remember? Where those great bookshelves are.'

'Oh,' she said, frowning. 'Doesn't it look a lot like a missile?'

'A missile?' I said.

'Isn't it sort of missile-shaped?'

I felt like I had a missile shooting through my forehead.

'That is definitely not missile-shaped,' I said. 'It's the shape of a beautiful loft.'

'Miss.' Storm called to the waitress. She came over. 'Do you think this drawing looks like a missile?'

'A what?'

'A missile, you know like from a submarine.'

'No,' the waitress said.

'I think it looks like a missile.'

The waitress stared hard at the floor plan. She turned it so that the angled part was facing upward. 'Oh, yeah yeah, I see what you mean now. It does sort of look like a miss-ile there, doesn't it?'

A group of four people came into the restaurant and stood near the door. The waitress went over to the two women and the little girl who were eating plates of cakes and finger sandwiches at our old table by the window 'You're going to have to switch tables,' she told them.

'What!' the old woman said in disbelief. 'We're in the middle of our meal.'

'Mom,' the other woman said. 'We'll just move.'

'That's ridiculous,' the old woman said. 'We're not going to move in the middle of our meal.'

'I'm afraid you're going to have to,' the waitress said. 'You're sitting at a table for four.'

'This little tiny table couldn't possibly be for four people. We practically have to hold our food on our laps as it is.'

'Look, you're going to have to move now.'

'Then we'll leave,' the old woman said.

'Fine,' the waitress said.

The little girl started to cry.

'Mom, you're upsetting Chloe. Why can't we just move to another table?'

'No!' the old lady said. 'We're leaving.'

She stood up, knocking over a cup of tea. The little girl was bawling.

'I don't think I could live in a loft shaped like a missile,' Storm said. I didn't think I could ever hate a client as much as Noah Bausch.

I paid the check, and Storm and I left the restaurant. Out on the street a pretty blond woman started to walk toward us. She was wearing a suit but she looked athletic, as if she had a tennis racket over her shoulder instead of a pocketbook.

'Jordan,' Storm said, stopping. 'Hi!'

I froze. It couldn't be Andrew's Jordan. This one was tall and wore a diamond engagement ring. She looked relaxed and content as if she had just had sex that morning.

'Storm, it's great to see you. You look great,' this Jordan said.

'Oh, you're sweet,' Storm said. 'Jordan, this is Liv, my real estate agent. I'm going to buy a loft if Liv can ever find me anything.'

'Oh, that's great,' Jordan said, completely ignoring me.

It was interesting that Storm had introduced me as her real estate agent instead of her friend even though we had been to countless parties together as children. I preferred it, though. I was glad that Storm realized there was some kind of business trying to happen between us. It was impossible to be someone's friend once you became their real estate agent even for five minutes.

I thought about Andrew in bed with this woman. It hadn't occurred to me before that Jordan could be beautiful. Where was the scowl I had imagined, and the frizzy gray hair? Her bag wasn't leather and her shoes were made of some new stretchy, micro-fiber material. I had to find out if this was the Jordan I had thought about for so many months. I considered asking her last name but then I remembered that Andrew had never told me Jordan's last name, all he had told me is that she was named after the Hemingway character.

'Jordan, that's a nice name,' I said.

'Thanks,' she said, enthusiastically.

'Were you named for the Hemingway character?'

'Yes, umm hmm,' she said, nodding her head sort of sympathetically as if I were a ladies' room attendant. 'My father is a Hemingway freak.'

Andrew had told me that Jordan's father collected first editions of famous American novels.

'Where do you two know each other from?' I asked.

'I know Jordan from New Haven,' Storm said. Storm never said the word 'Yale.' She always referred to it as New Haven or simply as Connecticut. It was her way of being modest. Andrew had never told me where Jordan went to school.

'If you don't mind my asking, what happened to you?' Jordan said. She was looking at my bandage.

'Her boyfriend bit her ear off,' Storm offered.

'Oh my God, you poor thing,' Jordan said. 'My fiancé can get quite overzealous sometimes, too. I'm going to have to tell him to be careful.'

Storm let out a fake squeal as if she had just then noticed the giant engagement ring. I couldn't picture Andrew buying anything that big.

'Same guy?' Storm squeaked.

'Same guy!' Jordan squeaked back.

'You've been living together for so long, I'm so happy he finally asked you.'

'What does he do?' I asked.

'He's an architect here in New York,' she said slowly.

I took a deep breath. 'Oh, what's his name?' I asked as casually as possible.

'His name?' Jordan said, curiously. 'It's Oren.' She said it as if she were embarrassed by it. 'Oren Mallis. Why do you ask?'

'Oh, no reason,' I said.

Jordan and Storm continued talking for a few minutes while I tried to relax. Suddenly New York seemed filled with potential Jordans. I finally excused myself and started to walk away. 'Don't worry,' I heard Jordan say, 'if she can't find you anything I know a really great broker from Halstead I can introduce you to.'

'Oh, would you do that?' Storm said. 'That's so sweet. I'd really appreciate that. I'm really desperate to find something.'

When I got home I found Andrew sitting on the front steps of my building holding a small plastic bag and a large square present of some sort badly wrapped in gold paper. He stood up.

'I can't see you anymore,' I said.

'I'm standing right in front of you, of course you can see me. You're not blind, are you?'

Suddenly I couldn't speak. I had no way to express to him how angry I was that he had bitten my ear off. I was blind. And my ear was bandaged. I was some kind of pathetic self-made Helen Keller. Helen Keller is alive and well and living on MacDougal Street, I thought. I felt like those three monkeys, one covering her eyes, one covering her ears, and one covering her mouth. I was one monkey, trying to cover all three, standing there in front of my own building.

'I think I have been blind,' I said.

'Well, then let's go on a blind date.'

'Every date with you is a blind date,' I said.

'I wanted to see how you're healing. Let's go upstairs,' he said

I shook my head no.

'Liv, I'm not going to hurt you. You're really acting like an idiot. He smiled at me and tried to take my hand.

'I can't see you now, Andrew, I have a date,' I said. I so clearly didn't have a date with that big bandage on the side of my head that I almost had to smile myself.

'Who is he?'

'He's from L.A. He's in New York every three weeks.'

'What does he do?'

I thought about telling him that he was the host of the television show *America's Funniest Home Videos* but I thought better of it. 'He's a television personality,' I said. 'I'd rather not say.'

I wished I had said he was a film producer of some sort who had taken a few things all the way to Sundance. It would have sounded more mysterious.

'I'll leave before he gets here. Come on, Liv, we have to talk.'

'No,' I said. 'I'm going upstairs without you.'

'I'll push my way in,' he said.

'Then I won't go up.' I sat on the steps and he sat down next to me. 'What's in the box?' I asked.

'I bought you a present. I'll show it to you upstairs.'

I grabbed the present out of his hands, ripped the paper off, lifted a green-and-white Official New York Jets football helmet out of the box. Least romantic I'm-sorry-I-bit-your-ear-off gift ever.

'What is this?' I asked as if I had never seen a football helmet before.

'What do you mean 'what is this'? I bought it so we can have sex again. You can wear it and then I won't be able to get at those delectable little ears. You'll be safe.'

'I won't be able to give you head through the mouth guard,' I said.

'I've already thought of that. You can take it off for that and then put it back on when we make love. It's the perfect solution.'

I was so mad I didn't know what to say. 'Grrrrrr,' I said, like some kind of angry animal.

'What was that?' he asked calmly.

'Grrrrrrr. Grrrrrrr.'

'Liv . . .'

'Grrrrrrr. Roar,' I growled at him. I was really acting insane. My animal sounds weren't even scary. They certainly weren't sexy, or even funny. They just came out sad.

'Liv, stop it. I brought you something else.'

He pulled out a pint of Häagen-Dazs and two plastic spoons from the bag. He peeled the lid off the ice cream and put it faceup on the step next to him. Then he took a spoonful and handed it to me.

I took a spoonful of ice cream and handed the container back to him. Vanilla Swiss Almond. We sat in silence, with the helmet between us, passing the pint back and forth and taking spoonfuls. It felt solemn, like a ceremony. I began to calm down. It was as if all I had needed all along was just a small kindness, a treat. I basked in the pleasure of it.

I had done it in bed with my husband from time to time. Passing the container back and forth, late at night, watching a video.

There was nothing wrong or dangerous about sharing a little ice cream with this man. There was nothing sarcastic, or hostile, or mean. It was somehow an equalizer. We were a couple like all couples before us, real and imagined, Beatrice and Benedick, Rhett and Scarlett, Beauty and the Beast, Diego and Frieda, Marv Albert and the woman who sued him for biting her.

Andrew put the empty container back in the plastic bag and handed me a paper napkin.

'Liv, I promise never to bite you that hard again.'

'You can never bite me again, period,' I said.

'Unless you die before me. Then I can take just a tiny morsel of cheek.'

He kissed my cheek gently. His lips were sticky.

I put on the helmet. It covered my eyes.

He kissed the top of it. 'I met Jordan today,' I said.

'Oh?' Andrew said, reining in his distress.

'She's getting married.'

'Don't kid around about Jordan, Liv.'

'Who's kidding?' I said. Then in one fast motion, like a star quarterback or whatever, I jumped up and managed the key in the front door and closed it behind me, before Andrew had a chance to go in for the tackle.

29
RAW SPACE

He buzzed and buzzed so finally I let him come upstairs. A relationship couldn't end with the terrible sound of buzzing. We lay in my bed. He had a headache even though I was the one still wearing the helmet.

I was nervous because it was four in the morning and he couldn't sleep. He had an eight o'clock breakfast meeting. As a woman, I took it as my personal responsibility to give him a good night's sleep. It must have been leftover from baby-sitting. Dating is a lot like babysitting, or having a pet. I wondered if he slept better with his girlfriend than he did with me.

'Liv.'

'Go to sleep, Andrew,' I said gently through the mouth guard.

'I love lying here with you.'

'I love it, too.'

'I sleep so soundly when I'm with you.'

I lay there silently not knowing what to make of that statement. In all the nights he had slept over he had gotten a total of about five minutes' sleep.

'Andrew, I don't think that's true. I don't think you sleep very well when you're here,' I said.

'I do,' he said. 'You relax me. I love sleeping with you. I love being with you. I love going out with you. I love fucking you. I love biting you.'

'I hate when you bite me.'

'No you don't, you love it.' He turned over and I ran my fingers over his back. I wished he would just go to sleep.

'Liv.'

'Go to sleep, Andrew,' I said.

'I'm not a good person.'

I sighed dramatically. Every man I have ever dated has told me that he is not a good person. At some point, as a last-ditch effort to get out of it, as they flail around in their minds trying to figure out a reason why they shouldn't get too involved, keeping their score cards and their lists of all the things that are wrong with you, they get the brilliant revelation that the solution lies within themselves, and they pull out a phrase like 'I'm not a good person.'

'I know you're not a good person,' I said. 'You're a man.'

'I'm serious, Liv.'

'I think you're a very good person,' I said. I would say it now, hoping we could both get some sleep, and worry if it was true later.

I wondered if Hitler had told Eva Braun, 'I'm not a good person,' when he was courting her and if she had assured him that he was.

'I'm not. I'm not worthy of you.' The sun was starting to come up. We were both aware of it. Some things just couldn't be stopped.

'Maybe you should tell your girlfriend about us. I think it will make you feel better,' I said.

'Maybe I should bite your ass.'

'If you bite me one more time, I'll call her and tell her about us,' I said.

He turned over and sat up. Then he straddled me and pinned my shoulders to the bed. 'If you *ever* call her and tell her about us,' he warned, 'I swear to God, I will have you killed.'

I let out a nervous laugh sound.

'You listen to me. If you ever upset her in any way, I will kill you. I may not do it myself, but I will have it done, and I will enjoy it just the same.'

'Well, this is a new low point,' I said.

In fact I considered this the lowest point of my dating career, including my divorce. And including having my ear bitten off. I lay flat on my back as he got up and got dressed. He brushed his teeth in the sink in the kitchen. I didn't say a word. I had never actually had my life threatened by a man before. There wasn't a chapter in *The Rules* entitled 'What to Do If Your Boyfriend Threatens to Have You Killed.'

He sat on the edge of the bed and leaned down to kiss my forehead. 'I'm going to the office to pick up something I need for the meeting. I'll call you later.'

He stood up. 'Bye,' he said.

I got out of bed so I could be careful to lock the door behind him. I watched him walk down the stairs in his low-riding jeans for what I decided would be the last time. I shut the door.

I sat on my couch and noticed the end of a white cable wire sticking out from the wall. I had lived here for months and never noticed the wires before. I started pulling. I pulled what seemed like miles of white and beige wires from the moldings, from the tops of doors, from along all the baseboards. It was like waking a thousand sleeping snakes. Staples flew out at me. The motion made me sick to my stomach. It just kept coming, longer and longer until it lay in a tangle on my living room floor. A coil of long intestines. A mountain of entrails. How had I lived there so long with those sickening wires? It would not have been long before they choked me like a boa constrictor.

I sat there thinking about the last thing I had read in Andrew's journal. *I told Liv that I was thinking of teaching an advanced architecture course at Columbia and she was extremely enthusiastic and said she thought I would be a great teacher and I should definitely do it. When we fucked she seemed especially turned on and called me Professor Lugar when she came. Of course this is a girl who considers watching a Woody Allen movie foreplay. I think I will tell her that I took*

the job and make up little stories about my students to titillate her.
Anyway she's a good little cheerleader.

Of everything I had read in his sloppy, tight, psycho handwriting, the sentence 'anyway she's a good little cheerleader' was the worst. I didn't want to be a cheerleader for Andrew or anyone. I hadn't called him Professor Lugar when I came. We hadn't even had sex that day.

I couldn't go on like this. I decided to call Jordan and tell her everything. I would call her and ask her to meet me for lunch. I wondered if she would know the minute she saw me that I was having sex with Andrew.

I remembered hearing a woman on TV talk about how she had gone to the airport to pick up her husband. She stood in the small crowd waiting for the plane to land when she spotted a beautiful woman standing there. That woman is sleeping with my husband, she thought suddenly, even though she had never suspected her husband of infidelity before. Just then her husband walked over to the other woman and greeted her passionately. 'I don't know why, I just knew that woman had been with him,' she had said.

I thought about Jordan knowing I was sleeping with Andrew. Maybe she wouldn't care. Maybe she would like me and we would drink sake and talk and laugh about him. I could find out if she really did have a lump in her breast. We could comfort each other. Maybe I would like Jordan. Maybe I would understand why Andrew couldn't leave her.

I picked up my phone but it no longer worked.

Maybe it was a sign I should go to the Upper West Side and ring her doorbell. I got dressed and put on velvet shoes instead of leather out of respect for Jordan because she was a vegetarian.

I walked down the street carrying the Tiffany shopping bag with the beehive honey pot in its light blue box with the white ribbon that I had bought for Andrew's mother. I could give it to Jordan as a house gift.

I have balls, I thought, surprising myself. I laughed out loud. I remembered the dream I had in my few minutes of sleep the night before. I was a dog, a brown boxer following a man on a sandy beach. I was a male dog with rather large balls that I think I was embarrassed about. My balls swung back and forth between my hind legs. I could almost still feel them there like ghost balls.

I stood on the corner of MacDougal Street trying to get a cab. MacDougal Street was dead. There were no cabs or cars. I turned to look down Bleecker Street when I thought I saw Andrew, talking on a cellular phone, turn the corner of the next block. I started to walk, almost run, in his direction to see if it was really him. Why was I doing this? I wondered. It couldn't have been Andrew, and who cared if it was? He couldn't really have been serious about having me killed. I stopped to catch my breath in the middle of the sidewalk.

I started to cross the street when a crazy bike messenger came speeding toward me.

There is a new sport in New York that the bicycle messengers love to play. They come right at you at full speed as you stand in the middle of the street mesmerized by fear. The messenger locks eyes with you. Just as they are about to hit you head-on they curse at you and swerve, just barely missing you. It is impossible to get out of their way – if you move one way or the other you could be hit. You are so panicked you stand like a statue for several minutes after the incident, until some stranger gives you a shove to help you snap out of it.

'That crazy a-hole was trying to kill you,' an Indian man said, touching my shoulder. 'Did you ever eat at Rose of India on Sixth Street?' He was holding a toilet plunger.

Rose of India? Pink and red lights, mirrors. I nodded slightly.

'I remember you,' he said. 'Chicken tikka masala.'

'I remember you, too,' I said dreamily. I walked over to a building and leaned against it.

'Do you need a doctor?' the Indian man said.

'I'm a doctor,' a man said, stopping. He took my chin in his hands and looked into my eyes. 'Who did these stitches?' he asked, looking at my ear.

'A vet,' I said.

'Nice job,' he said. 'Military doctors are usually very well trained.

After the attack of a bike messenger you usually have to cancel your plans for the day and go home and rest. I decided not to visit Jordan. I'd had enough excitement for one day.

I told the doctor and the Indian waiter I was fine and walked down the street past the theatrical costume store called Mayhem. Its windows were filled with rubber heads and bloody neck stumps and scarred body parts. I had only caught glimpses of it because every time I passed it, I forced myself to look the other way.

When I got home I opened my refrigerator to get a sweater and I suddenly remembered that I had never gotten around to cleaning out the freezer. I pulled the freezer door open and took out the warm ice cube tray. The tray was empty except for one dried, yellowish puddle where an ice cube should have been.

Once when Andrew was complaining after sex that he was in a high-risk category for a heart attack I decided to freeze his sperm in case he died before I could have his baby. I had emptied the contents of a come-filled condom into the ice cube tray. I had forgotten about the Spermcicle. I threw it in the garbage.

30
DOWNING ST — PNTHSE SANCTUARY

The next weekend was Andrew's birthday, and we were supposed to spend it together. We had planned it ages ago and I thought I might as well keep the date so we could talk. I called and made a half-hearted reservation for Saturday night at the River Café. 'Yes, for two.' I wished I hadn't had my phone restored. 'Yes, nonsmoking,' I told the 'reservationist,' which is what she called herself. I used my father's name. 'By the window, Miss Kellerman?' she offered. 'I guess,' I said. I already had a bad feeling, as Violet would say. Andrew was going to cancel.

Saturday night he called me from a pay phone. 'I can't get away,' he said.

'But I was taking you to the River Café to celebrate your birthday and all the deals I've done this month.'

'I can't get away. It's complicated.'

'But I have a cake for you,' I lied. I hadn't bothered with a cake. 'And a present.' I hadn't bothered with that, either.

'Oh, honey, what did you get me?'

'Fifty jazz CDs,' I said, recklessly.

'Oh my God, honey!' he said. 'That's too much.'

'What did Jordan get you?'

'She got me really nice sneakers.' His voice sounded funny.

'Sneakers! What kind of a gift is that?'

'Can I call you later?' he said.

'Yeah, you probably want to try out those sneakers and run away. Happy birthday,' I said and hung up.

On Monday babies in strollers kept looking at me and clapping. It was unnerving, all those big eyes focused on me, tiny hands cheering me on. 'If you're happy and you know it, clap your hands,' one little girl said, furiously, straining against the stroller's seat belt. It was a sign.

I was certain there was only one thing to do. I must never see Andrew again. I went to the office and e-mailed him: Andrew, Please don't contact me again for any reason – Liv.

He called a few minutes later.

'Did you get my e-mail?' I asked.

'Yes, I did.'

'Then why are you calling me?'

'We're going to get married. We're going to have the perfect marriage,' he said.

'Andrew, my idea of a perfect marriage is twin headstones side by side in a cemetery.'

'We're going to have that, Liv. We'll be buried together. Well, I'll probably get there first. But then you'll join me.'

I pictured myself standing over Andrew's grave. I pictured our headstones Andrew Lugar and Liv Lugar. I didn't want the last name Lugar.

Whenever I went to a cemetery I always looked jealously at the names on the tombstones. Michael Rafter and Helen Rafter, James Totheroh and Ada Totheroh, Max Block and Jennie Block, names in stone beside each other forever. That was my idea of commitment. That was marriage. After years of fighting and infidelity, sexlessness and dirty looks, you could end up together in a dignified manner.

'Will Jordan be buried between us?' I asked.

'We'll get a nice plot somewhere.'

'Did you know you have to be a licensed real estate agent to sell burial plots?' I said for no reason.

'No, I didn't know that.'

'I don't want you to call me again,' I said.

He was silent on the other end of the phone. 'All right,' he said gravely. 'I can't fight with you anymore. If that's what you want.' He hung up. It was really over.

I sat in my armless desk chair, stunned.

I wondered if when I died they could find a nice single tombstone to bury me next to. I wanted to be buried next to someone even if I didn't know the person. I could take his name. No one would know we hadn't been married in life.

I was already beginning to miss Andrew. I felt his final words to me in my solar plexus. I felt my stomach fill up with tears.

I let out a single sob just as Kim walked by my desk on one of her rare Nurse Ratched rounds.

'Bad deal?' she asked.

'Very bad deal,' I said.

'What property?' she asked. My heart, that's what property, I thought. My heart felt like a Hell's Kitchen tenement building under demolition. Hit by the swinging ball.

'It's not about real estate, Kim,' I said. 'Not everything's about real estate.'

'I have to disagree with you there, Liv. It's my experience that everything's about real estate.'

All week I wondered what Andrew was doing. I wondered if he was thinking about me and missing me. He didn't call, and it was better that way. Now I could meet someone new. I knew I probably wouldn't meet anyone new that week, however, so I let myself go a little bit. I drank hot chocolates with whipped cream every night at the Olive Tree. 'Keep them coming,' I told the waitress. She just giggled as if she were embarrassed for me.

'Can I tell you something?' she said. '*He* really likes you.' She pointed at someone behind me. I turned around slowly to see the cook who was right at that moment hacking away at the rotating shawarma. It looked like someone had hacked at his face. It was scarred and pockmarked. I had eaten there every day for months and never once looked at him. He was hideous.

I turned back to the waitress and just shook my head no.

'I know,' she said. 'But he's really nice. I guess I'll have to tell him.' She cleared my empty cup. ' 'Nother one?' she asked. I nodded.

I was insulted that the waitress could even think of such a thing. Were those my only choices? Andrew the wild dog-man or the elephant-man cook at the Olive Tree?

I cried in my apartment. Not over Andrew exactly. Fuck Andrew. More over the fact that I was alone, nobody loved me, nobody would ever love me, my ear was disfigured, I was a failure. All I did was show apartments for a living. I helped rich, happy people get richer and happier. I watched couples kissing, the man saying, 'Is this the place you want?' and the woman saying, 'Oh it is, darling, it really is.' I actually had to watch a man carry a woman over the threshold of a triplex in the Silk Building. It was too much to bear.

I lay in bed listening to the gobble gobble moaning sounds of the pigeons out my air shaft window. The window that must never be opened. They were so loud it was hard to believe the noises were coming from their round gray bodies. They sounded more like turkeys, or cows. Every morning I woke up to the terrifying flurry of feathers hitting brick There was nothing more depressing than the pigeons. Nothing made me feel lonelier. It was like hearing my parents fighting late at night or hearing strangers having sex through thin hotel walls.

Friday came, and I didn't want to face another weekend alone. I showed the Bausches a half-dozen more lofts I knew they wouldn't buy. I couldn't stop showing them things. I was addicted to listening to the different reasons why every loft was wrong. We saw one in Sandra Bernhard's building, one in Edward Albee's building, one in Isabella Rossellini's building, one in Susan Sarandon's building, one in Sarah Jessica Parker's building, and one in a building where nobody famous lived.

'Who lives here?' Noah Bausch asked.

'No one,' I said.

He frowned and thought for a moment. 'I guess that's not important,' he said, as if he had just found spirituality.

'But Robert De Niro lives across the street if that makes you feel better,' I said. He looked like it did.

The bathroom walls were lined with hundreds of colorful nightlights plugged into hundreds of electrical sockets. The Virgin Mary, Little Orphan Annie, the Statue of Liberty, Garfield, Snoopy, Tweety Bird, the Mona Lisa, Mickey Mouse.

'Liv, there's something we want to ask you. It's personal,' Noah Bausch said. I followed him out of the bathroom. I had learned never to lead a customer around an apartment, always to follow as if I were a guest in his (new) home.

Audrey came over with three-year-old Flannery. 'Why don't we all sit down,' she said, as if we were in her living room and not someone else's apartment that they had no intention of buying.

I wondered if they were going to tell me that they had decided to buy an apartment with another broker. I knew they were looking with brokers all over town. It would be a relief actually, never having to see them again. It was sort of comforting, though, showing them apartments month after month and knowing they would never make an offer. At least I never had to get my hopes up the way I did with everyone else.

We walked over to the two huge sofas facing each other, two white whales on the blue-green carpet. The Bausch family sat on one and I sat on the other. There they were, Dumb and Dumber. She was Dumb, but he was Dumber

They looked nervous. She had dark circles under her eyes worse than anybody, and his goatee was jagged. Flannery, the baby, had a flat face like a wooden Russian matryoshka doll. I wanted to open her and see if there was a smaller baby inside and an even smaller baby inside that one. Flannery went into the open kitchen and tried to swing from the handles of the Sub-zero refrigerator.

'Well, there's no way to make this easy. We might as well just say it,' Dumb said.

'What is it?' I asked. I was enjoying the drama of it.

'Liv,' Dumber said, 'Audrey and I like you very much and we were wondering if . . .' He stopped. I wondered if they were going to ask me to swing with them.

'We want you to consider donating your eggs for an in vitro fertilization procedure,' Audrey said, quickly. She took a deep breath as if she were in a Lamaze class.

I sat there unable to say anything. I had never thought about my eggs. I didn't want to think about them. The little girl smiled at me and clapped.

'You don't have to give us an answer now,' she said.

'We know it's a big decision. We would compensate you, of course,' he said.

'Of course,' I agreed.

'We're born with all of our eggs, if you can believe that,' Audrey said. She looked at her tiny daughter. 'Flannery's filled up with all her eggs, aren't you, sweetie, and once she starts menstruating she'll lose one every month until menopause,' she said in baby talk.

'Well, that's not for a while,' I said.

'You would undergo a series of injections,' she said. I didn't like the word 'undergo' or the word 'injections.' 'Then your eggs would be extracted and fertilized by Noah's sperm.' I put up my hand as if to stop her. I suddenly felt like I was going to throw up. 'Then they would be placed in *my* womb.'

My eggs in Audrey Bausch's womb. This was taking the term 'full-service broker' a step too far. 'So it would be half mine,' I said. I didn't want my half named anything like Flannery.

'And half Noah's,' she said quickly. 'But I would carry the baby. Or *babies*, as the case may be.' She had egg-sized circles under her eyes.

Why didn't they just adopt me? I wondered. I spent so much

time with them we might as well be a family. It was like Daddy Warbucks wanting Little Orphan Annie's eggs, instead of Little Orphan Annie.

But I had to admit I was slightly flattered. I suddenly felt rich. I was richer than the Bausches with my beautiful golden eggs. They were in a basket somewhere inside me, brightly painted and sitting on shredded green paper. I could give one to the Bausches or keep it for myself and scramble it up later for dinner.

You'd have to think someone was really smart and beautiful to want her eggs. 'Why me?' I asked, egging them on.

'We think you look a lot like Audrey,' Noah said. 'So we think the baby would look just like her, and like Flannery.'

I had never been so insulted in my entire life. I looked nothing like Audrey Bausch. My eyes, even after nights of crying, were wide awake-looking and sparkly. 'That's so nice,' I said. 'Thank you.'

'So what do you think, Liv?' Noah asked, as if I was the one apartment hunting for a place to house my egg.

'Well, it's certainly something to consider,' I said. 'So what do *you* think?'

'About what?' Noah said.

'About this loft,' I said.

'We would need to have an architect come look at it.' Their friend who was an architect finally stopped returning their phone calls because he got so tired of looking at dozens of apartments with them. 'Do you know a good one?'

'No.' But then I thought maybe I did.

I went home and called Andrew.

'I'm calling because that couple I hate, the Bausches, need an architect,' I said.

'Really,' he said. It was intensely infuriating the way it always is when you call a man you shouldn't be calling.

'Yes, really,' I said.

'Well, I'm flattered that with all the architects you know, you called me.' I knew he was smiling. I suddenly missed Andrew so much my heart felt like a claw-foot tub about to fall.

'I miss you,' I said.

'I've missed you, too,' he told me.

'What did you do this week?' I asked.

'Nothing.'

'You must have done something.'

'I went away for a few days.'

My blood started to boil. 'Where?' I asked.

'Just to Vermont with friends.'

'What friends?' I asked. The word 'friends' sounded unfriendly in his mouth.

'Just some friends you don't know,' he said.

'Was it fun?'

'It was fun. Really fun, actually. I flew a kite. I hadn't done that since I was a kid. It was life-affirming, running on a grassy field trying to catch the wind.'

I couldn't believe that while I was suffering all week Andrew was gleefully flying a kite.

'What did the kite look like?' I asked. I couldn't picture a kite, for some reason. I was having trouble remembering what a kite was exactly.

'It was a great kite,' Andrew said. 'A bright blue diamond. The perfect kite.' The way he said it, you'd think he had flown his own private jet.

I had pictured him locked in his study, fighting with Jordan, punching a wall. I couldn't stand the thought of him flying that kite. I had never been angrier. If I were a kite at that moment, I would have been shaped like a fire-breathing dragon.

I took my gun off my bedside table, handling it roughly. I was getting more used to holding it now; it was starting to feel smaller and lighter in my hands. At this moment it looked almost like a toy little Flannery would play with. I opened the chamber. It worked almost like a stapler with a spring inside it. I pulled at the handle and a part I had never seen before slid out. It was the part that held the bullets. They were silver with copper tops and had *Speer 9mm* engraved in tiny letters on each one. They were lined up like eggs in an egg crate. My Glock still had all fifteen of her eggs intact.

Suddenly there was something I wanted to tell Andrew but I couldn't remember what it was.

'There was something I wanted to say,' I said.

'What is it?'

'I don't know. It's right on the tip of my tongue.'

'The only thing that should be on the tip of your tongue is my cock.'

Then I remembered.

'Hey, Andrew,' I said. 'Go fly a kite.' I hung up.

31
NO FEE

I have a great loft I can show you,' I told Storm. It was all the way down on Duane Street between Greenwich and Hudson. We would have to take a cab. I had shown her five lofts that day already. I hailed a cab, opened the door, and got in after her. I leaned forward to give the driver the address.

'Duane Street between Greenwich and Husband.'

I realized what I had said.

Storm cackled. 'Husband Street. Husband Street,' she laughed. My head was spinning.

We didn't say a word for the rest of the trip.

I couldn't believe I was paying for yet another cab.

'Make a left on Duane,' I told the driver. 'A left on Duane,' I said again. 'Left on Duane. On Duane, you make a left. Okay, this is Duane. Here's Duane. Duane. Duane.' I watched the Duane Street sign go by. 'You passed Duane,' I screamed. 'Stop!'

The driver stopped.

No tip, I decided. I threw a few wadded-up singles at him and flung the door open.

'I'm sorry,' he said. He was Indian. 'I saw "Dune" Street. "Dune." "Dune." "Doon' Street. I did not see 'Duane.'" His brow was furrowed and he looked like a philosopher struggling with one of the mysteries of the universe. He looked gentle and kind, like an Indian Santa Claus. My eyes filled with tears. What had I done? He could be a swami, performing his *seva*. I got out and fumbled with my wallet trying to find a tip but he drove off. I felt like dropping to my knees and praying for forgiveness. No one could read a word like Duane. It was an impossible word. The world was cruel enough without me storming all over New York making things worse. That's what I had been doing lately, I realized, storming. I felt like it was Storm's fault.

As soon as we got into the loft Storm saw a problem with it.

'What is it?' I asked in my best real estate tone, ready to deflect any problem like a narcissist's mirror.

The best way to solve a buyer's problem was to stand back and let him solve the problem himself. It takes him by surprise and forces him to sell the place to himself. He realizes how much he wants it. He talks himself into it.

I always let the clients argue with themselves. If a client says there's no supermarket nearby, the worst thing you can do is start saying that there's a D'Agostino's not that far away and it has twenty-four-hour delivery, because then they argue right back at you. It's always better to say, 'You're right, there really is no supermarket nearby.' Then the client says, 'Well, there's a D'Agostino's and it's really not that far away and I can always have them deliver.' It gives them the benefit of being right and you the benefit of not being pushy.

'There's nowhere for my dining room table,' Storm said. Storm's dining room table had become the bane of my existence. I would have liked to set it on fire. It was an enormous gothic monstrosity that New York had no room for. Dining room tables are one of the biggest problems a New York real estate broker has to deal with.

'You're right, Storm, there really is no place for you to put that gigantic table.'

I had watched many couples come to terms with the fact that they were going to have to part with their dining room table. I waited patiently for Storm to part with hers.

Storm walked to the front door. 'Then let's get out of here,' she said.

We got out of our seventh cab on West Fourth Street right in front of the Pink Pussycat Boutique, a sex shop in the Village. I had bought a cupless bra there once to wear for my husband. She leaned against the store's window and a pink neon glow surrounded her.

'I've decided on the place I want,' Storm said.

I thought about all the lofts I had shown her. The only one she had liked was the one shaped like a missile.

'That's fantastic,' I said. 'Which one?'

'It's in the Dakota. You didn't show it to me.' My heart sank. All that time spent with her for nothing. I had even found myself starting to sound a little like her, saying, 'You're sweet,' and things like that. No commission in the world was worth that.

'Yes, I know I didn't show it to you. I don't show apartments in the Dakota.'

'Why not?'

'Well, they tend to be a little bit . . .' I thought of any number of words I could use. Run-down. Rickety. Decrepit. Disappointing. Slummish. I decided to use the one I thought she would hate the most. 'Overpriced.'

'Do you think so?' she asked, concerned.

'Yes I do, but that's beside the point. The important thing is that you'll be happy living there.'

'You're not mad that you won't be getting any commission?'

'No, Storm, of course I'm not mad. We're friends. All that matters is that you buy the right place. I have to say I'm a little surprised, though. I thought you had your heart set on a spacious glamorous chic downtown loft, not a decrepit, crumbling, overpriced apartment on the sleepy Upper West Side. I have a fantastic listing in the Apthorp. If I had known that's what you were looking for I could have shown you dozens of places like that,' I said.

I had explained to Storm a thousand times the concept of 'co-broking.' I could have shown her the Dakota apartment by simply calling the broker whose listing it was and making the appointment with her. We would have shared the commission.

'Well, the Dakota is New York's first luxury apartment building,' she said. I could tell she was parroting the other broker. 'I just saw it and it was so sweet and it had a beautiful velvet sofa in the living room and it has an amazing FDR, you know formal *dining room*.' I hated her so much I wished I had brought my gun. I could take it out and see if she thought getting shot in the head was sweet. I hated her more than I ever hated my husband.

She pulled out a floor plan. The other broker's business card was stapled to the corner of it. 'She's really sweet,' Storm said, pointing to the broker's name.

I looked at the drawing of the expensive three-bedroom apartment. It was L-shaped. 'Don't you think it's shaped a little bit like a gun?' I asked.

'Oh, I like that idea,' she said. 'It makes me feel safe.'

Behind her, dildos and vibrators made a funny halo around her head. Two inflatable sheep and several life-size blow-up women hung from the ceiling. Tiny red light bulbs blinked on and off.

'Liv,' she said, 'I'm sorry.'

'Oh, don't be,' I said.

Like being dumped.

The night I left my husband I lay awake in bed thinking about Yoko Ono. I thought about her lying in bed all alone at the Dakota after having her husband ripped from her. Every time I passed the Dakota I thought of her in there. I loved the Dakota. Now I would have to think of Storm in there making pasta with Parmesan cheese she stole from some restaurant. The Dakota was ruined. Now, even John Lennon's ghost would avoid it like the plague.

'Anyway, Storm, I'm happy for you.'

'You are?' she said. 'That's sweet.'

'But do you know why the Dakota was named the Dakota? Because when it was built it was so far uptown in nowheresville that everyone made fun of it and said you might as well live in

Dakota. If you wanted to visit someone there you had to make a day of it,' I added.

I left Storm standing there and got into another cab. It headed up Sixth Avenue, the sun beating down on my face through the window. I closed my eyes. What difference did it make if my eyes were open or closed? I only saw what I wanted to see. I knew everything I was passing by heart anyway. The buildings, the people, the brown high heels, briefcases, streetlights, signs – who really cared? What was the difference, really, if I was blind or if I could see?

'We're here,' the driver said. 'Okay. Here we are. Time to get out. Up and at 'em.'

I opened my eyes. It was raining. With my eyes closed it had been sunny, I had been better off. I crossed Central Park West so I could get a better look at the Dakota. I sat on a stone bench facing it. I took off my shoes and folded my legs into a half-lotus position. I wanted to say one last goodbye to the Dakota before Storm and her table got there.

I wanted things to be the way they used to be. The way they were before I went into real estate and New York was somehow cheapened for me. When the buildings were my friends, not to be bought and sold like slaves. Before I was forced to see too many insides of too many apartments. *TMI*, as my husband used to say. *Too much information*. I suddenly had an urge to call my ex-husband. Hearing his robust, unwavering voice might make me feel a little better.

I wanted him to walk by. To stand before me flattened and all shot up with holes like a slice of Swiss cheese. His coat smelling the same like airplane air-conditioning. With his usual William Hurt grimace on his face.

I wanted him to see me as a real estate agent. I wanted him to see me working. Once he had screamed at me, 'All you do all day is get manicures. You don't work!' I went right out and had 'F,' 'U,' 'C,' and 'K' painted in bright red glittery polish on four of the nails on my right hand, and 'Y,' 'O,' 'U,' and '!' painted on four of the nails on my left.

No, I would not call him. Losing a thirty-thousand-dollar commission was enough for one day. I didn't also have to lose my pride.

Night came and I sat on the cold bench shivering. The fat doorman gave me a little wave. I gave him a little wave back.

32
MONTAGUE ST

I went to the Olive Tree. I saw the cook who liked me. He was standing in his usual place in the open kitchen at the front of the restaurant. I hesitated. 'Hello,' I said, coolly.

He looked at me, startled. 'How are you?' he said. His eyes squinted under his backward baseball cap.

I nodded at him and took a seat in the back. His words stayed in my mind. 'How are you?' They washed over me. At this moment he probably cared more about me than anybody I knew. Even though I had rejected him so meanly, he still cared how I was. He was noble in his rejection. He was like a great swami graciously forgiving his most ignorant student. The waitress brought me a small plate of tabbouleh.

'This is on Frank,' she said.

I looked over at the cook but he put his head down shyly. I wanted to kneel in front of the table and pray, not sit at it and eat.

That night I dreamed that Woody Allen invited Andrew to his Country house but not me. 'Men only,' Woody said. I got to watch them through the window, sitting in armchairs in a pan-eled library, smoking cigars. I woke up so jealous I could hardly breathe. What are you jealous of? I said to myself. It was only a dream.

A bad dream was almost more than I could take most mornings. Every morning I woke up in a state of perpetual shock. I was not in bed with my husband. I was alone. I was not in eight rooms on Fifth Avenue. I was not in our old sleigh bed with the rising egg-yolk sun frying in the sky outside our greenhouse windows. I was alone on MacDougal Street thinking that if I flailed my arms and legs violently enough they might somehow get entangled in his again. He might climb on top of me for morning-hard-on sex. He might bring me a cup of Earl Grey. Every day I sat straight up in bed and rubbed my eyes with my fists like a bad actor indicating morning.

Every morning I woke up and started thinking about something I had done wrong. Once I had left the living room windows open a crack during a snowstorm when my husband had been away on business. He had called to remind me to close them but I hadn't. I went to sleep and in the morning found the living room filled with snow. The super had to come with a shovel.

I thought of the first dream I had in my MacDougal Street apartment. Jack had come home to me from a long journey. 'I'm back,' he said. 'How did you like it?' I asked him. 'I had a good time except for the crabs. There were too many crabs,' he said. At his feet was a pile of dried dead crabs. I swept them up with a broom.

The phone rang, and I sat up suddenly. It was Violet asking me to have brunch with her. 'Did I wake you?' she asked.

'No,' I said, excitedly, and told her my Woody Allen dream. People do not care about your dreams.

'Who cares about Woody Allen?' she said.

'The only thing that keeps me from committing suicide is not wanting to miss the next Woody Allen movie,' I said.

'Well, that doesn't say much for our friendship,' she said.

When I got up to pee I discovered that I had my period. My monthly egg had not been fertilized, Audrey Bausch would be interested to know. I sat on the toilet and cried.

I took a shower and washed my hair, coaxing the last drop of conditioner from the bottle like a porn star.

I met Violet in a restaurant she suggested in Chelsea. I got there first and sat at a table next to a window. Outside a dog was shitting as his owner stood behind him wearing a bag as a glove. To the owner's surprise, a green plastic cake decoration in the shape of a four-leaf clover that said, Happy St. Patrick's Day!' slid out of the dog's ass and stood upright on top of the pile of shit. The owner looked down at if in disbelief. Then he bent down and scooped the whole thing up with the bag.

I laughed and looked around to see if anyone else had noticed it. If I had been in a restaurant in Tokyo I wouldn't have been more of a minority. Men surrounded me in couples. They all looked so at ease and happy, kissing each other, waving, smiling. I couldn't think of a worse place to be. Why had Violet wanted to meet in hell? I wondered. I sat there bleeding, aware of the Tampax Super Plus inside me.

'Can I get you anything else?' the waiter asked the couple at the next table, completely ignoring me. He was wearing a pink apron tied around his slim waist. 'Hey, I felt that!' he said, putting his hand on his ass. He turned to two couples sitting at a table for four behind him. 'Never do that again.'

'John, did you pinch him?' one of the men at the table said.

'I couldn't help myself,' John said. He was big and fat with a receding hairline and a black mustache.

'I hate being touched,' the waiter said. 'Don't ever touch me. I am so serious about this.' He cleared their dishes and slinked away.

'Warren, don't forget your meds,' John said. The man sitting next to him took out a plastic baggie filled with dozens of different-colored pills. He swallowed them with three gulps of water.

Violet arrived with a *Time Out* magazine under her arm. I had a feeling she was going to try to talk me into calling a personal ad.

'I have the greatest idea,' she said. She opened to the personals. 'We're each going to answer one,' she said. I hated my clichéd life.

'No,' I said.

She started to tear out the personal ads, making little piles of them on the table. She saw the empty plastic baggie on the table next to us, which had held the man's meds. 'Can I borrow that?' she asked. She put the personal ad scraps in it and shook. 'Pick,' she said.

I reached in and took one. His headline said COME DRIVE WITH ME. *SWM, smart, goodlooking (really) ISO beaut, smart, 5'3+, funny, happy SWF for roadtrips and more. Valid Driver's License req'd.*

'Perfect,' she said.

'But, Violet,' I said, 'I don't know how to drive.'

'You picked him,' she said, as if I always had a knack for choosing the wrong men. As if I had *attracted* the wrong personal ad into my life.

'We're too old for this,' I said. 'We're too old to pretend we don't see how flawed all these guys really are. They're all so . . . flawed.'

They were as dishonest as real estate ads. You never saw a personal ad that said *short, cheap, bald, hates women and sex.* You never saw a real estate ad that said *dark shithole, rats, roaches, low ceils, high maint.*

Violet read all the headlines of the personal ads. Mr. Right. Handsome Physician. Affectionate Animal Lover. Professional Black Male. Prince Charming. She picked him. 'Prince Charming wasn't flawed,' Violet said.

'I'm sure he was flawed,' I said. 'Cinderella was just too young and accepting to see it. If Cinderella had dragged herself to the ball at twenty-six she would have seen that he's a closet fag with a shoe fetish, an entitlement complex, and obsessive-compulsive disorder – going from foot to foot like that, living at home with his parents. Even his name. *Prince Charming.* So gay. Prince Charming is beginning to make *Andrew* look good.'

'You have to call Mr. Roadtrip Guy. You picked him,' Violet

That night I called his box number and left a message. He called me back. We talked for two hours. He didn't mind that I was only 5'2". He didn't mind that I wasn't happy. I told him my dream about Woody Allen and my dream about my husband and the crabs. I really liked him. We made a plan to meet.

'I guess I should tell you,' I said, 'that I don't know how to drive.'

'You're kidding,' he said.

I laughed. 'No, when we go on our roadtrips you'll have to do the driving.' I caught a look at myself in the mirror. I was smiling. I had that embarrassingly intense concentrated look you have when you talk to a man you like for the first few times on the phone.

'Well, I'm sorry, Liv, but I'm afraid it's not going to work out.'

I laughed again.

'I think women who don't know how to drive are despicable. I think you want a man to take care of you while you sit around and get manicures and pedicures and waxing and massages and do nothing. You want to remain a child. But you're not a child, are you?'

'No,' I mumbled.

'No, you're not a child. You're a divorced twenty-six-year-old woman, if you're even telling me the truth about that. For all I know you're really thirty-six.'

His words were so forceful for a moment I wondered if I really was thirty-six, but then I realized that no, I was still twenty-six after all.

'You're the type of girl who doesn't want to take care of herself,' he continued 'You just want to sit around the spa getting waxes all day.'

That was the second time he'd mentioned getting waxed. I felt like I'd accidentally called my husband instead of this guy. I was always being accused of a terrible crime – good cuticle maintenance. If a man wanted to accuse you of this there was nothing you could do. All the deals in the world couldn't change that. Then next time I went on a date I'd have to wear my Transitions First Deal ribbon on my lapel. It was especially frustrating considering, with one phone call to my father, I could

spend the next two weeks getting massaged at Canyon Ranch
instead of showing the Bausches apartments .

'You're the third woman who's called without a license. Oh
and by the way, girlie, no, I'm not going to teach you. Do yourself
a favor. Learn how to drive.' He hung up. A regular Prince
Charming.

I wanted to kill Violet.

I sat in the Olive Tree watching Charlie Chaplin and eating a terrible salad. Charlie Chaplin had fallen in love with a blind girl.
He was staring at her and she was staring off into space. They
both moved their lips in conversation.

A couple sat down in the booth behind me, and the waitress
brought them menus.

'Well, this has been a perfectly lovely evening, hasn't it?' the
man said. He had an English accent.

'Yes it has!' the woman said. 'Full of surprises.'

'You've been an awfully good sport, haven't you?' the
Englishman said.

I wondered how he had surprised her and in what way she
had been a good sport. This sounded like it might be an interesting conversation to eavesdrop on. Usually in New York people
just talked about their apartments.

'These blind dates are so . . . Oh, I didn't mean to use that
word,' the woman said, laughing nervously. 'I was so nervous.
It's not often one has a date with a judge.'

'It's not often one has the good fortune to be out on a date with
a massage therapist, is it?' the English judge said.

I turned around and found Jerome blindly staring at me. He
was wearing his Friday suit even though it was Monday. He
must have gotten mixed up at the cleaner's. I stood up and
switched to the other side of my booth so I could watch him
without twisting around. The woman's back was to me.

'Well,' Jerome said, 'I've never been here before.'

'Oh, it's a great place,' the woman said. 'It's one of the oldest restaurants on MacDougal Street. Its Israeli food mostly.' She read him the whole menu. I knew he wished she would read faster. Then she described the entire restaurant to him the way I used to. She described the tall blond waitress with the tattoos, the grill in the front, the long bar in the back, the black slate tables and the little white bowls of chalk, the small Tiffany-style lamps hanging over the tables, the little black baby screaming in his stroller, the couple smoking cigarettes, the two Asian girls playing chess. When she finished she was exhausted. She slumped back in her seat the way I used to when I was with him.

'It's wonderful,' Jerome said.

Jerome was staring past her. She moved a few inches over to the right to meet his gaze. 'They play Charlie Chaplin movies round the clock. They have a screen on the wall and a projector.' When she spoke Jerome knew she had moved. He shifted his eyes, overshooting again. 'Charlie Chaplin is handing a woman a bouquet of flowers. She has light hair and her eyes are . . .' She stopped talking when she realized the woman was blind.

'I'm afraid silent movies aren't my cup of tea,' Jerome said.

'Oh, uh, of course they aren't,' the woman said, mortified.

'So was I what you expected?' Jerome said.

'To be honest with you, I thought you'd be, well, sighted.'

I couldn't believe Jerome hadn't told her he was blind.

'Is that a problem?' Jerome asked briskly.

'No, not at all,' the woman lied.

'I didn't think that was a necessary detail to put in my personal ad,' he said. 'I mean, does it matter to you?'

I couldn't believe Jerome had taken out a personal ad. What if I had picked him from Violet's baggie!

'It's not that it matters, it's just that, well, we did speak for two hours on the phone. You might have mentioned it.'

'Well, I'm terribly sorry, Iris,' Jerome said sulkily.

'Well, anyway, we're here now and we're having a nice time,' Iris said.

'I guess I'm not exactly Prince Charming,' Jerome said.

Iris laughed, and Jerome looked hurt.

'So do you like being a judge?' Iris asked. 'It must be hard . . .'

'What must be hard?' Jerome interrupted. 'You mean, because I'm blind? I have readers to assist me.'

'Oh, that's good,' Iris said.

'Yes, although I'm mourning the loss of my last one.'

'Did he die?'

'No *she* left to become a real estate agent.'

'Yuck,' Iris said.

'I couldn't have put it better myself. Yuck is quite correct. She had tremendous potential. She was a funny girl. Sort of morose, and smart as a whip. She was what they call high maintenance. I miss her. She was a character.'

Iris didn't say anything. I could tell she didn't want to hear anymore about this funny, morose, smart girl, but I did. I wanted to hear a lot more about her. This was great.

'So why did you break up with your last girlfriend? What was her name, Sarah?' Iris asked, to change the subject.

'Yes, her name was Sarah,' Jerome said. 'It's a long story really. Well, we were never that serious. The truth is I had an affair with a woman I worked with.'

An affair! I wondered who Jerome could possibly have had an affair with. It couldn't have been Ms. Howard at the front desk, or Elise, the insane court stenographer, or Cathy, the lady bailiff. It must have been his new reader. The woman he hired in my place.

'Oh?' Iris said. 'And what was her name?'

'Her name was Liv,' Jerome said. 'It's actually the girl I just told you about. My ex-reader.'

I almost choked on a tomato. I did a double take as broad as Charlie Chaplin. I wanted to scream but I pretended I was in a silent movie and kept my mouth shut.

'Liv,' Iris said. 'That's an unusual name. Liv Ullmann. Liv Tyler. Is she Norwegian?'

'No, she wasn't Norwegian,' Jerome said.

'So the two of you had an affair and you ended things with Sarah?' she said. 'We don't have to talk about this if I'm getting too personal.'

'Well, it wasn't an affair at first but then it became inevitable. She fell in love with me and –'

'How did you know?' Iris asked.

'Well, she did little things for me, you see. Insisted on accompanying me to the subway, brought me gifts, never neglected to bring me a hot apple cider each afternoon from Starbucks. Then one morning she simply confessed.'

'What did she say?'

'Oh, you don't want to hear about all this,' Jerome said.

Yes she does, I thought. 'Yes I do, tell me,' Iris said.

'Well, I'll spare you the sordid details. She just simply said she was in love with me and had been since she started working for me and, well, uh, described various effects I had on her body, et cetera. This is an odd conversation to be having on our date, isn't it?'

'What did you do?' Iris asked, with a hint of disgust in her voice.

'I told her that as she already knew I was involved with Sarah and that I didn't want to be unfaithful.'

'I thought you said you weren't that serious with Sarah.'

'Quite true. But I wasn't sure what to do under the circumstances. But then she sort of hopped up on my lap and threw her arms around me and I realized that she had removed her skirt and was wearing only a garter belt and stockings.' He felt for his glass and took a sip of water. I couldn't even imagine sitting on his lap. He didn't even really have a lap – just a round stomach with legs. 'And just at that moment Sarah paid me a surprise visit.'

'That's unbelievable,' Iris said. 'You mean she just showed up right when this girl jumped on you?'

'I'm afraid you've got it. Of course Sarah broke things off. Liv stopped working for me and became a real estate agent but she came to my office every day and described all the apartments she had seen. She saw wonderful places. Sometimes she even took me to a few of them when she had the keys.'

I suddenly felt bad that I hadn't visited Jerome and described the apartments to him. He would never see any of them. I had just packed up my eyes and left.

'Even though what she did was very immature. Of course I wished she wouldn't have been quite so wild,' Jerome continued. 'But she was very young. I do feel I taught her a lot. But of course she taught me a thing or two.'

'I'm sure she did,' Jerome's date said, sarcastically. 'Do you still see her?'

'No. I had to put a stop to it. It had to end. She still calls me, though,' Jerome said wistfully.

'What did she look like?' Iris asked.

'Plump,' Jerome said. 'Quite delightful.'

Plump! That was the last straw. I reached into my pocketbook and pulled out the gun, and held it on my lap. Why was Jerome under the strange impression that I was plump? I looked around and when I was sure no one was looking, I lifted the gun very casually and inconspicuously a couple of centimeters above the table and pointed it right at Jerome.

'She was fat?' Iris asked.

'Not exactly fat, but 'healthy' would be the right word, would-n't it?'

He had no idea that there was a loaded gun pointed at him. That was the truly amazing thing about being blind. A gun could pointed at you and you wouldn't know it. You would just keep talking. Which was worse, I wondered, seeing that a gun was pointed at you or not seeing it? Which made you more vulnerable? I put my gun away.

'Check, please,' I said, in a loud voice. Jerome looked startled.

'What's the matter?' Iris said.

'I need some change,' I told the waitress.

'Are you okay, Jerome?' Iris asked. 'You look like you've seen a ghost.' She laughed nervously when she realized she had said the 'seen.'

'Jerome, hello!' I said. 'It's me, Liv.'

'Hello,' he said in the back of his throat. He looked like he going to throw up.

'Hello, I'm Liv,' I said to Iris.

'Oh, uh, hello,' she said, tentatively. She looked me up and down to see if I was plump.

'Oh yes, Iris, this is Liv, an old employee of mine,' Jerome managed.

'Well, I was more than just an employee,' I said in a sexy voice. 'Wasn't I, Jerome?'

'Yes, yes of course,' he mumbled.

'Jerome, I've been meaning to call you. I finished your book.' I hadn't been able to read it. It was so wordy and filled with typos. Finally I just flipped to the last page where a man gets run over by a car on Montague Street in Brooklyn. 'I really loved it,' I said.

'You're being kind,' Jerome said.

'No, I'm not. It was a real page-turner.'

'What did you like about it?' Jerome asked.

'Uh,' I said. 'I loved the end, where the blind man gets run over on the street.'

'The man in my book isn't blind!' Jerome said.

'Oh, uh, of course I know he isn't blind,' I said. 'I'm just using the word as a sort of metaphor for his character. You know, getting run over and everything.'

'Yes,' Jerome said, miserably.

'See ya,' I said and walked out of the restaurant.

33

CONVRTD SYNAGOGUE — CATHDRL CEILS

I spent the whole next day at the Olive Tree thinking it was Saturday even though it was only Tuesday. It must have been Jerome's Friday suit that did it to me. Luckily, for an independent contractor, it didn't matter much what day it was.

I watched a man with a shaved head write notes on music paper.

I looked out the window and saw a tall, handsome man carrying an upright vacuum cleaner.

The cook turned a dozen eggplants on the grill.

Mike, the neighborhood crazy, came in and switched all the salt and pepper shakers around. He was thin with gray hair. His hands and face never stopped moving. 'Hello, Moses,' he said to me. Every time he saw me he called me Moses. He had a different name for everyone. They were all Biblical, or made up, except for one waiter he called Garibaldi. But my name was the best – Moses – and I personally loved it even though I didn't know much about who Moses was. I knew the real Moses had a white Santa Claus beard and stood on a hill with the Ten Commandments like a scary judge.

Mike slid into the seat across from me and slid out again in one motion. Then he continued on his restaurant rounds.

It all seemed like an omen. I felt close to God, closer than I had ever been. I hadn't spoken a word all day, just smiled and pointed to what I wanted on the menu when the waitress came by. I am Moses, I thought. I was surrounded by symbols of God – sheet music, vacuum cleaner, eggplants. The smell of lamb filled the air. The lamb rotated on its spit like a skein of wool being unwound. Strange place for a lamb to end up, MacDougal Street. On the screen Charlie Chaplin stood in a church preaching the story of David and Goliath.

I paid my check and left. As soon as I got out on the sidewalk a red Porsche pulled up in front of me. The car door swung open and a man who looked like he was about my age leaned all the way out with one foot on the street. He was gorgeous with dark brown hair and blue eyes. He was alone.

'Get in the car,' he said.

I stepped back. I wondered if this had something to do with Andrew. Recently a girl had been pushed onto the subway tracks and killed. On the news she was described as 'a well-liked receptionist.' I felt sorry for her, being summed up in that way. I wondered what they would say about me. She was a real estate agent last seen getting into a red Porsche.

'Just get in the car,' he said, evenly.

I smiled at him and then pointed to myself to ask if he meant me.

Suddenly Mike, the crazy, was at my side. 'Dad, get in the car,' the driver of the Porsche said.

Mike jumped behind me and put his hands on my waist, like a boy hiding behind a tree.

'Dad, will you please fucking get in the car?' the man said. Mike let go of me and spun around me in a circle. The man pulled some money out of his wallet. 'Then take this,' he said.

A few people had gathered to watch. Mike zigzagged around them.

'Ma'am,' the man said to me.

'It's Moses,' I said.

He looked at me as if I were crazy. He had no sense of humor.

'Would you please give this money to my father?' I knew I had ruined my chance to have a date with him.

I walked over to him, and he handed me a stack of one-hundred-dollar bills. 'Thank you,' he said. 'Take the money, Dad,' he yelled.

I stood for a moment holding the money. Then I walked over to Mike and held it out to him. 'Thank you, Moses,' he said, bowing. He took the wad of bills and threw them up into the air. They scattered all over the sidewalk. No one tried to grab any.

I admired Mike. He wanted to be independent from his son the way I wanted to be from my father.

His son slammed the car door and drove away. As soon as he was gone, Mike ran around chasing the hundreds and shoving them pockets.

'I like your father,' Mike said to me.

'You know him?' I asked.

'He's very generous,' Mike said. 'I saw him yesterday.'

'You saw my father yesterday?' I asked, confused. My heart was pounding. Was my father in town? Had he come to New York and not called me? Sometimes he rode around in the back of a cab or limo, looking at what kids were wearing in the Village and the Lower East Side. Had he stopped to talk to Mike?

'Tell your father I said thank you for the radio. Even though it's not working very well.'

'I don't understand, Mike, how do you know my father?' I couldn't keep my voice from shaking.

Mike looked annoyed. He put his hand on my shoulder. 'Moses, I'm surprised at you. Your *father*,' he said, pointing up to the sky. I looked up. 'You know your *fa-ther*,' he said, kindly. He was talking about God.

34

WASH SQ NORTH — LANDMRK TWNHSE

Right before he bit off my ear, Andrew had started bragging all the time about taking Pilates with a girl named Timothy who he said was extremely attractive and worked as a stripper on the side. I had never heard of Pilates.

'I'm planning to take Pilates,' I had said.

'No, you're not,' he said.

'Yes I am.'

'You just want to take Pilates because I'm taking Pilates.'

'That's not true. Everyone's taking it,' I said.

'If I ate shit would you eat shit?' he asked.

'I don't know, Andrew. Why don't you try eating some and we'll see.'

'If you go you can't tell Timothy about us because the owner of the studio knows Jordan,' he said, nervously.

I called the Pilates studio and made an appointment. 'Your name?' the woman on the phone asked.

'Moses,' I told her. I loved having a man's name.

The Pilates studio was a big open loft with a few strange pieces of equipment and a few mats scattered around the old painted floor. As soon as I got there I had to sign something saying that they weren't responsible if I got killed or injured. I wrote my name as 'Moses' on the medical questionnaire. I wrote 'God' as who to contact in an emergency and 'Father' as that person's relationship to me. I wrote 'Andrew Lugar' as the person who referred me.

'Put your feet in the strap,' Timothy said. 'Soften your ribs.'

'How the hell am I supposed to soften my ribs?' I lay there on the contraption staring up at the ceiling. I was supposed to slide myself back and forth using my legs. The apparatus was invented by Joseph Pilates, who, from what I could tell, was an insane male nurse in World War II who couldn't stand the thought of anyone resting, even sick people in the hospital, so he devised a way to exercise in bed.

I was lying on something that looked like a cross between a hospital bed and a torture device with pulleys and springs and attachments. It looked like something Andrew would have liked to have sex on. I told myself not to think about Andrew.

'Go,' Timothy said. She made her fingers into a 'V' and pointed them at me as if that would start me up. Then she began counting, 'One, and, two, and, three, and,' even though I hadn't moved. When she got to ten she took my feet out of the strap so we could get me into position for the next ordeal.

Timothy was Japanese. Tall and rail-thin with long black hair that was choppy on the bottom. Andrew never told you the important details about a person like the fact that she was Japanese. She was wearing a vintage one-piece bathing suit and platform sandals. Her toenails were long and painted metallic brown. She had long false eyelashes sprouting only from the corners of her eyes but she was beautiful despite all that. A metallic booze smell seeped from her pores. It was an honest girl smell. I was jealous of that smell. I would rather smell like smoke and booze than my own smell – shawarma and pathetic Oil of Olay.

'A guy I know told me to take Pilates with you,' I said, hoping Timothy would ask me who the guy was.

'That's good,' she said.

'Yes, so anyway this guy said you were a great trainer.'

'Okay, now we're going to do The Saw,' she said. 'Sit with your legs spread like this and pretend you're sawing off your right pinkie toe with your left hand.' That didn't sound pleasant.

I waited for her to ask Andrew's name. 'His name is Andrew Lugar,' I said.

'Andrew 'Strap me in, baby' Lugar?'

'That's him,' I said.

She laughed. 'Is he a friend of yours?'

'No!' I said.

'He's such a jerk,' she said. She pointed to the old black-and-white picture on the wall of a nurse helping a man to do some sort of a sit-up. 'He keeps telling me I should dress up like a nurse to be true to the tradition of Joseph Pilates. What a perv.' We both laughed. 'I hope he's really not a friend of yours.'

'He's not,' I assured her.

'I actually mentioned him to my shrink, and she said he's a psychopath. My boyfriend and I laugh about him,' she said.

'You have a boyfriend?' I asked. I wondered if her boyfriend knew that she was a stripper.

'We just moved in together in a loft in Williamsburg. We're having a fight because he's angry at me that I went to Bali a few months ago for three weeks and he felt all abandoned.'

'Maybe I should go to Bali,' I said.

'It's great,' she said. 'But one morning I woke up in my hut and I went to put on my panties. I was just about to pull them up when I looked down and saw a giant scorpion lying right in the cotton crotch.'

Andrew should be careful not to go through *her* hamper, I thought.

'I hate those married guys who come on to you. I just make it very clear to them that I have a boyfriend.'

'Andrew's not married,' I said. 'He just lives with someone.'

'Really? I thought he and Jordan recently got married. Who knows with him? I'm pretty sure I've seen him wear a ring.

Sometimes he says 'my girlfriend,' sometimes he says 'my wife.' But I know he has a lot of affairs.'

'What a jerk,' I said. 'Does he talk about them?'

'Well, you know the designer Peter Kellerman?' she asked. I nodded. 'He talks about Peter Kellerman's daughter, Liv Kellerman, a lot.' I smiled. Andrew had talked about me.

'So he's having an affair with Liv Kellerman?' I asked.

'Well, actually he says horrible things about her. He talks about her so much that lately I've been accusing him of being in love her. Whatever it is, he's obsessed.'

My heart bounced in my chest. Then it felt gripped like a pale red rubber ball in a dog's teeth, slimy and wet from saliva.

'What horrible things?' I asked.

'Well, apparently she lives in this really squalid tenement even though her father's so rich. He said not even her father can stand her. She pretends she doesn't want his help, but really he *won't* help her. He said she's like the girl in that book *Washington Square*, you know? Really ugly and untalented and oafish and dumb.'

I nodded to show that I had read the book even though I had only seen the old movie starring Olivia De Havilland in the part of me.

'She's a lowly real estate agent, too. I bet there are a lot of rich celebrities out there who have totally ordinary children. So it's sort of our little joke. I always accuse him of being in love with her and he always says she repulses him.'

Washington Square might have ended a little differently if Katherine had had a gun.

She made me do something called The Teaser. I was so angry I couldn't speak. I couldn't do it. I just lay there thinking.

'What do I have to do to get you to move?' Timothy asked. 'Hold a gun to your head?' I considered that idea. I could get the gun out of my pocketbook and she could hold it to my head. Maybe if I was lucky she would shoot me.

'Did you know that one of your hips is higher than the other?'

'No, I didn't,' I said.

She had me lie on my back with my legs together so she could measure if one leg was shorter than the other. It was. Then she spent the next twenty minutes pulling on my shorter leg trying to make it longer. Pilates was a lot like dating. I could be passive. Just simply lie there and let someone pull my leg.

Timothy ushered me over to another bed device she called the Cadillac. I didn't know if she was kidding. She put both my feet in fuzzy sheep's wool ankle straps and hoisted me up so I was hanging upside down. She stood over me holding my feet so they wouldn't slip out.

'Isn't this sort of advanced?' I asked.

'You can do it.'

'Can Andrew do this?'

'He can hardly do anything. He gets all sweaty and has to check his blood pressure every five minutes. You're already doing more than he is and he's been coming for almost a year.'

'Really,' I said. He had told me he had just started.

'He was just here right before you actually. I'm surprised you didn't see each other.'

I heard shrieks and laughter from the lower level. 'I'm not doing that. I just ate,' a woman was saying. The sound traveled up the spiral staircase. It was Robert De Niro's wife, Grace, down there with one of the other trainers, she told me.

Then a flower delivery man came with a big arrangement of cellophaned orchids. The delivery man looked at me hanging and sort of shook his head. I watched upside down as Timothy was called to the front desk. They were for her. I hung there with no one holding my feet.

Timothy opened the card. 'Oh, my God.' She went to the phone and dialed a number. 'Honey, it's me. Thank you so much, they're beautiful. I love you.'

'Timothy,' I said, upside down. Watching her get flowers was more than I could take. The last thing you want to see when you go somewhere to work out is a beautiful thin girl eating or getting flowers.

'I'm sorry, too,' she said into the phone.

Pilates cost eighty dollars an hour.

'No, I can talk until my next client gets here.' She looked at her watch. 'My session just ended. I'm going to smoke a cigarette outside. What are we going to do for dinner?'

'Timothy,' I said.

Timothy put a vintage kelly-green wool coat on over the bathing suit and took a cigarette out of a pack in her purse. She went out through the glass-and-chicken-wire door, still talking on the cordless phone.

Hanging there my body started to lengthen and even itself out. I became thinner and braver, like Timothy. Pilates was incredible, that's why all the celebrities did it. It was already working. There was a tingling sensation between my legs. It reminded me of how much I hated Andrew. I hated Andrew so much I wanted to kill him. He should be hanging here like a duck in the window of a Chinese restaurant, not me.

After a while Timothy walked back in and noticed 'Oops,' she said, letting me down. 'Oh, my God, I'm so sorry.'

'Don't worry about it,' I told her. 'I didn't mind.'

I changed in the tiny curtained-off dressing stall and went to the coatrack to get my coat and shoes. I noticed something familiar jammed into one of the cubbies on the bottom row. It was a blue duffel bag, just like Andrew's. There must be thousands of bags just like this, I thought. It couldn't be his. I stood there staring at it. Keeping my upper body completely still, I dragged it out of the cubby using only the foot of my longer leg. It was like a new Pilates exercise I had invented called The Duffel Bag. I looked around to make sure no one had seen me.

Then I let my coat fall right on top of the duffel bag. I bent down and scooped up my coat with the bag hidden underneath it. I smuggled the bag into the bathroom and locked the door behind me.

I unzipped the bag, and there, floating right on top, was Andrew's journal. I opened it and saw a sea of Livs. Livs dotted the pages. Liv this and Liv that. I couldn't focus.

Someone knocked on the door.

'Just a minute,' I said. I wasn't sure what to do. I didn't know if I should take just the journal home or the whole duffel bag with the journal in it. I was dying to read it but I was afraid Andrew would come back for it before I could smuggle it out. There wasn't time to read it now. I had to get out of there. I stared at the picture of Joseph Pilates on the edge of the sink as if he would tell me. He was standing in bikini underwear with his legs spread and his hands on his hips, proud to be sixty. I wanted to put his picture next to the picture of the swami on my desk so I slipped it into my pocketbook along with Andrew's journal.

I left the bathroom with the duffel bag wrapped up in my coat and flung the duffel bag, with the rest of its contents – his jockstrap and a Faulkner novel – back into the cubby, walked past the front desk with the sign reading 'Not responsible for lost or stolen property,' and right out the door.

Timothy was smoking again outside. 'I guess my next client is a no-show,' she said. 'Which way are you going?' she asked.

'I'm taking a cab to MacDougal Street,' I said.

'Do you mind if we share one? I'm meeting my boyfriend around there and I'll just kill time at a café until then.' She made me wait while she went back inside to get her flowers and hug the girl at the front desk goodbye. I could never work in a gym or at a restaurant because you have to hug all your co-workers all the time. You didn't see real estate agents hugging.

We walked to the corner of Hudson to get a cab.

'Moses is a strange name for a girl,' Timothy said.

And Timothy wasn't?

Finally a cab pulled over. The guy in the backseat paid the driver and then opened the door on the street side. I opened the door on the sidewalk side as he got out.

It was Andrew. He stared at me standing there with Timothy.

'Liv, what are you doing here?' he asked.

'Liv?' Timothy said, wide-eyed. 'Oh, my God.'

'Hi, Andrew,' I said.

'Hi,' he said. 'Uh, I've got to run. I left something at Pilates.'

'You don't have to run, Andrew,' I said. 'I've got it right here.' I pulled his diary out of my pocketbook, revealing just a corner of it.

'That belongs to me,' he said. He put his hand out for it

And that's when I saw his ring. It took me by surprise. I felt guilty, like I had accidentally come across something I wasn't supposed to find. It looked vulgar on his finger, as if it were a cockring instead of a wedding ring. But maybe he had worn it all along and I had just forgotten to look. Maybe the cold platinum band had grazed my nipple when we were in bed together and I hadn't even felt it.

When exactly had this happened? I wondered.

We all just stood there holding the cab doors open.

'Fuck you. Close my door, cheap asshole,' the cabdriver screamed at Andrew. He had some kind of Middle Eastern accent.

'Did you forget to tip the driver, Andrew?'

'I don't make turn and he make me take two dollar off meter,' the driver shouted.

'Andrew, I think you owe the driver – what is your name? – an apology.'

'Mohammed,' the driver said.

'Apologize to Mohammed.'

'Liv, I've got to go,' Andrew said.

'Apologize.'

'Can I have my book?'

'Get back in the cab,' I said.

Andrew just stood there.

I pulled the gun out of my pocketbook and pointed it at him, holding it close to my body. 'Get back in the cab,' I said.

Andrew looked at Timothy. I remembered that Andrew said that the owner of the Pilates studio was a friend of Jordan's. He looked more scared of Timothy telling on him than he did of my gun.

She gave him a disgusted look. 'Get in,' I said. Andrew got into the cab.

Timothy stood frozen on the sidewalk. I loved her hair, my color, but straight and choppy like that. 'Come on,' I said to her, 'it'll be fun.' She didn't look too convinced.

'Look,' she said, 'this is none of my business. I'm really sorry he said those things about you but I think you're both kind of wacko. I'll just get my own cab.'

I really didn't want to get in the cab alone with Andrew. 'He says things about you, too,' I said.

'Like what?' she asked.

'Well, only that you're a stripper.'

'What!' she said.

She got in the cab, and I got in after her. We all sat in the back-seat with Timothy in the middle.

'Please drive up the West Side Highway,' I told the cabdriver. I had never hijacked anything before but that seemed like a good route because we could move fast.

I leaned in front of Timothy and held the gun up to Andrew's head. 'Pardon my reach,' I said to Timothy. I was trying not to hurt the flowers on her lap.

'I'm going to kill you,' I said to Andrew. I shoved the gun into his ear. Even though it felt light in my right hand, I supported my wrist with my left.

'What is going on back there?' Mohammed said.

'Drive!' I said. 'Hurry.'

'I cannot make cab fly,' Mohammed said, angrily.

The cab started moving and the recorded celebrity announce-ment came on, but it wasn't my father. It was Judge Judy and Judge Jerry Sheindlin saying it was just plain 'stoopid' not to wear a seat belt.

'You heard the judge,' I told Andrew. 'Fasten your seat belt.' He fastened it.

'Why don't you tell Timothy and Mohammed how much you love me, and how you're going to leave your wife and marry me?' I said in a loud voice.

'Liv, you're really acting crazy,' Andrew said.

I pressed the gun into his ear as hard as I could.

'Cut it out,' he said.

'Shut up,' I said. 'It's loaded, and I *will* kill you.'

'I am not a stripper, Andrew,' Timothy said.

My wrist started to ache from holding it up for so long. I wanted to change hands but I was afraid he would see that as an opening.

It took all my strength and concentration to keep the gun steady. I would have to take a lot more Pilates if I was ever going to try using the gun on a regular basis. Suddenly it occurred to me that he could turn around quickly and knock the gun out of my hand. He could kill me. Without thinking, and without even really knowing what I was doing, I racked the slide back and sort of cocked the gun. It made a loud cocking sound that surprised all of us. I had never cocked a gun before.

Someone's cell phone rang. Timothy reached for her bag but it wasn't hers, it was Mohammed's. 'I can't talk right now,' I remembered how much Jerome hated cell phones. They were the bane of the blind man's existence. He was always veering around thinking there were twice as many people on the sidewalk than there actually were. Mohammed hung up.

'Tell Timothy and Mohammed how much you love to fuck me,' I said. 'Tell them how you lied to me. Tell them how much you love to bite me when we fuck.'

'Fuck you?' Andrew said, like he was thinking. Like he was stalling for time. I could tell all he was worried about was this information getting back to Jordan.

'Tell them!' I screamed.

'Come on, Liv,' Andrew said. 'Fuck you? I've never fucked you. I've tried to be a friend to you, Liv, but I've never fucked you. I've tried to help you as much as I can.'

I was stunned. 'Help me?' I said.

'You're a sick girl, Liv. You know there's never been anything sexual between us.' His voice was sickening, as if he was trying to talk down a lunatic. As if *I* was the lunatic.

I folded his earlobe over with the gun. 'Give me your ring,' I said.

'This is going too far.'

'Give it to me,' I screamed.

Andrew pulled at the ring on his finger until it came off. He handed it to me and I put it on my thumb.

'Tell me, Andrew, how long have you been married? Were you married when we sat in the sauna together on Laight Street? Were you married when you brought me my curtains? Were you married the night of the boxing match?'

He had ordered the fight on my pay-per-view and we watched it in my bed. It was fifty dollars but he said he would pay me back when my cable bill came. He never did.

'You owe me fifty dollars,' I said. 'Give it to me.' He struggled to pull his wallet out of his back pocket and handed me two twenties and a ten.

Suddenly he started to cry. He cried quietly with his head down. I wondered if he was crying over the fifty. Crying like that, he looked too young to be married. He looked like a little boy. He looked like a small little psychopath instead of a big grown-up one. I wondered if I had overreacted.

I softened my voice. 'Just tell me exactly how long you have been married,' I said. 'And I'll let you go.'

'Since the day I met you,' he said. 'I was married that day in the court building. Right after Judge Moody's retirement party. He was the one who married us. He's my father-in-law.'

I took the gun off his ear. 'Timothy, you don't happen to have a pair of scissors or something, do you? I want to cut off his ear so I can send it to his wife with his wedding ring.' Maybe I would cut the other one off for myself and keep it pinned to black velvet in a glass case like a butterfly. An ear for an ear.

'I think so,' she said. She transferred the flowers onto Andrew's lap and started going through her knapsack.

'I have knife,' Mohammed said. He handed me a Swiss Army knife with a blade pulled out as well as a tiny pair of scissors. Then he tossed a roll of paper towels over the partition. 'You make mess with blood and ear, you clean up,' he said.

I took it from him. 'Thank you, Mohammed,' I said. 'Andrew, you live around here somewhere, don't you? Where exactly do you live? Maybe it's time I got to see *your* wedding video. I really want to see your apartment.' But then it hit me. I didn't care about his apartment anymore. I didn't care where Andrew and his wife lived. 'Actually, Mohammed, why don't you just let him out here.'

Mohammed pulled over on the highway. Timothy took back her flowers. I figured we were around Ninety-fourth Street, not far from the statue of Joan of Arc. To our left the water looked like fool's gold. The Circle Line was going by. To our right were the buildings of Riverside Drive with their green copper roofs. The buildings of New York were built on jealousy. Each one wanted to be better and more successful than the one before it. The Ansonia, one of the most beautiful buildings on Broadway, was built for revenge. Its builder didn't get to move into the dream house he had just finished on the Upper East Side, due to his divorce. So he built the Ansonia and put live seals in a fountain in the lobby. 'Get out,' I said.

Andrew started to speak. 'Liv . . .'

Suddenly Mohammed turned around and shoved his own gun in Andrew's face. All three of us jumped in our seats. 'You heard the lady,' he shouted. 'Get out! I don't want to hear your mouth!'

Andrew unbuckled his seat belt and opened his door. He had a strange, infuriating little smile on his face.

I looked at the meter as Andrew started to get out. 'Don't worry, Andrew, I'll get this,' I said.

I wondered if I would ever see Andrew again, or if that was the way I would always remember him. He never even apologized to Mohammed.

'Short ugly man,' Mohammed said.

Timothy and I burst into laughter.

'No, it's terrible,' Mohammed said. 'I know these kind of men. I have daughter.'

I held Andrew's ring up and squinted to see the engraving on the inside. The initials J.M. & A.L. were written in tiny letters. I remembered judge Moody introducing me to Andrew. And Andrew lifting me on the balcony. I had been his bachelor party.

And then he married Jordan. J.M. Jordan Moody. Jerome's reader, my predecessor.

Mohammed drove us back downtown. He dropped us off on Sixth Avenue and Third Street in front of the basketball courts.

'Do you still want to take Pilates?' Timothy asked.

'Definitely.'

'I'm really sorry I left you hanging like that.'

'I'll see you next week.'

'Goodbye, funny girls,' Mohammed said.

35

*L*iv has a gun. I found it last night when she was in the shower. A *gun. It's a Glock 9mm Luger. I think it's what cops carry. It's loaded. Why would my Liv, my sweet little fuck-buddy, have a gun? Maybe she's an undercover police officer. No, she probably wanted to commit suicide because she can't have me all to herself: I'm sure she intended to pull it on me. She probably read somewhere that the best way to get me to leave Jordan was to get a gun.*

Fuck-buddy! I couldn't believe he had the nerve to call me that. And how dare he snoop through my things? A person couldn't have any privacy with a man like Andrew snooping everywhere. I turned the page.

I think I'll take it. I can't wait to see the look on her cute little Jewish face when she finds it gone. Maybe I'll kill someone and the cops will find her prints on it. It has occurred to me that she has read this diary. Liv, if you are reading this I am going to get your gun and I am going to murder someone with it – maybe even YOU. That's what happens to naughty little nosey parkers – remind me to give you a spanking.

I crossed Sixth Avenue, reading and sort of hyperventilating, taking dramatic Lamaze-type breaths and weaving drunkenly. I couldn't wait until I got home to read it. I couldn't wait another moment.

Yesterday a woman came into the office. She was interviewing to be Mark's secretary. I wanted to tear the pantyhose right off her. I need a lot of different women. No one person could satisfy all my needs. How can I make Liv understand that you can't do every position with everygirl? You can't do everything with everygirl. She just doesn't understand. When I shook her hand I leaned into her and she smelled like Liv. She must use the same shampoo, Pantene. I had to jerk off in the men's room even though I promised myself I wouldn't do that anymore.

He was right, I didn't understand. Why did he make every girl one word like that? It was the strangest thing I had ever seen, and I didn't use Pantene anymore.

I went to see the swami in Florida. I told Liv I was spending the weekend with Jordan but I flew to Miami to meet with him. He told a story in Hindi and even though I couldn't understand it I had an image in my mind of crossing a bridge made out of rope. Afterward he explained in English that the story was about a man crossing a bridge made out of rope. Then he pointed to me and told me to come forward and kneel before him. He placed his hand on the top of my head and I felt heat, like the sensation of a soft-boiled egg breaking and the warm yolk spilling down. The swami said you are involved with a woman with long dark hair. You two have a destiny together, but it is not a happy one. If you go to this woman you will harm her You might even kill her. But I love her, I told him. I know you do love her, he said. But you are not good for each other. I have to stop seeing Liv.

I stopped reading and looked around to see where I was. I was still in front of the basketball courts. A fat black woman in a red velvet unitard was playing handball by herself. My heart was beating so hard I had to rest. I didn't think I would ever be calm again. I stood with my hand on the receiver of a pay phone. I had to call someone and tell them what I had read. I wished I could call the swami himself but I called Violet instead.

'You'll never guess what I did,' I said, guiltily.

'What?' she asked with too much enthusiasm, as if she was hoping that this time I had done something really bad.

I tried to take a deep breath. 'I stole Andrew's diary.'

'You're kidding. What did it say?'

'A swami told him he was bad for me.'

'I've always thought that, Liv. At first I thought, Okay, Liv and this guy were meant to be teachers for each other –'

'Violet, what are you talking about?' Suddenly I regretted telling her about the diary.

'Well, you and Andrew probably have a karmic bond of some sort and you were meant to learn something from him.' Violet made love affairs as insignificant as a thirty-minute sitcom from the fifties, as if they could get all neatly wrapped up with a moral in the end. 'But I really have to say I'm agreeing with that swami. I'm feeling really strange about this whole thing.' She always said, 'I'm agreeing with,' instead of 'I agree with,' or 'I'm feeling,' instead of 'I feel.' I was definitely not loving this conversation. She expounded on her theory for a while as I read another page.

Last night, when I left Liv's rathole, I saw the most beautiful girl I have ever seen and I thought, Oh my God, this is the woman I am meant to spend the rest of my life with. She walked by me on the street and I could feel myself inside her, my fingers, my cock, before I had even said hello. She was stunningly beautiful. For the first time I understood the word flaxen. If I could invent a woman I wouldn't have dared to make her this beautiful. I said I like your shoes. I said those are really great shoes. Now I know that I can skydive. Her tits were my parachute. She said thank you and I knew she would let me fuck her. It was just starting to rain and I said your shoes are going to get ruined. She said no they're not. I said yes, they're going to get rained on. She said no, they're not. I said yes they are unless you live right here. We were standing in front of a townhouse on Washington Square North. 19 Washington Square North. She took me up to her bedroom and what a bedroom. Hundreds of peacock feathers! And I didn't have to endure interminable babble. Just unbelievable wetness and her smell on my face. I am going to rub my face on this page so I will always remember it.

Slowly, I brought the book up to my nose. It smelled like paper.

'Promise me you won't read any more of that diary,' I heard Violet say. 'It's just not right.'

'What?' I said.

'You have to respect his privacy. You wouldn't want him going through your things. It's bad karma. If you keep reading it and you get upset it's your own fault,' Violet said.

'I know. I won't read it anymore.'

'How'd you get it from him, anyway?'

I didn't know what to say. I didn't want to tell her the whole story because I knew she would not be approving of it. But I didn't want to have to lie. So I told her what had happened with Andrew and Timothy. We took a moment to marvel about what it would be like to be a girl named Timothy.

'You know, that really wasn't funny,' Violet said.

'Funny? I wasn't trying to be funny.'

'You put yourself and Timothy in danger.'

'Oh, I did not,' I said. Lorna wouldn't have minded. She might even have thought it was funny. I made a mental note to call Lorna instead of Violet next time I used my gun.

'You could have gotten yourself arrested.'

'Arrested,' I said. 'No one in New York gets arrested.'

'I'm just not understanding you lately, Liv. Lately you've been so . . .' She searched through her blond head for the right word. 'Negative.'

'I don't think I've been negative,' I said. 'I think you're being negative, saying I was going to get arrested.'

A recorded voice told me to make a twenty-five-cent deposit. I fished in my bag for a quarter.

'What did you think would happen when you date a married man?'

Her new boyfriend played Dungeons & Dragons with two other guys every Sunday night. I'd rather date a married psychopath than a man who did that. Violet wasn't really my friend if she couldn't take a little gunplay. I was working on a theory that a New Yorker could never truly be friends with a Texan.

Violet and I had nothing in common. But how did you break up with a girlfriend? One little gun couldn't help me do it. I would need a cannon. It was the hardest thing in the world, much harder than breaking up with a man. Millions of women were friends with women they couldn't stand but couldn't bring themselves to hurt. It was a worldwide epidemic. 'I'll call you if I ever get less negative,' I said.

I clutched the quarter in my hand until the phone went dead.

A ll night phrases from Andrew's diary ran through my mind. *How can I tell her that she's not going to be in my life very much longer?*

I will miss her plump little body.

Last night I slept in my study and called Liv as soon as I woke up.

Jordan made vegetarian chili.

I know Liv is reading this. I'm going to start making entries on the PC. Liv, if I find out you are reading this I'm going to stick your gun up your cunt and kill you.

Friends, Romans, Liv, lend me your ear.

Maybe Liv's adopted. It's hard to believe she's Jewish. It's hard to believe a Jew could be that stupid.

I stood up and turned on my overhead light. I reread the part about the girl with the parachutes on Washington Square North over and over.

Even when I finally stopped reading it I was still reading it. *Liv, I know you are reading this . . . Liv, if you are reading this . . . If you are reading this . . .* And then it finally hit me. He knew I was reading this. The whole thing was simply a joke. A gag, Andy Kaufman-style. A trick a teenage boy would play on his little sister. He only wrote these things because he knew I was reading them. They didn't mean anything. They weren't true.

Or maybe they were.

19 Washington Square North didn't even exist. There wasn't even any such address. I knew because I had canvassed the entire area. A lot of those buildings were owned by NYU. There was 20 Washington Square North, then a parking garage, then 18 through 14 Washington Square North, which was a postwar building pressed up against the side of Two Fifth Avenue, the

home of Mayor Ed Koch. There was no 19. There was a number 9, which was definitely an NYU building, but no 19. And a person couldn't have sex in a house that wasn't there. Real estate was necessary for actual sex to take place.

In the morning I got dressed and put my gun and Andrew's diary in my bag.

It was beautiful out so I decided to walk to the office. I walked along MacDougal Street and turned at the corner of the park. There were new birds with strange long yellow beaks. There were black squirrels, scary. And there was a townhouse, right there on Washington Square North, with a big number 19 above the door.

I stood on the street staring up at the house. There were eleven steps and a landing and then two more. Ever since walking Jerome I always counted steps. I had to think for a minute. The existence of the house didn't necessarily mean that the diary was true. But it didn't prove that it was false. I paced back and forth like a lawyer. I stared up at the windows. I half-expected to see a flood of wetness pouring out of them. I decided I couldn't go to work in this condition. I went to Caffe Reggio and drank a pot of Earl Grey with about three tea leaves in it. I looked through the damn diary.

Jordan found a kitten and we found out it is dying. I hate this world. I told Liv I couldn't see her because I had to stay with the kitten, Sammy. She was a cunt about it. I said, you're being a cunt about this. She said so what are you going to do? I said I am going to hang up the phone.

'Is that your journal?' a good-looking man sitting at the next table asked.

'Yes it is, I said. It was my journal now. I looked to see if he was wearing a wedding ring. He was, but it was on the ring finger of his right hand. That's where European men wore their wedding rings. He was probably European. 'Where are you from?' I asked.

'Oregon.'

He wasn't European, just a nice, normal single man. I congratulated myself on my ability to size a person up so fast.

We talked for an hour, and I told him Louisa May Alcott was across the street and that Caffe Reggio was famous for having the first cappuccino machine in America. 'Once, a claw-foot tub fell through the ceiling,' I said. 'Right here where we're sitting.' I pointed above us to the unpainted patch of tin.

'No. I don't believe you,' he said.

I told him unfortunately I had to get to work.

'What do you do?' he asked.

'I'm a real estate agent.'

'So's my wife,' he said.

Wife! I checked his left hand one more time for a ring and noticed that he didn't have a left hand. He didn't have a left arm. No wonder he wore his wedding band on his right hand. It was his only hand. How could I spend an hour talking to someone and not notice a thing like that? When would I ever learn to be more careful?

Part III

Let every eye negotiate for itself
And trust no agent . . .

WILLIAM SHAKESPEARE,
Much Ado About Nothing, II, 1

36
24HR DRMN

At the meeting on Monday Kim said there was a new property coming on the market. She wanted us to make a strong pitch for it. She said the owner seemed difficult and she wanted to pick the broker she thought would best match his personality and then she would accompany that broker personally and assist in the pitch.

'What do you mean "difficult"?' I asked.

A couple of the agents laughed.

Kim scowled at me as if only I could pick out the negative detail in all of this. 'Not difficult, just a little particular. He's a real fusspot,' she said.

She held up a glossy eight-by-ten photo of someone's living room. The floor was covered with soft sandy carpet and strewn with magnificent kilims. Sun streamed through the twenty-foot-high greenhouse window. I could see part of the curved banister, the ladder from Bali leaning against the bookshelves my husband had built, a stupid gold owl from our wedding, the coffee table I had chosen on Greene Street.

It was mine. My husband's. My ex-apartment. A picture of my old life. I had almost forgotten how beautiful it was.

Kim gave details and rattled off comps. 'We can all go there as a group tomorrow morning,' she said. 'I added it to the bus tour. It will be our first stop.' A few times a month Kim hired a bus and we all had to travel together to preview six or seven apartments. 'We'll get to it at nine A.M.'

'We'll all have to take our shoes off at the front door,' I said.

'How did you know that?' Kim asked suspiciously.

'I just know,' I said.

In the morning I watched a little girl in a pink down jacket walk down the street clutching a Winnie-the-Pooh doll under one arm and talking on a cellular phone. The coat made a shiny down sound when she walked. She had a knit hat that tied under her chin with two pompoms shaped like strawberries. She couldn't have been more than seven.

'May I speak to my daddy, please,' she said. I followed after her. 'I'm on my cell phone and I'm supposed to talk to him while I'm walking to school,' she said crossly into the phone. She kept marching along. 'Hi, Daddy, I can't stay on too long or my ear gets hot.'

We stopped at a red light. She had a clear plastic change purse with a blue plastic diamond ring in it dangling from a clip on her knapsack.

'Are you coming home tonight?' she asked, excitedly. I looked at her face to see if I could tell what his answer was. Her face didn't change.

'Daddy, guess what. I have something exciting to tell you. Oh wait, that's my call waiting, hold on a second.' She took the phone from her ear and pressed a button. 'Hello? Hi, Mommy, I'm on the other line with Daddy. We're having a nice conversation. Can I call you back later? Okay.' She pressed the button again. 'Hi, Daddy, are you still there? It was just Mommy. I decided that when you pick my new room it should have a nice view and a big walk-in closet. Because, because, because it makes me feel happy if I can see the Umpire State Building and some dogs. I can't talk anymore, I'm here.'

I looked up and found that we had reached the school. 'Bye,' she said. She put the phone in her big coat pocket and joined a group of other children climbing down the three steps to the door.

It occurred to me that I should have given her my card.

The Liberty Lines bus was parked outside the office, waiting to take all the agents to my old apartment. I stood across the street trying to decide what to do. Part of me dreaded it but part of me felt excited, like it was show-and-tell day at school. I pictured the bus pulling up in front of the building's canopy and me filing out last, the smallest clown in a circus Volkswagen. I would march past the doorman, proud to be with my dignified colleagues. 'Hi, honey, I'm home,' I would say to my husband, as I slipped off my boots at the door.

Kim spotted me across the street. 'What are you waiting for?' she shouted.

I boarded the bus and took a seat across from Marti Landesman in the second row.

As I sat there I looked at myself in the bus's wide rearview mirror and straightened my posture. I was in the unfortunate seat where the whole bus can see you in the mirror. I thought about a girl I knew in high school who told me that I had a short neck. If I asked her now, she probably wouldn't remember saying it. Sometimes a person can say something to you and you never see yourself the same way again.

Kim balanced herself in the front and passed out sheets of paper with addresses for six other apartments that we would look at that day with brief descriptions, maintenance charges for the co-ops, taxes/common charges for the condos, and asking prices.

I wondered if he would be home. I suddenly imagined us all parading into the bedroom and finding Jack on our old bed with some kind of girl. I remembered everything. The day we bought the bed, the day the bed was delivered, the day we bought the air conditioner, the day the air conditioner was delivered, the day we had sex in the walk-in closet because we didn't have curtains yet, the day we bought the curtains, the day the curtains were installed.

I looked over at Marti Landesman writing confidently in her organizer. She handled it crudely and expertly, like an old woman handles raw chicken.

'Is your Forty-nine West Tenth Street still available?' the woman sitting behind her asked.

'Accepted offer, but I'm taking backups,' Marti said, without looking up. Her voice was the worst of New York, gravelly, flat, uncaring, like a shit-bottomed shoe being scraped on the sidewalk.

I had actually had a dream about her. When I woke up I couldn't believe that Marti Landesman had gotten into my dream. In the dream we were in separate elevators that moved horizontally and she was chasing me with a syringe like a crazed nurse.

I thought about telling her about my dream. 'Marti,' I said.

'Yup,' she said, without looking up.

'I had a dream about you.'

She looked at me. 'Oh yeah?' she said. She wore an expression of complete disgust.

'So what was the dream?' she asked a few minutes later.

'Oh, you were trying to kill me with a big needle.'

I could tell she was pleased.

'Isn't that a little pathetic?' she said. She looked over her shoulder as if she might need a witness.

I wished more than anything that I hadn't told her my dream. I didn't know what I could have been thinking. It was my worst real estate faux pas since I showed an apartment to an entire Japanese family and accidentally called it a condom instead of a condo.

'I think you oughta have your head examined,' she said.

A cell phone rang. Of course it was Marti's.

'Marti Landesman,' she said loudly, as if she were the only person on the bus. 'No, Harrison Street is a good street because it's nice and wide. Thomas Street is narrow.' She hung up.

I wanted to know what streets were wide and what streets were narrow.

We rode the rest of the way in silence.

Go on up, he's expecting you,' the doorman said to Kim. He was new, I had never seen him before. We all followed after Kim and stood reverently waiting for the elevator.

I compared this lobby to my new lobby, a tiny vestibule that smelled like cat urine and shawarma. I had felt safe in this lobby, with its big brass trolley to carry my bags. Now I carried laundry up five flights of-stairs. My husband hadn't liked to talk in front of the doormen or the neighbors. I had kissed Andrew in my new vestibule one night when we were fighting and I wouldn't let him come upstairs. I was wearing a cocktail dress and no bra. He slipped the straps off my shoulders and the dress fell down to my waist and we stayed that way, kissing, for an hour.

You don't realize how fake fake flowers look until you see them again after six months have passed.

When the elevator opened onto my old floor, a boy, about eight or nine, was playing with marbles. He had placed eleven trophies in an S shape like cones on an obstacle course.

'Hi,' I said as if I were his new neighbor. The other agents clucked over the trophies and headed toward my old front door. 'Are all those yours?' I asked the kid.

'Yes,' he said. 'Plus one more that's silver that's in my house.'

'What did you win them for?'

'Soccer, basketball, and baseball, and bowling,' he said.

'How long have you been living here?'

He thought for a moment. 'I don't know.'

'That's how I feel,' I said.

I walked down the hall, careful not to knock over the trophies. I knocked one over. I bent down to fix it.

'I'll do it,' he said, annoyed.

'Sorry,' I said.

'It's okay, I'm a klutz, too,' the little boy said. I had never thought of myself as a klutz.

The door was open a couple of inches. I pushed it tentatively and found myself standing where I had stood so many times before.

When we first moved in my husband marked both of our heights on the wall with a pen. 'This way we can measure every year to see if we're shrinking,' he said. It was the first time I liked the idea of growing old with someone. We had kept those marks through two paint jobs. Now they were gone.

The apartment was a duplex. The front door was on the upper level and opened onto a sort of grand mezzanine landing that overlooked the huge living room with its double-height ceiling. It made for a dramatic entry.

'I know, it's like a castle,' an agent said to me when she saw the look on my face. 'I feel like it should have a suit of armor somewhere.'

It does, I thought: its owner.

'I wonder what these are,' one agent said. She lifted a large egg made out of some kind of polished stone from a large wooden eggcup stand. There were dozens of them all over the living room like evil pods. I had never seen them before.

There were only a dozen agents on the bus but now it seemed as if they had multiplied. They were crawling all over my things.

I decided not to go in the bedroom. Watching Marti Landesman in there measuring it with her big feet would give me another nightmare. I went to the kitchen. Kim was looking in the pantry.

'Is the owner at home?' I asked.

'Whoever designed this kitchen is an idiot,' Kim said.

The granite, the marble, the paint, the tiles, the glass, the shelves, the island, the fridge, the faucets, the recycling bin. I had spent days, weeks, months personally choosing each one. The ice maker was still set to 'crushed.'

'Look,' Kim said, 'the refrigerator opens the wrong way.'

'No it doesn't,' I said.

'Yes it does.'

'The owner's left-handed,' I said.

'Oh, you think that's why they did it?'

'I know that's why they did it.'

'All right, Liv, how do you know that?' Kim asked, annoyed.

'Because I married him,' I said.

'You married the owner.'

'Yes. He was my husband.'

'Did you live here?' she asked. 'That's right,' I said. 'I'm the idiot who designed this kitchen. And that's why I think I should be the one to sell it.'

Our maid, Charitable, stood in the doorway.

'Hello, Miss Liv,' she said to me.

'Is Jack at home?' I asked her.

'No, he left before I got here this morning.' I wondered if she was just too polite to tell me that Jack's bed hadn't been slept in. 'Would you like me to make you a cup of coffee?'

'Yes, thank you, Charitable, please make coffee for everyone.' Kim watched the conversation like she was at Wimbledon.

'We don't have time for coffee,' she said. 'But thank you,' she added awkwardly.

'So, I'd like to be the one to sell it,' I repeated.

'If it's all right with the own . . . your husband, it's all right with me,' she said.

I suddenly felt dizzy and sat on a metal stool. Charitable brought me a cup of coffee.

And then it hit me. Jack was selling the apartment. It would no longer be our apartment. It would no longer even be his apartment. He was going somewhere else. I would no longer know exactly what chair he was sitting in or hear his cereal bowl hit the sink at three A.M. all the way from my tiny apartment. He would sit in new chairs and have new sinks. He would be unchartable. Our marriage would be like a plane crash with the black box left undiscovered somewhere on the bottom of the ocean. It had meant nothing.

The least I could do was get a commission.

The phone rang, and Charitable, Kim, and I all jumped as if

we were going to answer it. I was closest. It was my phone. I bought it. The receipt was in a drawer somewhere. Charitable took a step toward my phone.

'Hello?' I said.

'Hello?' It was Jack. 'I'm sorry, I must have the wrong number,' he said and hung up.

I hung up, too. 'Wrong number,' I told Kim and Charitable.

The phone rang again. 'Hello?' I said.

'Hello?' It was Jack again. 'Liv?'

'Hi, Jack,' I said. We had a bad connection. 'Where are you?'

'I'm on an airplane. I was calling to tell Charitable that I had to go out of town for a week. Is she there?' he asked, sounding worried that I had tied her up and stuffed her in a closet.

'Yes,' I said.

'Do you mind if I ask why you dropped in? Did you come for the curtain rods?'

'Never mind that,' I said. 'I'm here with Smoothe Transitions to preview the apartment. I'm a broker now.'

'Good for you.'

'Good for you,' I mimicked.

Kim looked like she was going to take the phone away from me. She obviously thought I was going to keep Transitions from getting the exclusive.

'Liv, be nice,' Jack said.

'So you were just going to move without talking to me?'

'I was going to talk to you. There's a lot I want to talk to you about. I started meditating. I'm moving to India. I'm moving to India to live with a swami.'

'Really,' I said. How did a man void of emotion suddenly become interested in meditating? I pictured a group of robots sitting crosslegged in front of another robot wearing a turban. 'Does this have something to do with all these new stone eggs you've got?'

'Those are *lingums*, Liv. A symbol of male sexual energy.'

'Really,' I said. I move out and he fills the house with male eggs.

'I'd love to talk to you about it. Maybe we could sit down and –'

'Maybe.' I stood up. 'Jack, I want you to give me the exclusive.'

He laughed. 'Well! The exclusive! Don't you sound different.'

'No, I do not sound different,' I said, mimicking him again.

'So you're a broker now,' he said. 'All grown up.'

'I want the exclusive. Don't give it to anyone else.' I felt like I was begging him not to cheat on me.

'How long do you think it will take you to sell it?'

'We generally ask for a six-month exclusive right to sell.'

'I'll give you one week.'

'One week,' I said.

'Let's see if you can do it in one week. I'll fax Kim from the hotel and you can send me any papers that need signing.'

'Fine,' I said.

'I have to go. Can you please tell Charitable that I'll be back Wednesday and ask her to come to the apartment every day while I'm gone? Tell her it's okay for her to stay in the guest room.'

'Sure,' I said.

'Bye, honey,' he said and hung up.

'That was Jack,' I told Kim and Charitable. 'He gave me the exclusive, for a week,' I told Kim. 'And, Charitable, Jack said there's no need for you to come to work this week but he'll pay you anyway when he gets back.'

Charitable took off her apron. 'You're a good man, Charlie Brown,' she told me.

37

OPEN HOUSE WED 12-2

There is one last apartment I could show you,' I told Noah Bausch.

'Where is it?' he asked.

'Well, that's the thing. I really don't think you'd like it. It's not in your preferred neighborhood and it's way out of your price range.'

When you look at apartments in Manhattan for as long as the Bausches had looked, an extra half-mil here and there doesn't seem like a lot.

'It's on the Upper East Side,' I said, for the first time making that sound like a good thing. 'It's on Fifth Avenue. And it's easily over a million dollars.'

'No,' Noah Bausch said.

The next day Noah and Audrey Bausch met me in my husband's lobby, as I knew they would. We walked into the apartment silently. It looked beautiful, even with them in it.

For once they weren't condescending. They didn't knock on any walls or turn on any faucets to check for water pressure. They didn't open any closet doors and shake their heads in disgust or look up at the bathroom ceiling as if something might be dripping on them. They just *assumed* all the windows opened and that they could in fact get cable. As much as I loved lofts, there was something reassuring about a real apartment. Lofts had a certain smoke-and-mirror aspect to them.

'These are nice,' Audrey mumbled, about the bathroom tiles I had brought home from Provence.

'Aren't they?' I said.

'We'd like to see it again,' Noah said. 'And we'd like to bring Flannery.'

I wasn't aware that their three-year-old daughter had been the decision-maker all along.

Then I called Storm. 'How's life treating you at the Dakota?' I asked. I had heard from another broker who also hated her that the deal had fallen through. She had annoyed the owner with her endless inane questions and insulted him by offering him tiny amounts of money for his furniture, which he had no intention of selling. Storm had behaved so horribly that the deal had become infamous among brokers, a sort of case study.

'It didn't work out,' Storm said.

'You're kidding, that's awful. I had no idea. Well, that's all water under the bridge, Storm. You know, something just occurred to me. I actually just thought of a place I could show you . . .'

Storm's limo pulled up at my husband's building and I brought her into the apartment.

'Your dining room table could go here,' I said, opening the French doors to the dining room. 'Or here,' I said, on the landing at the top of the stairs that led down to the living room. 'Or here,' I said, in my husband's study, climbing a few rungs of a bookcase ladder and making a dramatic sweeping gesture with my arm as the ladder slid across the bookcase like we were in a musical.

This apartment could even weather Storm.

'It smells so nice here,' Storm said in the kitchen. I turned off the cider on the stove. I put a cinnamon stick in a mug and poured her a cup. I had been simmering the cider for hours, an old realtors' trick that would only work on someone like Storm.

It made the whole house smell like Christmas. 'I don't know why I feel so cozy here,' she said. 'I love these mugs.'

'Of course the owner said whoever buys the apartment can have them,' I said.

'Hmmm,' she said, examining the mug more closely. 'The only thing is I'm not sure Fifth Avenue is safe. That was one of the problems I had with the Dakota. I've heard Central Park can be dangerous. I'd like to see this apartment again at night,' she said.

When the Bausches came back for their second showing I noticed that they had dressed up. Noah was wearing a sport coat, and Audrey had made an attempt with concealer. They shuttled Flannery around from room to room.

I gave her the stuffed sheep my husband had bought for me on a drive Upstate and some wooden bracelets he had brought me from Japan and his childhood toy train he kept wrapped in tissue paper, which he considered his prize possession. I found a present for her in every room.

'You're so wonderful with children,' Audrey said. 'Have you put any more thought into what we discussed?'

They were still obsessed with my eggs. I hadn't given them a definite no yet because I knew once I did they would go with another broker and try to get her eggs. It felt strange to be talking about my eggs in my old apartment surrounded by eggs. I had pictured the baby I would have had with Jack so often, I could almost hear it breathing in the second bedroom through the Fisher-Price intercom in my mind. Strange to think of Mrs. Bausch waking in the middle of the night to check on her, walking down the corridor in her nightgown, instead of me in mine.

'I have thought about it a lot,' I said. 'But I haven't made a final decision. I must say that if you bought this place I'd certainly be tempted. Any child who got to grow up here would be so lucky.'

When Storm Shapiro came back to see the apartment at night, I got there early and turned on every light and boiled water on the stove for pasta. I wanted her to feel that if she bought this apartment she would never be hungry again, there would always be a home-cooked meal.

The doorman buzzed. 'Stormy Shappy eess here.'

'Send her up, Eddie,' I said.

'Yes, Mees, eess nice to have you home.' It made me feel like Scarlett returning to Tara. I considered giving Eddie my husband's gold pocket watch he had inherited from his father, the way Scarlett does when her father dies and she can't pay the help, but I thought better of it.

Storm came in and I presented her with the floor plan. I had it enlarged in the copy shop so it would be bigger than all the other floor plans she had gotten.

'It's so sweet. It looks like a castle!' she said. 'A big square castle with four towers.'

'That's exactly what I was going to say,' I said.

'This is a nice loft,' she said.

'It's not a loft, Storm.'

'It looks like a loft to me,' she said.

I told her to make herself at home, to try out the furniture, to open the drawers. I couldn't bear to look. I stayed in the kitchen. I didn't want to see her open those drawers. If I saw my husband's socks and underwear I might start compulsively folding them again through force of habit.

I ladled pasta onto plates that matched the mugs. 'Would you like some dinner?' I asked, when she found me in the kitchen.

'Oh, that's sweet,' she said. 'That bed was so comfortable.'

We sat at the kitchen table, and I poured red wine.

'So this is what it's like at night,' she said. 'I really feel at home here.' She looked at the plate. 'These plates are so . . .'

'They're yours,' I said.

The next morning, instead of our regular weekly meeting, a strange Chinese woman came to give us a seminar about Feng Shui.

She pushed the table to one side and made us all sit facing north. Her whole body tilted east.

She held up a few floor plans as examples. 'In this apartment,' she said, holding up a picture of Marti Landesman's new exclusive, 'the Qi will get caught in the corner of the L-shaped corridor. Qi will become enraged.'

'That's ridiculous,' Marti said. We all looked at her pityingly. If there was any Qi around, Marti would find a way to enrage it.

'This apartment,' the Chinese woman said, holding up Tony Amoroso's new exclusive, 'has such a small kitchen, no spiritual growth can ever be possible.'

'Uh, I disagree with that,' Tony said, standing up. 'It's quite a large kitchen by New York standards, with granite counters, a Sub-zero refrigerator, a six-burner Vulcan stove, and one of the only garbage dispose-alls in New York. And the owner is a very spiritual yoga instructor.'

'I don't care if owner is Dalai Lama,' the woman said. 'There will be no growth.'

'I'm sorry but I really beg to differ. I don't mean to argue but . . .'

'There is no arguing with the Qi!' the woman said.

Then she held up the floor plan to my husband's apartment. She shook her head. Everyone turned to look at me.

'Big huge large window opposite front door,' she said.

She threw the floor plan down as if even touching it for one more second would be hazardous.

'Qi comes in door and flies right out window! When Qi flies right out window all opportunity flies right out with Qi. No love, no family, children die, no sex! Out the window. Out the window.'

'What should I do?' I whispered.

'Curtains can help to contain Qi,' she said. 'But for you, you should try to live in a round bid-ing.'

'Where am I going to find a round building?' I asked, alarmed, looking imploringly at the other brokers.

'Your only chance is a round bid-ing with round windows. Everything else, bad luck!'

Just then I was paged over the loudspeaker. I had an important call. For one split second I wondered if it was Andrew. It had occurred to me that Andrew might really believe those things he said. That he had really convinced himself that we had never had sex. But history could not be rebuilt, even by a master architect. 'Remember our first kiss?' I had asked my husband at our wedding, as we danced our first dance as man and wife. Our first kiss had taken place leaning against a wall outside John's pizzeria. 'That must be some good pizza,' a man on the street had said.

'Of course I remember,' my husband said. 'It wasn't very good.'

'What do you mean?' I asked. I stopped dancing.

'You were too tentative,' he said, trying to start me up again.

I had kept my head down and sort of smiled as we kissed. I was shy. I had been *purposely* tentative.

'Fuck you,' I whispered in his ear. Our first kiss had been incredible. Shy and smiling and incredible. His words couldn't change that. But somehow they did.

I left the conference room and took the call at my desk. It was Noah Bausch with an offer on my husband's apartment. 'Eight hundred thousand,' he said.

'Of course I'll convey your offer to the owner,' I said, 'but I'm sure he won't accept. As you know, he wants one point two million.' I wished I had just said one point two and left off the word 'million.' I swiveled my chair around to face north, the wealth direction. 'Perhaps you should come up at least one or two more hundred.' I meant hundred thousand.

'Well, I'm not going to negotiate against myself!' Noah said, irately.

In every single deal I did, at one point the owner and the buyer would each come out with, 'I refuse to negotiate against myself.' No one was asking them to. It's the one thing all people seemed to know about the rules of successful deal making. The phrase reminded me of how my husband had refused to go to couples therapy with me, and I had to go alone every week. 'Well, what do you wish you could say to your husband?' the therapist said. 'And what do you think your husband wishes he could say to you?' Now, that's what I would call negotiating against myself.

'I'm not axing you to negotiate against yourself,' I said to Noah. Not that you're not your own worst enemy, I wanted to say.

'Did you just say 'axing'?' Noah said, contemptuously.

'Of course not,' I said. 'I think I know how to speak English.' My call waiting went off. 'I have another call,' I said curtly.

'Offer him nine hundred thousand dollars,' Noah said. 'But we're not going up much higher than that.'

'Fine,' I said. 'Bye, I mean, hold on.' I answered the call waiting.

It was Mr. Shapiro, Storm's father. 'We'll take the Fifth Avenue apartment,' he said.

'I'm afraid I'm on the other line with a customer who's making an offer right now.'

'Eight hundred thousand,' Mr. Shapiro said.

'Oh, I'm sorry but my other customer already bid nine hundred and fifty thousand and that's just his opening,' I said.

'Please inform the owner that our offer is one million dollars,' Mr. Shapiro said.

'Would you mind holding,' I said, and went back to Bausch.

I explained to him that unfortunately he had been outbid and would have to go higher.

'One million dollars. Cash,' he said.

I gasped at the word 'cash.' I had no idea they had that much money. Dale always said I didn't qualify the customers carefully enough. 'Hold on just a sec,' I said and clicked over to Storm's daddy.

'Sir, I'll make your offer to the owner but I'm afraid we've got a cash offer on the table.' He could definitely afford to pay cash, too, but there were tax benefits or something for carrying a mortgage. I couldn't remember what they had said in real estate school about that.

Mr. Shapiro paused. 'One point one,' he said.

'Cash?'

'No, not cash! Fuck him if he thinks he's getting cash.'

'Of course,' I said. 'I'll relay the message.'

'Wait a minute,' Mr. Shapiro said.

'Yes?' I asked, hopefully.

'My financials are impeccable. A cash offer doesn't mean anything in this case.'

'I'm aware of what difference cash makes, sir,' I said.

'Make sure you give him my offer, Liv.'

'That's my job,' I said, cheerily, and returned to Bausch.

'He's up to one point one,' I said to Noah.

'One million cash is our final offer,' he said.

'That's a shame,' I said. 'Are you sure you won't come up a little more?'

Noah didn't say anything.

'Hello?' I said. There was silence. 'Hello?'

'I'm here,' he said. 'I can't go any higher.'

'Well, I'll give him both offers,' I said, like a nursery school teacher saying she liked both children equally.

'Thank you,' he said meekly.

'You're welcome,' I said and hung up.

When I leaned back in my chair I noticed Carla for the first time. I hadn't been aware that the meeting let out. She was just staring at me with her chin hitting her half of the shelf.

'Jesus Christ,' I said. 'Haven't you ever seen a deal before? Take a picture, it lasts longer.' I picked up my bag and headed for the door.

I walked down the aisle between rows of desks and brokers yelling on phones and finishing bagels. I had never felt so much a part of anything in my life. With two million-dollar offers on the table I had definitely secured my place in the Millionaires

Circle, which I was pretty sure came with a luncheon at Tavern on the Green and maybe a weekend at Samantha Smoothe's own weekend house in Connecticut.

Every month Smoothe Transitions ran a full-page ad in the *Times* featuring its best agents doing seasonal things like gardening in the spring or ice skating in the winter. Now I would be in one of those ads, and Dale would see it, and Lorna, and maybe even my father. Jerome wouldn't see it, of course.

38

WHY RENT??? POSTWAR STU LOW MAINT

I might as well have stayed at the office because Noah and Storm both called me late into the night, whining and complaining about why they couldn't come up any higher.

'Why don't you just come up ten more thousand,' I said.

'We caaaan't,' Noah simpered. 'Hold on, sweetie.' He was talking to little Flannery. 'Liv, Flannery wants to talk to you,' Noah said to me in baby talk.

'Hello?' I said gently into the phone. 'Flannery, Flannery,' I sang. 'Are you getting ready for beddy bye?' I hated when people put their babies on the phone. Flannery didn't say anything, she just breathed, so after a while I just stopped saying anything. We just stayed on the phone in silence. Finally I said, 'Can you put Daddy back on the phone?'

'Guess what she named her favorite teddy bear?' Noah said.

'I don't know, Noah,' I said. 'Eggbert?'

'No. She named it Liv Kellerman. She sleeps with Liv Kellerman every night and takes Liv Kellerman with her to the doctor's. In fact the other day she left Liv Kellerman in the playground and I had to go get it in the middle of the night. Anyway, when do we find out if we've got an accepted offer?'

I told him for the hundredth time that I would call him as soon as I spoke with the owner. I told the same thing to Storm.

The more they called, the angrier I got. I couldn't stand the thought of them living in the apartment I loved. I had chosen the carpet. I had polished the floors and the banisters. I didn't want Storm sleeping in my bedroom. I didn't want the Bausches putting window guards on my beautiful windows. Madonna and Lourdes should live in that apartment, not Noah, Audrey, and Flannery Bausch, and their future egg. I was more jealous of Storm or the Bausches getting to live there than I had ever been of Jordan. They could issue a new street sign. 'Jealousy Street.' 'Envy Ave.' 'Longing Lane.' 'Despair District.' I could just avoid the whole neighborhood.

I had thought it would help me to broker the deal, like a pregnant woman choosing the couple who will adopt her baby. But I just couldn't stand it. I hated Storm and the Bausches so much. How dare they refuse to come up ten more thousand?

The phone rang. 'Hello?' I said.

'Did you talk to the owner?' It was Noah again.

'No, I didn't,' I said, 'but I'm afraid there's a new development that I don't think you're going to be too happy about.'

'What is it?' he asked, panic-stricken.

'There's another buyer who has come in with a very high bid and I think she's going to get it, especially since you won't come up even five more dollars.'

'What's her bid?' he said angrily.

'I'm afraid I can't release that number until I speak to the owner,' I said.

'I thought you weren't showing it to anybody else. Who is this woman? Where did she come from?'

I considered the question for a moment. 'Actually, Noah, it's Liv Kellerman. The person, not the teddy bear.'

'What!'

'Well, you said you couldn't go up any higher and I got to thinking about it and I just really think it's worth a lot more than you could afford, so I decided to buy it myself.'

'That's outrageous. That's illegal!'

Actually it was sort of illegal, I was pretty sure. But they hadn't discussed bidding against your own client in real estate school.

'I'm sorry, Noah. The apartment is as good as mine.'

I heard a crumbling sound in my kitchen. I couldn't take it if there was a mouse. I reached for my gun on my bedside table. 'Anyway, I've got to go. But good luck in your search,' I said and hung up.

I went into the kitchen and saw a small pile of rubble on the floor. It looked like a dune in the middle of my kitchen. I looked up at the ceiling. Debris was slowly pouring down like sand in an hourglass. Dune Street.

There was all kinds of construction being done in the building. The bricks were being pointed. Sheets of black mesh hung from scaffolding out my window, like a widow's veil. My building was an Afghani woman imprisoned in her shroud.

I lay on my bed and waited for my husband to call. There was a crumbling sound from the kitchen ceiling again. Then it was more of a rumble. It sounded like a tub was going to fall through at any moment. I got up and put on my sturdiest boots and my only hat, my straw sombrero from Mexico. When I took the apartment I didn't know I would require a hard hat. I trudged through the rubble on the kitchen floor and began to gather my things. Suddenly I found myself packing.

Before I left, I poked curiously at the kitchen ceiling with a broom handle. Giant rocks rained down like candy from a piñata. I was covered in pale soot, the color and consistency of cremated bodies.

I stepped out of the kitchen just as the whole ceiling caved in. 6F's refrigerator and stove came crashing into my kitchen in another New York City tin-and-porcelain avalanche.

I didn't bother to lock the door behind me.

I loaded my bags and a couple of boxes into a limo I had ordered from the Tel Aviv car service. The limo was white, and inside there were cocktail napkins with wedding bells printed on them wrapped around champagne glasses. The chauffeur had given me a nasty look when I carried down the last garbage bag of shoes. There was no champagne .

I took possession of my husband's apartment, wheeling my things over the threshold on the doorman's gold hotel cart. I was glad Andrew wasn't there lifting me over it. The phone rang and I answered it. It was Jack.

'Did we get any offers?' he asked.

'No,' I said. 'No one wanted it.'

'What are you doing there at this time of night?' he asked.

'I live here,' I said.

'You're staying there while you show it this week?' he asked, sounding annoyed. 'Where's Charitable?'

'No, I live here,' I said. 'And I'm not ever leaving here again.'

'Do you do that with all your exclusives? Just move in and force the owner out? Is that the policy at Smoothe Transitions? Does Kim let all her brokers do that?'

'Jack, I'm serious. I'm really not leaving. I'm staying put.' I smiled when I said that because it was what my father used to say – 'I'm staying put.' On those rare occasions when I found him in the living room and we'd listen to a set of records he bought me of an English guy reading *Through the Looking Glass*, he'd say, 'Today you and I are just staying put.'

'You've always been obsessed with the apartment,' Jack said.

'I love it,' I said.

'I love it, too.'

It was the most passionate we'd been with each other in a long time.

'I think it's fair, Jack. I have a right to live here. This apartment is a part of me, and I can't leave it again.'

'Liv, you know I'm a good guy,' Jack said. 'I'm not just going to turn you out on your ear.'

'Thanks,' I said, laughing. 'God knows my ear's already been through enough. You're welcome to take my place on MacDougal Street,' I offered.

I perused my divorce agreement standing at the counter in Ray's Pizzeria. Jack gave me the apartment and some of the furniture and, much to the chagrin of my attorney, who came recommended by Marti Landesman, I agreed to no support.

I also retained sole custody of the video I had rented but never returned, *The Long, Long Trailer*. I kept meaning to watch it.

My father had helped his models get at least a hundred divorces, and I knew he would be hurt that I hadn't asked his advice. But I wanted to do it alone. He had turned the wedding into his party, and I didn't want my divorce to become his party too.

I asked the pizza man to lend me a pen so I could sign. I wanted to do it quickly, alone and without ceremony.

'You need a witness for that,' the pizza man said. 'And a notary public.'

I looked at the last page. 'You're right.'

'I'm a notary,' he said. He opened a drawer behind the counter and pulled out two big stamps and an inkpad.

Romeo Manuel Ernesto Montego signed as my notary and Jesus Jorge De La Cruz, the boy smoking cigarettes outside the door, signed as my witness. I put the divorce decree back in its manila envelope and left. It was a good deal. My wedding band had slid off like a whore's panties, while my husband's had to be cut off his finger by a surly locksmith.

39
ALL ORIG DETAILS

The day Jack came to pack up his clothes and eggs and things, I left the apartment so I wouldn't have to see him.

When I came home, a woman was entering the lobby at the same time I was. She had a conservative blond haircut and was wearing a light raincoat, carrying a Ghurka briefcase and half-reading a newspaper. She had on low-heeled navy shoes.

'Hello,' she said to the doorman, and kept walking past him, rumpling her newspaper.

'Can I help you?' the doorman asked, rising from his wooden stool. His hair was pulled back into a ponytail under his doorman's cap. He picked up the receiver of the intercom system and got his finger ready to buzz someone.

The woman stopped. 'I live here. You know you do this every time,' she said. Her voice was filled with the hurt and frustration of a little girl whose parents were always away. The girl whose bedroom was so far away from her parents' master bedroom suite that even if they were home they couldn't hear her crying desperately once when there was a cockroach in her glass of milk. I recognized her tone of voice. It was mine, throughout my childhood.

'I've lived here for nine months,' I heard her saying desperately, as I stood waiting for the elevator.

I couldn't stand to witness her embarrassment. I suddenly realized there were terribly unfortunate people in this world. Sick people and lonely people and people so invisible their own doormen didn't recognize them. Your husband might as well call you by a different name in bed.

It was one thing if your own parents or husband couldn't bear to see you. They had a lot invested, after all. They had a lot to be frightened of because what they saw was a reflection of themselves. But your doorman? He was just a neutral figure in your life. He had nothing to lose by seeing you. His whole job was to remember you, remember your apartment number, and sign for an occasional package.

If your doorman couldn't even recognize you, even after you pointed yourself out to him, you were as good as homeless. You had not made a home for yourself. Even with a lease and rent bill stubs and a bed and a couch, you were homeless until your doorman said hello to you at the end of the day.

I didn't know what I would do if my doorman had ever said, 'Can I help you?' to me. But he hadn't said that. He had said, 'Hello, Liv, good to have you back in the building.' He had remembered me even though I had been gone for so long. Even if I had accomplished nothing in my life so far, if I was only a tacky real estate agent, if I had failed at my marriage, not even had a baby, not done any of the things I thought I would do, if nothing else, at least my own doorman knew me.

I wondered if Jack would ever come crawling back into the lobby and have to ask the doorman to buzz up.

I didn't want to take the elevator with the woman who had just been humiliated by the doorman, so I stopped to get my mail. A sign on the bulletin board read, 'Dale the Handywoman – no job to small.' I wondered if Dale had left real estate. I ripped one of the tabs with Dale the Handywoman's number on it. I would need help hanging the curtains Andrew took down. I opened my mailbox. There were a few official-looking letters that were addressed to my husband, which I promptly stuffed into the mouth of the chrome garbage can, and one large envelope hand-addressed to 'Occupant.' I took it upstairs with me as excited as if it were my own invitation to the White House. In my apartment, I tore the envelope and pulled out a letter written in a woman's flowery handwriting.

> Dear 'Occupant,'
>
> I hope you won't think this is too 'wacky' but . . .
>
> My aunt was a singer and actress who lived in your apartment from 1947 until 1963. The days in your apartment were the happiest days of her life until the 'bottom' dropped out and she was forced to leave.
>
> My aunt died three months ago, at eighty years old, from cancer. It was her last wish to see the apartment again but 'alas' that was not 'to be.' A few days before she died I took her to your building and she went so far as to step inside the lobby and 'visit' the elevators and the mailbox, but she did not want to 'intrude.'
>
> I feel very fortunate that I was able to come to New York from St. Louis (where I am a social worker) to 'help' her die.
>
> I thought you might like to know about the 'life' of your apartment so I have enclosed some black-and-white photos for you to keep.
>
> > Sincerely,
> > Cynthia (Oberon) Otis

In the envelope was an 8×10 glossy publicity shot of a beautiful blonde in a mink stole clasped with a diamond brooch. Her name, Olivia Oberon, and the words 'Ric Records' were printed on the bottom.

There was a picture of a party. Men in tuxedos and women in gowns filled my living room, smoking cigarettes and holding champagne saucers. Every single man wore a tux. It was the most fabulous party I had ever seen. The picture was taken from the mezzanine, looking down into my living room. There was a grand piano with a Christmas tree on it and a bamboo bar cart in the corner. Olivia stood in the center, smiling up at the camera.

There was a photo of 'move-in day' with boxes everywhere and the couch lying precariously on the stairs, and Olivia, in a leopard suit and high heels, holding her hands to her temples, laughing, triumphant. I loved the idea of wearing a leopard suit and heels to move in.

The last photo was of my living room window, with giant lace curtains sweeping down on either side and the beautiful view. 'View in 1947' was written on the back.

I walked down the stairs to the living room window clutching the black-and-white picture. I held the picture up to the window and moved my eyes from the park to the picture and back again. It was the exact same view. The lake was there. Not one tree had been added.

Nothing had changed.

I called St. Louis information and got the number of Cynthia Otis. She answered right away.

'Hello,' I said. 'This is Liv, the occupant. I don't think you're wacky at all.' I told her that I would frame her aunt's picture and hang it by the window so she would always be there in the apartment.

Cynthia Otis burst into tears. 'Thank you,' she cried. 'Oh, thank you. I've heard so much about the apartment. I'm very grateful. I know my aunt would love to be remembered to it.'

I got chills down my back and I felt like my head was going to lift off. I let the woman cry for a few moments.

'Did you say your name was Liv?' she asked.

'Yes. Liv Kellerman.'

'But that was my aunt's name!' she said. 'Two Livs in the apartment? That's unbelievable. Is the wall above the fireplace still mirrored?' she asked.

Suddenly I got a picture in my head of my own first 'move-in day' five years before. I am not smiling, triumphant, in a leopard suit. I am eating a bagel in sweatpants and sulking while my husband is single-handedly pulling down the mirrors. They covered the whole wall from floor to ceiling and were smoked and veined as blue cheese. I had begged him to let us keep them. 'It's the mirrors or me,' he had said. I should have picked the mirrors. I should have sliced his throat with a jagged shard. Taking down those mirrors was the single worst thing my husband had ever done and I hated him for it. Olivia Oberon should never have moved out and I should never have moved in. I felt so sorry for both us Livs that my eyes welled up with tears.

'My husband made us take the mirrors down,' I cried. 'I'm so sorry we took them down.'

'Aunt Liv had a tragic life,' the woman said. 'She had a terrible divorce in that apartment. Terrible, terrible, violent fights. Her husband left her for the nurse who oversaw the adoption of their daughter. Then he and the nurse took the little girl and left. She ended her career for him. She nearly died of sadness when she was forced to leave the apartment. Literally.'

'But that's exactly what happened to me!' I said.

'Your husband left you for the nurse who oversaw the adoption of your daughter?' she asked, amazed.

'He had an affair with a nurse at the hospital where he had a disk removed.'

It was the first time I had ever admitted it to anybody. It sounded almost funny. There was something inherently evil about nurses. I had always hated nurses, even when I was a little girl.

'Is he still with her?'

'No,' I said.

'At least you got to keep the apartment. Aunt Liv spent the rest of her life alone giving singing lessons in a tiny rental on Eighth Avenue.' I couldn't think of a worse end. 'You're lucky to get to live there,' Cynthia said.

When I got off the phone I didn't feel like staying in the apartment even though I had so much to do. I went outside to get some split pea soup at the old lady diner on the corner of Madison. Young boys were trying to throw a small beanbag on top of my building's blue canopy.

A gorgeous Con-Ed man smiled at me. The whole street was being ripped up. I was beginning to think construction would always follow me wherever I went. Men were pouring concrete. I wanted to walk in the wet concrete, making fresh footprints. Moving back into my old apartment was like walking in my own footsteps. I lifted my foot, ready to do it, but a worker grabbed me and pulled me back. Everyone else in New York was constantly writing their initials in cement, but I never got to.

I went back home and propped Olivia Oberon's pictures on the mantelpiece. Then I wandered around from room to room. I could do it with my eyes closed. Moving into my old apartment was like going on a blind date with my ex-husband. It was redundant. A double negative. I wondered if I had made a mistake.

When I looked at my watch I realized I was too late to go to the protest to save the Edgar Allan Poe house on West Third Street. I had enough to worry about. Edgar Allan Poe would have to fend for himself.

I realized I was holding my cordless phone even though I didn't feel like calling anyone. 'Hello?' I said out loud as if someone were calling me. 'Hello?' I just kept walking around saying 'Hello?' to no one. I looked at the gold curtains in a heap in the corner. But it seemed silly to call Dale the Handywoman if I wasn't even sure if I should stay.

I looked at the couch my husband had left. Under it was the hole in the carpet that Andrew had made when he stole the piece for me. Jack had never lifted the couch to discover it gone. I lay on the couch to see if I could somehow feel the carpet missing like the princess and the pea. I thought maybe I could.

I stood and managed to move the couch, exposing the patch of missing carpet. I smiled when I saw it. It was like the new bald spot on the head of the man you love. It was the only thing about the apartment that was new.

I lay on the askew couch. I had gotten what I wanted. I had prayed to lie on this couch again one day. I had sat in Jerome's chambers praying. I had prayed at my desk at Dale's. I had cried in apartments all over New York thinking how inferior they were to this one. I looked at poor Olivia propped up there on the mantel. Liv, the ghost, living here again with Liv, the girl. Then I realized that Liv, the girl, was a ghost, too. I was merely a ghost haunting my own apartment.

I had to get out of there and save both of us. I could almost see the Qi flying out the window.

40

NO FLIP TAX

At the sales meeting on Monday, Kim asked if anyone had a new listing. My stomach clutched a little bit. I raised my hand, then took it down, then raised it. I was starting to take it down again when Kim said, 'Liv, do you have a listing you would like to tell us about?'

'Yes, I'm putting my apartment back on the market,' I said. 'Flipping it.' I said 'flipping it' as if I were flipping it the bird. Technically you had to pay for something in order to flip it, but I liked the word. Besides, I really had paid, hadn't I?

'All right,' Kim said. 'We'll keep it in-house for as long as we can before co-broking.'

'And don't forget,' I added, 'as a Transitions agent I only have to split three percent instead of six.' It was the only part of the three-volume employees manual I had bothered to read.

'What's the listing price?' Kim asked.

'Asking price is one point one,' I said.

I accepted an offer of one million dollars from Marti Landesman's customers, a Mr. and Mrs. Wolfe. I didn't show them the pictures of Olivia or tell them about myself. We didn't discuss the 'life' of the apartment, just the co-op board, the school district, and my 'thinking' behind the layout of the master bath.

I didn't take anything they said personally I didn't care who lived there .

I picked up my kitchen phone and called my office voice mail. There were two messages. The first was a company-wide message from Sam Smoothe herself saying she was going to be interviewed on *Good Morning America* about market trends and we should all wake up tomorrow at the crack of dawn to watch. She also asked if anyone knew of a good place to hold this year's annual party.

The second message was from Juliet Flagg, the original owner of the Loft of My Life on Liberty Street, asking me to call her back. 'I tried calling you at that other firm several times and finally your secretary, Lorna, called me back and told me you had moved to a new number.' I laughed thinking about Lorna saying she was my secretary. She had helped me out.

First I called Samantha Smoothe and said I would love to have the party in my apartment. What better way to remember it than filled with a couple of hundred brokers? She assured me that she would provide full catering, flowers, and clean-up service, and I would be nominated for the 'good guy award' the following Christmas. It was set.

'You know there's someone I think would make a great member of the Transitions team,' I told Samantha. 'Her name is Lorna and she was sort of a mentor to me when I started in the business.'

'Bring her in,' Samantha Smoothe said. 'We'd love to have her.' I thanked her and hung up. I would get Lorna a job, and Valashenko, and then, one day, maybe even Dale.

Then I called Juliet.

'I'm back in the loft,' she said. 'It's a long story but my marriage didn't work out.'

I admired her for saying it like that, outright.

'And,' she continued, 'I really missed my apartment so I called that couple, the Zeislofts, who you sold it to and made them an offer. They packed up their snow globes or whatever those stupid things are called and moved to Washington, D.C., and I moved back in. But now I realize I made a mistake and I want to put it back on the market.'

I couldn't believe my ears. The Loft of My Life was for sale again.

'I wanted to talk to you before I make any decisions,' she said. 'I met a woman at my yoga class who is also a real estate agent but I don't know how experienced she is. I think she may have just started.'

'What's her name?' I asked.

'Storm Shapiro. She talked me into letting her come by with a client and now she says the client wants to make an offer. But then I thought maybe I should give you the exclusive because you sold it the first time.'

'Her name is Storm Shapiro?' I said. I couldn't believe the world's most annoying real estate client had become an agent.

'Yes, Storm. But I'm not sure I like her because she told the client that I would sell my furniture and I really don't think I want to sell my furniture.'

It was Storm all right. How could she be a real estate agent? She wasn't exactly good with people.

'Well, Juliet. I don't think I can be your broker.'

'Why not?' she asked.

'Because I want to be your buyer.'

'Oh?'

'How's six hundred thousand sound?' I said.

'Shouldn't I have a broker?'

'You don't need a broker, Juliet. All we need is a couple of lawyers. I can get my own mortgage, I can do the board packets myself, and besides, we're friends.'

Juliet's call waiting went off and she asked me to hold.

'I have Storm on the other line,' she said. 'Her client matched your six hundred.'

'I'll go to six hundred and fifty thousand,' I said. 'But you know it has a really high maintenance.' It was a very high maintenance but I had faith in myself. I knew I'd be able to handle it.

'The market's really good right now. It's a seller's market,' Juliet said.

'Liberty Street is a terrible location.'

'That's not what you said the last time I saw you. Tribeca is so hot.'

'It's not in Tribeca.'

'It's southern Tribeca.'

'Hah!' I said. 'It's nowhere near Tribeca. You can't even get a cab down there.'

'So you're not going to go any higher than six-fifty?'

'Well, I'm not going to negotiate against myself,' I said.

She told me to hold again.

In less than a minute she was back. 'Storm's up to seven,' she said. 'But she said her client wants me to throw in my grandmother's armoire.

'Seven-fifty,' I said, cheerfully. 'Buckass neckid.'

'What?'

'No armoire. No furniture. No dishes. No Parmesan cheese. Broom clean. Totally empty.'

'You might not be too happy about something.'

'What?' I said.

'They put in a strange fridge. The shelves rotate.'

'I don't care,' I said. 'I've had worse.'

'Hold on,' she said. I waited. Finally Juliet came back on the line. 'Storm said her client's at seven-fifty but she won't go any higher.'

'Is Storm still on the other line?'

'No,' she said. 'But she said her client would pay the whole seven hundred and fifty thousand in cash. She's going to call me back.'

'Juliet, a cash offer doesn't make any difference in this case. Storm probably hasn't even qualified her customers properly. And do you really want a stranger living there?'

'I don't care anymore,' she said. I knew how she felt.

'I'll give you eight hundred thousand dollars but you have to accept my offer right now,' I said.

Suddenly she laughed. 'Offer accepted,' she said.

41
FULLY RENOVATED

Juliet and I closed in a lawyer's office on lower Broadway. The lawyer, whose nickname was Oz, was known in the business as a deal maker rather than a deal breaker. He was a legend in real estate law. I had heard so much about him I was surprised when I saw him, just a nice, gentle-looking man with a framed picture of himself on a boat off Montauk. He reminded me of my father. Deep down my father was just like this man. He wasn't a larger-than-life celebrity you had to look perfect for. He was just a man behind the curtain. Maybe I had been afraid to see that all along, to see that all men, including Peter Kellerman, were just men behind their curtains.

Before I signed up for real estate school I had thought about calling my father and asking him to stop me from disgracing myself and the family by becoming the worst thing a person could be. He could get me a job in his fashion house or even hook me up with a job on a movie set.

Just as I was about to hand over my check for the real estate course, I said, 'Just a second,' to the woman at the desk, and ran to a pay phone in the lobby. I called him.

'Dad,' I said, 'I have something to ask you.'

'Anything,' he said.

'It's a really big favor,' I said, my voice getting higher and higher. 'Whatever it is, it's yours,' he said.

I want you to love me, Dad, I thought. Be my father. We'll start over. Spend time together. Get to know each other. We'll have Chinese food and you can teach me to use chopsticks all over again, put makeup on me, show me India, zip up my raincoat. Look at me, Dad, I wanted to say, I'm still the same girl you used to love.

What was the point of being loved as a child if it just petered out in the end? With every year more of the love evaporated until it was all condensed to a small 'love you' the size of a bullet at the end of a phone call. Suddenly I understood why I cried every time I got off the phone with him. My father hated me. He hated me for the same reason my husband hated me, and Andrew hated me. Because I had glimpsed them, albeit briefly, behind their curtains.

'What is it, Liv?' he asked.

'Uh,' I stopped. 'Can you get me tickets to Lion King?' I asked.

'Of course. That's it?' he asked.

'That's it,' I said.

'Bye,' he said. 'Love you.'

'Love you, too,' I said.

What had I been so afraid of? I wondered. Maybe never seeing him at all was better than seeing him drunk, the last to leave Spago, each arm wrapped around a blond model. I was better off with my eyes closed. What I wanted didn't even exist. What would happen if I finally tracked him down in a fog of dry ice on a fashion runway in Paris or Miami or Milan? The answer was nothing. Nothing would happen. In my best dress, in my highest heels, even packing my gun, nothing would happen. He wasn't there. I couldn't see him and he couldn't see me. We were as blind as Jerome. The best I could do was tell it to the judge.

When we left Oz, Juliet and I went to lunch at a diner where the waitresses wore beehives and the photos of the winners of the old annual 'Miss Subway' beauty queen competition lined the walls. I had eaten there after I took the real estate exam.

'Where's your new apartment?' I asked Juliet.

'It's in Brooklyn and it's so exotic. The building is round!' she said. 'It even has round windows.'

Before we said goodbye she asked for the name of the real estate school I had gone to. 'I've been thinking about it ever since my divorce. It just seems like the thing to do,' she said.

With my new keys in my pocket, I stopped in at Tortolla to have Tom do my hair. He blew it out straight for the first time. My long black wavy hair became as straight and Japanese-looking as Timothy's. I had him chop it up a little on the bottom. I loved it. I sat beaming in the chair. 'I always want my hair like this,' I said.

'You can't do this all the time,' Tom said. 'It's much too much work. You'll never be able to blow it out like this yourself.'

'Then I'll come here and have you do it,' I said. I had been going to him for seven years and he had never done anything new to my hair, except for one terrible French braid incident. He had never done anything new to his hair either. I loved Tom but I was starting to think the only thing worse than a reluctant bridegroom was a reluctant hairdresser.

'You'll have to book two appointments back to back in order for me to do this. It's way too high maintenance for you,' he said.

'I want high-maintenance hair,' I said. 'I can handle it.'

'What have I done?' Tom asked, smiling back at me in the mirror. 'I created a monster.'

On my birthday I moved to Liberty Street.

It was my birthday but it felt like Independence Day. I stood on my roof deck in the tight vintage leopard suit I had bought for the occasion. I half-expected to see fireworks. I was sure the city would provide fireworks for my housewarming. I looked for them over the East River, in Brooklyn, and all the way over in New Jersey. I could see them in my mind. The sky turned into a giant screensaver. I imagined the waterfalls of stars and stripes and sparkling chrysanthemums.

With my own hammer and nails I hung the freshly framed photographs of Olivia in our new loft. 'Who knows,' I told her, 'maybe we'll even move again. This isn't the only apartment in the world.' One thing real estate had taught me was that there was always another apartment. And if there were other apartments, then maybe there were other men.

And if there were other apartments and other men, maybe there were even other cities. But then I caught a glimpse of my new view. No, I thought. There are no other cities.

In just two weeks the maintenance would be due and I would mail it from my own shiny brass mail chute in my own private foyer. But I would need stamps. I would have to go to the post office to buy myself some Love stamps. I unpacked the box I had labeled 'firearms' and lifted the gun out of its nest of bubble wrap and *New York Times* real estate sections. I had heard that if you brought a gun into a police station they took it, no questions asked, and even gave you a small amount of reward money, which most people probably used for sneakers or crack, not Love stamps.

I got on the elevator and pressed L, fingering the Braille dots. The elevator went down one floor and then stopped. A great-looking man got on. He was wearing a tie with puppies on it and no wedding ring. 'Nice suit,' he said.

We went down one more floor and the elevator stopped again. And another great-looking guy got on. This one was tall with beautiful black moussed-up hair like a model.

On the next floor down, a man with hair as long and dark and straight as mine got on. I had never dated a man with long hair. The thought made me nervous.

On every single floor the elevator stopped and another gorgeous man got on. They made cute little comments. 'Room for one more?' 'I see we have a full house.' 'I guess this is the local.' Standing in my suit, with my gun in my pocket, I felt like a female leopard on a man-watching safari. I felt grateful for everything that had happened, grateful to be alive with my eyes and ears and eggs still intact.

Liberty Street was not a terrible location at all. It was in the financial district! For a single girl in New York, there was no such thing as living too far south. All the men in New York filtered down here to the bottom. I just prayed that the elevator had a habit of getting stuck.

I'd do my errands and come home later and unpack. I'd call my father and tell him my new address. Explain that the only thing left of my marriage was the wedding video, which I would send him for his archives. And ask him if he happened to know anybody who wanted to buy an apartment, or sell one.

Maybe I'd even watch the video, *The Long, Long Trailer*. I finally felt ready to watch it alone. Because I wasn't alone; I was in New York.